D0938436

THE
IONIA
SANCTION

ALSO BY GARY CORBY

The Pericles Commission

THE
IONIA
SANCTION

Gary Corby

Minotaur Books

New York

THE IONIA SANCTION. Copyright © 2011 by Gary Corby. All rights reserved. Printed in the United States of America. For information, address St. Martin's Press, 175 Fifth Avenue, New York, NY 10010.

www.minotaurbooks.com

Library of Congress Cataloging-in-Publication Data

Corby, Gary.
    The Ionia sanction / Gary Corby. — 1st ed.
        p. cm.
    ISBN 978-0-312-59901-0
    1. Private investigators—Fiction.   2. Murder—Investigation—Fiction.
3. Athens (Greece)—Fiction.   4. Greece—History—Athenian supremacy,
479-431 B.C.—Fiction.   I. Title.
    PR9619.4.C665I57 2011
    823'.92—dc23

                                                                    2011026221

First Edition: November 2011

10   9   8   7   6   5   4   3   2   1

For Helen, Catriona, and Megan

ACKNOWLEDGMENTS

The author is merely the point man in the team that creates a book. So many talented people have contributed to these mysteries.

First and foremost, thank you to my wife, Helen, and my daughters, Megan and Catriona. Without their support, love, and encouragement, there would be no books.

Janet Reid is the best literary agent any author could have. How she manages to do what she does is beyond me. She must be superhuman.

Joanna Volpe most generously critiqued *The Ionia Sanction*, taking time out from her own vastly successful agenting career to help me, with no hope of reward but my thanks.

Judith Engracia probed for logic holes in the plot and did an outstanding job. Meredith Barnes is lucky to retain her sanity after assisting with the booking of author events.

Kathleen Conn and Keith Kahla at St. Martin's Press are dream editors. Countless people at St. Martin's Press contributed to the book, from design to printing to shipping, and I'm sorry to say that in many cases I don't even know who they are. Thank you to a great organization.

Anneke Klein and Bill Kirton read early versions of the book, and as always provided invaluable comments. Tehmina Goskar helped me with advice on early Zoroastrian rituals and beliefs.

Belinda Byrne, editor of the Australian edition at Penguin, has been an amazing support and provided great advice on the manuscript.

And finally, a big thank-you to the countless people who follow my book adventures online: who read and comment on my blog, and talk to me on the social networks. There are far too many to list, but you know who you are, and your support and encouragement make writing all the more fun.

A NOTE ON NAMES

Most modern names come from the Bible, a book which had yet to be written when my hero, Nico, walked the mean streets of Classical Athens. Quite a few people have asked me what's the "right" way to say the ancient names in these stories. I'll be getting hate mail from classical linguists for this, but the truth is, there is no right way. I hope you'll pick whatever sounds happiest to you, and have fun reading the story.

For those who'd like a little more guidance, I've suggested a way to say each name in the character list. My suggestions do not match ancient pronunciation. They're how I think the names will sound best in an English sentence.

That's all you need to read the book. For those who'd like to know more about Greek names, I've included a short reference on page 333.

THE ACTORS

Characters with an asterisk by their name were real historical people.

Thorion THOR-ION	Proxenos for Ephesus	He just hangs around.
Nicolaos NEE-CO-LAY-OS (Nicholas)	Our protagonist	"I'm Nicolaos, son of Sophroniscus, of the deme Alopece."
Socrates* SOCK-RA-TEEZ	An irritant	"For one night only, I'll be your slave."
Pericles* PERRY-CLEEZ	Leader of Athens	"It's a disaster, Nicolaos, a bloody disaster."
Diotima* DEO-TEEMA	A Priestess of Artemis	"You vile, disgusting goat, you make me sick!"

Onteles ON-TELL-EEZ	Son of Thorion	"There'll be a strange but innocent explanation."
Callias* KALL-EE-US	The richest man in Athens	"Ah, the lack of imagination of youth."
Sophroniscus* SOFF-RON-ISK-US	Father of Nicolaos	"A father has to do what's best for his son."
Phaenarete* FAIN-A-RET-EE	Mother of Nicolaos	"Don't be such a baby."
Araxes ARAX-EEZ	A bandit leader	"May I call you Nico? I feel we're forming a bond."
Asia* ASIA	A slave girl	"I'm afraid you'll have to take payment on delivery."
Anaxagoras* ANAX-A-GOR-US	Philosopher	"A philosopher should always praise his host. The Gods know where his next meal is coming from."

A cloth seller	He's from Phrygia	"I got a family to feed."
Orbanos ORB-AN-OS	Harbormaster at Piraeus	"Don't bother me till I've eaten."
Koppa KOPPA	A slave with an interesting rod	"Now pay close attention, young man."
Pollion POLLY-ON	A merchant trader	"How did an inexperienced young man like you get such a responsible job?"
Macrobianos MACRO-BEE- ARN-OS "Mac"	A small-time hustler	"Hey mister, my sister's lonely! You wanna come with me?"
Geros GEROS	A eunuch	"It's not infectious."
Brion BREE-ON	Proxenos for Athens	"His fingernails are always trimmed and clean."
Philodios FILL-O-DEE-US	A torturer	"The horses, my lord? Or shall I remove his toes?"

Barzanes	A Persian official	"I congratulate you, Athenian. I have rarely seen a man so completely engineer his own destruction."
BAR-ZANE-EEZ		
Themistocles*	Satrap of Magnesia	"We would have been undone, had we not been undone!"
THEM-IST-		
O-CLEEZ		
Mnesip- tolema*	Daughter of Themistocles	"You've been a naughty boy, Nicolaos. I like naughty boys."
NESSIE-TOLEMA		
"Nessie"		
Cleophantus*	Son of Themistocles	"I *told* Nessie this was a bad idea."
CLEO-FAN-TUS		
Archeptolis*	Son of Themistocles	"My favorite scene: slaves being tortured."
ARK-EE-TOL-IS		
Nicomache*	Daughter of Themistocles	"They call it a paradise."
NEE-CO-MASH		
Ajax	A horse	"Snort"

The Chorus

Assorted traders, slaves, bandits, eunuchs, soldiers, sailors, and drunken barroom brawlers.

The voyage of *Salaminia,*
Athens to Ephesus

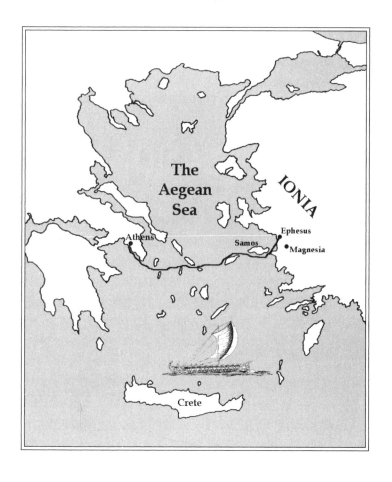

The Aegean Sea

IONIA

Athens

Samos

Ephesus

Magnesia

Crete

The voyage of Ajax the Horse,
Ephesus to Magnesia

ATHENS

1

Evil deeds do not prosper;
the slow man catches up with the swift.

I ran my finger along one foot of the corpse, then the other, making the body swing with a lazy, uncaring rhythm. I stared at his feet, my nose so close I went cross-eyed as the toes swung my way.

"He was like this when you found him?" I asked.

"I touched nothing," Pericles said, "except to confirm Thorion was dead."

"Are there any sons?" I asked.

"One, of twenty-four years. He's at the family estate, according to the head slave."

Thorion had died hard. He hung from a rope tied to a crossbeam in the low ceiling. A stool lay toppled below. The fall was nowhere near enough to snap his neck; instead he'd strangled. He must have changed his mind after the air was cut off, because there were deep red scratch marks in his throat where he'd tried and failed to relieve the pressure. Yet his arms were long enough to have reached the beam to pull himself up and call for help. Why hadn't he?

There was no answer to my question, except the high-pitched

wails and long, low moans that had assaulted my ears ever since I arrived. They came from the women's quarters across the inner courtyard. The wife and girl-children had begun screaming the moment they'd learned their husband and father was dead. They would screech, tear their clothes, and pull their shorn hair every waking moment until he was cremated. The caterwauling meant that by now the whole street knew Thorion was dead.

I stepped across to the narrow window facing onto the street. A small group stood below; citizens, and their slaves holding torches, the black smoke floating up to me with the distinctive bittersweet aroma of burning rag soaked in olive oil. The crowd would have entered the house by now but for the two city guards who stood at the door. The moment they were allowed, these neighbors would cut down Thorion and carry him to the courtyard, laying him out with his feet pointing toward the door to prevent the dead man's psyche from straying. Then the women would come downstairs to wash the body and dress it for eternity, with no more than three changes of clothes, as the law demands. They would place an obol in his mouth, the coin as payment for the ferryman of the dead, Charon, to carry Thorion across the Acheron, the river of woe.

The pressure would be building on the guards to let through the crowd and allow the rituals to begin. I might have only moments left to learn what I could.

"Did you know him?"

"No, not really." Pericles handed me a torn scrap of parchment. "This is the message which brought me."

THORION SAYS THIS TO PERICLES. I HAVE BETRAYED MY OFFICE AND MY CITY. NEWS OF A THREAT TO ATHENS. COME AT ONCE.

"It's not the sort of message anyone could ignore," Pericles said. "The head slave led me up here to Thorion's private office, where we found him dead. Is it reasonable for a man who intends suicide to summon someone he barely knows, purely to make him discover the body?"

"It might be if the man summoned is you." Pericles at the young age of thirty-three was recently elevated to leadership of the new democracy. Though he held no official position, already men came to him, to seek his approval before any important decision was made. I knew Pericles fairly well, might even claim to be a minor confidant, which was no easy position. The last time Pericles and I had been together in the presence of death, it had very nearly resulted in my own execution.

"The slave boy who carried the message says Thorion had a scroll with handles carved as lion heads open before him. Thorion appeared upset, shocked even. It seems obvious whatever this news is, it's written in the scroll, but there's no such scroll here. I've looked. How could it have disappeared? Something is wrong."

"You're correct, something is indeed wrong. His feet are dry." I pointed at the dry floor beneath the corpse. "Where's the urine? Everyone knows a dying man releases whatever he holds."

Pericles shrugged. "Not everyone does; not if they relieved themselves shortly before they died."

I lifted the hem of Thorion's chiton, which fell all the way to his ankles. I kept lifting until I found what I sought, at thigh level. I took a big sniff.

"He let go all right. It's on his thighs, but it didn't run down his leg."

Pericles stepped forward for a closer look, careful not to touch the body. He grunted. "You're right." He cast about the room, and so did I. Ceramics and pots and amphorae and jars stood on every possible surface, on benches and tables and even on the floor, giving the room more the look of a small warehouse than a man's private office. They must all have been imported; none had the look of the famous Athenian red figure pottery. Many appeared delicate and had small bases, yet not a single one was out of place or knocked over.

"Whatever happened, there wasn't a fight."

I lifted each pot and shook to see if the missing scroll had been dropped inside. Only one amphora rattled, and it proved to hold three old coins, not even Athenian.

I got down on all fours and crawled about, paying particular attention to the areas where a man might ordinarily stand or sit. Pericles watched from the entrance as I nosed about like a hunting dog searching for scent.

"Here, under the desk. The floor is damp, the smell is obvious."

"Let me see." Pericles, not one to fret about form when an important matter was at stake, shoved me aside and checked beneath the desk for himself. He surfaced to say, "It seems you are correct. Thorion died at his desk."

"And likely was murdered to prevent him passing on this intelligence. How could a comfortable citizen in the middle of Athens come to learn of a threat to the city?"

Pericles said, "Do you know what a proxenos is?"

"A citizen who acts for another city."

"A citizen who represents the interests of another city in its dealings with Athens. Thorion is . . . was . . . the proxenos for Ephesus."

Ephesus is a major city, across the sea on the east coast of the Aegean. The Ephesians speak Greek—they're as Hellene as we Athenians—but their city lies just within the Persian Empire.

"You think the summons had something to do with Ephesus."

"Don't you? Every proxenos receives regular news from his client city."

I nodded. "If your theory is good, then Thorion received letters today."

Pericles summoned the head slave of the household.

The man was thin, balding, and middle-aged. He shook with dread as his dead master hung before his eyes, and the most powerful man in Athens stared at him grim-faced. At twenty-one I was unimportant, and certainly less threatening to a slave, so I said, "Did your master receive any letters or packages today?"

The slave turned to me and said, "Oh, yes sir. The regular courier from Ephesus arrived at dusk, straight from the boat. He still smelled of the sea."

"You've seen this man before?"

"The same man always brings the mailbag, sir."

I glanced at Pericles. He glanced at me. This was progress.

"Was that when you last saw your master alive?"

"No sir, he was alive when I announced the second courier."

"The *second* courier?"

"The first left, taking the mailbag with him back to Ephesus. The master stayed in his office. I was summoned again later to bring a boy, and the master gave him a note for Pericles."

Pericles nodded.

"Then a second courier walked in as the boy went out the door, I hadn't even time to shut it. The second courier said he had an urgent message, sir, from Ephesus."

"What did Thorion say to that?"

"It's never happened before, sir. The master was startled when I told him."

"This second man must have given a name."

"Araxes, sir. He said his name was Araxes."

"Did he too smell of the sea?"

The slave thought for a moment. "Yes sir, now that you mention it, he did. He stayed longer than the first—I suppose he had more to say—and when he walked down the stairs he told me the master didn't wish to be disturbed until supper. I opened the door for him and he left."

"You didn't think to speak to your master after that, to check with him?"

"No sir, I always obey orders."

I sighed.

"Describe the second courier," I ordered.

"He had white hair," the slave said without hesitation.

"You mean he was old?" Pericles asked.

"No sir, I'd guess his age to be thirty, maybe thirty-five. The hair wasn't gray, it was white."

"Was he Hellene?" I asked.

"He spoke like us."

"What did he wear?"

"A chitoniskos. 'Twasn't worn either. It looked new."

The chitoniskos is cut short at the shoulders and thighs for easy movement. I wore one myself. Since the material is never cut to fit the body, there are always extra folds of material in which you could hide anything, such as a scroll for example.

"So the murderer tricked his way into Thorion's office. He slipped a loop around Thorion's neck, strangled him, and strung him up to make it look like suicide. Then he tucked the missing scroll inside his clothing and walked out."

"Oh, sir!" said the slave. "Did you say murderer? You're not suggesting the courier had something to do with the master's death are you? No, it's impossible."

His tone intrigued me. "What makes you so sure?"

"Because he spoke so nicely. I've never known a man who minded his pleases and thank-yous so well."

"You liked him?"

"Yes sir, who wouldn't?"

Pericles said, "Nicolaos, the murder of Thorion is important, but not as important as recovering the contents of the scroll. The safety of Athens depends upon it."

I nodded and rubbed my hands. "Any chance of sending a slave to Piraeus for a jar of seawater?" I had touched a dead man, and so would be considered ritually unclean and not permitted to eat until I'd washed my hands in seawater. The call from Pericles had made me miss dinner, and I was hungry.

Pericles shook his head. "The city gates closed long ago."

Why couldn't Thorion have died at a more convenient time? That was the way my luck went these days. But—"Say that again?"

Pericles wrinkled his brow. "What? The city gates closed long ago? It's true. So?"

"So Thorion was killed at night, *after the city gates closed.* The murderer is trapped inside Athens."

There was silence while Pericles absorbed that.

"The gates open at dawn," he said, his manner snappier than before, his back straighter. He glanced out the window into the dark night. "Can we catch him before then?"

"In a city as large as Athens? Not a hope in Hades, unless the murderer makes a mistake, and this man's no idiot."

Pericles' shoulders slumped.

"We could keep the gates closed in the morning," I suggested.

"Lock in Athens during the day?" Pericles shook his head. "The people wouldn't stand for it."

I nodded unhappy agreement. "Besides, that would tell the killer we're looking for him. He'd only go to ground until we were forced to reopen the gates. No, we have to let him come out into the open."

"You have a plan," Pericles deduced from my tone. "What is it?"

"The slave said the killer smelled of the sea, as did the real courier. Their boats docked at the port town of Piraeus, and they walked uphill to Athens. I'd be willing to bet our man will be lined up with the normal crowd to walk downhill back to Piraeus at first light. All we have to do is watch the traffic pass by."

"There are two roads to Piraeus," Pericles pointed out.

"So there are. I suggest that tomorrow morning, there will be a problem with the gate to the northern road."

Pericles nodded. "That can be arranged. You want everyone down the south road?"

"The south road is enclosed every step of the way within the Long Walls. If he goes that route then he can't escape; he'll be trapped in a tunnel where we control both ends."

"Brilliant," Pericles said.

"I'll be at the south gate to watch every man who passes," I said, pleased with myself. There were those who said I was too young and inexperienced for my position. This operation would prove them wrong.

I could imagine Pericles' reaction if I lost the scroll because I'd overslept. Yet dawn was far enough away that the wait would be tedious, particularly since I couldn't eat.

I solved the problem by shaking awake a slave when I returned to my father's home, and ordered the bleary-eyed man to stand over me—so he wouldn't fall asleep himself—and wake me in the predawn. I was so tired I went to sleep immediately, despite being on edge about my mission.

The slave got his revenge by kicking me in the stomach when the time came, but I didn't mind. I'd completed my two years of compulsory service in the army as an ephebe; broken sleep and rough awakenings had been the norm then.

One glance upward showed me the rosy-fingered dawn, as Homer would have called it, lighting the otherwise dark sky. I rose naked and wrapped the short material of a gray exomis about myself from the right side and tied it over my left shoulder. Such clothing is favored by artisans; I would be merely another workman, waiting at the gates to make my way to Piraeus for the day's employment.

I hurried through the dark streets, stepping in more than one pool of sewage, soaking my sandals in the stale wash water, the urine, the feces, and the rotting, rancid leftovers that neighbors had tossed out their doorways. I cursed as my feet plunged into yet another sticky, squelchy mess up past my ankles.

At the south gate, men were already lined up, shivering, yawning, and scratching themselves. Two guards stood at the head, waiting for Apollo's rays to appear in the east, when they would pull back the gates so the men could shamble through. I had visited these guards after leaving Thorion's house. They knew of my investigation and what to expect.

I walked from the end of the line in the direction of the guards, reminding myself every few steps to amble, to not appear as if I had any purpose, nodding or wishing good morning to the men I passed.

"*Kalimera.*"

"*Kalimera.* Good morning."

Most nodded back; some gave me queer or hostile looks. They probably thought I was a line jumper, something that could end with a fistfight. To them I explained I was looking for my workmate: had they seen a man with white hair? They would shake their heads and I would pass on.

Among one group were some women, haggard-looking, with unwashed hair and wearing patched linen. I couldn't imagine why they were waiting, until it occurred to me these were probably drudges whose men were too ill to work, or couldn't be bothered. One of them looked me up and down and smiled, then she blew me a kiss and said, "Gorgeous." The few teeth she retained were black. I felt myself blushing; had I been staring?

It was all too easy to pass by my suspects without even breaking step. Some wore hats, and these I had to stare at a little longer. Others held the leads of donkeys harnessed to carts, or sat atop protesting mules. A very few had horses, a luxury item.

The artisans among them had a slave or two to carry their tools and wore an exomis like mine. The common laborers wore nothing but short leather cloaks and surly expressions. The slaves stood together and told jokes. What man would rather be a slave than free? Yet the slaves did not seem hungry, and the free men whose only skill was to sell their labor looked thin and their faces were taut—I could see the ribs beneath the flesh, so perhaps slavery was to be preferred over being useless.

These men, as I say, were easily dismissed, and if a man owned slaves it was all the more easy to ignore him, because no one arriving in an afternoon can both murder someone and acquire slaves before the next dawn. The front of the line came ever closer, and still no Araxes. Had I made a mistake?

There were only two in the line before me now, a man leading a donkey, and a flattop cart pulled by a horse. Apollo peaked over the hills, and on cue in the weak light the guards lifted the heavy bar and carried it to the side.

Where had I gone wrong? The only thing I could think was that Araxes had arrived late, or perhaps wanted to hide himself in the crowd. I would stand by the gates and watch as the men passed through. Despite the chill I felt the irritating trickle of sweat in my armpits and down my back.

The man with the donkey had dark hair and beard. He grinned as I passed.

The distinct aroma of dead fish surrounded the horse cart. It was probably on its way to collect the morning's catch. Two men sat at the front, the one on the left held the reins. He was slumped forward and wore a full-length cloak to keep out the chill. The man on the right was fast asleep, leaning back in the seat with his hat over his face.

Behind the driver and his companion was a rack holding amphorae: clay pots with narrow lids, wide middles, and long tails that taper to a point; they looked like a row of pregnant worms standing upright. The amphorae exuded the strong, pungent, salty fish sauce called garos, which the fishwives make from gutted intestines fermented in large vats with seawater. No doubt the cart carried empties to be refilled. Anyone buying fresh fish would want the popular sauce to go with it. The smell made me ravenous.

The man under the hat was suspect. I leaned over and said to the driver, "*Kalimera.* I wanted to ask you—" I knocked the sleeping man's hat, which fell onto the seat and I jumped back.

His hair was disappointingly dark. But he didn't wake. His eyes stared, and his jaw hung slack, his tongue limp in his mouth. Across his throat was a dull red band, almost like a tight necklace, and there were claw marks in the flesh about it.

I stared for one shocked moment, then looked to the driver. His cloak had a hood. With the sun rising at his back he was a faceless silhouette.

I said, "*Kalimera,* Araxes."

He replied, "And a good morning to you, dear fellow." Araxes shoved. The dead man fell on me. I hit the ground with a corpse on top; the lifeless eyes stared into mine.

"Gah!" I pushed him off.

One of the guards grabbed Araxes' left arm. In a blink, Araxes had pulled a knife with his right and driven it into the guard's shoulder. The guard staggered back.

The other guard tried to snatch the harness but failed when Araxes lashed out with his whip.

The horse surged through the gateway, onto the road to Piraeus; the road that, according to my plan, Araxes would never reach.

I had no backup plan. None at all.

The unwounded guard grabbed his spear and ran into the middle of the road. It was a soldier's spear, not a javelin, not weighted for throwing, but the cart had not gone far. Araxes' back was crouched over, shrouded in his light leather cloak. The guard stood, legs apart. He considered his target for a heartbeat, hefted the spear, left arm pointing where he wanted to hit and eyes locked on the target, took three rapid steps forward and threw in a controlled arc, elbow firm. His right arm followed through. He kept his head up and his eyes never left the target.

It was a beautiful throw. I saw at once it would make the distance.

The spear arced across space, wobbling as it did, and passed over the shoulder of Araxes, so close I thought for a moment it would take him in the skull. But it passed him by, only the Gods know how, and landed, *thwack,* into the horse's rump.

The horse screamed. It half-reared, held by the harness, stumbled then recovered. The shaft flailed wildly. The wound opened to inflict even more pain.

The spear fell from the fleshy hole and the cartwheels clattered over it. The horse whinnied and accelerated away.

The guard beside me cursed. "I aimed for the man; all I did was scare the shit out of the animal!"

2

But Sarpedon missed him with his bright spear,
which smote the horse Pedasus on the right shoulder;
and the horse shrieked aloud as he gasped forth his life . . .
and the two warriors came together again
in soul-devouring strife.

We took off after the disappearing cart. The guard was as young as me and in tip-top condition. Between us we had a good chance of running down our prey.

Araxes looked over his shoulder, probably in fear of another spear. Instead he saw us chasing. He clambered into the tray of the cart. The frightened horse stayed on the path, trapped between the Long Walls.

Araxes picked up one of the empty amphorae and threw it.

The amphora bounced with a hollow thud. It veered from side to side. At the last moment it went straight for the guard.

He leaped, magnificent, strong as a deer. The guard came down safe and kept running as if nothing could stop him. Whoever this man was, he was a top athlete.

Araxes threw another amphora.

The guard jumped again, but this time the amphora ricocheted straight up into his knee. I heard a sharp crack. The guard went down screaming. He'd deserved better.

It was up to me now.

The next amphora shattered on the first bounce and I easily leaped over the shards.

One left.

I swore a sheep sacrifice to Zeus, if only the last amphora shattered.

Araxes stood with bent knees to compensate for the swaying cart. He threw.

The amphora bounced straight at me. I canceled the sacrifice.

When the amphora filled my vision, I threw myself at it, *under* it, rolling in the dirt. The hard clay whistled over my head.

When I came back up Araxes had returned to the driver's seat, his back to me. He must've thought the amphora had brought me down.

I sprinted to the tail end, hauled myself up. The platform was smooth and varnished dark from years of fish oil.

Araxes looked back in surprise. He dropped the reins and pulled out his knife. The blade was still red from the shoulder of the wounded guard.

The driverless cart slammed into the right wall. We both fell over and I scrabbled for a hold to stop being thrown off.

The cart veered wildly to smash into the opposite wall. The metal rims of the wheels squealed against the wood and made my teeth hurt.

The whole contraption settled and picked up speed. We'd reached a steep descent.

We picked ourselves up off the slippery, bouncing surface. The first of us to fall would get a knife in his back.

He tried to stab me. I blocked his forearm with my left, and then did something you should never do: I threw down my knife.

No, I wasn't surrendering; I'd aimed at his foot.

I missed cleanly. The knife quivered point first in the wooden tray. But the throw forced him to dance, and as he did, I grabbed the scroll case from beneath his chiton.

"Thanks a lot, Araxes. See you!"

Mission accomplished. I jumped off the back and—

Bang. My chin hit the floor and rattled my teeth. He'd pulled my feet out from under me.

The scroll case rolled from my hand. Araxes stamped on it as it skidded past.

I snatched the hilt of my knife and rose. I kicked at the case, hoping to send it over the side. Araxes blocked my kick, then tried to drag the case to him.

I was having none of that. I stamped on the case myself and dragged it back to center. It was like playing a boys' ball game in the street, with the added distraction of knives on a bouncing, slippery surface.

We'd rushed downhill at great speed. Over my enemy's shoulder I saw the closed gates at the Piraeus end of the road and the two guards who defended them.

With a sinking feeling, I realized nobody had briefed those guards. It never occurred to me Araxes would get this far.

Araxes saw it too. He grabbed the whip and deliberately cracked it against the horse's wound, goading the already panicking animal into going faster.

The guards held their spears with points facing us and ends dug into the earth. I could hear one of them shouting, "Halt! I order you to halt!"

He didn't have a hope in Hades.

Araxes said, "Good luck." Then he jumped. His body slammed into the Long Wall and disappeared to the rear as the cart sped onwards.

I wanted to pick up the scroll case. But if I did, I would die on the cart. I turned and jumped.

Hitting the wall pushed the air out of my lungs. I hooked my arms over the top to stop from falling under the wheels.

Splinters embedded in the flesh of my forearms. I tried to scream but there was no air.

The horse ran headlong into the gates and squealed, a terrible, sickening sound.

I heard cracking, whether wood or bones I don't know. One guard went down. His body jerked as a wheel drove over him. Then the other. He lay still.

The cart left the ground. It spun in the air, smashed into the gates. They cracked and flew outward. Men on the other side screamed.

Araxes had bounced off the wall and landed on a roll. He picked himself up and waded through the bloodied wreck of horse, cart, and men.

The scroll case had been thrown clear. It lay in plain sight on the other side of the ruined gates. Araxes picked it up as he stumbled past.

I cursed and let go of the wall. There were a hundred tiny wooden splinters sticking out of my flesh, each one a painful red dot of blood.

On the other side, men lay with wounds, or stood in simple shock. I ignored them.

Araxes veered away from the streets of Piraeus. He headed right, to the commercial docks.

I felt a small surge of relief. If he tried to hide in the warehouses, he would be trapped, and a small army would eventually root him out.

I was exhausted and shaking, but surely he had to be too. Araxes staggered and came to a stop.

I'd run him down.

Araxes stood on the wooden docks and waved to me as if he hadn't a care in the world.

Suddenly I was aware of the sea-salt air, the crisp breeze tossing my hair, the wash of the sea against the wharves, and the large ship docked right next to where Araxes waved.

It was stern-to-wharf, which some ships will do when they're ready to depart. A gangplank led from the wharf to the stern.

Araxes turned and walked up. They didn't even stop for the gangplank. A sailor kicked it crashing to the wharf.

I heard the call, "Oars out!" A single row of oars appeared over both sides.

I came to a juddering halt at the gangplank, gasping for breath. The ship was five paces away. I thought about jumping, but it would have been suicidal. Even if I made the leap, there was a boatful of sailors to fight.

The ship on which Araxes slipped away was long, but with only a single row of oars. She was either a diplomatic boat, the sort that belonged to a city, or . . . and this seemed all too depressingly likely . . . before me was a Phoenician warship, or maybe a pirate.

Araxes appeared at the stern. He waved cheerily, and then, with his left hand, held up the scroll for me to see. He cupped a hand to his mouth and shouted, "So pleased you made it. Take care, dear fellow. Bye!"

I gritted my teeth, but couldn't prevent myself from screaming in frustration. Araxes had escaped, and taken with him the information that had killed at least three men, maybe more, plus he'd made me look incompetent. I watched as whatever fledgling reputation I had for investigation departed on that boat.

I swore on the spot, by Zeus, by Athena, by every God that knew revenge, that I would track down Araxes.

Then a trickle of sweat and a cold shiver ran down my back. I'd promised Pericles success.

I'd actually said, "He can't escape."

What was Pericles going to say?

3

*There is a strength in the union
even of very sorry men.*

"It's a disaster, Nicolaos, a bloody disaster."

Pericles stalked back and forth in his office, as if he could find the source of his anguish underfoot and grind it out of existence.

I shifted in my seat. My arms were on fire from the splintering they'd taken. They had a crust of blood over them, but the scabs broke and bled every time I moved. My forehead sported a lump—I had no idea how it got there—and my chest muscles ached with every breath.

"How could you have let him get away so easily?" Pericles demanded.

"We did our best," I muttered. "I didn't get these injuries sitting still."

"Don't whine," he said testily. He turned his back and gazed out the window.

"There are men worse off than you. Two of those guards are dead. One has his kneecap shattered and will probably never walk straight again. He was chosen to run at the next Olympics. How am I supposed to explain this to their fathers?" He turned back to me.

"And how in Hades did a Phoenician ship get alongside the commercial docks without anyone noticing?"

"I'll ask the harbormaster, but Pericles, is there a law against it?"

"If there isn't, there will be now!"

I decided not to point out that horse had bolted. In fact, any mention of a bolting horse would probably be a bad idea.

"I'm disappointed, Nicolaos. I trusted you with a vital, delicate mission, and this is the result you bring me. I'm reconsidering our arrangement."

Disaster. If Pericles dismissed me, it would prove my father's contention—that there was no future to be made from investigation—and I would be bound by our agreement to return to his sculptor's workshop.

"Pericles, this is unfair. The investigation has barely begun."

"It should be over. Look at the mess you've made so far."

Shouting would be the fastest route to my dismissal. "All right, that's a fair point," I conceded. "Araxes proved to be more able than anyone could reasonably have expected."

It sounded weak even to my ears, but I had to try something. "Who's going to catch him, if I don't?"

"I've been asking myself that same question, but with a slightly different emphasis."

I dredged my brain for some morsel of progress, to show I was not a complete failure. "At least we know his name is Araxes."

"We know nothing." Pericles glared at me. "Araxes is the name of a river in Asia."

"Oh."

Pericles drummed his fingers on his desk while I contemplated life as a sculptor and rehearsed the words I would use to tell my father I had failed. Then Pericles spoke.

"We have wars with four cities dragging on. *Four at once,*

how many cities could manage that? Plus there's talk of a major war with Corinth or Sparta. If it gets any worse, we'll have to think about bringing old men and boys into the army." Pericles glared at me. "The only reason I'm retaining you, Nicolaos—for now—is we're stretched so thin. You're the only man available. That's the *only* reason. When this commission is over, you can consider our agreement terminated."

"Unless I succeed," I said at once.

Pericles paused, while my heart gyrated about my chest.

"Unless you are *spectacularly* successful," he said at last, and I breathed again. "Which, frankly, I doubt."

It was the best deal I could hope for, perhaps better than I deserved, because Pericles was right; I had comprehensively underestimated my opponent, and been comprehensively defeated. I wasn't planning on anything less than total success before I finished.

He said, "You're going to Ephesus. I'll arrange transport."

That made me sit up. "Can't we send the navy after the Phoenician?"

"Do you know how many ports there are in the Aegean Sea? No? Neither does anyone else, there are that many. We may have the largest navy in the world, but even we don't have enough ships to cover every hiding place. Besides, we have two hundred triremes committed against Cyprus, and that's the bulk of the fleet."

It was true. Cyprus was still pro-Persian and agitating against Athens on the seas. Worse, the news from the fleet was not encouraging.

"Ephesus is the source of the letter. We can't retrieve the letter, so find whoever sent it, and recover the information." Pericles paused and studied me for a moment. "I'd have thought you'd be overjoyed to go to Ephesus. Isn't that where your girl-friend is?"

"Diotima's not my girlfriend," I said.

"But she's in Ephesus, is she not?"

So she was. Diotima was in Ephesus because she'd left me three months before, and I still hadn't got over it.

Diotima was the result of a long-standing affair between one of our statesmen and a high-class prostitute. Not the most regular of pedigrees. Yet when her father had been murdered, Diotima had hunted down his killers with a relentless determination that would have done credit to a firstborn son, let alone a disregarded daughter. By the time the two of us had caught the killer, my heart was set. Diotima was the girl for me.

In Athens, such things are arranged between the fathers. I'd been so sure my father would agree to a betrothal that I'd told Diotima my intention before I asked him.

Then he'd said no. Father had thought only of the shame of his son married to the daughter of a noncitizen prostitute. When Diotima had eagerly pressed me next day, I'd had no choice but to tell her why she was not an acceptable bride. It was a conversation I cringed to recall.

Diotima disappeared without a trace. I was eventually driven to ask her mother, who told me she'd left for Ephesus. My girl had been a priestess of Artemis in Athens; now she was a priestess at the Artemision in Ephesus. I didn't have to ask why she'd gone, nor why she'd left without a goodbye. I hadn't heard a thing from her in the three months since. I'd thought never to hear from her again.

Pericles said to me, "You'll be able to see her when you arrive."

I wasn't about to tell Pericles the last thing I wanted was to see Diotima. At least, not until I'd worked out what to say to her.

"Oh, and Nicolaos, you are invited to a symposium tomorrow night, at the home of Callias."

Callias? He was the richest man in Athens; a man far above my station. "Whatever for?" I asked.

Pericles snorted. "Callias has about thirty years' more experience with foreign missions than you do. Whatever advice he has, I suggest you take it."

Any other man, when he's been wounded in battle, visits a doctor at the gymnasium, an expert in treating sword cuts, spear punctures, broken bones, and bruises. The doctor tends the hero's honorable wounds while his comrades in arms stand about, recounting his bravery on the field of battle and singing his praises.

I, on the other hand, having risked life and limb in the shadowy world of investigation, went home to my mother.

Phaenarete is a midwife. She sat me down with a bowl of hot water and a clean rag, and used bronze tweezers to pull out the splinters in my arms, one by one, all the while describing my various defects, intellectual and physical. It was a long list. Whenever she made a particular point she squeezed harder and I yelped. My mother told me not to be a baby.

When she finished she applied a sticky, smelly lotion to my forearms and told me to lie still and let the lotion soak in, or I would die of the flesh-eating sickness. "Which would be no less than your own fault," she sniffed, and walked off, leaving me to feel sorry for myself.

I'd ritually cleansed my hands in the sea while I was at Piraeus. That allowed me to eat my fill, so I had a slave girl bring me yesterday's bread soaked in wine, with olives, figs, and cheese. I lay there digesting, which gave my mind all too much time to replay the disastrous scene with Pericles and worry about my future.

I'd known Pericles would be angry, but the strength of his backlash had shocked me. I hadn't noticed during the argument, because I'd been too concerned for myself, but now I recalled the dark rings under his eyes. His movements, always graceful in public, had been twitchy in the privacy of his office. The voice of Pericles was the most beautiful and serene instrument the world had ever heard, but with me he'd had the grating, angry tone of a cornered man. Pericles had looked and sounded like a man under pressure, and no wonder.

Pericles had come to the leadership of Athens at a moment of extreme crisis, when our new democracy had been only days old, and the man who founded it had been murdered. In the wake of the murder the city might have collapsed in civil war, but Pericles had stepped into the breach and saved us.

Pericles had inherited a city that barely functioned. Men loved the new democracy, but they didn't know how to run it. Citizen committees had sprung up. It would have been nice if some of the committees had actually worked. Men couldn't agree, officials overstepped their powers, gaps appeared where everyone thought someone else had been responsible for something. Fingers pointed in every direction. The democracy was like some giant machine with levers that didn't fit and not enough oil to stop the friction. Pericles spent his days being the oil. He went from one committee to another, to persuade where he could, correct where he had to.

Then too, many cities had taken advantage of the turmoil within Athens to act against us. The army and navy were stretched beyond the limit. The agora seemed half empty. Women were conspicuous among the stalls because so many men were away, serving in the army or the navy. The stoas where men met to gossip and discuss politics were almost empty.

So if Pericles shouted at me because I had failed in the one task assigned to me, who was I to complain? On the other hand, like Pericles, I was new to my job, and I was an apprentice with no master from whom to learn, because no one before had taken the trade I'd assumed: to be an agent when the truth was needed. Wasn't an apprentice permitted a few mistakes? It was all terribly unfair.

My twelve-year-old brother entered the courtyard.

He took one look at me and said, "What happened to you, Nico?"

I closed my eyes. "Go away, Socrates."

He sat down beside me. "You get in a fight?"

"Yes, and the other guy got hurt too."

"Did you win?"

"It was a draw." I refused to admit Araxes had defeated me.

"You look like you'll be lying there for days."

"It's only a few scratches. Anyway, I have work to do. I'm to go to a symposium tomorrow night at the home of Callias. Pericles invited me along."

"Wow!" Socrates was right to wow. Callias and Pericles were not normally given to socializing with young men of no consequence.

"I want to go to the symposium too," Socrates said, surprising me.

"In case you haven't noticed, you're still a child."

"If I was a slave boy I'd be able to come, wouldn't I?" he wheedled. "You're taking an attendant, aren't you?"

I was so young and inexperienced in the field of formal socializing that I hadn't even thought about it. But Socrates was right. No citizen would dream of going to a symposium without at least one slave to see him home.

"Of course I meant to take an attendant," I lied without hesitation. "I'll ask Father for one of his slaves."

He smiled. "Don't bother. For one night only, I'll be your slave."

The idea of having my irritating younger brother as my slave held a certain appeal, and it meant I wouldn't have to ask a favor of my father, with whom I was at odds, but, "Why are you so desperate to go?" I asked, suspicious.

He shrugged his shoulders and said, "I want to see what goes on. I've never been to a symposium before. Do you think I'll be good at it when I'm old enough?"

"No Socrates, you'd be rotten," I said, quite certain.

It was an earthquake. No, it was one of my father's slaves, shaking me awake next morning. I opened a bleary eye to see a grimy foot on my chest, and above it the same slave whom I'd ordered to stand over me the night before. I suspected the slave disliked me, and I was certain he needed to cut his toenails, they were digging into my skin.

"There's a man outside on a horse," he said it as if he were announcing plague. "He says he needs to see you."

I groaned. Every bruised and abused muscle whined when I sat up.

"Did you get his name?"

"No, but he says his father's dead."

The son of Thorion. "Bring him in."

"What about the horse?"

"Bring it in too."

"Through the front door?"

"No, you idiot, through the window."

But still he looked blank. I took pity upon him. Our family doesn't keep horses and he had no experience. I said, "Open the gates to the courtyard. Show him in through the back lane."

"I came as fast as I could," said Onteles, the son of Thorion.

He had indeed. His hair was damp and hung like seaweed. I could smell the sweat of the ride upon him.

"Where were you when you heard?"

"At our country estate, to the north."

"How did you get here so quickly?"

"I rode hard. I stopped at home only to confirm the news my father was dead and learn you are investigating the crime, though the Gods know why. I rode here at once."

The horse breathed heavily and had drunk buckets of water but was sleek and looked fit for more. The muscles rippled beneath the skin, a powerful beast.

"This is a magnificent horse."

"One of the best. Father bought him for me."

I was instantly jealous. I'd always wanted a horse. After I left the army I begged my father, Sophroniscus, to buy one, but he refused, saying what possible need had the son of a sculptor for a horse?

"Thorion must have been a wealthy man."

"He did well from trade. Import, export, anything that was profitable."

"Recently it was pottery."

"If you say so. I never paid much attention. The estate is my future. Father had less interest in it. The farmland has become rather run-down." Onteles looked me over. "You're younger than me."

"Twenty-one."

"Then why are you avenging the crime? Does my family know you?"

"Pericles asked me, for the good of the state."

"You?"

"I've done this sort of thing before. It seems your father wanted to confess to a crime against Athens. Now we'd like to know, what crime?" I told Onteles about the note.

Onteles snorted like his horse and said, "Ridiculous. Whatever this note, there'll be a strange but innocent explanation."

I couldn't agree, but an argument with the son would be pointless.

"What are your plans?" I asked him.

"To bury my father. After that"—he shrugged—"there's the estate, and to be a citizen of Athens. I have responsibilities now."

Onteles, son of Thorion, was only three years older than me, but already an adult. In Athens, a man is a child in the eyes of the law so long as his father lives. Pericles himself was still a legal child, and he'd been the foremost man of the city for months.

By the death of his father, Onteles, son of Thorion, became responsible for his mother for the rest of her life, and for his sisters until he found them husbands, which he would probably do as quickly as possible to relieve himself of the burden.

I asked, "You won't trade?"

"That was always my father's business. I'll wind it down."

"Or continue as proxenos for Ephesus?"

"Gods no! I have enough to keep me busy." He paused in thought. "I think I'll marry."

I felt a pang of envy. Onteles no longer needed his father's permission to marry as he chose. If only that were me.

Onteles departed to see to his household. I ate breakfast and then hobbled my way down to Piraeus to find the harbormaster. I chose the southern route to see again the places where I'd fought for my life. It was an odd experience. I irrationally felt the struggle should have left its mark deep in every step of the way, yet the hard surface of the road was untouched. The same did not apply to the Long Walls, which were satisfyingly gouged where the cart had crashed into them, and strange cyclic marks showed where the wheels had scraped the wood.

Men swarmed over the broken lower gate. Carpenters worked on the shattered support posts, prying off the heavy, metal hinges to be reused. The frame for a new gate was already taking shape on the ground. Men with hammers and chisels and drills kneeled over it, working to fit the joints. There was more than the usual amount of swearing.

As I stepped over planking, a fellow traveler stopped to ask a workman what had happened. The workman wiped the sweat from his brow, spat in the dust, and said, "Some idiot drove a horse and cart right into the gates. It'll take a month to fix." He spat again. "I'd love to get my hands on the asshole who did this."

I tiptoed through.

At the docks I was directed to the harbormaster, a stocky, older man perched on a small, three-legged, wooden stool in a small alcove, which was nestled between two large warehouses, one of which reeked of spice, and the other of oil. His entire attention was upon a tarnished bronze brazier, in which something sizzled over a respectable fire. He held a metal skewer in his right hand, which he used to poke his lunch. His face was fleshed out and ruddy, either from the heat of the fire or naturally, I didn't know which.

He looked up as I stopped before him, and his face fell at once.

"Are you the harb—"

"Oh Gods, what is it now?"

"Huh?"

"I walk away for the briefest moment to have a quiet bite, and the first thing that happens is someone interrupts me. Is some ship blocking you in?"

"Me? No."

"Got a problem with your pier allocation?"

"No."

"Other captains bitching about dock space again? Oh Zeus, I hate that."

"No one said anything to me."

"If the street kids are stealing your cargo, that's your problem."

"I don't have any problems with street kids."

"Anyone drowned?"

"No."

"Your ship sank?"

"No."

"So you got no problems?"

"I need—"

"Good. Then don't bother me till I've eaten." He turned back to the brazier and did his best to ignore me.

I stood and watched him stir the sizzling food. The aroma overwhelmed me. Eventually I had to ask, "That smells great. What is it?"

He said without looking up, "Eel in garos sauce, with some extra spices. My own recipe."

I licked my lips. "Hey, you know what would go well with that?"

He looked up. "No, what?"

"Neither do I. I thought you'd know. Wait a moment."

I stepped out of the alcove, and ran through the narrow alleys that squeezed between the warehouses and the Emporion, which divides the docklands from the town. On the other side was the larger of the two agoras in Piraeus. I searched among the stalls until I found a small amphora of spiced wine from Chios, and a chunk of goat cheese.

I carried these back to the harbormaster in time to see him ladle the eel into a bowl. I held up the wine and cheese and said, "Share?" I jiggled the amphora to show it was full.

He looked at the amphora suspiciously. "What wine is that? I won't touch bad stuff."

"Chian."

He nodded. "But you leave the amphora behind, all right?"

"Sure, no problem. I'm Nicolaos, son of Sophroniscus, of the deme Alopece," I said, naming my father and my family's district.

"Orbanos, son of Polymenotos—may the bastard rot in Hades—of the deme Piraeus. Take a seat, Nicolaos."

"There isn't one."

He pointed to a packing box that was too high to be comfortable. I broke the cheese while he halved the eel into a second bowl, then reached behind him to pull out two cups. He spat in each and rubbed his finger round to get the dust out before putting them on another packing crate. I levered the wax plug out of the neck of the amphora with my knife and poured for us both.

We held up our cups.

"Ships and women."

"Athena confound our enemies."

Orbanos sipped, and then sipped again. "Not a bad vintage," he conceded. "The fenugreek really comes through on the aftertaste, don't it? Maybe one part in fifty seawater, maybe two parts?" He swirled the wine in the cup. "This could cellar." Orbanos looked at me with something approaching respect. "I see you know something about wine."

If it was good, it was a fluke, because I didn't know the first thing. I'd merely bought the most expensive amphora I could find. Pericles had given me a large bag of coins for expenses, and I had no objection to spending his money.

We reached for our steaming bowls. The eel was hot enough to burn my fingers as I picked up a chunk coated in garos sauce and small flecks of extra spices. I put it to my lips, wondering what a rough-looking man like Orbanos might have produced.

It was brilliant. I had my doubts about Orbanos as a harbormaster, but as a cook he was first-class. I began to shovel in the food. Orbanos ate delicately, picking a small piece with his fingers, and taking his time over each mouthful.

As I chewed I said, "This is delicious, Orbanos. How did you learn to cook like this?"

"I was a sailor in my younger days, saw a lot of the world.

Any port we laid over at, I'd try the local food, anything different. Got to be a hobby with me. I talked to the cooks and learned their recipes. I passed on what I learned in one place to guys in another, and I always tried everything for myself."

"Have you thought about becoming a cook yourself?"

He snorted. "I'd rather swallow anchovies than waste my time cooking for men who can't tell goat meat from a decent tuna. The only place you can get work as a cook is in the taverns. By the time the customers order food, they're so drunk they'll eat whatever the pigs turned down. I've even seen unscrupulous innkeepers serve rat and call it a traditional local dish, and the idiots ate it."

"Maybe you should start your own place, purely for eating?"

He thought about it for a moment, but said, "Nah, it'd never catch on. If a man wants to eat out, he visits a friend."

"Write a book then. Tell other people how to cook this delicious food."

"A book about cooking? Who in their right mind would want something like that?" Orbanos belched. "So, what do you want with me?"

"I'm searching for a man. He left on a boat that was here, the other day—"

"No there wasn't."

I blinked in surprise. "There wasn't?"

"Look, if you're going to turn up here asking questions, at least get the terms right. We don't allow boats to dock here, only ships."

"What's the difference?"

"You don't *know*?"

"Not about boats . . . ships. I've never been on a boat or a ship in my life."

Orbanos dropped his empty bowl on the ground in shock, where it clattered. "Poseidon's nuts! You, an Athenian, never rowed for the navy?"

"No, but I was an ephebe in the army. Does that count?"

He spat in the dirt. "No, it don't. Can't stomach those use-less bloody army fools. Show me your hands."

I held out my hands.

"Not that way, you dolt. Turn 'em over."

Orbanos inspected my palms and fingers and grimaced. "Not a proper callus on 'em. In my day lad we fought the Persians on ships—our ships—in the navy. You know what I mean?"

"I don't care about—" I saw the expression on his face. "Er . . . yes, of course."

"It was us common men beat the Persians, lad, 'cause a hundred and seventy men pulling hard, and a steersman who knows his business, can put a ship's ram in an enemy before the dozy bastards can blink. *Pulling.* Getting calluses on our hands, like you haven't got." He thrust his hands out at me. Horrible, misshapen things. The fingers were curled in on themselves. The palms were a solid mass of . . . well, he said callus, but I would have called it scar tissue. "Now those are the hands of a man who fought for his city," he said with pride. Then his eyes narrowed. "You're not the son of a wealthy man. Are you?"

"My father's a sculptor."

Orbanos relaxed. "One of us, then. A poor man."

"He's not rich," I said.

"Good. The rich are trash, the only decent man among them was Themistocles."

"But he ran to the Persians."

"Wouldn't you run if your own city turned against you? We veterans know who gave us victory. He built the fleet. Before Themistocles, this place was a tiny village. Today, it's the big-gest port in Hellas."

"And that's how we beat the Persians?" I asked.

"Hades take me if I lie."

He paused. Since the Lord of the Dead failed to carry him

off, Orbanos took it as proof of his truthfulness. "There, you see? How old were you when the Persians came?"

"Uh, I was one year old," I admitted reluctantly. Whenever I talked of such things to older men, or listened to them as they reminisced, I always felt a slight, irrational shame that they had fought and I had not.

To change the subject, I said, "You manage the ships, don't you? You tell them where to tie up."

"Twelve yesterday. Fourteen the day before that. You've got no idea how much business this place does."

"I'm looking for a long, narrow one, not like a cargo ship, with a single row of oars."

"You mean a pentekonter."

"A what?"

"*Fifty* oars. *Pentekonta*. Twenty-five on each side. Katafrakta class."

The question was in my expression.

He sighed. "Means she has a deck for men to walk upon. If she'd been only a hull with seats she'd have been an afrakta class. The pentekonter's an old design but she's good for lots of things."

"What was this one?"

"Ship for hire, if you ask me. Not a trader, that's for sure. The pentekonter hull's not the best for trading, not enough cargo space."

"Ship for hire?"

"Like a mercenary, only on water. You see?"

I saw. "Any idea where she came from?"

He shook his head. "No."

"Name of the captain?"

"He didn't say."

"Did they say what they were doing here?"

"Didn't ask."

I sighed. "Is there anything you do know?"

"She arrived two days ago. Rowed into harbor nice and quiet, not like some dumbass captains who come in under canvas and drop sail at the last moment—had a collision 'cause of that last month. This guy only wanted to touch long enough to off-load a couple of passengers. It was barely worth taking his docking fee."

"*Couple?*"

"Man and a girl."

A *girl*? "Tell me about the girl."

He shrugged. "I dunno. Who pays attention to slaves?"

"How do you know she was a slave?"

"Because he stopped and asked me for directions to the slave market. Said he wanted to sell her. She didn't look none too happy about it either."

"She might have been captured in a pirate raid."

"Then that would make her a slave, wouldn't it?" he said, reasonably enough. "As long as she isn't Athenian."

"Was she?"

"Dunno."

"Thanks, Orbanos, I'm off to find that slave girl."

"You better hurry then."

"Why?"

"The market was shut yesterday, but it opened this morning. She could be sold by now."

4

You ought not to practice childish ways,
since you are no longer that age.

The girl stood on the auction block, naked but for a sign hung around her neck, and I knew that before the day was out she would be raped. The sign gave her name, age, state of health, and certified that she was a legitimate slave and not a free citizen. The law of Athens says they have to hang the sign, but everyone knows the seller always lies about the age and health. There's a saying, "No one ever sold a sick slave."

The dealer pushed the sign to the side, the better for the crowd to view this particular asset. He had no need to lie this time.

The slave market is run in one corner of the large agora at Piraeus, between the corn exchange and the rest of the vegetables. I'd sprinted all the way there in time to hear the dealer declaim the girl's virtues: young, pretty, virgin, in good health, the perfect spice to brighten any brothel. He was probably right.

She was perhaps fourteen, give or take a year, and she wasn't too skinny, quite rounded in fact; light brown hair, slightly curly, thin face, large, scared eyes; but her posture was defiant, her back straight, chin up. The girl had the attention of every man there, all of whom were bored.

One man had a go at feeling her behind. She kicked out at him and swore. Men laughed. I'm sure I hadn't known those words when I was her age.

The dealer tugged on her chain, and snarled something at her. She snarled back.

That stopped me. I didn't speak Persian, but I knew it when I heard it, and she'd been speaking it. She seemed Hellene, but she spoke Persian. I pushed my way through the crowd, to the edge of the platform.

"What's your name?" I asked. I could have read it off her sign, but I wanted to hear her say it.

"Asia," she replied in perfect Greek. She looked down at me in contempt.

"You speak Persian?"

She replied with a rapid flow that was unintelligible to me.

"Listen," I said to the slave dealer, "I need to talk to this girl."

He was a large man with a bushy beard. He looked down at me from the platform and said, "Talk all you like until the auction starts, then you have to stand back. You a buyer?"

"How much do you expect she'll go for?" I asked.

He told me. I winced. How could I hide this on the accounts? No, it wasn't possible. Pericles would have me take the hemlock if I listed "purchase slave girl" under state expenses.

"No, I'm not a buyer."

I said to the girl, "Listen, you came here on a boat—ship—two days ago, didn't you?"

She nodded and said, "Yes."

"The man who brought you, who is he?"

"He said his name was Araxes, but that's a river in—"

"The Persian Empire. Yes, I know." Why did everyone have to know more geography than me? "Who is he really?"

"I don't know."

"Then how come he owned you?"

"He didn't own me. I was taken. I'm not a slave, I was free, I shouldn't be here."

"Are you Athenian? If you're Athenian I can get you freed."

She hesitated. "No."

"Where are you from, then?"

Silence. She didn't open her mouth.

"Your name . . . Asia was a Titan, the daughter of Oceanos and Tethys, but it's also the name we use for the land of the Persians. Is that where you're from?"

Silence again, but I was sure of it. How else could she speak Persian? I didn't even know if Asia was her real name; she may have adopted it, as Araxes surely had his.

"Listen, I'm an agent working on an investigation. What you know could help me."

"What's an agent?"

"Someone who carries out commissions for others."

Her eyes brightened. "Can I hire you?"

I laughed. "No. How could you pay me? Do you know why this Araxes came to Athens?"

"I have no idea."

"Do you know what he intended to do?"

"To sell me."

"Do you know what he did after?"

"How could I?"

"Why did he bring you?"

"I don't know."

"Is Araxes your father?"

"*No!*"

That reaction, at least, was real. "Did Araxes take you off a boat?"

"On land."

"Who's your father?"

Silence. The fact she refused to discuss him or her home

only increased the likelihood her father had sold her. Such things happened. Maybe she was in denial about it.

"Did your father sell you?"

Silence.

"Are you going to tell me anything?"

"No."

"You have to tell me something."

"Why? Would it get me out of here?"

The dealer said to me, "It's time."

The auction commenced. The slave dealer called, "What am I bid?"

A man not far away from me bellowed, "One hundred drachmae!"

Another on the other side of the crowd immediately replied, "One hundred and twenty!"

Someone I couldn't see shouted, "One hundred twenty-five!"

The crowd murmured in appreciation. That was a decent price for any child, and this auction had barely begun.

They edged each other up, until the third man dropped out and it became a two-horse race. Or rather, a two brothel keeper race. The man closest to me was fat, his chiton was stained with sweat, and he reeked of the sickly sweet incense the brothels use to cover other smells. There was no doubting what he was. I assumed the other man was a competitor, since they seemed to know each other, and both called to the dealer by name.

Finally the one I could see called, "Two hundred and five drachmae!"

Silence.

The owner is often the one to break in a new purchase. This one stared up at the girl and licked his lips; it was obvious he couldn't wait to get on top of her. After that, he'd turn her over to the clients. The girl stood upright, and stared over the heads of the crowd, her face a mask of nothing.

The slave dealer allowed the silence to continue for heartbeats. He looked back and forth among the crowd. When he spotted me, he raised an eyebrow.

I shook my head.

The girl began to weep.

He called, "For two hundred and five drachmae, going to—"

"Two hundred and fifty drachmae!"

Did I say that?

The dealer didn't look at all surprised.

The brothel keeper did. I glanced at him, he glanced at me. The brothel keeper licked his lips, called, "Two hundred and fifty-five drachmae!"

"Three hundred drachmae!" I winced at the sound of my own voice.

A poor family could live for a year on what I had paid for the child. Now I owned her, Asia would have no choice but to tell me what I wanted to know, and I couldn't wait to find out. She was my link to Araxes.

The dealers always hand over a slave with a wristlock so no one can blame them if the slave later escapes. My first action was to unpeg the lock. I wanted her cooperation, I didn't want to hear coerced lies.

Asia rubbed her wrists and said, "Thank you," her expression neutral. I couldn't tell if she was pleased or disappointed to be my property, but there was one thing that had to be sorted out at once.

"Thank you, *master*."

She looked at me blankly.

"I am your master. You will address me correctly."

I thought for a moment she would argue, but she seemed to get control of herself and said, "Yes, *master*." She didn't quite spit it out.

"Master, are you really an agent?"

"Yes, of course."

"In that case, master, I want to hire you."

I laughed. "Asia, I think we might have this master-slave relationship thing around the wrong way."

"No, I mean it, master. I need you to return me to my father."

"Your father's the one who sold you."

"My father loves me. He'd never sell me."

Sure he wouldn't. That's why I'd found the girl in a slave market. "All right then, I'll humor you for a moment. Who is your father?"

She drew herself up to her full height, which wasn't much, and announced, "I swear destruction for the man who enslaved me. As my father did to his enemies, so I follow his example. I am Asia, daughter of Themistocles. My father is Satrap of Magnesia in the name of the Great King, and I am hiring you to take me home." She paused, then said anxiously, "I'm afraid you'll have to take payment on delivery."

5

A man of substance dear to his fellows;
for his dwelling was by the road-side
and he entertained all men.

Was she telling the truth? I didn't have time to quiz Asia on the spot, I barely had time to deposit her at home before preparing for the symposium. I ushered her in through the front door, having warned her to tell no one her father's name.

"Where did you get her?" It was Socrates. He'd wandered into the entrance hall, and looked Asia up and down appreciatively. It occurred to me my little brother was growing up.

"She's a slave. I bought her. Today."

"*You* bought her?"

"Yes."

Socrates inspected my purchase once more, and said, "I wouldn't want to be in your place when Diotima sees her!"

"Who's Diotima?" Asia asked.

"His girlfriend," Socrates said to Asia.

"No, she's not," I said. "Diotima will never see her, and anyway I don't care if she does."

"That's bad logic," Socrates said. "Either you don't care if Diotima sees her, or else you do care but you're not worried they'll meet. They can't both be true; it's an exclusion principle, you see—"

"Socrates, I need you to do something for me," I said, cutting him off before he could go on about his principle, whatever it was. "I have to get ready for the symposium. Get Asia some food and a proper tunic, will you? The tunic the slave dealer threw in is so moth-eaten it's ready to fall apart. She needs something tough enough for travel." I paused. "Sandals too." Sandals were a major extravagance for a slave, but I reasoned we had some hard traveling to do.

"Can I take the slave girl to the agora?"

"I have a name, it's Asia." She glared at Socrates.

Socrates would be there to watch her, but Socrates . . . hmm.

I said, "Run along and play, children."

Asia ran into the street at once. I grabbed Socrates' arm as he followed her, looked into his eyes, and said firmly, "She was a virgin when I bought her. She better still be a virgin when you bring her back. Got it?"

Socrates grinned. "Yes Nico."

I washed at the gymnasium and had a barber cut my hair and shave me. One doesn't call upon the mighty without looking one's best, especially if one is as low as one can get and still be a citizen.

My mother's slaves laundered my best chiton. It was a rush job, so the smell of the laundry still hung about the cloth—they use urine to bleach, and it lingers—but they sprinkled me with scented water that almost erased the smell. The chiton was tied about my waist with clean ceremonial rope, into which strands of blue ribbon had been threaded. The only sandals I owned were old, scuffed, and had been soaked in blood on more than one occasion. I sent a male slave to the agora with my old sandals for comparison, and orders to buy a decent pair of formal wear. The ones he returned with were pretty, made of highly polished light leather with silver buckles, and minutely embossed with a Dionysiac scene. They would fall apart after a day's hard walking, and cost five times what my sturdy pair had done. I sighed and reflected that the slave had done exactly what I'd ordered. Next time I would think before I sent a slave to market with general instructions.

Callias rose as I was shown into his courtyard. He was graying, well dressed, and manicured, showing none of the paunch an older man might acquire. Callias made his money mostly from renting slaves to the silver mines run by the state. That was his private business, but he was also a man who took part in public affairs. He was probably Athens' most experienced diplomat, and certainly the smoothest.

He gave me a broad smile and said, "Nicolaos, so good to see you. Pericles told me you were coming. I'm glad."

The home of Callias is remarkable for its size, and its beautiful courtyards and garden.

"I could work for a hundred years and never afford the equal of this," I said, looking around in appreciation.

"You are too kind."

"Merely realistic." I paused for a moment, not sure how to broach the subject. "Callias, did Pericles tell you why he asked me here?"

"Pericles has told me everything. It was I who suggested he invite you. Now hush, don't mention it until after dinner. I think you will enjoy your fellow guests. Among them will be Anaxagoras, the philosopher. You may know he's a friend of Pericles. The others are my son Hipponax and his friend Telemides. Hipponax is a good lad and in high spirits. He's recently married."

At that moment Pericles and Anaxagoras were announced and walked into the courtyard side by side. Pericles nodded his head to Callias, turned an ice-cold smile on me, and uttered a few simple words; Anaxagoras greeted his host by taking Callias' hands and quoting Homer, "'A man of substance dear to his fellows; for his dwelling was by the road-side and he entertained all men.' Thank you, dear Callias, for this invitation. Would that Homer were alive today so that he could describe you in such language."

Hipponax and Telemides arrived before Anaxagoras could continue with more flowery words, and we all settled onto our couches. It was a warm night so they'd been moved into the courtyard and torches lit. Slaves brought out scented garlands, which we placed around our heads, and cups of aromatic wine. A flute girl emerged from the colonnades and played something soft and lilting.

Slaves brought in the first of the dishes: plates of fish, eels, octopus, vegetables, and two hares. We ate with little conversation, as is the custom. Revelry waits upon the removal of the dishes.

As we ate, I looked sideways with interest at Anaxagoras. He was a famous man, not for his wealth, politics, or military prowess, but because Athens had never seen his like before: a professional philosopher, a man who earned his living by telling other men what he thought of things, as if his views were better than anyone else's. Everyone knew Pericles funded Anaxagoras. The philosopher had arrived in Athens five years ago and attached himself to the young politician long before he had risen to the top. Was it luck, or had Anaxagoras seen something in Pericles right from the start?

The philosopher wore a rather bushy beard but was half bald. What hair he had on top and his beard were a light brown, almost blond. His eyes were a dark blue, his manner lively, and his paunch particularly visible as he lay upon his dining couch. I guessed him to be about forty years old, or perhaps a little older. That made him five to ten years older than Pericles.

Anaxagoras belched and declared, "Callias, my friend, that was the most delightful meal I have enjoyed in a long time. Thank you." He turned to me and stage-whispered, "A philosopher should always praise his host. The Gods know where his next meal is coming from."

Socrates stood as my attendant, behind my couch. Even without turning my head I could feel him taking all this in.

Slave boys carried a krater into the middle of the gathering. Callias, as host, would be the symposiarch, who would determine the ratio of water to wine to be poured in. A symposiarch controlled the nature of the evening with this single decision.

Callias ordered the boys, "I think we will begin with three to one." Three parts water to one of wine meant a refined, cultured evening of discussion rather than a raucous party, but with enough wine to keep everyone glowing happy. The boys poured water and wine into the krater and stirred slowly before handing out cups. I took my first sip. The wine was excellent, heavily spiced with fenugreek.

"This is excellent, Callias, as good as anything we have at home," Anaxagoras said as he swirled the wine in his cup.

"Anaxagoras comes to us from the other side of the Aegean Sea," Callias said to me. "From the city of Clazomenae."

Anaxagoras sighed. "Oh, for my own estates and my own wine. I miss them so."

"Have you ever considered going home, Anaxagoras?" I asked. Perhaps if he went, Athens might lose its obsession with philosophy.

He looked at me in surprise and said, "Do you know why I moved to Athens?"

"I imagine because Athens is richer, and you were more likely to find a host here to act as your patron."

He snorted. "It was to save my skin. The Persians wanted me dead after the Hellenes of Ionia rebelled thirty years ago. The Persians crushed the revolt and then went looking for the troublemakers who started it. One of them was me."

"Every city rebelled?"

"Every city under Persian rule, which meant all the provinces on the Asian side of the Aegean Sea. All except Ephesus. The Ephesians decided to remain quiet and subservient. The reward for their cowardice was permission to govern themselves. They have the illusion of freedom as long as they do nothing to offend the Great King."

"The Athenians supported the revolt," said Callias. "But alas, it came to nothing. Many of our friends suffered."

"I had a fine house, a farm for olives and another for sheep, an orchard, and a vineyard. It's all gone. Fortunately I have my philosophy to sustain me." Anaxagoras knocked back his wine and called for more.

The slave boys mixed more wine, and I took a moment to admire the krater. Like everything else in the house of Callias, it was a thing of beauty. The krater was painted with red figures and showed a battle scene, Hellenes fighting in phalanx against Persians.

Callias said, "I see you are admiring my krater, Nicolaos. It comes from the workshops of Ceramicus. I commissioned it years ago from Hieron the potter and had Makron paint the scenes to my direction. He was a touchy man, old Makron."

Callias had named two of the greatest craftsmen of the past generation. This pot was worth more than most houses.

He was still speaking. "I couldn't make a single suggestion without touching off his temperament. Why is it so many artists must be temperamental? Your own artistic father is a delight to deal with. All I wanted was a particular scene."

"It's very beautiful. But what is particular about the scene?"

"Look closely."

I did. Something was odd about the Hellenes in the scene, but for a moment I couldn't put my finger on it. Then I inspected the leading figure in the phalanx. He carried a spear and hoplon shield like all the others, but he wasn't wearing armor. In fact, he was dressed in the robes of a priest.

I laughed. "Oh, Callias, this is the battle at Marathon, and the man leading the charge is you."

Callias smiled. "So nice to be recognized."

Callias had been one of the heroes who fought at Marathon, and some eccentricity of his had led him to fight not as a soldier, but as a priest. The krater spoke volumes about the subtle byways of his mind. Any man of the previous generation would immediately recognize Callias in the scene. The krater displayed his wealth and discrimination, but it also advertised that here was a man who served the state in every way, not only as diplomat and wealthy backer, but a man not afraid to put his own life on the line for Athens.

I had planned to say to Callias that Pericles' anger with me over my failed attempt to capture Araxes was unfair, and suggest he might persuade Pericles against dismissing me when the mission was over. Now I put away that idea. No man who had stood in the line at Marathon would accept adversity, or bad luck, or a tough opponent, or overwhelming odds as an excuse for failure.

It occurred to me that every important leader in Athens had fought both at Marathon and the later sea battle at Salamis. The only exception was Pericles, who like me had been too young. If I wanted to be worthy to join them as a leader of Athens, I would have to fight my own Marathon.

My question about the krater had caused Pericles and Anaxagoras to fall into a discussion of pottery art. Anaxagoras said, "All those terribly practical men with their practical tools and practical wares in their practical houses." Anaxagoras gave a mock shudder. "Practical men scare me. I shall stick to my philosophy."

I said, "Philosophy isn't practical?"

"You certainly can't use it to make a pot. Now, if you wanted to know what the pot is made of . . ."

"The pot is made of clay," I said, thinking the question quite obvious. If this is what philosophy was, then why did men make such a big thing of it?

"Ah now, but what is the clay made of?"

"Er . . . more clay?" I ventured.

"And if you take a pinch of the clay, what do you have? And what if you take a pinch of the pinch?"

"If I tear away a small pinch, then it's still clay, so I guess if I tear away a small pinch from the small pinch it will be clay again."

"And if you continue to take pinches from the pinches?"

"Obviously that will never work. My fingers are too large—"

"Bah," Anaxagoras snorted. "You are thinking in practical terms. Forget the size of your fingers. Use your *imagination,* man. What if your fingers were no impediment?"

"Then I suppose it would still be clay no matter how small the pinch, but I must say this isn't very pract—"

"Excellent. You begin to understand philosophy, young man. You have proven matter is infinitely divisible."

"I have?" I said, perplexed.

"You have," he said, with a firm voice. "Clay must consist of infinitesimally small particles of clay. You could continue taking pinches from the pinches for the rest of your life, and all you would get is an ever-decreasing amount of clay. So it is that water must consist of infinitesimally small particles of water. Air must consist of infinitesimally small particles of air."

He reached for his wine cup and took a hefty swallow of infinitesimally small particles of wine. Callias had upped the ratio to two to one with the latest krater. I wondered if Anaxagoras had begun to feel the effect, or did he always talk like this? Anaxagoras rubbed his hands. "Now we get to the serious points," he announced. "If all matter consists of infinitesimally small pieces, then how could all those clay particles have come together in a lump? Why aren't all the different types of particle mixed together in an amorphous soup? How is it possible a clay pot consists of only clay particles?"

"Don't ask me."

"I won't. I'll tell you. Because it doesn't!" He laughed as if he had won some triumph. "There must be infinitesimally small pieces of all the other types of matter in the pot as well, but because the vast majority of the pot consists of clay particles, it seems to us to be all clay. We don't notice the other particles, the impurities, which could be of stone, or water, or—"

"Horsehair?" I suggested, smiling. "Or nose hair?" The man was clearly mad. But I noticed Socrates had stopped serving and leaned over my couch in a most unslavelike manner, hanging on his every word.

"Correct, you understand. And now then, young man, what made most of the clay particles come together to form clay, and most of the air particles come together to form air?"

"Hmm. Anaxagoras, I am so stunned by your blinding revelation, I can barely think . . ."

"It was the Mind, young man, the universal Mind! There is a Mind that moves the parts of matter to form the world we experience!" He was almost shouting, and he waved his arms about.

Socrates was so totally absorbed that he forgot himself and said, "But sir, how does the Mind know what to make, and why does it do it?"

Anaxagoras stopped in mid-exult, and looked at me with a quizzical expression. "You allow your slave to speak?"

"I'll beat him when I return home. In the meantime, I would take it as a favor if you could bestow your wisdom to answer his no doubt ridiculous question."

Anaxagoras rubbed his chin and said, "On the contrary, the question is a deep one and would require considerable time to answer fully. It is true there are some fools, claiming to be philosophers, who make this very objection to my theory. To hear the same point from the mouth of this simpleton slave boy only goes to prove my belief that their arguments are worthless. Nevertheless, there are some subtle points involved. Let us begin."

I wish I could record the ensuing conversation, but I confess my eyes glazed over within moments. Anaxagoras spoke at length, and when he was finished, Socrates responded with something I didn't follow at all. Anaxagoras however did, and forgetting that he talked with a boy, and a supposed slave, the two of them became immersed in their argument. I gave up and held out my cup for a refill.

"Your slave boy appears to be a lad of some talent," Callias remarked.

"Callias, I have a confession to make—"

He laughed. "I noticed early in the evening. Also, I met your brother previously, when he was here with your father. It would not be the first time an inquisitive lad entered a symposium before his time." He glanced over at his other guests. "They will be in conversation for some time. Let me see if I can untangle Pericles from my admiring son. Have you noticed everyone wants to know Pericles now that he's the most influential man in Athens?"

Callias ordered two slaves to carry Pericles' dining couch next to his own, thus placing himself, Pericles, and me slightly apart from the others.

Callias said, "We must speak of state affairs, and the death of Thorion, of which Pericles has told me. Forgive me for raising such matters at a symposium, but time rushes."

I said, "I have important news." I began to tell them of Asia the slave girl.

"You paid *how much for her*?" Pericles fairly shrieked, loud enough that everyone in the courtyard stopped their own talk to look our way.

It was an awkward silence. Callias quickly motioned to the

slave boys to refill cups, and called for flute girls to play music. Two girls appeared from the shadows of the porch. They began a lilting, soothing tune and walked among the couches. The other guests turned back to their neighbors.

I said quietly, so that only we three could hear, "She was worth every drachma, Pericles, I swear it. Listen to what she had to say."

I was gratified to hear exclamations of surprise from both Pericles and Callias.

"Is she telling the truth?" Pericles asked when I finished. The puzzle of the girl's origin had at least made him forget for the moment the bill that was coming his way.

Callias looked thoughtful. "Themistocles did have a young daughter at the time he was ostracized. Your woman-child would be the right age, and I happen to know the infant's name was Asia. The family was spirited away after Themistocles was condemned for treason."

"How did they escape Athens?"

"A friend named Epicrates smuggled the wife and children out of the city. There was suspicion he had help, but he was the only one discovered."

"Then Epicrates might recognize the girl. Would he speak to us?"

"I'd be surprised if he said anything at all. He's dead. The Athenians took the view that a man who aids a traitor is a traitor himself and applied the usual penalty."

I shook my head and said, "Epicrates got what he deserved. I don't understand how anyone could do anything so obviously wrong."

"Sometimes the pressures on a man can be intense," said Callias mildly.

"Intense enough to turn him against his own city? It's hard to credit."

"Ah, the lack of imagination of youth."

All three of us stopped to drink, each thinking his own thoughts. I had passed from the point of being careful how much I drank, to the point of telling myself another one wouldn't hurt. As the slave took away my cup to refill I said, "If the family of Themistocles had to escape, then what of the family of Thorion?"

Pericles said, "The son will be suspect for years to come. He can forget about holding public office. His neighbors will turn against him. The household will probably be harassed. Any daughters will find it hard to get husbands."

"It hardly seems fair. The whole family aren't criminals."

"It's the way in Athens," said Callias.

Pericles said, "Nicolaos, I'm expanding your mission. Find whoever wrote that letter, learn what was in it. When you've done that, return the girl to Themistocles in Magnesia, and while you're there, find out what in Hades the man is up to."

"But wouldn't that be spying?"

"You understand. Excellent."

"No need to think of it in quite such blunt terms," Callias said smoothly. "Themistocles will naturally be grateful when you return his daughter. Take the opportunity to stay a few days and observe anything of interest. Nothing could be simpler. When you return to Athens, tell us what you saw."

"When you put it like that . . . very well. As you say, it would be perfectly natural."

Callias said, "At Ephesus there will be a proxenos for Athens, whose duties are the same as Thorion's, only in the opposite direction, including forwarding mail. He will know at least the names of everyone who sent something in the last batch. The proxenoi of two cities deal with each other frequently."

"What if the proxenoi get too friendly?"

"It's their *job* to be friendly. The rest of us supply all the mutual suspicion you could want."

Pericles said, "Someone has to tell the Ephesians their proxenos here in Athens is dead. That can be you. It's the perfect excuse to arrive and ask a few questions."

I asked, "Are you a proxenos, Callias?"

"I am indeed. I assumed the proxeny of Sparta after the man who held it, my brother-in-law Cimon, was ostracized. The proxenos normally has some family connection with the city he acts for."

"What was Thorion's connection with Ephesus?"

"I don't know."

I made a note to find out.

"Why was Themistocles condemned?"

Callias sighed. "Never has a man risen so high and fallen so low, nor been more dedicated to his own self-interest. At the first Olympics after the war, the whole stadium rose to give him a standing ovation. The Spartans gave him an honor guard of three hundred citizens, an unprecedented compliment. But then he made a lot of enemies in Athens by his arrogance. The actual charge was treason with the Persians, but his real crime was fear he would make himself tyrant over us."

"I met a man who said it was jealousy of his genius."

"There may be a touch of truth in that. Of course, it didn't help when he built a temple in honor of himself."

"You're joking, aren't you?"

"I'm afraid not. Themistocles built a temple to Artemis Aristoboulë—Artemis Of Wise Counsel—a small temple in his own deme, practically next door to his house. He clearly intended the dedication as an outright boast that he was most clever, which was true, but the people didn't want to be reminded. They ostracized him, and then ordered him to return to stand trial for treason. Instead, he disappeared without a trace, and surfaced a year later in the court of the Great King of Persia. Rumor has it he learned Persian during that missing year."

"He learned their language? Is that useful?" I asked.

Callias smiled. "I speak it myself. Yes, of course it's useful. In diplomacy, when you speak the enemy's language, you take the fight onto their own ground."

I made a mental note of that. "Go on."

"The Great King was favorably disposed toward Themistocles and granted him a minor satrapy—that is a governorship—of three cities in the western part of the empire. It's said he was granted the city of Magnesia to supply his bread, Myus for his meat, and Lampsacus for his wine. At a conservative estimate I would say those three among them should be delivering at least a hundred talents a year in taxes, so he is eating and drinking rather well."

"Then he certainly doesn't need to sell his daughters for the cash."

"No, whatever reason the girl is here, that is not it."

"He lives in Magnesia?"

"His family is there too. By all accounts his family is a model of harmony. He's had none of the problems of unruly sons and disobedient daughters that the rest of us suffer. If anything, he's too indulgent to them." Callias laughed. "Well, I'm hardly in a position to criticize him on that score."

Callias had been the talk of Athens a few years before, when he had allowed his daughters to marry whomever they wished. The daughters named their choice in husbands and Callias bought the young men by offering dowries so large no father could refuse.

Callias sipped his wine and thought. "Two of the sons live with Themistocles: Archeptolis and Cleophantus. He's had enough daughters to populate a brothel; I believe some are yet unmarried. I don't know their names, and in any case they need not concern us."

"No, of course not," I agreed. A woman could never play a part in politics.

"Archeptolis indulges in trade. Since Themistocles appeared

in Persia he's used his father's influence to expand his business in that direction. If the reports I've received are accurate then he's doing quite well for himself. That seems to be as much from sharp dealing as good business."

"Likes to cheat his friends?"

"Not so obviously that he could be taken to court. My impression is the son has the father's character but not his intelligence. I caution you I've never met the man, but, judging from what I've heard, I won't be rushing to do business with him."

"And the second son?"

"Cleophantus is an effete dilettante and is believed to be a coward. He passes all the requirements to join the army as a hoplite, yet he's eschewed every opportunity to fight. He spends his days under the protection of his father, showing not the slightest ambition. I know of nothing else against him, unless you count his appalling taste in fathers; but I suppose he can't be blamed for that. One final piece of trivia; Archeptolis married his own sister, a woman called Mnesiptolema; half sister, in fact."

I blinked at that. "Well, I suppose it simplifies negotiation of the dowry."

Pericles said, "Ephesus and Magnesia are on the other side of the Aegean Sea, in the province of Ionia."

Callias nodded. Both men obviously expected a reaction. I had none to give.

I said, "I don't understand your implication."

Pericles sighed. "Ionia was colonized by men as Hellene as you or I. But there are many barbarians too, and the whole province is ruled by the Persians." Pericles paused and studied me for a moment. "You'll be subject to the whims of whatever Persian official rules, far beyond the protection of Athens."

Better and better, I thought to myself. Pericles liked to look over my shoulder as I worked, and critique everything I did. In

Ionia I'd be free of his daily interference. For the first time I began to look forward to this mission.

Because I wanted to hear Pericles confirm it out loud, I said, "So I'll be a free agent."

Pericles pursed his lips as if he'd eaten something sour. "In Ionia, you are sanctioned to act as you think best, within tight restrictions. Under no circumstances must the Persians discover you act for Athens. Whatever weakness or threat we face, the Persians are not to learn of it. Also . . ." Pericles nodded to Callias.

Callias whispered to a slave, who hurried off, returning with a small, balding man who waddled from the back of the house, carrying a bag. A slave, but a valued one, because he was well fed.

Callias said, "Nicolaos, this is Koppa. He has something for you."

Koppa eyed me and said, "Now pay close attention, young man." He spoke as if he held little such hope.

"This," he said, holding out a short, round rod, "is a skytale."

"It looks like a short round rod," I said.

Koppa sighed. "So it is. Now watch."

Koppa pulled a leather cord from the bag. He pushed the end of the cord into a notch at the end of the rod, and proceeded to wind the cord tight until the rod was covered in leather. He pushed the remaining cord into a notch at the other end.

"You see?" he demanded.

I nodded.

He produced a very thin brush and a jar of ink, of the type scribes use to write on parchment. This he used to write tiny letters along the length of the rod, squinting as he did in the poor light. When he was finished he unwrapped the cord and handed it to me.

"Read it," he commanded.

I took the cord in both hands and tried to read, but I

couldn't. Koppa had written across the wrapped leather cord. Unwound, the letters of the words were jumbled together.

"I can't," I said.

Koppa handed me the rod. "Try it now."

Within moments I had placed the thong in the notch, wound the leather around the wood, and read off the message. It was a quote from Homer.

AS SOON AS OUR PEOPLE ARE INSIDE AND IN SAFETY, CLOSE THE STRONG GATES, FOR I FEAR LEST THAT TERRIBLE MAN SHOULD COME BOUNDING INSIDE ALONG WITH THE OTHERS.

"That's very clever," I marveled.

"You can use it to report back during your mission," said Callias.

"Report back?" I repeated.

Callias must have seen I was about to bristle, because he said at once, "I use the same system myself, when I'm on a mission for Athens. Of course we have every trust in you, Nicolaos."

Koppa handed me the bag he'd carried from the house. "A present from my master."

It was the sort of bag a man can carry on his back, made of tooled leather with a wooden frame. Koppa reached into the leather folds of the frame and pulled out a rod. "This is your skytale. As you can see I've disguised it as part of the frame." He slid it back in.

Pericles said, "I've arranged your transport. A fast ship will be waiting for you at the naval dockyard at high tide tomorrow morning. Don't be late."

Callias raised his hands and clapped. "The Loving Cup," he called. Hipponax and Telemides turned their attention to us. Anaxagoras had to be called twice to tear his attention away from his argument with my little brother.

Slaves hurried in with a kylix, a shallow but very wide drinking cup, shaped almost like a dish on a stand. It was a beautiful thing, painted in the fashionable red figure style of the krater with scenes of Dionysiac revelry among a group of satyrs and nymphs. A slave dipped a ladle into the krater and filled the kylix.

This is the rule of the Loving Cup: each man drinks and passes it on to his neighbor. Sometimes it is accompanied with a game of some sort, sometimes with conversation.

"Nicolaos first," Callias commanded.

I took the smallest sip I felt I could get away with, and I'm sure Callias and Pericles did the same, because the cup did not stay long with either. The kylix passed on to Hipponax and Telemides, who had no reason for inhibition. Anaxagoras too gave it a healthy nudge, though not so much that he could not resume his argument with Socrates. As the cup emptied, the boys refilled using the dipper. By the time the cup had gone around twice, the wine had well and truly gone to the heads of the other guests.

On the next round, Anaxagoras took the kylix and declared, "I want to buy your slave."

I needed a moment to understand. Then, "You want to buy *Socrates*?" I said, aghast.

"Is that his name? Yes, I want him."

"Whatever for?"

"Can you imagine any better slave for a philosopher? No, perhaps you can't, not having the wit yourself to understand. Then let me tell you this boy has more philosophy in him than all the dullards combined that I am compelled to speak with every day." Then Anaxagoras probably recollected to whom he spoke, because he added hurriedly, "Excepting you, of course, great Pericles. A truer mind never walked the earth, but excepting Pericles, this boy-slave is the only mind in Athens who can put up a decent argument."

Oh, the temptation! I imagined the conversation. *Yes, Father, I sold Socrates, but I got a good price for him!*

Socrates gave me an anguished stare. I smiled back, letting the silence linger and enjoying every moment.

I said with some regret, "I'm afraid, Anaxagoras, the boy isn't for sale."

"Name your price."

What if I did? No, don't do it, Nicolaos.

"He belongs to my father."

"Your father, eh? I'll call on him in the morning."

"Er—"

"The boy is special to the father," Callias intervened. "*Very* special."

Anaxagoras misunderstood, as I'm sure Callias intended. "Ah, it's like that, is it?"

"I'm afraid so," Callias said.

"No hope of him parting with the boy?"

"It would be like losing a son."

The Loving Cup passed around many more times and, despite my best efforts, it was impossible not to feel the effects. But the same was even more true for the other guests who, as the moon reached its highest point, were close to passing out. The symposium was over.

Anaxagoras departed as he had come, saying, " 'True friendship's laws are by this rule express'd; Welcome the coming, speed the parting guest.' Thank you, dear Callias." At which point he fell over backward, and had to be carried away by his slaves.

6

For of himself had the king of men, Agamemnon,
given them benched ships wherewith to cross
the wine-dark sea,

Early next morning I found my father, Sophroniscus, already
in his workshop. He sat on a high stool, hunched, paunched,
balding. His hands were a deep, muddy brown. Before him sat
a clay model of his next work, a votive statue of Zeus. It was
probably destined for someone's courtyard as their altar to
Zeus Herkios; which every proper home must have. He pinched
bits here, adding there, and standing back to see how his cre-
ation looked.

"Father."

He looked up. "Nico. What do you think of this piece?"

"It looks fine," I said without glancing at it. "Father, I need
to talk to you. I am required to travel to Ephesus, part of an
investigation for Pericles." I didn't tell him it would be my
last.

By rights I should have asked my father's permission the
day before, straight after Pericles and I had discussed it, but I
knew Father would permit my travel since it was in accordance
with our agreement, granting me two years to make a success
of investigation. Father could not reasonably deny me if I was

to receive a fair chance, and for all our differences, he was a fair man.

He grunted. "Ephesus, eh? That's a long way for a young man who's never been outside Attica."

"Yes, Father, it is."

"You might learn something of the world. It's not all like Athens, you know."

"May I ask a favor? If I send you any mail, could you please pass the wrapping cord on to Pericles?"

"The wrapping cord?" He looked at me strangely.

"Don't cut it, untie the knot and have a slave carry the cord to Pericles. He'll know what to do with it."

"This is something to do with your work?"

"Yes."

"I'll do as you ask. But I won't change my mind about that woman you want, Diotima. That's what you've really come to see me about, isn't it? Whether I'll change my mind about this girl you're so besotted with?"

"No. I . . . well, yes, I did," I said, though I hadn't realized it myself until that moment. If Father relented, then when I arrived in Ephesus there'd be something I could say to Diotima without having to flinch. Perhaps I could even bring her home. This was my last chance.

"Father, I admit it, I do want Diotima—"

"No." He put down his tools and laid a cloth over the model, then sat back on his stool.

"Son, Diotima is the daughter of a prostitute."

"A hetaera," I corrected him.

"A high-class prostitute then, but still a prostitute. Granted, the mother's not a pornê walking the streets—"

"She's wealthier than we are."

"That's not the point. Nicolaos, you're not listening to me. *She's not a citizen*."

"I don't care."

"I do."

Father lifted the cloth off the model and resumed his work. He was not good at dealing with conflict at the best of times. I knew this was his way of avoiding any more conversation on the subject. I said, "Thank you, Father, for your permission to travel."

"It's my pleasure, son." He raised his eyes from his work one more time. "A father has to do what's best for his son. You understand?"

"I do."

He said, "By the way, I received a note requesting an appointment from a man called Anaxagoras. He says he knows you. Any idea what he wants?"

"Anaxagoras? Er . . . no, I can't imagine," I said, as innocently as possible.

With any luck, by the time Father found out, I would be overseas and well out of reach, but I regretted not being there to hear Father's reaction when a complete stranger offered to buy Socrates. I looked at the model before him, into which he pressed his fingers with the most delicate care. You could never find two men more different than my single-minded, practical father, and the abstruse philosopher, nor two men less likely to have even a single point of view in common.

"Father, will you listen to my advice on one thing?"

I was bound to accept my father's decision on Diotima, but . . .

"Certainly."

"When Anaxagoras visits, why don't you ask him what your clay is made of?"

The house was too quiet. You don't notice the noise slaves make until they're gone. Onteles and I might have been sitting in a house of the dead, but in fact it was the andron of his own home, the public room at the front reserved for men. We both nursed a cup of watered wine that he had served himself.

Onteles said, "Do you know how many people came to my father's funeral?"

"No."

"Not one. Not a single person outside the family."

With a pang of guilt, I realized I hadn't thought to go. I'd been involved in the deaths of six people in the past and attended the funerals of every one of them, even the slaves. This was the first I'd missed.

"I'm sorry."

"Someone is spreading the word Father was a traitor to Athens. Is that your doing?"

"Not me." I guessed it was their own house slave. He had probably heard every word Pericles and I said that night.

Onteles tore at his hair, which was shorn short in grief. "What are we to do? Our neighbors, the men of our own deme, are shunning us. I sent a slave to the agora for food and she was pelted with stones by local children. Yesterday we woke to find threats scrawled across our front wall. I sent my mother and sisters to the country the moment the funeral was over. It's an insult to my father's memory, but what can I do? They're safer away."

Onteles grabbed me by the arm. "Nicolaos, you must prove my father was not a traitor."

"By his own admission he *was*. How do you explain his wealth? How did he pay for that fast horse of yours?"

"I know what my father was. He liked money. Who doesn't? Probably he took advantage of the proxeny to cheat a little. I don't know. He must have had opportunities, and I could believe he took them. But I can't believe for one moment my father would have turned against Athens. Father never said what his crime was, did he?"

"Only that he'd betrayed."

"His position was hardly high enough to do much damage. Whatever he did, maybe it's not so bad."

Onteles made a good point.

I said, "Whatever he knew, it was bad enough to send an assassin."

"Please help us."

I'd read the message scrawled across the front wall on the way in. Someone had threatened to torch the building at night, with the family in it.

"I'll try," I agreed reluctantly. After all, I told myself, I had to work out what the man had done anyway.

"Thank you."

I nodded. "Whoever wrote the letter to your father might have written to him in the past. Maybe there's a clue. I want to go through your father's correspondence."

"Anything to end this nightmare."

Back in the room where it all began, I spread out Thorion's papers and read every word. There were many notes about importing pottery from Ephesus. I glanced over at the pots sitting in the room; I was probably looking at some of the merchandise. The import business was in partnership with a man from Ephesus called Brion, who was the equivalent of Thorion in his own city: their proxenos for Athens. Excellent; now I had a name.

Everything else on the desk was public business. By the time I finished, I knew more than I ever wanted to about the work of a proxenos. There were complaints from citizens of Ephesus, who felt they'd been hard done by in deals with Athenians, and wanted redress in the courts; men who looked for business contacts; lists of incoming cargo shipments, with requests for Thorion to see the goods safely into the warehouses; men who wanted maritime insurance from Athenian bankers; men who demanded an introduction to high-placed Athenians; men in search of husbands for their daughters.

I pushed the lot away from me and sighed. If I'd had to deal with all these demands, day after day, I might have viewed a murderer come to throttle me as a welcome relief. Maybe Diotima could have made sense of the documents—she was so good with written words—but it was beyond me. I missed her, and not for the first time. I wondered what she was doing in Ephesus, and whether she was happy there.

The thought of Ephesus reminded me of the question that had occurred to me at the symposium. I said to Onteles, "How did Thorion come to be proxenos for Ephesus?"

"I wish he never had been. It's a family connection. Nothing wrong with that."

"Nothing at all," I agreed. "So what's the connection?"

"Through my mother. She came from a good Ephesian family."

"The family's still there, I suppose."

"Her brother, my uncle, is head of the family now. He's a merchant trader."

"His name?"

"Pollion, son of Hegerandros. But you can't speak with him. He's in Ephesus."

"That's not a problem. I'm going to him."

Asia had stayed in our home for a mere day and a night, in which short time she'd managed to irritate every other slave with her superior airs. No slave, not even a temporary one, can afford to do that. I kept her apart for her own safety, and to teach me a few of the more common words of Persian. The idea of speaking another language fascinated me and I made rapid progress on the basic phrases.

We departed at first light the next morning to begin the long journey back to Asia's home. Asia wore a secondhand chiton and sturdy sandals and had no other possessions. I carried spare clothing and basic supplies in the backpack given me by Callias, the skytale hidden within the frame.

A huge warship waited for me at the docks, and not just any warship, but the most famous one of all. I was to ride to Ephesus on *Salaminia,* the fastest ship in the world.

Salaminia is a trireme, fitted out with only the best equipment, crewed only by Athenian citizens who volunteered for the job. The men are paid double to be available at a moment's notice to go anywhere a ship can go. She is used for delicate diplomatic missions, when getting the ambassador where he needs to go quickly is of the greatest importance. Each year too, *Salaminia* and her sister ship, *Paralos,* carry gifts to the Sanctuary of Apollo on the isle of Delos, one of the holiest places in all Hellas.

The crew saw us coming, and loosened the lines holding them to land even before we'd reached the gangplank. I handed Asia over, then stepped in myself, and the helmsman standing beside me at the tiller called, "Pull!" The singer began his song, the aulos player began blowing his pipes to accompany and keep the rhythm, and *Salaminia* moved before I'd taken my second step on board.

Two hundred men stared at me. Most of those were rowing, but all that could looked up at me on the slack of their pulls, to see what manner of man had caused them to prepare their ship for sea. I must have been a major disappointment. These men were used to carrying the highest leaders, the best generals, and the most important priests. For me to be the point of their muscle-aching efforts was a step down.

Asia had no such delusion about who was the center of attention. "What are you all staring at?" she challenged them.

I said, "Be quiet, Asia. Slaves don't talk like that to citizens."

As I said it, I realized she was right. None of the crew were looking at me; they were all staring at her.

My woman-child slave was dressed in a modest chiton of

ankle-length, but not even the usual extra folds could prevent her curves pressing out the material in interesting places, and nothing could hide her young red lips and those wide, round, dark eyes. It made me glad of the twenty soldiers on board—archers and spearmen—except they too were staring at Asia. The two chiefs of the rowers, one on each side, both shouted at the men to pay attention to their work. I silently prayed to Poseidon for a quick trip.

The trierarch stepped easily around or over the various things attached to the deck, and said, "Good morning. I believe our destination is Ephesus. Correct?"

It was all I could do to nod and say, "Yes please," as if it were normal for a young man to be the sole purpose of the most prestigious ship in the most prestigious navy.

The trierarch nodded back. "The helmsman tells me it should be a fast passage, the weather will be fair. Sit down and relax." He looked down at Asia and added, "And try to keep your slave under control."

Sitting was easy. There was a covered deck running down the center, an unheard-of luxury on any other ship. Both sides of the deck were open so light and air could filter down to the three rows of oarsmen. I wanted to look down and watch, but manners prevented me. They might be poor—surely the only reason a man would volunteer for this duty—but these were citizens of Athens.

I asked the trierarch—the captain—quietly, why slaves were not used to pull the oars, particularly on the lowest level.

He smiled and said, "You're not the first person to ask that question. Let me ask you one back. What do you think would happen if we put slaves in a position to take control of a warship?"

"Oh. Good point."

"So we never allow slaves to row, only free men. On *Salaminia* and *Paralos* we restrict it further to citizens, no mercenaries or hired laborers, but that's only because we also have sacred duties."

He rubbed his jaw. "Mind you, I take your point. It's tough, nasty work, better suited to slaves. Smelly too. The thranites on the top row are all right, but they practically sit against the faces of the zygios on the middle row, and the thalamios on the bottom have legs and bums dangling all over them. More than one deadly fight has broken out over a man who farts too much. The veterans fart on new recruits on purpose."

"How do they decide who's at the bottom and top?"

"It's decided on seniority and reward for excellent service. A man starts in thalamio, progresses to zygio and if he's good is promoted to thranite. There are strict rules for promotion, or there'd be mutiny."

"Have you been a sailor all your life, sir?"

The trierarch laughed. "Me? A sailor? Poseidon protect me, no."

"Then, why are you . . . that is, what—"

"What am I doing here? I paid for the ship, young man; every board, every rope, every fitting, every plank. It's my gift to the state, because I am wealthy, part of my obligations under the liturgy, the convention that says wealthy men must spend their wealth to the benefit of the state. So I get to call myself trierarch, and strut about the deck as if I know what I'm doing. The truth is, the best sailor on this ship is him." The trierarch pointed to the helmsman; a grizzled, burned, unsmiling man. "I'm the one who gets the glory of command; he's the one who gives the orders when it really matters."

The trierarch wandered off to do some more strutting and glorying.

"*Salaminia,*" Asia said thoughtfully. "That means the *Girl From Salamis.* Is that where she was built?"

"So are you from Salamis, girlie?" one of the nearby rowers called out. The men around him laughed.

"Shut your mouth!" the portside chief shouted at the caller before I could intervene. Everyone knows a girl from Salamis will spread her legs for any man.

The proreus, who is the officer in charge of the foredeck and therefore in charge of looking where we were going, said to Asia, "No, the ship is named in honor of our greatest victory at sea, over those scum the Persians in the straits of Salamis."

Asia bristled. "You don't like Persians?" she said.

"Does anyone?" the proreus replied.

Asia was a living, breathing, walking clue. I was sure I could get important information from her before I returned her to her father, if only she wasn't drowned first by irritated naval officers. I pulled her away from the proreus and sat her down in the middle of the deck.

"Tell me how you were kidnapped," I ordered. "And don't even think about lying to me."

Asia hesitated, and already I could imagine the lies assembling within her mind.

"It was in a dark alley," she began.

"You walked down a dark alley?"

"The main streets were bright and sunny. They were boring."

"Did you have a slave with you?"

She looked up at me with big, innocent eyes.

"What sort of an idiot would walk down a dark alley on their own?" I asked, incredulous.

"Master, I liked to explore the city. Some days I would wander about. It wasn't that dangerous. What could go wrong?"

"You could be captured by slavers and sold to a brothel in foreign city, to pick a random example. Did your father let you walk about the city on your own? No wonder he lost you."

Asia blushed. "He . . . er . . . didn't always know I was gone."

"Ah. He beat you when you returned?"

"No."

Themistocles, it seemed, was one of those weak, indulgent

fathers who lets his children run riot. I had no trouble imagining Asia wrapping him around her little finger.

"Very well. Go on."

"The alley ran off the main road, which ran off the agora. It was narrow, lots of shadow, and there were boxes and things you had to walk around. It looked interesting, so I decided to see what was there. A man appeared at the other end. He walked toward me, watching. I got scared and decided to turn and run. A hand from behind went over my mouth, a big man's hand. I tried to scream, but I couldn't. I almost couldn't breathe because he covered my nose too. He was big and I was small and, well, it was useless. I got my mouth open and one of the fingers covering my mouth slipped in and I bit down hard before I could think about it."

"What happened then?"

"He swore and let go. A huge blow to my head threw me to the ground, and that's the last I remember. When I woke up, I was a slave, and Araxes had me."

I gave her a hard look. There was a certain consistency to Asia's tale, it sounded like the sort of child capture that happened every day, to some child somewhere in the world, but it didn't explain her abandonment in Athens, unless it was merely a way to earn some extra coins.

Asia seemed oblivious to my study of her. She did her own musing, staring across the sea in the direction we traveled, to Ephesus.

EPHESUS

7

A multitude of rulers is not a good thing.
Let there be one ruler, one king.

We drifted into Ephesus port with the sun at our backs. The boat touched lightly, a sailor jumped onto the wharf to wind a rope, and our journey came to a gentle end. I called farewell to the trierarch and stepped off, hauling Asia after me. *Salaminia* would touch only long enough to take on more water. Pericles had given orders the ship was not to call attention to my mission by tarrying.

Merchant ships were being loaded and unloaded all about me. Next to us was a crew of Phoenicians, a people famed for their seagoing prowess. They were bare-chested and barefoot, wearing bronze armbands, bronze bracelets, and loincloths. Their skins were as burned and weather-beaten as the ships they served. All had beards, dark, layered, and ringleted.

On the other side of us was an Egyptian ship. Her sailors had hung about them necklaces full of charms. They chattered away to one another in their own language in between much shouting and confusion. Among the crew were men who were black. I knew at once they were Ethiopians. I had heard the Ethiopians sung of by the bards in Athens. They were impressive men, tall and thin and strong and seemingly oblivious to the heat. They seemed always to smile.

Behind the wharves were warehouses and shops, different but similar to the ones I knew so well at Piraeus. Everywhere, men were in motion. Pedestrians walked past in a stream, talking with each other or engrossed in their own business. Beggars sat by the side with palms outstretched. No one paid attention to anyone in their way, and I was pushed about twice. A hand tugged at my chiton.

"What are you staring at?" said Asia. "The road into the city is this way."

She walked off, leaving our bags behind. I stayed where I was and called, "Aren't you forgetting something?"

She turned and looked puzzled.

"Our bags," I prodded.

Asia drew herself up to her full, unremarkable height. "Have you forgotten I am—"

"A slave."

I thought she was about to argue, but she controlled herself and said, "Yes, master."

Asia picked up our bags and I followed her into the famed city of Ephesus.

The road from the docks led straight inland. We came at once upon a gymnasium and baths to our left, situated so close to the port that the air was still wet with sea spray. The road turned right and on the outer bend was an amphitheater that dwarfed the one at Athens. Did the Ephesians really have so many people?

On the right was what looked and sounded like an agora. Well-dressed men stood about, gesticulating, shouting, arguing, conferring, reading scrolls, writing notes, and paying each other money. It all looked highly confused to me, and there wasn't a single stall to be seen.

I asked Asia, "What is that place?"

She looked at it with a confused expression and said, "Master, I don't know."

I stopped a passing citizen, who told me we stood at the commercial agora, where men traded entire shiploads or warehouses of goods. I'd never heard of such a thing; Athens had nothing like it.

We passed through some ornamental gates onto a smooth road. I took ten steps before I realized I walked on marble. People pushed past me as if it was perfectly normal to be treading on the most expensive road in the world. The marble road twisted left, and we walked uphill to the second agora, much more reminiscent of the one I'd left behind at home.

The agora of Ephesus was long and thin. The road we'd walked from the docks entered at the west end, and exited on the east. I found it odd pushing my way through the streams of people without being able to look up at the Acropolis. The stallholders were Hellene. They sold vegetables, olives, and olive oil in stacked amphorae; fish and eels and squid. Pottery and bronze ware had its own section, as had something you don't see much of in Athens: apples. There were entire stalls of apples. They were a delicacy back home, where most people preferred quince. I picked up an apple and inspected it, a mottled yellow, then bit in. The sweet juice trickled down my throat. You could give me apple over quince any day. I pulled out a coin and was about to toss it to the stall owner when I realized there was a problem, a problem I'd never experienced before.

I had the wrong money.

"I'm sorry, I only have Athenian coins," I said to the stallholder.

"No problem," he replied. "I'll take your owls." All Athenian coins are stamped with the sacred bird of Athena.

"How much?"

"Seven obols."

I almost dropped the apple in shock. "You could feed a family for a day for that much!"

"Hey mate, you bit into it!"

The error was mine; I should have changed my coins the moment I arrived. The stallholder charged a premium for accepting foreign currency; any shopkeeper in Athens would do the same. I had laughed at the rubes who tried to use their own coins in the agora at Athens often enough. Now it was my turn.

I grimaced and tossed seven coins to the man. He caught them all and I turned away, biting into the most expensive apple I would ever eat.

I almost walked straight into two men, coming the other way. All three of us stopped in time, face-to-face, practically nose-to-nose.

They wore shirts, and trousers, and carried a shield on their backs and a spear in their right hands. Their beards were barbered and curled into ringlets, their skin dark beneath the weathering, their noses large and bulbous. For the first time in my life, I faced Persian soldiers. Throughout my ephebe training, over and over the instinct had been drilled into us: see Persian, kill Persian. My hand went to where my sword would be if I'd still been a soldier in the army. Luckily for me, it wasn't there.

The one on the right said, "Excuse me," in the language of the Medes. I understood because Asia had continued to teach me the rudiments of the language as we traveled. The Persian stepped around me. The other did the same on the other side.

I nodded, not trusting myself to speak, but they were already gone.

I'd known, intellectually, that I'd passed from the free city-states of Hellas into the rigidly ruled superstate of the Great King's empire, but the transition had been so smooth that until that moment I hadn't noticed. The Persians ruled all the land from the ground on which I stood, all the way to the east.

For all I knew, their empire extended to the ends of the earth. The Hellenes controlled every island in the Aegean Sea. When I stepped off *Salaminia* onto dry land, I had stepped into the empire of our enemy.

The two soldiers stopped at the stalls of the vegetable growers. They chatted with the vendors, who from their looks and dress were Hellene. But they all spoke Persian together. A stall owner said something I couldn't understand, and they all laughed.

I backed away, and almost tripped over a funeral stele poking up out of the ground. It was so bizarre I stood staring. Everyone else walked around it as if it were perfectly normal to bury your dead in the middle of the market. The memorial stone had one word on it: HERACLITUS.

I shook my head. I'd come to a strange place.

We walked into the side streets and chose an inn that seemed clean. In Athens, it's the inns closest to the agora that are the best and most expensive. I paid for a private room, which was even more expensive. The innkeeper looked at Asia and smirked, displaying broken, black teeth. The room was on the second floor at the back, small but with sound walls and a decent bed in one corner. I sent Asia down to collect straw for her bedding. She returned with the innkeeper.

"What ye want straw for?" he asked. "Ye've got a bed." He pointed at it, as if I might not recognize the item.

I told him, "That's for me. The girl needs something to lie on."

He leered. "That's you, ain't it? No need to pretend with me."

I sent him on his way with firm instructions to send a slave with straw.

"Now we can see the city," I said to Asia. I was eager to go out and be a tourist.

Asia led me farther along the road we'd walked before. Our path took us out by an eastern gate. Asia said, in an offhand way, "This is the road to Magnesia. If you continue on this way you'll come to the city in two days."

I climbed a hill to view Ephesus from the landward side. The city was shaped like a centipede bent in the middle. The wide, curving road Asia had led me up when we arrived was the body, all the buildings to each side and a surprisingly small number of side streets made the legs. There was no high defensive ground of any sort, no acropolis. There was a wall about the city, a bit like a semicircular bubble poking inland, but I doubted it would provide any serious resistance to any passing army.

We followed a well-worn path outside the city walls, for perhaps nine or ten stadia, a bit short of a thousand paces, until we came to a large temple, the largest I had ever seen.

"The Temple of Artemis," Asia announced. "Your girlfriend is probably here."

"She's not my—" I broke off.

I looked at the temple nervously. It was huge. People were walking in and out all the time. Asia was probably right, Diotima would be in there somewhere. She might walk down those steps at any moment. I glanced down to see Asia staring up at me with big, round eyes, fourteen and pretty.

"Socrates says you only came to Ephesus to see her."

"I think I'll avoid—that is, I'll surprise Diotima later, not now."

Asia shrugged. She turned and led me back into the city.

At the eastern gates, the ones called the Magnesia Gates, I detected a certain aroma.

"Is there a horse market here?" I asked Asia.

She shrugged. "I don't know. I suppose so."

We followed our noses, and came to a small paddock of turf littered with wads of mud and horse droppings. Horses, mules, and donkeys were tethered to poles, most standing quietly, some protesting volubly. Men stood beside the animals, talking, inspecting, or walking from one to the next.

I thought back to the fast horse of Onteles, of which I'd been so envious. Here I was on my own in Ephesus, and it wasn't my father's money in my bag, it was Pericles'.

I picked my way across the paddock, and inspected the animals, trying to look as if I knew what I was doing.

"There's a top breed, yes sir." The man beside me broke in on my thoughts. "I can tell you're a man who knows his horseflesh."

I had stopped beside the largest animal I could see, reasoning that a big horse would be faster than a small horse. This one was colored red-brown. Beyond size and color, I couldn't tell the difference between any of the animals on display.

"She looks good," I said.

"He. Have a look underneath."

I bent down. "Oh, yes."

"So, what're you looking for, my man?"

"Er—"

"Hunter? Racehorse? I can see at once you're not a plowman. You'll be looking for a sophisticated beast, sleek, light on the touch, instant response, fast."

I imagined myself racing across the fields on an important mission. "Yes, I want fast!"

"You've come to the right place, yes sir." He slapped the animal's back and smiled. "This here is the fastest thing on four legs you're likely to see anywhere in Ephesus, or even Ionia. Why, he's good enough for the King's Messengers, so he is."

"The King's Messengers?"

The man took out the strand of hay he'd been chewing on, and looked me in the eye. "You're not from these parts, sir?"

"Hellas. Mainland."

"Ah, that explains it. Well, young man, the King's Messengers are the fastest men around. They carry the Great King's commands from one end of the empire to the other. If you were standing by the road, and a King's Messenger came over the horizon, why, if you blinked, you'd miss him. A Messenger carrying a message is not allowed to sleep, or eat, or even piss unless he can do it at full gallop. The Messengers have a saying: 'Neither snow nor rain nor heat nor darkness of night will stop us.' The Great King can have his words delivered to any part of the empire in only two days. And this beast here," he slapped the horse again, "Ajax here is good enough for the King's Messengers. But you know what's happened? I've gone and sold them so many great horses that they don't need no more. So now I'm reduced to selling top quality stallions at a discount, just to make ends meet. It isn't fair, sir, no it isn't."

A discount sounded good to me. I bought Ajax. He even threw in the bridle.

I led my new horse through the streets of Ephesus, taking special care to be seen. I was so proud of my new possession. Ajax followed my lead, docile as a lamb. He knew at once who his master was. Men pointed and talked among themselves as we passed by. I noticed he was larger and more powerful than every other horse we passed. The stable hand at the inn demanded extra money to handle such a powerful stallion, which I willingly paid.

The sky had darkened toward dusk. I decided to celebrate my purchase of Ajax and see something of the nightlife of Ephesus, so I left Asia with bread and cheese in our room and walked down to the docks where, if Ephesus was like Athens, I knew most of the excitement would be. Men of every class were stopping work and pushing their way into the taverns. One particularly large one seemed popular, a board outside proclaimed THE GREAT KING, not a name you would ever see in Athens.

I could hear raucous laughter, and as I watched a man came flying through the window and thudded to a halt in the dirt. He picked himself up and staggered down the road, no doubt to find another drinking hole. The half-open shutter on the window dangled crookedly, as if a previous throw may have been less accurate.

I joined the steady stream pushing their way in.

The Great King was large but crowded. I breathed the humid fog of sweaty men, talking all about me. The fug was not helped by the fact that the innkeeper had lit pitch torches, which added a pungent aroma and enough light to drink by. The moonlight coming through the open window and door had better effect. Words drifted past, confusing me with their different accents. Standing near the window, where they could get fresh air, was a group of locals. They were drinking, talking, and laughing simultaneously, a few men were already swaying on their feet.

A party of travelers sat in the near corner with their backs to the wall. They were dressed for riding and talked to no one but themselves. Their hair was long and hung in oily plaits. They held large drinking horns and ate from bowls of stew that smelled good. They watched the room with suspicious eyes. In the middle a pair of dark Ethiopians and three olive-skinned Karians—all obviously sailors—stood talking together loudly in a language I didn't recognize, but from the tone the conversation was heated and might turn into an argument at any moment. Two huge men, their skin covered in blue tattoos, even their faces, sat at the long common bench, facing each other, drinking wine, being surly, and ignoring everyone about. Both had swords strapped to their backs in leather scabbards that were faded and worn with use.

The innkeeper came and served me wine—very cheap—and then offered me some of the stew, a house specialty that he assured me was a traditional local dish. I jumped at the chance. A slave brought out a bowl of hot, steaming, delicious smelling stew. I ate it at the common bench. I considered carrying my bowl and cup into a corner, but the air was thicker there and a space opened up close to the surly, tattooed pair with the swords. No one in their right mind would start anything that might annoy those two, so I sat down next to them. The air grew hotter with all those bodies crowded together. The volume got louder as men became inebriated. A belligerent drunk left via the window exit, with the help of the men he'd annoyed.

A man sat down opposite me.

"I hope you've recovered from your exertions. I confess I've had sore muscles ever since."

I reached for my dagger.

Instantly two hands clapped down on my shoulders from behind and *squeezed*. The pain paralyzed me. I let go and my dagger dropped to the straw-covered floor. All about us, men continued to drink and talk loudly; no one had noticed.

Araxes, sitting before me, said, "My man standing behind you is possessed of remarkable strength. I've seen him snap the collarbones of someone in the position you currently occupy. I wouldn't recommend any sudden moves."

If I hadn't known better, I'd have taken Araxes to be a successful middle-class trader, not a killer and slaver. He was clean, his white hair hung loose to his shoulders, he wore a colorful tunic of good trim. When he spoke I saw he had good teeth. He had a pleasant face with a small nose and blue eyes. I still couldn't tell his nationality.

Araxes smiled, settled back on his stool, and said, "How good to see you again. Tell me, what's your name?"

"Nicolaos."

"May I call you Nico?"

"No," I said through gritted teeth.

Araxes glanced up at the man behind me and the pressure eased, but did not disappear. He glanced down at my half-empty bowl.

"You've not been eating that stuff, have you?" he asked in unfeigned horror.

"Why not?"

"I hope you like rat." He shuddered. "Gah!"

I blinked, then realized he was only saying that to unbalance me. "Rubbish. You don't know it's rat."

"I do. I used to catch them. I wasn't always the successful businessman you see now. I began in the streets, on the docks, Nicolaos. We boys used to make our living catching rats. The better taverns paid us to catch and dispose of them. The worst kind paid us for the bodies. This is one of the worst kind. It's amazing what a drunk sailor will eat, or a foreigner, especially if they use that old saw about 'traditional local dish.'" He peered at the half-eaten stew for a moment, then stuck the point of his dagger in and pulled it out with a tiny bone hanging on the point, and an even tinier sliver dangling by a sinew. "No doubt about it, that's the pelvis and the bone from its penis."

My stomach lurched but, love him or hate him (I selected hate), Araxes was an impressive, highly educated man. One part of his story was hard to swallow. "*You* were a rat catcher?"

"I was an orphan," he said shortly.

"Oh." He had my sympathies. In Athens, orphans are the responsibility of the archon who runs the city, but even in Athens that was only true for the children of citizens. Other orphans were on their own. If they were lucky, they would be picked up as slaves. The ones who weren't ended up as criminals or grew to be very, very tough men, good only for mercenary work.

"I killed my first man, right over there." Araxes pointed to the far end of the docks.

"Back when I was a boy. I'd had a brother, we'd looked after each other for as long as I could remember, but he'd been taken from me and now I was on my own. I was hungry, I hadn't eaten in days. A drunk sailor had staggered there and collapsed to sleep off his wine. I *needed* his coins. But I misjudged his stupor. He opened his eyes as I was bent over him. He grabbed my wrist, my left one, luckily. I snatched his dagger with my right and stabbed him in the throat. It was an awful blow, all I cut was his windpipe. I was inexperienced, you see. I took everything of value while he lay there asphyxiating and then rolled his body into the water. No one heard the splash. That was when I realized if I wanted to get anything out of my life, I would have to stop catching rats and start improving myself, so I could move on to more profitable activities."

"Tough childhood."

He sighed. "Good times, Nicolaos. Good times. Though of course, back then I certainly didn't think so. I was young, no responsibilities, free to do whatever I wanted, no father to tell me nay. You have a father, don't you? Of course you do. I'd wager he gives you grief. I never had that. But I wanted more from life. Have you noticed the young are never happy with their lot? Always ambitious, always wanting more."

"Not like you and me at all."

"Precisely. I, for example, would be perfectly content with a villa somewhere in the country, nothing too large, a nice, quiet estate with enough land to grow my own food and a little extra to sell at market."

"I wish you luck."

"I must ask you Nico—"

"It's Nicolaos."

"I must ask, Nicolaos, what are you doing here?"

"Having dinner."

The pressure on my shoulders returned at once and I grunted with pain.

Araxes said, "Oh, no, no, no. This won't do at all. You have no one watching your back—if you did they'd be on me already—and here you are trying to play the tough man. Dear boy, it simply won't do. Save the pretense and the smart-ass comments for the amateurs who might be impressed by it. Let's start again, shall we? What are you doing here?"

The pressure eased. "Looking for you, of course."

"But you brought the girl with you. That was a bad mistake."

I blinked. Araxes had just told me I'd been followed.

"I'm returning the girl to her father."

"Don't. She's in the greatest danger here."

"From you?"

"No."

"Then why do you care?"

"She's a child. She doesn't deserve to be a player in this game, but if she remains, she will be. My advice is, take the girl and get out. Go back to your work in Athens."

"That's all very well for you to say, Araxes, but I don't have any more work. I lost my job because of you."

"What's this?"

I found myself in the odd—bizarre would be more like it—position of spilling my heart out to my enemy.

"But this is dreadful," he commiserated. "Has your employer no idea how the game is played? Would he sack a general of the army for a single reversal in a long war? No, of course not. Yet he sacks a fine agent like yourself at the first mishap that comes by. It's outrageous! This Pericles of yours is not entering into the spirit of the thing. I've a good mind to write him a letter of protest on your behalf."

"I'm not sure that would be helpful, coming from you. No offense intended."

"None taken. Fair warning, Nicolaos: if you remain, I may eventually have to kill you."

"Then why not do it now while I'm helpless in your underling's hands? Not that I want to encourage you . . ."

"The answer to that is simplicity itself. I am a businessman. At the moment, no one is offering to pay for your death, but if you continue as you intend, then I see you as not so much a threat as a maturing revenue stream."

A commotion at the door made Araxes look up. I followed his gaze. A man stood there, a Persian, with the nose of a hawk and expressionless eyes under hair that was black as Hades. Though there were men of many different lands in The Great King, few of them were Persians.

Araxes turned back to me and said, "And now, I must leave you."

Araxes had ruined my reputation with Pericles and I'd sworn to get my revenge. Instead, he'd walked in front of me, made me helpless, talked down to me, and now he would walk away as carelessly as if he had nothing to fear from me.

I looked down at the formerly delicious, now cold, bowl of stewed rat. I could feel some of the gristle still in my mouth. I worked it around with my tongue, sucked in for a moment, and spat.

I spat right into the face of the blue-tattooed barbarian next to me. He turned to me in surprise, put his hand to his face, and felt the spittle running down his cheek. He snarled.

I rolled my eyes upward, to the thug holding down my shoulders, and jerked my head upward as if to say, "It was him."

Either I was about to lose most of my teeth or . . .

The barbarian smashed a fist into the thug behind me. The thug let go and took two steps backward, yelling in surprise.

I didn't hesitate. I pushed the bench back and launched myself over the table at Araxes. He was totally surprised. He made to stand, but didn't have time. I dived into him headfirst and we both went tumbling, me on top. Good. I straddled and punched him one-two in the face, enjoying every moment.

I got two more punches in, just for fun, before I was whacked from the right. The blue-tattooed man on Araxes' side of the table hadn't been fooled by my trick; he'd seen me spit on his friend. He picked me up and roared—I felt like a child's doll in his hands—and threw me across the room.

Except I didn't go far. I landed smack into the Ethiopians

and Karians who'd been arguing. They dropped their argument in favor of beating me. I had to hit back to defend myself while stepping aside, anxious to get back to Araxes before he got away.

I needn't have feared. The barbarian had stood Araxes up against a wooden pillar, the better to beat him. I laughed. The barbarian had seen us talking together and thought he was my friend. Meanwhile the other barbarian and Araxes' thug were throttling each other, to the cheers of the onlookers. They were both huge, heavily muscled men, and both had rictus grins of determination.

A tall man landed on my back and tried to get his arm across my throat. It was one of the Ethiopians. I staggered but didn't fall. I reached behind me to grab at him, fell to one knee, and pulled. He flipped over my shoulder.

I looked up to see Araxes get control of his situation. He planted a hard knee into the barbarian's groin and then clubbed him doublehanded on the back of the neck. A stiletto appeared in his hand.

I shouted, "No!" and charged him, which knocked us both into the crowd of locals by the window. They weren't amused and set about us both. We found ourselves back to back. There were too many punching; I had to put my hands up to defend my head. The Ethiopian had charged again—I think he must have gone berserk—and ran into the recovering barbarian, who backhanded his new attacker away, straight into the oily plaited riders, who'd formed a defensive ring about their corner and were striking anyone who came near. The Karians were hitting at the remaining Ethiopian.

Other men, all of them drunk, had decided to join in. I saw the innkeeper, wielding a club in one hand and a hydria of water in the other, stepping over struggling bodies to get to the torches and douse them before someone knocked one over and started a fire.

Someone pushed me from behind and I was ejected from the group hitting me, back into the room. I staggered straight into the barbarian, who smiled to see me again and took me by the throat with both hands and pressed in hard with his thumbs. I couldn't breathe. My hands flew to his and tried to pry them away, but it was like trying to bend iron. He grinned through his tattooed face and I saw his teeth were stained black.

At the window the locals had tired of beating Araxes. They picked him up, and as one, they tossed him out the window. He flew out cleanly.

My vision began to fade. I tried to kick the barbarian's groin like Araxes had but he was ready and blocked me. At any moment my eyes were going to roll upward.

From nowhere, a bowl smashed over the barbarian's head. He looked puzzled, then woozy. His hands relaxed and I could breathe again. He collapsed, like a mountain falling sideways, to reveal the Ethiopian standing on the table behind, holding the broken pieces of the smashed bowl and spattered with leftover stew.

I gasped, "Thanks, I owe you."

He replied with gibberish and grinned.

I looked to the door, between me and it were men fighting and men looking for a fight. I hadn't the slightest chance of getting through.

There was only one thing to do. I picked out the nearest local in the group, turned him around, and punched him in the face. He hit back, but his friends grabbed me by my clothing and lifted me high. I told myself to keep my arms and legs in. They ran me two steps and then I flew. I remember passing through the window and then hitting the ground.

I rolled to a halt before a pair of boots. Above the boots were trousers.

Hellenes don't wear trousers.

I looked up from my prostrate position in the dirt to see the Persian. Two soldiers stood at his back.

He stared down at me. I stood at once, because Hellenes do not prostrate themselves before any Persian, not even by accident.

"Did you see a man come flying by here a moment ago?"

As I said it, two more flew out the window. The Persian and I watched them hit with dull thuds and lie still.

He said, "A man rolled, as you did, and jumped up and ran away. Perhaps that was your friend."

His hair was black but his skin very pale. This was not a man who worked in the light of day. His eyes were dark—they could not have been any other color. His age I guessed to be somewhere between late twenties and midthirties. His hair hung ringleted, and his beard curled, in a style you would never find on a Hellene. The robe he wore had large sleeves and flowing folds and was striped in dark red and yellow. Obviously he was a high-ranking officer but he wore his rank as if it were of no account.

"You are?" He spoke perfect Greek.

"Nicolaos, son of Sophroniscus."

"You started the fight in there."

"I didn't."

"I saw you. Know this, Hellene, lawlessness is hateful to the Great King."

The officer turned and walked into the night, his soldiers following. I watched him fade to black. Most officers I have seen swaggered in their importance, but he simply walked as if he were impatient to be done with another detail. Dear Gods, if all the Persian commanders were like this man, how had we managed to beat them?

I toed three unconscious bodies, just in case, but none were Araxes.

I looked back. The Great King was a heaving mass of struggling men, thrashing each other in the near dark, because the innkeeper had managed to douse the last of the torches.

The Persian had delayed me too long. Araxes would know paths and places to hide that I could never find. He'd got away.

"With Araxes on the prowl I don't want you out on your own," I said to Asia back in our room, as I washed my cuts and bruises. In fact, the sooner we cleared Ephesus the better, but I had too much work to do to leave for a few days.

"The man you met," Asia said. "I think I know him. His name is Barzanes. He . . . works with my father."

"Works with?"

"Barzanes arrived at Father's palace about three months ago, not long after my mother died."

"Oh. I didn't know about your mother. I'm sorry."

Asia shrugged. "So am I. Barzanes arrived, and things changed."

"Changed how?"

"I don't know. Father became distracted. He always used to talk to me, telling me things, about politics, about how he ruled. It was like he meant to train me, though I'm only a girl. But then he stopped. He spent all his time working. Well, he worked all the time anyway, but he worked even harder, spent so much time in his office and only came out to rule the city. I never saw him and he seemed a bit different. At the time I thought the way he acted was because of Mother dying, but looking back on it later I wondered if Barzanes had something to do with it."

"In what way?"

"My father has commanded armies and faced powerful enemies and always he's won. But I think Father is scared of Barzanes."

I lay in bed that night, pondering. I tried to concentrate on my mission, but my thoughts kept reverting to Diotima. Could I pass through Ephesus without seeing her? Did I want to? No, it was unthinkable. But what would I say to her?

"Yaahh!" A piercing scream ripped through the air and tore me from sleep. I sat bolt upright. A girl's voice. Who?

"Father, no! Help me!"

Asia. In my addled state I'd forgotten Asia. She tossed and turned in the straw on the other side of the room, as if someone attacked her.

I shook her and said, "It's all right. You're safe." My words hadn't the slightest effect.

She continued to buck and cry. "No! Father!"

Asia was still asleep, yet she talked. Had Themistocles been beating her? I held her tight so she wouldn't hurt herself and shouted over and over, "Wake up, Asia. You're safe. Wake up!"

"What? Where am I? Who are—" She threw her arms about me and held on tight.

"You were having a nightmare."

"Yes." She shivered despite the warm night.

I brought her some water from the hydria in the corner. Asia drank it, staring at the floor, and the shivering stopped.

"All right. Try and get some sleep," I said as gently as I could. I rose to go.

"No, wait . . ."

"Yes?"

"Let me . . . let me sleep with you . . . please?"

"No."

"At home . . . I always slept with my sister Nicomache. I'm not used to a bed on my own. Please, master?"

It was bad enough I had her in the same room, though

that was obviously necessary for her own safety, but any father would kill me for this.

A tear trickled down her face.

I sighed. "You'll have to squeeze in the side."

She dived into my bed before I'd finished the sentence.

I walked over to find there was barely any room for me. "Move over."

She wriggled to the far edge and I pushed my way in.

"But I warn you, if I can't sleep, out you go."

I was in bed with the wrong woman.

I lay back and tried to pretend there wasn't a girl sleeping below my armpit. I could feel her move against me as she made herself comfortable.

Asia was of marriageable age, and she was well developed for it too. I had the natural reaction any man would with a young woman wriggling beside him. I reminded myself of the words I'd used to Socrates: she was a virgin when I found her, she'd better still be a virgin when I returned her to Themistocles. At last she settled down and I could close my eyes and go back to sleep.

I rolled over to put my back to her and thought of Diotima.

Sex was a problem. Of course, a woman couldn't afford to lose her virginity if she expected a good marriage, I understood that. Fathers had been known to kill men for deflowering their daughters, and afterward the courts approved the killing. Jurors are men with daughters too.

It made sense Diotima had refused to have sex. Perfectly normal. Very frustrating.

"Master?"

I opened my eyes. "What is it, Asia?"

"Why did you buy me?"

"I'm returning you to your father."

"Why?" she persisted.

To find out why she had arrived in Athens with a murderer. To uncover a secret which killed a man. To spy on her father.

I said, "It's partly a goodwill gesture. Your father is still well respected by many in Athens, and you are, technically, a citizen of Athens. The Athenians would not allow one of their own to be a slave without reason; there's a law against it. The best thing to do is return you."

"Are you going to invite Father back to Athens?"

"No."

"He wants to go home, more than anything. I know he does."

"That's not for me to decide. The Ecclesia and the courts are in charge."

"Father will reward you for bringing me back."

"That's nice."

"What reward will you ask for?"

My job back with Pericles? A position among the leaders of Athens? My marriage? Themistocles had nothing I wanted.

"I haven't thought about it."

"You should. Father's sure to ask. I'm his favorite daughter."

"Fine, I'll think about it in the morning." I closed my eyes.

"Master?"

I opened my eyes. "What is it now?" I droned.

"When are we leaving for Magnesia?"

"I have some things to do here first. I'll know more *in the morning.*"

"Master, will you—"

"Asia!"

"Yes, master?"

"Shut up and go to sleep."

"Yes, master."

I woke next morning to find Asia had somehow migrated to the other end of the bed and was curled up, peaceful and asleep against my legs. I didn't want to wake her so I lay thinking.

Here I was, outside Athens for the first time in my life, and not only in a new city, but inside the Persian Empire. Granted, Ephesus was as close to being independent as you could get and still make obeisance to the Great King, but in no free Hellene city could I come face-to-face with Persian soldiers, like I had the day before.

Anything was possible, even the success of my mission, even the saving of my career, even a new beginning. Perhaps a new beginning to everything. I had to find Diotima and talk to her. Things had gone wrong between us, horribly wrong. Today was the day I would put them right.

I meant to mention this to Asia that morning, as we sat at the bench eating our breakfast of stale bread soaked in a little wine, but I didn't because although I knew in a general way what I wanted to say when I found Diotima, I hadn't quite worked out the precise words. I rehearsed the conversation over and over in my mind, but it never sounded as good as I expected. I gave myself a little more time by telling Asia we would spend the morning investigating.

She shrugged and said, "I thought you wanted to find this woman?"

"We will, later this afternoon for sure."

We walked down the road to find Pollion, the brother-in-law of Thorion, whom I guessed would be at the commercial agora. We were coming down Marble Road when walking uphill I saw the one and only person I expected to recognize in Ephesus: the long, dark, curly hair, the confident walk, the pretty face with the thin nose and the full lips, and the pleasing way her dress stretched across her breasts. Diotima was about to turn the bend in the road; any moment now she would see me standing in the road.

Well, that was all right, wasn't it? After all, I'd resolved to talk to Diotima some time today. All I needed was a prepared speech. Then I looked down at Asia who stood beside me, and

I thought back to the words of Socrates. "I wouldn't want to be in your place when Diotima sees her!"

Perhaps this wasn't the right time to talk to Diotima.

Yes, that's what I'd do. I would let Diotima pass by, and approach her when I didn't have Asia with me, when I'd decided what to say. But where to go?

Behind us lay the commercial agora, with nowhere to hide. Other than that there was only the wide open theater. On the lower side of the road was what looked like a large private residence. On the uphill side, a low building stood, into which I had seen others pass; obviously a public building of some sort.

"Quick, come this way."

I grabbed Asia by her left arm and dragged her up the steps.

Asia protested. "What are you doing?"

"Shut up and do as I say."

We passed through the open gates into a small courtyard, open to the street, in the middle of which sat a water well. The stonework and the flowering vines twined around it to provide fragrant aroma were a thing of beauty, but I didn't stop to admire. Diotima would see us as she passed, and I hadn't yet decided what I'd say to her. A door exited the courtyard to our right. I didn't hesitate. I slammed it shut the moment I'd pulled Asia inside.

I stood there, panting from the sudden fright. There was a shutter in the door. I opened it and peered out.

"If you like this girl so much, why are we hiding from her?" Asia asked loudly.

"Shh!"

"I'm sorry. We don't permit clients to bring their own women." It was a rich, vibrant, sultry voice.

I whirled about to find a lady standing behind us. She was dressed in . . . not very much. Her face was painted and her red hair flowed in ringlets down to her bosom, which was exposed.

We had come to a brothel.

"My apologies, er, lady. I only want to stay for a few moments."

"That's what they all say, dear, but they pay all the same."

"No, you don't understand. I—"

"He's hiding from his girlfriend," said Asia.

"She's not my girlfriend," I said quickly.

But the lady had only one interest. "You haven't come for our services?"

"No, I said it was an accident."

"Well, you can't stay here. Out."

"But—"

"I don't care. Heracles!"

Heracles was well-named. He was a hulking great man in Persian dress. He was at least a hand's width taller than me and wide, so wide he almost waddled. There was almost no hair on him, no sign of a beard. His facial skin was as smooth as a woman's. I suspected I'd met a eunuch for the first time, but I was not tempted to lift his tunic and see.

"You leave now, master." He spoke Greek heavily accented with Persian. The words were polite but the tone was unmistakable. It left no doubt I was leaving now.

To assist me in my understanding, Heracles picked me up by the neck of my chiton, and carried me, using one hand, through the doorway and into the courtyard. Asia walked alongside. I dangled like a kitten in the mouth of its mother. There he dropped me.

"Try to keep him out of trouble, dearie," the brothel keeper called to Asia from the doorway.

"I'll do my best," Asia promised.

The door slammed behind us.

We stood in the courtyard with the well. The paved path descended on a gentle slope back to Marble Road. Diotima was out there, somewhere on the street, probably about to pass by at any moment. To give her time to walk past, I said to Asia, "Why don't we drink from this well?"

"You mean that? Oh, master! But—"

"Don't argue, just drink, and take your time about it."

I pulled up the bucket and used the tureen tied to the well wall to proffer a drink to Asia, then took a large drink for myself. The water was cool, even more than I expected, and tasted pure and did a great deal to calm me down. I dropped the tureen. Heracles stood at the entrance to the brothel. I congratulated myself I had delayed long enough to be sure Diotima would be gone.

She stood there, with her back to us, staring at the house opposite the brothel. I squealed in surprise and she whirled about.

"Nicolaos!" Diotima cried in delight, a broad smile appearing. "You've come to see me. Have you just arrived? Listen, I have a case to solve. A missing man and, oh, I'm so *pleased* to see—"

She stopped, realizing where she stood, where I stood. She'd been living in Ephesus long enough to know all the businesses on the main street. I watched her eyes as they followed my path back to the building I had exited. The scantily clad lady who had ordered me thrown out walked into the courtyard to collect water. She gave me a friendly wave and retreated. Diotima's smile vanished. She looked down, to see pretty little Asia holding my hand and looking up with wide, innocent eyes.

"Hello Diotima," Asia said. "I've heard so much about you!"

8

But curb thou the high spirit in thy breast,
for gentle ways are best,
and keep aloof from sharp contentions.

"You vile, disgusting goat, you make me sick!"

Diotima delivered a well-chosen curse on behalf of her deity, the Goddess Artemis, one which involved certain parts of my anatomy catching boils and falling off. Men who walked down the street smirked as they passed. This probably wasn't the first time they'd heard a woman curse a man outside this particular address. She finished with, "I suppose you were hiding in that brothel, waiting to jump out at me."

"No. Well, I *was* hiding, but—"

"I thought as much. You traveled all the way to Ephesus to make me miserable. Desperate to flaunt your new woman in my face, were you?"

"Asia? She's a slave."

"Is that supposed to make it better?"

Asia had been looking from one to the other of us as we argued. "Can I make a suggestion?"

"No," Diotima and I said in unison.

Diotima said, "I suppose you picked her up in some brothel?"

"No, but I saved her from one."

"Oh, sure. I've heard that before!"

"I'm on a case, Diotima. There's been a murder. She's my clue."

"That means if I weren't with him, he'd be clueless," Asia said.

Diotima ignored Asia and said to me, "She reminds me of Socrates."

"You mean the way she interrupts with irritating comments?"

"Yes."

"At last, something we can agree on. She's not a witness—she didn't see a thing—but her presence must mean something, like leaving your cloak at the scene of the crime, only a cloak that talks too much."

"You don't seriously expect me to believe you came here for a murder?"

I told her of the death of Thorion in as few words as possible. "No one you know. The victim was our proxenos for Ephesus. Now I'm looking for his equivalent on this side of the sea, the proxenos for Athens here. His name is Brion."

"You won't find Brion," she said with such utter certainty it made me angry.

"Oh, come on, Diotima. What makes you think an experienced agent like me can't find one simple man, a public official at that?"

"Because he's the missing man I told you about, *my* case I told you I'm investigating."

My jaw dropped. I closed it. It dropped again.

"You look like a dying fish, Nicolaos."

I said, "There's something you need to know." I explained to her about the odd pottery in Thorion's room, and how Brion had shipped it to Thorion. I finished by saying, "There has to be some connection."

"Maybe."

"When did Brion go missing?"

"It could be as many as six days ago. He's a merchant, he

has interests all over the place, it took a while for people to realize he wasn't anywhere."

I counted back. "The timing's tight, but it's doable, Brion could have been taken here, and then the same man could have made it to Athens in time to murder Thorion. Is Brion the sort of man who would stare death in the face to protect the privacy of the mail?"

"I doubt it."

"What say we share? You can have half my murder. We can be a team again!"

"I wouldn't want your poxy murder if it was the last one on earth. We *were* a team. What did I get out of it last time?"

"You avoided being forcibly married to an uneducated boor who would have beaten you every day."

"Besides that."

"What more do you want?"

"You promised your father would negotiate for me, and then came back next day, looking like some naughty boy who'd been caught stealing food from the kitchen, and said no he wasn't after all. How do you think I felt?"

"That was my father's doing, not me."

"You made me feel like dirt when you told me why."

"You can't blame me for your parentage."

"I've spent my whole life not being my mother, and I still can't escape her. Anyway, who'd want you now? That was before you took to traveling with this—" She looked down at Asia. "This combination child and floozy sexpot."

"I resent that!" Asia said. "I'm not a child, I'm fourteen. Besides, we drank from the well." She pointed up the path to the well that stood before the brothel.

Diotima looked stunned.

"I don't see that you have any basis for complaint," I pointed out. "What claim do you have on me that I shouldn't do what I want, or see who I want?"

Perhaps not the most intelligent thing to say, but Diotima's tirade had turned my confusion and awkward feelings to anger. What I had meant to say was, we might still be friends if she'd stayed in Athens. It was the wrong thing to say, but I'd said it, and I wasn't going to back down and unsay it.

She said, "That includes having children with this girl, does it?"

"Who said anything about having children?"

Diotima pointed at Asia. "She did. Just then. The Goddess Aphrodite charmed that well . . . any local could tell you . . . if a man and woman drink from the well together, then the woman will bear the man's child. Congratulations."

Asia looked up to me with those big, round eyes of hers. "Isn't it wonderful?" she said with a smile.

Diotima turned and walked away.

I called, "Wait, Diotima, wait!"

She turned, already twenty paces away. "Yes?"

"You need to listen to me," I said.

"But Nicolaos," she said sweetly. "What possible claim do you have on me, that I should do as you say?"

Diotima turned her back on me for a final time and flounced off in a cloud of anger so palpable men coming the opposite way walked around rather than risk being within her arm's length.

"That didn't go too well, did it?" Asia observed.

"Shut up," I suggested, feeling morose.

"Yes, master."

I spent the rest of the day and all of the evening drowning my sorrows at the inn. My life was destroyed: Pericles would sack me for incompetence when I returned—I couldn't hide from the fact that my error had cost two men their lives; I was estranged from my father over a woman, and I admitted to myself—now—that I'd been hoping to patch things up with Diotima, but that chance was gone too.

I left Asia in our room, but I suppose she became bored, or hungry, because she came to me and watched as I sat, getting drunk.

She said, "Do you want to talk about it?"

"No. You're my slave, not my mother."

I downed my cup in one draft, slammed it down on the table, and beckoned for the house slave to refill it.

"How come you two broke up?"

"I asked my father to negotiate for her. He refused. I looked like a total idiot in front of the girl I wanted to marry."

"Oh." She knew as well as I did, it was unheard of for a man to marry against the will of his father. Not that it was unusual, but that it *never happened.* "Then she really isn't your girl-friend."

"I keep telling you that."

"I think you need to move on, master. You should find someone else. Then you'll stop thinking about her."

Now I was getting relationship advice from a fourteen-year-old. How low can a man sink?

I refused to talk anymore to Asia. After a while she tired of watching me drink and went back to bed.

The only time I spent away from the bar that night was when I went to see to Ajax. He whinnied happily and ate the apples I brought him. Then he nuzzled my shoulder. I put my arms around his neck. At least my horse still loved me.

9

It is not right to glory in the slain.

The innkeeper woke me next morning with a sharp kick in the back. I groaned, rolled over, and opened my eyes to see another drunk beside me, a drooling unshaven man with blood-red eyeballs and the sallow look of a plague victim. He stared back at me. No, that *was me;* I stared with gritty eyes at my reflection in a polished bronze urn.

I must have slid off the bench at some point in the night and not noticed. My head was pounding, pounding, pounding with the curse of cheap red wine. The world spun around, and around, and around, and that was while I lay flat on my back in the urine-soaked straw of the dirty floor. The Gods only knew what would happen if I sat up. Focusing only made it worse. I felt nauseous.

The only solution was a trip to the baths, if I could make it that far.

I left Asia at the inn—I had sufficient trust in her common sense now to expect her to stay out of trouble as long as she didn't wander—and shambled, a decrepit creature, down the road to the gymnasium and baths that we had passed on the day we arrived, close by the docks.

The bath attendant smirked—he'd seen it all before, especially at that hour of the morning. He was a slave, but I paid him extra coins because I knew if I didn't, my clothes would go missing, and because I knew what he would soon be cleaning up. He knew too; he handed me a bowl, which I carried to the cold pool. I ordered the slave to fill two buckets with the cold water.

Best get it over with quickly. I picked up the first bucket and poured it over my head. The icy water ran over my head, down my back and front, cleaning off the grime of the inn, washing away the sour smell of the wine, and waking me up as nothing else could have.

That was the last straw for my poor stomach. I doubled over by reflex and heaved the contents into the bowl and across the floor. I used the second bucket to wash out my mouth while the slave sluiced away the mess with a resigned expression of distaste.

"That's better," I said. My head was still pounding, but I knew that with the poison out of my system I would heal faster. I was fit now to walk into the pool, shivering as I did, but kept on walking until I was immersed up to the neck. I closed my eyes and let the water support me for I don't know how long, concentrating on surviving the throbbing in my head until it subsided to a manageable level.

I stayed until my lips and fingers were blue, then hauled myself out, shivering, and stepped into the next room. This was the laconica, shaped like a cone, with a round hole in the high, pointed ceiling. Trays of coals glowed in the semidark and heated the air so hot that I passed within a few heartbeats from shivering, to a comfortable glow, and then to sweating. I sat on the shelf that ran around the edge of the room.

A slave approached me, a naked and very thin slave. No surprise since he worked in this oven every day. He carried a tray with a hydria full of water and a cup. I drank three cups in a row without pausing. He put down the tray and brought out the real tools of his trade: a flask of oil, a sponge, a strigil, and soap.

I said at once, "The rest is fine, but skip the soap." I hate soap. It's made from goat fat and ashes. Even if the man who cleans you is thorough about scraping away every bit, you still walk out of the baths smelling like a dead goat.

The slave nodded and began to rub olive oil from the flask into my back. I lay facedown on the bench so he could do the same for my arms and legs. When I was fully oiled, he picked up the strigil and proceeded to scrape away from every part of me the oil, dead skin, and the grime of my travel, leaving behind fresh, clean skin. A bad strigil man can pinch and cut you until it feels like torture, a skilled man can make being washed one of life's great pleasures. This man was competent. The last vestiges of my hangover were gone.

He began to rub me down, soothing the skin where the strigil had scraped, over my back and chest, arms and legs. Then his hands began rubbing areas the strigil hadn't touched.

"What are you doing?"

"If the master wishes, for a few coins I can relax him some more."

Paying a slave for sex? I was desperate, but not *that* desperate.

I shook my head and said, "No thanks."

He let go.

I drank more water, then left the laconica for the fresh air, where I found my chitoniskos and dressed.

The commercial agora was right across the road from the baths. Men were standing about the edge, mostly in pairs but sometimes in small groups, talking with one another, arguing, waving their arms, or bent over scrolls. Some were doing all four things at once.

Other men stood in the center, each shouting at the top of his voice.

"Grain, fifty baskets!"

"Ceramics, in the warehouse and ready to go!"

"*Dolphin,* solid ship, empty hold!"

"Wine! Two hundred amphorae of the best!"

I asked after Pollion, son of Hegerandros, and was directed to a statue of Hermes looking down upon the merchants, larger than life high on a plinth. Standing beneath was a man carrying scrolls tucked under his left arm and one open before him in which he scratched notes.

"Are you Pollion, son of Hegerandros?"

"I am." A tall man with graying hair, he looked me up and down, trying to place me.

"I am Nicolaos, son of Sophroniscus, come from Athens. I'm sorry to tell you, Pollion, that your brother-in-law Thorion is dead."

"Dear Gods, I didn't even know he was sick."

"He was murdered."

Pollion raised an eyebrow. A man approached wanting to do business but Pollion waved him away.

He grabbed me by the arm and led me to sit on the low boundary wall of the agora. "Tell me everything," he ordered.

I didn't. I carefully omitted Thorion's note claiming to be a traitor.

When I finished my edited tale Pollion said, "This is terrible. Who killed him?"

"That's why I'm here. I have some questions."

"Go on."

"I need to understand the work Thorion did as proxenos."

"You suspect a disgruntled trader?"

"It's a possibility," I said. "Did you yourself trade with your brother-in-law?"

Pollion laughed. "Your question is less than subtle. How did an inexperienced young man like you get such a responsible job?"

"My employer is correcting that mistake."

"Oh? Well let me give you a piece of advice, young man. *Never* do business with relatives."

"I see. Did you learn that the hard way?"

"Many years ago, and my teacher was a worthless cousin, literally worthless as it turned out when he went down with his ship, taking my loan with him."

"Do you know of anyone with reason to hate Thorion?"

Pollion thought for a moment before saying, "There are always disputes. Litigation is constant. But I know of no one who'd risk harming a proxenos. Word gets around and it's not the sort of reputation any trader can afford to have."

"How did Thorion come by his position?"

"Through my father, at the time my sister married. Our family is prominent, and everyone agreed a proxenos with family ties to Ephesus gives him a certain interest in our welfare."

"It must be an advantage for you personally."

"Thorion looked after my interests in Athens for no fee, in court cases for example."

"Did that happen?"

"All too often. It's amazing what unscrupulous merchants will do. I had a problem with Telemenes of Athens only last month. He claimed spoilage far above reasonable expectation on a cargo of grain he carried for me on one of his ships. I suspected him of faking the loss and selling my grain for himself. I took him to court."

"Did you win your case?"

"As Thorion advised I would. He told me Telemenes' reputation, even within Athens, is, shall we say, more a question than a statement. As you say, having a proxenos in the family helps." Pollion pulled a face. "This is a disaster. My nephew Onteles isn't old enough to assume the proxeny, it will go to another family."

"Do you by any chance happen to know Brion, the proxenos for Athens?"

He looked at me oddly. "Brion trades here, a charming and very successful man of business."

"Excellent! Where is he?"

"I have no idea, he hasn't been seen for days, and that's a funny thing. I owe him money, profit from a joint venture. Quite a substantial sum, too, and it's not like Brion to miss out on money. He's rather fond of it."

"Isn't his wife worried?"

"He isn't married." Pollion chuckled. "Brion extends his charming nature to the women, who seem to find him attractive. Everyone loves Brion, if you get my drift."

Pollion stood up. "I will write to my nephew at once. Thank you for bringing me this news."

I stood too, looked out over the confused mass of men, and said, "I still don't understand this trading. How can anyone follow what's happening?"

"It's simple enough. A man comes here with a cargo, which he stores in the warehouse behind the docks. Perhaps he has grain from his farm. He could make a handsome profit if he sold it in Kos, where the crops have failed, but he has no boat. Another man arrives. He has a boat but no cargo. They find each other in this agora and agree to a joint venture, sharing the profits and the risks.

"Or another man comes with money to invest, but no cargo or boat. He buys a cargo from a farmer who prefers to take the certainty of hard coins now for his produce, but fewer of them, incurring no risk himself. The farmer departs with his coins. The investor finds a captain to carry his venture, which he sells at higher than he bought.

"Or perhaps the investor has money to risk, but not enough to fill a hold. So he clubs together with his friends and they form a venture with many owners.

"Or perhaps the investor has no friends with money to risk. So he comes here to find men of a like mind, and they agree to invest together. They split the profits according to how much each contributes. Sometimes the captain is a partner, sometimes their employee."

My head reeled. "You mean I could come here with a bit of money. I could join with men I've never met before, to buy something I didn't make myself, to ship it on a boat I don't own to a place I've never been, and the captain could sell the cargo and I'd make a profit?"

"Just so."

"But that's . . . that's . . . immoral." It wasn't quite what I meant, but I couldn't think of a better word for it.

"What do you find so objectionable?"

"Because I didn't do anything to earn the money. I didn't make anything, or move it, or sell it, but I made money."

"On the contrary, you *did* do something. You and your fellow owners selected the cargo, and you selected the captain, and you probably chose the destination for your produce. Granted you performed no physical labor, but you did something much more valuable, for you are to consider, a cargo sent to the wrong place—grain to a city with a surplus, for example, or wine to Chios, or pottery to Athens—would be as wasteful as throwing your product into the sea. The work you have done as owner is to allocate resources to the places that need them most."

"Because that's where the most profit lies."

"And the greatest need, or the profit would not be there."

"Did I hear you correctly, a moment ago? You said that sending pottery to Athens would be a waste, like sending wine to Chios."

Pollion laughed. "Athens is the largest producer of pottery in the civilized world. Athens *exports* pottery of every type by the boatload. No one in their right mind would ship pottery to Athens."

"That's funny, because Thorion imported pottery, from here—Ephesus—in fact."

"You must be mistaken. He of all men would certainly know better." He peered into the crowd. "Ah now, some trades are beginning. Observe the men in the middle. Each shouts what he has to offer. Those seeking approach and, if there is interest on both sides, they move to the edge to negotiate. Sometimes they agree, sometimes not. See? That man there returns to the center, he could not agree with his partners."

"I suppose Brion used the warehouse you mentioned."

"As does every man. A merchant rents space only when he requires it. The idea, after all, is for the goods to be on ships going elsewhere, and we already tithe the temple enough without having to pay those exorbitant storage fees."

"The temple?"

"The Temple of Artemis owns the warehouse."

I took a shortcut across the commercial agora to the warehouse. I wanted to see what Brion traded, and in particular if anything else was destined for Thorion. Diotima was far too competent to have missed so obvious a lead, but I knew more now than she had mere days ago and perhaps I could find something she hadn't.

I entered through a rear door and wandered about, looking for the manager. The warehouse was a huge but flimsy looking structure, so wide it needed rough wooden pillars—tree logs that had been barely shaved—set at regular intervals to hold up the roof. It was hot. We were nearing the middle of summer, and there were practically no windows and only the large doors at the front and small ones at the back and side. The floor space had been divided into rectangles—you could see the scuffed and faded lines painted on the floor—and it was obvious each represented the space for a merchant, because each was piled with wildly different goods. To move around you had to squeeze between the gaps. There were boxes of tools in one spot, tents in another. Many held amphorae stacked in pyramids, some with olive oil, some with wine, some with preserved fruits. You could tell what was what by the smell and the puddles where amphorae had been dropped and cracked. I came across one rectangle with nothing but bronze ware, and another with giant pots, like the ones used to make garos fish sauce. How they were going to ship those I didn't know.

I found the manager, a harried-looking man with a stack of wax tablets. He pointed me to the back corner where Brion had space.

In the far corner I found a man in rough clothing with ragged hair and an instantly suspicious expression.

"What do you want?" he demanded at once.

"I'm looking for Brion," I said, peering over his shoulder. Brion's goods had been covered by a wide cloth sheet that had the look of a ship's sail. Whatever Brion had here, he wanted hidden. "Where is he?"

"Got no idea. If I did I wouldn't tell you."

"For a slave you're very good at being rude."

"I ain't his slave," the man said.

Of course, the obvious answer: "You're a hired guard."

He nodded.

"Not exactly a prestigious job, is it?" I taunted him. Mercenaries consider sentry duty one short step above begging. Or mugging.

"What I'm doing's my business, ain't it?" he said.

"If you haven't seen him for days how are you getting paid? I would have thought you'd be gone by now." Mercenaries are not noted for extending credit.

"That's my business too."

He might have been a man down on his luck, but I didn't think so from his attitude.

"So you stand here all day and all night. Must get boring."

"It's a day job. They got night watchmen for the warehouse."

"What's underneath the sheet?"

"If you gotta ask, you don't need to know. So push off." He gave me a small push, daring me to make something of it.

"All right! All right!" There was no point in staying, and causing trouble wouldn't take me any further. "Tell Brion that Nicolaos has a message for him, from Thorion."

"Thorion. Right."

I walked toward the back door, which was close by, but at the last moment turned to hide behind some tapestries that hung from the ceiling almost to the ground, down the back wall.

I parted the heavy materials to find someone already there. A woman.

"Diotima?"

"Don't just stand there or someone will see!" She grabbed my tunic and pulled me in.

I let the layers of thick material fall together behind me and whispered, "What are you doing here?"

She whispered back, "The same thing you are, of course. When you told me Brion shipped ceramics to Thorion, I knew I had to get a closer look at his goods. I checked this warehouse two days ago, but then I only thought to ask after Brion. It was the same guard who's standing there now, and he was as rude to me as he was to you."

"I need more room. Move over."

She wriggled over. We both peered around the edge of the

tapestry at Brion's corner, where the guard paced back and forth and looked bored.

The tapestry we hid behind was dusty. I'd brushed against it when I pushed in, and a gray cloud had erupted. Didn't they ever clean this place? The front of my exomis was smeared with the stuff and I wanted to sneeze. I turned my head to the side. Diotima stood so close that her hair was directly below my nose. The perfume of her dark hair soothed the urge to sneeze. She always did smell nice. She in turn grabbed the material of my exomis and jammed her face into it to escape the dust. Through the material I could feel the warmth of her breath on my chest. It was oddly pleasant. Then she gave a little sneeze, fortunately muffled.

When the dust had settled she let go and we stood slightly apart.

I said, "The guard can't keep up that pacing forever. Sooner or later he'll get hungry, or need a toilet."

Even as I said it, the guard stopped pacing, walked over to the covering sheet, and reached under. He pulled a low krater out from underneath, lifted his exomis, and proceeded to urinate into it.

Diotima said, "So much for that theory."

The guard took a swig from a leather water pouch and resumed his pacing.

I said, "There's still hunger. Or nightfall. He told me night watchmen take over. They'd be easier to elude."

"With a light on? We'd need a torch to see anything. We'd be spotted in an instant."

"Good point." It would have to be daylight. "You can lure him away with your feminine wiles."

"I don't have any."

"Yes, you do," I said with feeling. Diotima looked up at me, and her eyes were large and dark and round and I wanted to kiss her, but I couldn't; she wasn't mine to be kissed. In my confusion I said to her what worried me most, "You didn't tell me Brion isn't married."

"Let me rephrase that, my wiles aren't available for commercial purposes, and what's Brion's marital status to do with you?"

I said, "I'll wait forever if I have to."

"To marry Brion?"

"For the guard to move."

We waited, and waited. And waited. We sweltered in the hot air, made worse from being covered front and back by the heavy material of the tapestries. We took turns peering out, hoping the wretch would get hungry, or bored, or die.

He did none of those things. He paced back and forth, and when he got tired, he sat on a stool.

As we waited I whispered, "Diotima?"

"Yes?"

"Why did you leave Athens?"

For a moment I thought she wouldn't answer, but then she whispered back, "After the disaster with you I realized no father would let his son marry me. I thought if I got far enough away, it wouldn't matter."

"So you do want to marry."

"Do I get a choice? Women aren't permitted to own property. It's marry or join my mother as a prostitute."

"I thought that was why you became a priestess."

She didn't reply except to say, "Has the guard moved?"

We both peered around the corner. The guard had his back to us but he wasn't moving. We pulled back.

A question had been burning in my mind. "Diotima, if he doesn't have a wife, who hired you to find Brion?"

She blushed. "No one hired me. I said right at the start, this is my own investigation. Brion is a friend."

"A friend?" I didn't like the sound of that.

"I wrote to him as proxenos to help arrange my move to Ephesus. After I arrived, he asked for me by name whenever he came to the temple. At first, he was the only one who was nice to me, and now he's missing. I won't stop until I find him."

Diotima had woven a one-woman path of destruction through Athens in her determination to find her own father's killer. I contemplated what would happen if she were left to find Brion on her own. Ephesus might never be the same again; I'd hate to see the place in ruins.

"What was Brion doing at the Artemision?"

"Reading the book."

"What book?"

"I'll show you when we get to the temple."

I said, "Listen Diotima, nothing happened between me and the slave girl. I swear by Artemis, by Zeus, and Athena." I put as much force into my whisper as I could.

She replied with as much contempt, "Oh, sure. I suppose next you'll tell me you went into that brothel by mistake."

"As it happens—"

Footsteps. A man walked from the front of the warehouse. We both fell silent and stood still, and I thought thin thoughts so the bump wouldn't show in the material. Our faces were turned sideways so we could breathe, staring at each other in midargument but unable to speak.

Whoever he was, the footsteps passed by.

Diotima whispered, "When I saw you standing in the road, I thought you'd come to take me home. I was so happy, for that moment. I thought—"

She cut herself off, and her voice hardened. "Then I saw you were outside the brothel, with *that girl*."

I whispered back, "Do you want to know why I ran in there? Because I was scared. Of *you*. There you were walking down the road, and I had no idea what I'd to say to you."

The man returned and stopped right in front of us. If he bent down, he'd see our feet. Instead, after some loud heart-beats, he walked on.

"My feet hurt," Diotima complained.

"Why don't you go back to the temple? I can handle this."

"And leave you to get all the information? I'll see my feet fall off first."

The sweat ran down her face and neither of us had water. I didn't think she'd last much longer. Something had to be done.

"I have an idea."

"You'll lure him away with your manly wiles?"

"When he runs, go check the goods. You'll be safe. Promise."

"What do you mean, safe?"

I edged along the tapestries to the exit on the other side.

"Nico!" But I ignored her and slipped out.

I walked across the warehouse to the different stacks of am-phorae, wandered along until I found the ones I wanted, then stopped and looked around. No one watched me. Apparently olive oil was too boring to guard. I pulled an amphora off the top and walked away with it balanced on my shoulder, whis-tling as if everything were normal.

I carried the oil over to the empty garos vat, unplugged the stopper of the amphora, and dropped it inside. While the oil poured I worked my way to the camping supplies. Sure enough, there were boxes of flints and tinder. I carried a box of flints back to the vat, and along the way snatched a handful of dry rags. Back at the vat, I dropped the rags into the oil to soak, then draped the three longest over the side to act as wicks. The garos vat had been turned into a giant oil lamp. I used the flint fire starters to light the wicks.

The fire flared high. I screamed, "Fire! Fire!" and ran away, waving my arms. Anyone among the piles of goods would see only the bright flame, and smell the acrid, black smoke that began to fill the air. The conclusion was obvious: the high piles of flammable oil had caught alight. Other men took up the call of fire and ran for the exits in panic. They pushed me aside, knocking things over as they ran and adding to the confusion.

Diotima had the covers off by the time I returned to the corner.

She said, as she threw the sheet to the side, "He ran. Please tell me this is your trick."

"It's safe. Someone will soon put it out."

Beneath the sheet was pottery. In the same style as the pieces I'd seen in Thorion's office. Fired in browns and pastel reds and fauns, it looked nothing like the red and black of Athenian work.

Diotima said, "Brion set a guard over pottery?"

"Maybe it's expensive."

"Doesn't look it to me. It looks old, and weird. Look, there are barely any figures in the decoration. It's all patterns."

The pieces ranged from small hydriai for storing water to large kraters. I bent to pick up a hydria, and stopped in surprise. "Zeus, this is heavy." I yanked it up, but it was even heavier than I'd realized. The hydria slipped from my fingers and crashed to the floor. The stopper fell out and small coins tinkled across the floorboards in a stream. The jar was full of them. Diotima and I looked at each other in surprise. She snatched a handful of coins off the floor and put them in her pouch while I restoppered the rest.

"Are they all like this?"

We tried a few more.

"No, most of them are empty."

"Nico." Diotima took a step back from the largest piece, a krater with a lid, sitting in the very corner. She removed the lid and looked in. I joined her.

At the bottom of the krater was a jumble of human bones, and a skull staring up at us.

I said, "Do you think that was Brion?"

"No. The bones were too old."

I nodded. In fact they were brown with age and jumbled together.

We'd replaced all the lids and stoppers, thrown the sail sheet over everything, and got out through the back door just as the fire was extinguished. Now we walked uphill to the Artemision.

I said, "The bones are old, but that stuff hasn't been there long."

"How do you know?"

"There was very little dust on the cover sheet, but lots of dust in the air of the warehouse. I saw things covered in it."

Diotima nodded and said, "There's still a chance Brion's alive. I like to think he is, I hope so."

"Then who's the guy in the krater?"

"I have no idea."

"Did Brion ever talk to you about this pottery business?"

"No, but why would he? It was merely another trade."

"A rather odd one." I hesitated, then, "What *did* you talk about?"

"With Brion? Oh, philosophy mostly. He's talked with many famous thinkers, even Anaxagoras. Brion's nice, he's courteous. He shaves every day. His fingernails are always trimmed and clean."

"Easy enough for him," I said, putting my hands behind my back. "He's rich."

So Brion had been charming, handsome, wealthy, *and* fascinating about philosophy. I'd never met the man, but already I loathed him.

I said, "Anyway, that's nothing. Just the other day back in Athens I discussed philosophy with Anaxagoras myself."

"*You* talked philosophy?" Diotima choked back laughter.

"It's true!"

"Oh sure."

"We discussed theories of matter." I repeated what little I could remember about tiny particles all mixed together.

Diotima looked at me with surprised respect. "That's actually very good. You know, I almost believe you."

We passed through the agora, stopping to drink our fill from the public fountain, before she went on, "Did you recognize the coins?"

"No. We could take them to a money changer of course, but—"

"That would be insane. Word would spread and we'd have half the city on us before the day was out."

"The coins . . . another body . . . I don't know if any of this will lead me to Araxes."

"Pericles is being harsh on you, Nico, you did everything humanly possible. It's not your fault Araxes got away."

"No, Diotima, Pericles was right. It was my responsibility and I failed. I would have sacked me, if I were him. The only chance to redeem myself is to find the information Thorion died trying to reveal, return Asia to her home, and find out what Themistocles is up to, if anything. Araxes is my own personal mission, like your Brion."

"Your slave's story puts Araxes in Magnesia, right before he traveled to commit murder."

"Correct, but Araxes is merely an agent, acting for someone else."

"Like you."

"Like me."

"Could Araxes' client be Themistocles?" Diotima said.

"Let's think about that. Araxes works for Themistocles.

Themistocles orders Araxes to kill Thorion. So, right before he leaves, Araxes kidnaps Themistocles' daughter, because he likes having a *really angry* boss. Umm . . . no."

"When you put it like that . . ."

We had reached the Artemision, the largest building I had ever seen. It sat between two streams, both of which were called the Selinus although they approached the temple from different directions and came together farther downstream. The red-painted wooden columns holding up the roof were vast, I could not have put my arms around one, and they towered into the sky. The style was old and elegant. People were coming and going, young, old, male, female, different races too, not only Hellenes but those who were obviously from far away.

The building was immaculately clean, which was easily explained by the small army of men scampering about. Several of them greeted Diotima in a friendly manner, but I shrank from all of them. Diotima noticed. "What's wrong?" she asked.

"Are they what I think they are?"

"They're the Megabyzoi; they're the property of the temple, and they're as bad as the women."

I raised an eyebrow. Diotima answered my unspoken question. "The Megabyzoi are eunuchs who serve at the temple. And before you ask, no, we don't have them in Athens. The Megabyzoi are a specialty of Ephesus. It's considered a high honor to be selected."

I nodded, and decided I would forgo that honor. "They make my skin crawl," I muttered.

"Don't worry, you won't be asked to join them. You'll be free to continue your sordid adventures in the brothels." She gave me a calculating look. "Though come to think of it, a few slashes might fix certain undesirable traits . . ."

"Please, Diotima," I pleaded, wincing. "Must you go on about it?"

She smiled and brushed back the dark curly locks that fell across her face, then took me by the hand and led me through the entrance of the Artemision. "This temple is deeply sacred. Not as sacred as where the Goddess was born on Delos, but except for Delos, you couldn't find anywhere more holy. People from all over the world come to see it. In the months I've been here I've met people from Carthage and Massilia. Did you know there's a city called Massilia? It's Hellene, but I'd never heard of it. Then there are people from the far side of the Empire. They don't look remotely like us. I've met Medes and Babylonians and people you could never hope to see in Athens. The barbarians call her Cybele rather than Artemis, but they seem to think it's the same goddess."

Diotima's eyes shone as she spoke, and her speech was fast and excited. I said, surprised, "You like meeting the barbarians?"

"It's exciting, Nico. All over the world, people are living in different ways, speaking different prayers, in strange cities, and we don't even know about it. Don't you wonder what might be happening in other parts of the world?"

"I have enough trouble with my own piece of it."

We stopped at an immense red curtain, hung from the ceiling but drawn up, with great folds of material spilling over the ends, to reveal the statue of the Goddess. Artemis stood high and proud, her arms outstretched like a supplicant, or a mother welcoming her children. Her chest was covered with breasts, not merely the standard two, but more than I could count at a glance, all hard and full of milk.

I admired the Goddess for some time while Diotima waited patiently beside me. I cleared my throat. "I take it we are not viewing Artemis here in her guise as the Huntress?"

"Hardly," Diotima murmured.

In Athens, Diotima had been a priestess at the temple of

Artemis of the Hunt. There the Goddess is depicted as a fit young maiden armed with a bow, accompanied by a deer as she runs through the forest.

"The Artemis of Ephesus is a Mother Goddess, and a Goddess of Fertility," Diotima lectured.

"You don't say," I muttered, counting the breasts. "Twenty-one, twenty-two . . ."

Diotima glared. "Keep it pious, Nicolaos. Just because the Goddess appears to these people as the Mother is no reason she can't transform for your benefit to something more likely to put an arrow through you. She's still the same person, you know. The Gods appear to us in many forms but they're each a single deity within."

I commented, "The cult statue looks a little old." The stone and wood was stained and cracked and aged, despite their efforts to keep it pristine. The style was stiff and, well, wooden; noticeably of a period long, long ago.

"This statue of the Goddess was dedicated by the Amazons."

"What, as in Troy?"

"Oh yes. The Amazons worshiped Artemis. They came here to the Artemision several times, the first during their war against King Theseus of Athens, and that was a generation before the war against the Trojans."

I studied the Goddess in new appreciation. "This place is that old?"

"Older. The Artemision was built by the demigod Ephesos, who founded the city under the protection of the Goddess. Since that day, it's been the greatest ill deed to lay a hand against anyone who claims protection of the temple. The whole civilized world knows of the sanctuary of the Artemision."

"I didn't."

"I said 'civilized.'"

She led me through into a courtyard at the back, where there was a smaller building which looked like another temple.

"This is where we keep the Book."

I heard the significance in her words before, but had no idea what she meant.

"The Book of Heraclitus."

Where had I heard that name before? Then I remembered. "The funeral stele in the agora?"

"Yes, that's where they buried the author."

"Tough critics they have around here."

One of the Megabyzoi guarded the entrance. He inclined his shaven head to Diotima and said, "Priestess," in a voice so high and effeminate it could have been a woman's, though he was taller and wider than me, and had a massive chest. I imagined he must be very strong. I doubted there was even a single trace of fat in him.

Diotima said, "*Kalimera,* Geros."

He bowed and replied, "*Kalimera,* Priestess."

Diotima passed within. I followed, but I couldn't help staring at him as I went by. He looked back at me with the bland expression of contempt one sometimes sees from a slave. I'm sure he knew my thoughts, the poor wretch.

The building was indeed a temple of sorts, a miniature one, built upon the same kind of stepped platform, with the same external pillars in rows about all four sides, holding up the same peaked roof, and with the same rectangular room shielded by the roof. But within the temple, in place of where the cult statue should have been, was a scroll upon an altar.

"So this is the Book. What did Heraclitus say that's so interesting?"

"It's a book of philosophy. They say Heraclitus was a great sage. He died, oh, fifteen years ago, and left this book he wrote to the Artemision. The priests built this small temple purely to keep the Book, for anyone to come and read it, though the original has to remain here. Sometimes a rich man in another city will pay a scribe to make a fresh copy. The scribe has to work there," Diotima pointed to the table at the side of the room, "and when it's done the copy is sent away to the client. It's the Keeper's job to see the original remains inside the temple and in good condition, and you saw the guard outside."

I put my hand on the scroll to open it, and hesitated. "Can I look?"

"That's why it's here."

I opened the scroll and rolled the words past me.

On those who step in the same river, different and different waters flow.

I looked back to Diotima. "This is gibberish."

"They say Heraclitus wrote in puzzles because he believed his wisdom should only be learned by people smart enough to understand it. What you read means, 'You can't step in the same river twice.'"

"Then he's obviously wrong. I can step in to any river, get out, and step back in again."

"He doesn't mean it like that. What he's saying is, the river flows all the time, water moves, leaves and twigs floating in the river are carried along. When you step back in, the river has changed. You can't step out of the river and step back in to *exactly the same river.*"

"Obvious."

"He's using the river as a metaphor for the whole world. Everything changes, all the time. We all age, the trees sway, the wind blows, rocks crumble. It's quite profound when you think about it."

"You're not going to tell me the stars change."

"He's obviously wrong about them, but they're not part of the world, are they? Not like the sun and moon are."

A man's voice began calling in a singsong. Diotima said at once, "A sacrifice is about to begin. I must attend. You can come if you want."

"I'd rather stay and look at more of this book, if it's permitted."

"It is, on one condition." She walked across the room to the entrance, opened the door, and spoke to the eunuch outside. The eunuch stepped in and shut the door behind him.

Diotima said, "While I'm away, it's the rule another must be here."

"Fine with me."

Diotima departed for her ritual, and I was left alone with the eunuch. The room felt distinctly warmer, and I shifted about in an uncomfortable way. Without paying any attention to the eunuch, without looking at him, I rolled to the beginning of the scroll and read. I scrolled forward and read at random, "They do not understand that what differs agrees with itself; it is a back-stretched connection such as the bow or the lyre."

I'd always thought it, and this book was the proof: philosophy was a waste of time. I hoped Socrates would get over his obsession before he grew to adulthood.

I'd thought there must be a clue in here, if Brion had read so much of it, but I was wrong. I was done with this twaddle, but I was entirely unwilling to turn and make small talk with a eunuch. I shifted back and forth on my feet, very much aware that Geros watched me. What was he thinking? Was he staring at me? I felt an itch, on my behind. I ignored it, turned the scroll, and read random words to keep my mind off the irritation. The itch became worse, until it screamed at me to scratch, but I'd be cursed before I let him see me scratch my backside.

"It's not infectious," a voice behind me said. A high-pitched boy's voice.

I turned around, startled (and rubbed my backside against the altar bench). He stood with his arms folded across his massive chest, leaning back against the wall.

"What isn't?"

"Eunuchy."

"I'm not concerned."

"Yes, you are. We see your kind all the time. Men afraid to come near us, who won't look into our eyes. I've learned to smell it. You're scared."

"Have it your way, slave," I said, forcing myself to look straight into his eyes, and not liking it for a moment. He might read my thoughts. "Look, your unfortunate condition is nothing to do with me—"

"Unfortunate. Is that how you think of it?"

"A man who can't be with a woman? Yes."

Geros laughed. "Merely because our balls are missing, it doesn't mean we cannot pleasure a woman."

I blanched. "You mean there are women who will . . . will . . ."

"Some women prefer us, especially the married ones, because there's no risk they'll fall pregnant."

A horrible thought assailed me. "You didn't . . . with Diotima, did you?"

Geros said nothing, but smiled.

My hand went to the hilt of my dagger.

"What's wrong, don't you like my choice of lover?" Diotima said from the doorway.

"You mean you . . . you . . ." I went red. How much had she overheard?

"Anyone who takes slave girls into brothels is in no position to complain about what I do."

"But, Diotima, a eunuch?"

"Eunuchs are people too, you know."

"They're not *men*."

Diotima laughed, and so did Geros. "Nico, you moron, Geros is winding you up, and so am I. There's absolutely nothing between him and me, not that it's any of your business."

But I noticed the way Geros looked at her as she spoke and I said, "Are you *sure* you're not having an affair?"

"I think I would have noticed."

I took my hand off the hilt of my dagger.

"The priestess speaks truth," said Geros. "Indeed she spent more time with the merchant than she did me."

"Oh, is that so?" I looked hard as Diotima.

"Come with me," she said. "I have an idea."

Diotima led me around the side of the main complex, to a place where marble steps began at ground level and descended, ending at bronze doors set underneath the temple. Geros had been the sole guardian of the Book, here there were two guards, more Megabyzoi, and they looked like they meant business, with spears and shields but bare chests.

Diotima said, "I have the permission of the High Priest." She handed over a piece of parchment, which one of the guards read before hitting the door with the butt of his spear. A resonating bang on the other side told me someone had lifted a bar, and the doors swung to reveal two more guards within.

"What is this place?" I asked.

"The Treasury of the Artemision," Diotima said. "Welcome to the building fund."

We stood among piles of coins, gold decorations, silver masks, you name it, and all unbelievable wealth. The guards never took their eyes off us.

"Why are we here?"

"They never stop building this place," Diotima said. "There's always something more to do. Like the small temple of the Book, for example, it was built only fifteen years ago using funds from the treasury. When visitors bring gifts for the Goddess they are stored here. Some of it goes to running the place, but most is saved against the next project."

I picked up a child's mask, made of gold. "People donate this?"

"Dedications are stored, gifts are used, and the priests keep records. The point is, this has been happening for decades, maybe hundreds of years. What are the chances someone in the past gifted coins the same as the old ones we found in the warehouse? We can find out where they came from."

"That's almost brilliant."

We sifted through jars of coins by upending each in turn and keeping an eye out as we reloaded. Much of what I handled was gold. If there hadn't been two silent eunuchs standing over me with spears I would have been tempted to pocket some of the coins.

"Got it," Diotima said in triumph from her end of the floor.

"Where?"

She held out a handful of coins from the jar before her. I took one and compared it to our sample. Both were heavy in the hand and bore the image of a lion's head face-on.

Diotima already had the temple records open. She ran her finger down the lists. She had to read back a long way. "It's very old. This jar contains electrum staters—that's gold and silver— from"—she looked up at me—"from the island of Samos?" She finished as if it were a question.

"That doesn't make sense. Samos is a free state in the Aegean. My ship passed it on the way here."

"Nico, this jar is sixty years old."

"Maybe they still make the same coins?"

Diotima scrolled forward. "According to this, the Samians stopped donating coins in electrum fifty years ago and now they give silver tetradrachms."

Diotima looked up from the scroll. "What was Brion doing with ancient coins?"

There was something I had to do, and soon. The trierarch of *Salaminia* would have reported my safe arrival, but three days had passed, and they'd had nothing from me since. It was time to let Pericles know the situation in Ephesus.

I'd noticed a leather working stall in the agora when I'd explored the place with Asia. I went there now and bought some leather cord. I asked for directions to the quarter where the scribes worked. There I purchased two small wax tablets and a stylus to go with them, a jar of ink, and the smallest brush they had.

In the privacy of my room I pulled the skytale from the bag and wrapped the leather cord around it as Koppa had showed me. I thought for a moment, dipped the brush in the ink, and began.

NICOLAOS, SON OF SOPHRONISCUS, GREETS PERICLES, THE SON OF XANTHIPPUS, AND SAYS THIS TO HIM. BRION HAS DISAPPEARED. ARAXES IS IN EPHESUS. NICOLAOS WILL MOVE ON TO MAGNESIA TO DELIVER THE GIRL. HE HOPES TO LEARN MORE THERE. IF HE LEARNS NOTHING USEFUL IN MAGNESIA, HE WILL HAVE TO FIND BRION OR THE SOURCE OF BRION'S INFORMATION.

I wrote nothing about Diotima. Her situation had nothing to do with my mission for Pericles, and if I told him of her connection with Brion it would only serve to make him suspicious of her.

I hesitated. If I sent blank tablets, and someone snapped the cord and saw they were blank, it would be instantly suspicious. To cover my tracks I should write something on the tablets.

But what? Obviously it must be nothing about the mission. It had to appear innocent, boring even. Aha! What would be more natural than a son writing home to ask for more money? I picked up the stylus and scratched into the wax.

NICOLAOS GREETS HIS FATHER, SOPHRONISCUS, AND PRAYS TO ZEUS FOR HIS GOOD HEALTH. FATHER, I HAVE ARRIVED IN EPHESUS. THE JOURNEY WAS PLEASANT. THE WEATHER HERE IS FINE AND THE PEOPLE ARE FRIENDLY, ESPECIALLY ONE YOUNG LADY I MET. I STOPPED HER TO ASK DIREC-TIONS AND AFTER SHE SUGGESTED I GO WITH HER TO HER HOME . . . I'M SURE YOU WILL APPROVE WHEN YOU MEET HER, AND . . . YOU WILL BE PLEASED TO HEAR I HAVE INVESTED IN A FINE HORSE, A TRUE RACING BEAST . . . SPEAKING OF RACING . . . AND SO IF YOU COULD SEND MORE MONEY BY RETURN I SHALL BE ABLE TO PAY MY HON-ORABLE DEBTS AND . . . YOUR DEVOTED SON, NICOLAOS

I reviewed my work of fiction. Excellent. Anyone who cracked open the tablets would think these were the words of a naïve young man who had blundered his way about a new city, with little idea of what went on about him, nor of the true characters of the people he met.

I placed the written faces of the two tablets together and bound them tight with the cord, and carried my package down to the docks. On the way I passed the commercial agora, where I saw Pollion, and he saw me. Pollion beckoned me over.

"You deliberately didn't tell me there is a charge of treason against my late brother-in-law," he accused me in a cold voice.

"I'm sorry. Since he's dead, it hardly seemed right to upset you," I dodged. "I take it you've had word from your nephew."

"Onteles sends his regards to you and asks if there is prog-ress in clearing his father's name."

"Oh."

"Well?"

"I'm afraid not. We don't even know what the nature of this treason might be, only that he confessed to it before his death."

"Then there may be no treason at all."

"That's what Onteles thinks. He might be right, but I don't hold out hope. How's the family doing?"

"They suffer, as the family of a traitor always suffers. Onteles writes of damage to property and frightened womenfolk."

"Oh, I see. Another question for you, if I may, Pollion. The Ephesians chose Thorion for their proxenos because he had ties with Ephesus. Does that mean Brion has a connection with Athens?"

"There was such when he was appointed, more than ten years ago. Brion had a tie with one of the most powerful families in Athens. It's all over and done with now."

"Who?"

"The man who recommended Brion for proxenos was Themistocles. Why, does it matter?"

I carried on, my head in a whirl with the possibilities, and asked directions to any ship heading toward Piraeus. There were two leaving at first light next day, and I picked the larger, sturdier-looking craft. I negotiated with the captain to carry my package, and arranged for one of his crew to deliver the tablets to the home of my father. I knew I could rely on Father to pass the cord on to Pericles as he'd agreed.

As I turned away from the salty ship, I saw the diverse range of men who inhabited the docks of Ephesus: the tough sailors and wealthy merchants, slaves and free laborers and destitute beggars.

The beggars. They gave me an idea.

I wandered over to the wide front entrance of the warehouse, which I was pleased to see looked none the worse for its near incineration at my hand. A number of thin, haggard beggars sat outside. Every time someone walked through, the beggars stretched out their hands in supplication and called out their tales of misfortune, most of which no doubt were lies. A slave with a stick guarded the door; I could only imagine what would happen if the beggars got loose inside.

I found the one I wanted. It was hard to judge his age, because his hair was long and his beard straggly, but I guessed him to be in his late twenties. His clothes were not quite rags and he seemed alert. His right arm was off at the shoulder in a misshapen stump that was red and scarred.

"You." I pointed at him and held up a drachma.

At once the others rushed me, but my chosen beggar clubbed them back with his strong left arm, and we walked apart from the wailing crowd.

"What happened to your arm?" I asked. Now we were close I could see the face beneath the beard had ugly red, puckered scars.

"Sea fight." When he spoke I saw his broken teeth. "We got hit by pirates. One of them had a sword."

I'd guessed right. This was a man of my own class who'd been struck down by misfortune. I said, "You're lucky to be alive."

"If you call this luck."

"How come they didn't kill you?"

"Our side won. But by then I was down and screaming. My mate held a torch against the wound, and for a wonder I lived. Can't work again, though."

"No, of course not." No one in their right mind would hire a man who couldn't do his fair share. This fellow would live so long as he could squeeze coins from passersby, and then he would die.

I handed him the drachma. "This is your down payment. I want information, and I want correct information. I'll pay you the same no matter the answer, so don't tell me what I want to hear, tell me the truth."

"If you say."

"Do you know of a man called Brion?"

"Yes."

"I thought you might. They tell me everyone loves Brion, so I guess he's one of the few who throws you coins."

He laughed. "The beggars could tell you a different story. Brion's like all the other rich men, he's only good to people he thinks might be useful to him. You want to know which people give the most? It's the poor."

"I guess you see most things coming and going from the warehouse."

"Yes."

"And steal what you can."

"It isn't much. The merchants watch their merchandise too closely."

"I'll bet. Brion stored some pottery, I don't know when, maybe a few days ago, maybe a month ago, I doubt longer than that."

He nodded. "I remember. Fifteen days ago, sixteen maybe."

I handed him another drachma. "Good. Did the pots come off a ship?"

"No, from inland, on carts, three of them, pulled by donkeys."

"Not from Ephesus?"

He shook his head. "The donkeys were tired and dirty. So were the men leading them."

"Any idea where they came from?"

"Yes." He put out his hand. My one-armed friend had become confident.

I dropped in two drachmae.

"Magnesia."

"You sure?"

"The donkey men talked about staying overnight before going back. Anyway, it makes sense, doesn't it? Magnesia's the closest town inland."

That was what I wanted to know. "All right, I won't pay you any more money—"

He opened his wounded mouth to protest but I held up my hand. "Wait. I won't pay you more money because I have something even better for you. I suppose you plan to spend those coins on food and wine?"

"I can stretch out this much for a month, maybe get me a cheap woman too." He smiled.

"Don't do any of that."

"What?"

"Take this money and get a decent haircut at the gymnasium and a wash at the laconica, and buy a new chiton."

"I need the food more."

"When you come back," I said, ignoring him, "no one will recognize you, except maybe for the arm. You'll have to disguise that somehow. Go in the back door of the warehouse and turn right." I gave him directions to Brion's space.

"Under the cover is a jar full of coins." I described the jar. "They're all yours if you can take them."

He said, "How many coins are we talking about?"

"I don't know. A lot. Maybe enough to buy a small farm and a couple of slaves."

"Zeus!"

"The jar's heavy. With only one hand you might need help to carry it."

"No, I won't. I'll find a way."

I was sure he would too, because half a farm is not as good as a whole one, and I had just offered this man his life.

"There's a guard," I warned, "and he's aggressive. You'll have to deal with him."

"Not a problem," he said confidently. He thought for a moment. "Maybe I'll buy a long knife too."

"Do that."

"Why do you tell me this?" he asked, suspicious.

"Because I like you."

And because the dangers of my profession were not so different to his. If I did this man a favor, maybe the Gods would send someone to help me, if I was ever in the same straits.

He said, "You have something against this Brion?"

"No. Funnily enough, I'm trying to save his life, if he still has one." I didn't know what had happened to Brion, nor fully understand why the self-confessed traitor Thorion had died, but I did know these pots had something to do with it. It was time to strike a blow, anything that might disrupt the enemy.

"If these pots are all that important to you, you might want to check with the man who met him. Half-man, rather. One of the ones from the temple with his balls missing."

"Huh?"

"A eunuch was hanging around the doors, and when the donkeys arrived and Brion turned up to supervise, they talked like they knew each other as the slaves unloaded."

"Describe him."

"Tall, big chest, head shaved. One of the Megabyzoi for sure."

"He gave me a message from my family," Geros said. "It's quite true, I did meet Brion at the warehouse."

I'd ambushed Geros by walking up to him as he stood guard on the steps of the small temple. He hadn't shown the slightest surprise when I appeared, and he spoke to me in a mild voice, which made me wonder if he'd been expecting this conversation.

"*You* have a family?" I failed to hide my surprise.

A woman's voice behind us said, "Of course he has a family.

You don't think eunuchs come from Mommy eunuchs and Daddy eunuchs, do you?"

Geros and I both turned to see Diotima. I felt myself blush. I'd been hoping to avoid her presence.

"What do you think you're doing?" she demanded.

"Geros and I are chatting," I said, avoiding her real question.

"Without me?" Her voice rose.

"I thought we established last time he isn't yours to protect."

"That's not the point. You deliberately went behind my back."

"Because you have a soft spot for the eunuchs when right now you need to be suspicious."

"You're the one I suspect. Of bigotry. Geros, I order you to throw Nicolaos off the temple grounds."

"I claim sanctuary," I said at once.

"What? That's for criminals."

"Is there any rule says so?" I countered.

Geros looked from one to the other of us and rubbed his chin. "Priestess, technically, the man is right. Anyone can claim sanctuary and the temple has no right to refuse."

Diotima opened her mouth, shut it again, then said, "You mean he can wander about bothering you and you can't stop him?"

"It seems so, but truly, there is no difficulty, Priestess. He asks me what I'm not ashamed to tell."

"I'd never thought about eunuchs having parents," I confessed. "Did your father donate you?"

"I was taken at eight years and cut at once."

"Did it hurt?"

"Nico!"

"Yes, it hurt. I was brought here with other boys. They rested us for a few days, and gave us good food so we would be strong, and then they cut us, one by one, in a ceremony, with a knife they held in flame."

I winced and crossed my knees.

"It's for the Goddess," Diotima said gently. "It's what She requires."

"I know this, lady. All we boys cried, and afterwards they took us to lie on good beds. The fever came by next day, and for days afterwards we lay there and others of the Megabyzoi, who had been cut long ago, tended us. One of the boys died. The rest of us lived."

"So when you met Brion at the warehouse?"

"He gave me a message from my brother. As a proxenos Brion was used to sending mail, but it was kindness in him to do this for a slave."

Diotima said, "There, you see, Nico? Nothing to worry about at all. Now leave him alone."

I hadn't expected such an explanation, and it was impossible to check. Either Geros had been prepared with a clever story, or he was innocent.

"It's my brother I miss most," he said, almost musing to himself.

"Can you confirm any of this, Diotima?" I asked, a last-ditch attempt to shake his story.

Geros said, "I would never discuss my problems with the priestess. She has enough worries of her own."

"Drop it, Geros," Diotima said at once, before I could ask what he meant.

I led her aside and whispered, "Diotima, do you want to know what else I learned? The pottery was brought to Ephesus from Magnesia." I related the story of the cart drivers and their conversation.

"Magnesia again." Diotima looked thoughtful. "This makes it worse. Why are coins minted in Samos, an island in the Aegean Sea, appearing from Magnesia, an inland city?"

"Why is your friend Brion the one importing them?"

Diotima thought for a moment, then seemed to come to

some decision because she turned back to Geros and said, "Wait here. Geros, don't answer any more questions until I return."

We watched her walk, almost run in fact, into the main temple. The moment she was out of sight I said, "Good, she's gone. Now Geros, tell me what you meant about Diotima's worries."

"The priestess said—"

"Forget what the priestess said. If she has problems, I want to know about them."

Geros considered me for some time, and I let him. He needed to trust me on this. Then he looked over to the temple where Diotima had disappeared. "The priestess is not popular with her colleagues. It is well you should know. Though you hate eunuchs, I know you have her best interests at heart."

"What's the problem? Diotima was unpopular when she'd served at the Temple of Artemis in Athens but that was because of her parentage. She should have escaped that here."

Geros said, "The priestess doesn't tend to notice when others find her high competence a trifle . . . confronting. It was I who pulled them apart. It is how we met."

"There was a fight?"

He nodded. "Between her and the other new priestesses, when it became clear she had outperformed them in all learning and prayers and rituals."

"She said nothing to me of this."

"Would you expect her to?"

No, of course not. Diotima was not one to admit a problem she couldn't solve. "She should have pretended to be like the rest of them."

"If you think that, then you do not know the Priestess Diotima."

We both nodded our heads glumly.

I said, "You're in love with her, aren't you?"

"The Megabyzoi can't have the emotion as you know it. There is no lust, but there is kind regard."

"So what you said before about being able to pleasure a woman was—"

"Absolutely true. But it's not something we *need* to do, unlike you. I may be a slave to the temple, but *you* are a slave to your lusts. I know which of us is the freer."

"I'm perfectly rational."

Geros smiled his insulting smile.

Why was I arguing about my sex life with a eunuch slave?

Diotima walked out of the temple toward us. She announced, "I've just informed the High Priest I'm leaving Ephesus. When you go, Nicolaos, I'm going with you."

Geros let out a small cry of astonishment. "But Priestess—"

"It's decided, Geros. Everything leads to Magnesia. I have to follow."

Geros began to argue, then bowed his head and said, "You will be missed."

"I'll miss you too, Geros."

Geros turned to me and said, "You must keep her safe."

"I will," I promised him.

Next morning, Diotima met Asia and me at the southeast gate. Diotima wore an old, patched chiton, suitable for hard travel on a dry, dusty road. She'd rolled up the hem to her knees to make it easier to walk. Not the most elegant arrangement, but she was a practical girl. I noted with approval that she wore a pair of thick leather sandals. Over her back she'd slung a soft leather sack, stuffed with what I guessed to be clothes and whatever things a woman needed.

I led Ajax. She took one look at what was on the end of the lead rope and said, "You bought a horse? Why?"

I explained, finishing, "Ajax could be very useful." I felt put out when Diotima laughed.

"How do you plan to get him home?" she asked. "He can hardly go by boat."

"I thought of that. I'll ride him home."

"What? North, past Byzantion, across all of Thrace, through Macedonia and Thessaly? It would take *months.*"

"Only a few, and after I've finished this job I'll have the time. It'll be a holiday."

"I've never even seen you ride a horse. I didn't know you could."

"Of course I can ride. I'm a man, aren't I?"

Diotima rolled her eyes.

"Let me take that sack for you."

Diotima handed me her sack and I slung it over Ajax. I hauled myself up, swung my leg over, and grabbed the reins. "All right, here we—"

I don't know what happened next. All I recall is the world passing by in a blur.

When I came to I was on the ground. My head hurt. The bits of me between my legs hurt. Everything else hurt too, my elbows and knees were grazed and my chiton torn, but the head and groin were special hurts. I put my hands between my legs and groaned.

"What happened?" I asked. I pushed myself up with my elbows. Three Diotimas frowned and put their hands to their mouths. Their heads spun around me.

Three was more than I could cope with. I closed my eyes, which didn't stop the world spinning around, but at least I couldn't see it happening. When I opened them again things were more stable. The Diotimas were reduced to one; a much more manageable number.

The place where I had mounted Ajax was a hundred paces

away. Ajax stood nearby, grazing on some wild grass. He looked at me through one eye and snorted.

"You left without us," Asia accused. She hesitated. "May I speak frankly, master?"

"Go ahead."

"When you said you could ride, I think you might have been telling a teensy little fib."

Diotima said, "The horse bolted, you hung on, screaming something I couldn't quite catch. I saw you let go the reins and grab his neck. Then you fell off."

I stood up, refusing to wince, and walked cautiously toward Ajax, my right hand held out. I coaxed, "Here, boy . . . here, boy . . . that's a good boy."

"Master, he's a horse, not a dog."

Ajax watched me with apparent indifference. He bent to take another mouthful of grass and chewed on it while I edged up to him. He didn't move at all when I grabbed his bridle.

I said, "Right, this time we'll see who's boss."

We walked to Magnesia. I led Ajax by his lead rope. The journey would take two days, but as I pointed out to Diotima and Asia, this was good news because there'd be time for my contusions to heal.

The road east out of Ephesus crossed a bridge over a small stream and remained flat for only a few hundred paces before rising into the hills that surrounded the city. After that, it was up and down all the way. Diotima walked ahead, Asia behind. They never spoke to each other. I tried to walk alongside Diotima, but she was still surly over my suspicions of Geros and angry I had gone behind her back, so instead I kept Asia company.

We slept the night under the stars, without much conversation, beside the road in a depression invisible to anyone passing by. Luckily it was a warm night.

Next day, Asia skipped along and sang songs. She had been understandably scared, then solemn, back in Athens. Now she was positively happy, and no surprise, soon she'd be home with a family she'd expected never to see again.

As midday approached I started believing we were close to Magnesia, I predicted we would see the city at the crest of every hill we climbed, and around every bend we trudged. Asia became increasingly amused at my irritation when I was invariably wrong, but I kept it up. Eventually I'd be right. I watched forward in the pleasant anticipation of seeing Magnesia and knowing the journey would soon be at an end.

As we rounded one bend, we saw another hill to the right of the road, this one low and covered in grass. Standing upon the hill was a man, in a curious position, his legs spread, his arms stretched wide, nor did he change position in all the time we walked his way. The closer we came, the more audible his moans.

Diotima spotted him too. We exchanged glances but said nothing.

A rude, narrow trail split from the main road and led up the hill. I tied Ajax to a bush. "Something's wrong," I said to the women. "Wait here."

Asia ignored my order and walked along behind me. Diotima turned to our packs, which we'd slung across Ajax. On the ground I recognized footprints: man, donkey, and horse. Obviously we were not the only ones to have stopped.

As I walked uphill toward him I saw that a wooden stake, of a width you could barely get the fingers of both hands around, stood upright between his legs, embedded deep in the ground and reaching up to penetrate his anus. It was a tight fit.

Dried blood stained the pole, and some blood not so dry

dribbled down. Feces were scattered along its length, some lay in a steaming heap upon the ground. Blackflies covered the pole, the blood, the feces, and the man. A loud buzz came from behind him. I held my breath, held on to my courage, and walked around to view him from behind. His anus was covered in swarms of flies. I knew maggots would be crawling there soon; possibly they already were, underneath the filth. His inner legs were a mass of sores from rubbing up and down the pole; he had been standing as high as possible to keep the stake from penetrating further, and to do that he had to keep his legs as close to the stake as he could.

A pole had been placed across his shoulders and along his arms, tied to his wrists and elbows with leather thongs that had probably been wet when his tormentors drew them tight.

I completed the tour and returned to face the poor bastard. His head hung, unmoving. The shock of what had been done to him must have shut down my senses, because only now, looking into his face, did I realize that where his nose had been was a gaping hole, and his ears had been removed.

They'd left his eyes alone. I couldn't imagine why until it occurred to me he would probably suffer more if he could see.

How long can a man stand on his tiptoes? A day? Two days? How long can a man stand without falling asleep, or fainting? It's only a matter of time before he sinks lower and lower, and the stake penetrates further and further.

The head rose.

I jumped back, I'd been sure he was dead, but now the awful face stared at me. I tried to read the expression in his eyes, but it is impossible for any man who hasn't experienced such torture to imagine how this man felt.

I said, "What is your name?"

He opened his mouth to speak. Within was a blackened stump. They had cut out his tongue. He made grunting noises and moans.

"His name is Brion," Diotima said from behind me in a flat, emotionless tone. She had caught us up, with her bow in hand.

"*This* is Brion? How long has he been here?"

"The whole time I've been looking for him." She was visibly holding back her tears.

"We could get you off," I said to Brion. "I think you know you're not going to live even if we do. But if you wish, I can end it for you."

"No!" Asia exclaimed.

"No? Why not?" I asked in surprise. Asia had never struck me as the bloodthirsty type, and I was sure she wasn't sadistic.

"This is what the Persians do to some criminals," Asia said in an offhand way. "If we lift him off the stake, or if we let him die early, it's a crime against the Great King and the person who does it has to take his place."

"You mean this is a state execution?"

"Only the officials of the Great King are permitted to kill with the pole."

"Dear Gods, these people are . . . are barbarians!"

Diotima said, "Yes, that's exactly what they are; barbarians, non-Hellenes."

"At least in Athens, if someone needs killing we're quick about it. Painless too, if it's hemlock. What can possibly be the point of prolonging the agony? He'd be just as dead if they snapped his neck."

"The Persians would say they're sending a message to anyone else thinking about committing the same crime."

I shuddered. "So while all this time you feared he was the victim of a crime, he was in fact a condemned criminal. What did he do?"

Asia said, "There's usually a sign, to say. But I don't see one."

"This tells me everything I need to know about the Persians. What sort of a vile, disgusting barbarian would kill a man like this?"

"Well, my father would," Asia said. "And you know he's Hellene."

I stared at her. "Themistocles?"

"Father is the satrap of this region," Asia explained. "Only he could order an execution like this." She looked up at Brion with little expression on her face. "You must have been a very bad man," she said. "What did you do that was so evil?"

The man's head rolled until his eyes fetched upon Asia. They widened at once. He opened his mouth and tried to say something.

"Ung . . . guh, arrh." He bent his right wrist to point at Asia. With his left he pointed the way we'd come. He tried once more to speak, but the effort was too much. He gave up. Tears rolled down his cheeks. His eyes held inexpressible sadness within that face of horror, but they didn't waver from Asia.

I asked her, "Have you ever seen this man before?"

"No."

"He seems to be reacting to you."

"I don't know why."

"Perhaps he's saying he doesn't want a girl-child to be upset by the sight of him." But Asia was hardly upset; if anything she was disinterested.

Brion shut his eyes. His head slumped forward and his legs began to give way. He slipped further down the pole, perhaps a handsbreadth. His head snapped up at once and a piercing scream surged from his gaping mouth.

"Aaaiiieee!"

The sound cut off in an instant and his body arched, despite the pole up inside him. The pain must have been excruciating. Then his muscles seemed to collapse, he slumped forward, and I saw the reason for his spasm. An arrow was embedded in his back, precisely where his heart would be.

Diotima stood behind the body, bow in hand and tears running down her cheeks.

I ran to her and hugged her tight, turning her away from Brion.

"What are you doing!" Asia shouted. "My father will put *you* on the pole."

Diotima shouted back, "If your bloody father ordered this, then I'll shoot him too!"

"My father's not evil. He's a ruler."

"Shut up Asia," I ordered. "Diotima did right. If it's a problem, I'll deal with it."

When she'd calmed, I took Diotima by the shoulders and said, "Come away," and led her back to the road.

We left Brion's body there, without an audience to stare at him as a curiosity. There was nothing else we could do. I didn't turn as we marched onward at the fastest pace we could manage.

Twenty paces later we passed the low hill. There before us, not far away, lay Magnesia.

MAGNESIA

10

Miserable mortals who, like leaves,
at one moment flame with life,
eating the produce of the land,
and at another moment weakly perish.

We entered Magnesia at midday. Asia had tired, so I placed her atop Ajax and led him by his lead rope. He wouldn't have me on his back, but he was perfectly happy to have Asia. I wondered what thanks Themistocles would offer for the return of his young daughter.

We had no trouble entering, because there was no wall around the city. How on earth did they defend the place? Instead, the countryside merged into city, and we went from passing farms to a steadily increasing number of houses. It made me uneasy. Cities are supposed to have walls, it's the natural order of things.

I had a sudden thought. "Do they speak Greek here?"

Diotima said, "Of course they do, we're still in Ionia. We *are* inside the Empire, but most people will be Hellene and they'll speak Aeolian Greek; you won't have a problem understanding them."

"What about the Persians?"

"All the government officials will be Persian, and they're *totally* different."

Magnesia was not as large as Ephesus. It wasn't as beautiful, nor as well designed. But then, Ephesus was famed for its size, beauty, and wealth. I could hardly blame the nearest neighbor for being a poor relation. The streets were the standard dirt and gravel, much the same as Athens, but better maintained. The houses were much the same too, with whitewashed mud adobe walls and thatched roofs.

People stopped what they were doing and watched as we passed. A few pointed and spoke to each other. Asia waved and I began to feel as if we were part of a parade.

"You, halt!" Two guards stepped in my path, their spears at the ready.

The murmuring among the onlookers rose to a loud buzz. Asia slid off Ajax.

I said, "What's the problem, gentlemen?"

A man walked toward us from the direction of the agora, a pair of Persian soldiers flanking him. Dark hair against pale skin and a face without emotion; it was Barzanes the sinister Persian, at whose feet I'd fallen outside the Great King. How had he got to Magnesia so quickly?

Barzanes said, "Whoever you are, you are in a great deal of trouble."

Before I had a chance to answer, the crowd parted for a bodyguard of six men, three on each side flanking an older man whom I recognized. I breathed a sigh of relief. Now we were safe from Barzanes.

Asia cried, "Daddy! Daddy!" She broke away from me, and ran straight into the arms of Themistocles.

Themistocles held Asia close to him and glanced at Diotima and me. I was the obvious leader. Now for my reward.

Themistocles pointed at me and said, "Take him away. Imprison him."

I was chained to a wall by both wrists, somewhere deep within the palace to the south of the city. I hadn't had a chance to see much along the route because the soldiers had dragged me through the dirt with my head forced down.

I knew I was underground because the moisture gathered on the wall and ran down my back. My feet didn't reach the floor, the entire weight of my body was on my wrists, which felt like they might snap at any moment.

I swore to myself, the moment I got out of here—if I did—I would collect Diotima and make a beeline straight for Ephesus. I'd come to Magnesia to deliver Asia and report on Themistocles for Pericles. Asia was home, and if Pericles wanted to know more, he could come look for himself, because it was obvious there was nothing further I could do. My objective now was to talk my way out of this prison and out of Magnesia.

Once before, I'd been imprisoned, in a cell for the condemned, where I'd paced back and forth all night awaiting a gruesome execution at dawn. I'd been lucky to escape my fate then and I didn't know if I could be lucky twice. My latest prison was significantly larger and appeared to have fewer rats, but what it made up for in airiness it lost in atmosphere, and the décor was disturbing. The rack I recognized, also the whips and the stocks with their special screw to strain the victim's vertebrae until they were crushed. The other items were unknown to me, but if the dark staining was anything to go by then I would be happy to remain ignorant.

The door creaked open.

Barzanes walked in. Two soldiers and another man wearing a leather apron followed him.

He studied me as I studied him. When our eyes met, I was as careful as I could be to register neither fear nor insolence.

He said, in excellent Greek, "I congratulate you, Athenian.

I have rarely seen a man so completely engineer his own destruction."

"I have done nothing wrong, nothing to offend."

"No? You merely walk into Magnesia with a stolen horse. To complete your arrogance, stolen from our own stables, an expensive, prime beast dedicated to the King's Messengers."

The charge was so unexpected I reacted without thought.

"Ajax belongs to you?"

"He went missing from the King's grazing field last month. Men have been searching for him since."

"I bought that horse only a few days ago at the market in Ephesus, and he cost a small fortune."

"So." He did not seem impressed. He moved around the rack, ran his hand along the winches. "Our empire is a law-abiding one. The people enjoy order, detest lawlessness. The penalty for horse thieves is death. The penalty for stealing from the Great King is a lingering, painful death. The penalty for a horse thief who steals from the stables of the Great King is even worse. Philodios?"

"Lord Barzanes?" the man in the leather apron said. The muscles of his arms bulged like a blacksmith.

"The last man who tried to steal a horse of the King's Messengers, what happened to him?"

"It was long ago, my lord."

"Stretch your memory."

The man thought. "Torn apart by the King's Horses, my lord. In the agora. One horse per limb. Shall I summon the stable master?"

"Not yet."

Barzanes turned back to me. "So you see, Athenian, your position is unenviable."

I sweated despite the chill. I put all the conviction I could into my voice. "Listen, I didn't steal the animal. If I had, would I be so stupid as to walk him back into town in full daylight?"

He said nothing, merely stared at me with those black, unblinking eyes.

I continued, "I bought him from a man at the horse markets of Ephesus. He must be the thief. I can give you a complete description." I proceeded to shop the horse trader to Barzanes, for a fate I could imagine all too well, but I had no qualms; the bastard had set me up and I was happy to return the favor.

Barzanes said nothing.

"What in Hades do I have to say to convince you?"

He waited. "Tell me about the girl," he said at last.

"Asia? I brought her back to Themistocles."

His dark eyes bore into me, expressionless. "Did you steal her too?"

"I bought her as a slave, in the market at Piraeus. I didn't know then she was the daughter of Themistocles."

The dark eyes gave nothing away but a look of utter contempt. "I see. The horse was stolen, but you bought it innocently at the market, not knowing it was stolen. The girl was stolen, but you bought her innocently at the market, not knowing she was kidnapped. You have an unfortunate habit of buying stolen goods, don't you?"

When he put it like that, even I had to agree it didn't sound good.

"I think there is a great deal more you will tell," Barzanes said to me. "What is your purpose here, what happened to the girl, who are you acting for? It will be painful, but we can stop this now if you tell me the truth. Truth, Athenian, is the highest good the Wise Lord demands of us."

Philodios said, "The horses, my lord? Or shall I remove his toes?" I cursed his helpful attitude.

"What's happening here, Barzanes?" Themistocles stood in the entrance. He descended the steps into the chamber.

Barzanes' mouth was a thin line of displeasure. "My lord,

you have many demands on your time. Leave this to me and I will bring you truth."

"These are hardly details. The man brought back Asia to us. I will interrogate him."

Barzanes bowed. "As the Lord Satrap wishes."

Themistocles walked to my side. He looked up at me, hanging on the wall. I looked down at him.

Themistocles had put on weight, and lots of it, but as unhealthy as he looked, his eyes were intelligent and wide-awake within the puffy flesh. He had a bushy gray beard with only flecks of its original color as also his hair, which he mostly retained and wore in curls. The hair served to hide his expression, although by all accounts no man could tell the thoughts of Themistocles in any case.

I recalled Brion, dying on the stake, and Asia's statement that only her father could have ordered such a death.

"I will learn from my daughter everything of substance concerning her kidnap. You can tell me about yourself."

"I am Nicolaos, son of Sophroniscus the sculptor, of the deme Alopece."

Themistocles paused for a moment. "Yes, I remember your father. Asia tells me you are not yourself a sculptor; that you are an . . . agent? This must be some new trade they didn't have when I was in Athens. Does it pay well?"

"Not anymore."

"Oh?"

"These days I am an unemployed agent."

"By implication therefore, you once had an employer. He was?"

"Pericles."

"Pericles?" Themistocles paused before saying, "He was an insignificant young man when I left Athens, much the same age you are now, I should think. The stories say he's become a force."

"The stories are right."

"What did you do to displease him?"

"I made a mistake on an assignment, and as a consequence Pericles terminated our agreement."

"What sort of mistake?"

"A fatal one, for the men with me."

"Then you are not here acting for Pericles."

"No, Themistocles, I'm here acting for *you*. I brought your daughter home."

Themistocles scowled. "I have no cause to trust the Athenians. I led them to greatness. They ostracized me, then they condemned me. When an Athenian arrives in Magnesia, unannounced, should I not assume he intends me harm?"

"I'm no threat to anyone. I'll be happy if I can walk away from Magnesia and not end up like the dead man by the road."

"What is this?" Barzanes exclaimed.

Themistocles' eyebrows shot up and his brow creased.

I said, "He's dead now."

"I have no idea what you're talking about," Themistocles said. "Do you, Barzanes?"

"No, Lord Themistocles."

Neither Barzanes nor Themistocles knew Brion was dead? I glanced from one to the other, unable to determine if they were telling the truth, and said, "There's a man on a pole by the roadside. We passed him on the way here, not a thousand paces from the city. Asia said it was a method of execution only you had the right to use, Lord Satrap. The man's name is Brion."

Themistocles frowned. "Brion the merchant? I know him well. But I've executed no one recently, I assure you. Probably brigands on the road. It happens, no matter how often we chase them."

"My Lord Satrap?"

"Yes, Barzanes?"

"Will you not investigate this? If the Athenian speaks truth then a murder has been committed."

Themistocles nodded. "See to it."

"I will, lord, as soon as we are finished here."

Themistocles turned back to me. "My daughter tells me you saved her life."

"Not entirely true. I saved her from the brothels." I related the story of finding her on the auction block in sufficient detail for the point to sink in, before saying, "If I might be permitted a question from a position of severe disadvantage, I'm curious to know how the daughter of Themistocles came to be on the auction block at Piraeus."

His eyes bore into me. I returned his look as blandly as I could manage.

He said, "I share your curiosity." He paused for a moment, then said, "So my daughter was your slave."

"I've rarely had a worse."

His lips twitched. "I'm glad to hear that. Your girlfriend has begged me for your life."

"She's not my girlfriend."

"She said the same thing when I asked." He paused, then said, "Asia makes the same request. Your tale beggars belief, but at each point there is a tenuous wisp of credibility; I have heard of more ridiculous things happening. Indeed, a few of them have happened to me. Very well, I am going to believe you, Nicolaos, son of Sophroniscus, because only an idiot would enter Magnesia intending me harm, with a stolen horse and carrying my daughter in full view."

I solemnly agreed only an idiot would do such a thing.

"There is a condition. You will remain in my court or within the city at all times. You are not to depart without my order. Let me be clear about this. If you leave the city, your life is forfeit."

What an odd demand. Why would Themistocles want to keep me here if he didn't trust me? But he was the boss. "I understand."

So much for escaping Magnesia to report back to Pericles. We were trapped here.

11

But when the bright light of the sun was set,
they went each to his own house to take their rest,
where for each one a palace had been built
with cunning skill.

Themistocles lived in a palace that made the home of Callias look like a deserted hut on a windy night. At three stories it was taller than anything I'd ever seen, I wondered how they held up the third floor. The building formed a rectangle with a paved inner courtyard and a fountain in the middle that shot water higher than a man. Misty droplets fell on everyone's head and kept the air cool.

All my possessions awaited me in my room, with the notable exception of Ajax, who had been repossessed. The room was bright and airy, on the third floor, in the wing reserved for honored guests. It made for a bizarre contrast with where I'd just been. I fell back on the bed and it was the best bed I'd ever lain in.

There were two windows, covered with shutters. I hung my head out to see an extensive garden of trees and ponds and green grass. The garden began at the palace and went all the way out to the surrounding wall, which was as high as two men. Within the gardens, next to the main building, I could see workshops, a barracks, and stables, where I supposed Ajax relaxed at that very moment in a stall. I wondered if he remembered me.

The slave who'd shown me to my room made a point of telling me where to find the baths. I took the hint and spent a long time soaking off the grime of the road and the stinking sweat of fear. My own clothes were no longer fit after their treatment in the torture chamber—I felt somewhat the same myself—so a slave brought me a fresh chiton. Then I wandered about the palace, happy to be free.

I found Diotima in the gardens, on a bench beneath the branches of an apple tree. She sat slumped and downcast. I sat beside her.

"Thanks for getting me out of prison."

"I didn't. I tried, but Themistocles wouldn't listen to me. Asia swore you'd saved her, then she burst into tears and Themistocles promised to release you. She has him twisted around her little finger. I, on the other hand, was as useless to you as I was to Brion."

I moved to put an arm around her, then thought better of it. "Diotima, I'm sorry about Brion."

"I feel bad about the arrow."

"Don't."

"It's such a horrible way to repay all his friendship."

"No, it's not. It's what any sane man would have wanted. If you ever find me in the same situation"—I shuddered—"I hope you'll kill me before I know it."

I paused, because I didn't want to say it, but, "It must be tough to lose the man you were going to marry, especially like that."

She sat up with a jerk and stared at me, openmouthed. "Marry him? What made you think that? He wasn't the marrying sort. Believe me, I could tell."

"You mean he preferred boys?"

"Hardly. Too many girlfriends. A man like that uses women."

I didn't understand. "Then why were you seeing him?"

She shrugged, and returned to her slumped position. "I don't know. For practice, I suppose."

"Er, practice at what, precisely?"

"Not *that,* you cretin."

"Well then?"

She mumbled something that sounded like, "At attracting men. It makes me nervous."

I must have misheard. A lion might be nervous. An army of Spartans could conceivably get nervous. But Diotima?

"I don't know, Nico. A year ago, I would have said I didn't want to be married. But, you know, it's hard to avoid when a woman isn't allowed to own property, and not having a husband is social death. I thought . . . well, I thought it was all sorted out. Then when you told me your father had refused—"

"I understand. You must have been devastated at losing me."

"I was put out, because now I'd have to attract someone decent, and I had no idea how to do it. You would have been very convenient."

"Convenient?" I said, hurt. "Is that all I was, convenient?"

"No. Well, yes, but also no."

"Thanks a lot."

"I'm being honest with you. A girl has to think about these things. Don't look so shocked, Nicolaos. Everyone knows men care more for the dowry and the father's status than they do the woman. If she can't improve the man's social standing then the marriage isn't going to happen, is it? Look what happened when you asked your father for me."

"I never realized the way you thought about us was so . . . clinical."

Diotima stood up. "Nicolaos, son of Sophroniscus, I would

have been perfectly happy to marry you. I mean, not many men would listen to me the way you do. And you're ambitious. I like that. You're reasonably presentable, good-looking even, especially when you're only wearing a loincloth and I can see your chest."

I puffed out my chest.

"Also you're not quite as dumb as most men—"

"I think you should have stopped at the chest."

"Hey, Athenian!" Philodios approached us, the man who had been so eager to fetch horses to have me torn to pieces, or to cut off my toes. He stopped before me, put his hands on his hips, and said, "Dinner is served."

I stared at him for a moment before I comprehended. "*You* are announcing dinner?"

"That's my job."

"What happened to your other one?"

"I don't get to do it full time, not enough demand. If you ask me, this Lord Satrap is too easygoing."

"Who is this man?" Diotima asked.

"This is Philodios, my personal, in-house torturer. Philodios, I'd like you to meet the woman who thinks I'm convenient."

Philodios led Diotima and me to the dinner hall. As we walked in I thought to myself, Diotima hadn't been planning to marry Brion. Somehow I felt better about his death.

I hoped to see some sign that Themistocles and his family missed their old lives, something—anything—to show they knew they'd made an error when they turned against Athens.

The dining hall was filled with military officers from the local garrison, dressed in gaudy ankle-length robes with large sleeves, jeweled rings, bracelets of silver and gold, and torcs hung about their necks. My plain Hellene chiton had only an edge pattern for decoration. I didn't even have a himation cloak with me. I felt distinctly out of place, but I was determined not to show it.

The Persians milled about, kissing each other on the lips or on the cheeks, talking together. Here were the men the Hellenes feared above all others, my hereditary enemies. It was these men, or their fathers, who had burned Athens to the ground. I was like a man swimming with sharks.

Themistocles entered from another door, followed by Barzanes and five Hellenes ranging in age from teenage to middle years. Among these was Asia, holding the hand of a young woman whose face, posture, and expression shouted sister to the world. This was Nicomache. Asia had prattled about her brothers and sisters during the march from Ephesus, and I was able to match names against faces without difficulty. The middle-aged man with gray-tinged hair was Archeptolis. He wore rich clothes and rings upon his fingers for which, if he had dared wear them in the streets of Athens, he would have been bashed and robbed.

The woman beside him was therefore his wife and half sister, Mnesiptolema, Asia had told me her nickname was Nessie. Nessie's mouth was pinched in disapproval, her chin overstrong, but what Mnesiptolema lost in her unfriendly face she made up in her figure, which was spectacular in its curves. Her breasts were large, her shoulders wide, and her waist narrow. More voluptuous than attractive, and aware of it.

Behind them walked the other son, Cleophantus, whom I guessed to be in his early twenties. This was the man Callias said was a coward.

I whispered to Diotima, "That's the full family, everyone who's still living with Themistocles in any case."

"Yes."

"I'm going to mention Brion."

"At a banquet? Nico, you're only just out of jail."

"Every important person in Magnesia is in this room. Can you think of a better time to get everyone's reaction?"

The room fell silent and everyone made a curious motion toward Themistocles, bending at the waist with stiff bodies and touching their hearts. Diotima copied them. I didn't. A free Athenian makes obeisance to no man.

Themistocles seated himself at the end, Barzanes at his right hand and the children of Themistocles following. The room fell silent.

"I rejoice to announce what everyone here already knows. My daughter Asia has been returned to us." Themistocles looked about the room. He saw me.

"Nicolaos, son of Sophroniscus, and Diotima, Priestess of Artemis, you will join us at this end."

Everyone sat at a long, low table in the middle of the room, about which the diners were expected to sit on cushions. I realized then there was a precedence, which everyone assumed so naturally that it was not obvious to a visitor. Themistocles had moved us to the position below his children and Barzanes, but higher than everyone else present. Barzanes was expressionless as I sat down opposite him.

What's the etiquette for dining with someone who's been torturing you that afternoon? Does one mention in passing that one had been hanging in chains? Or is that a minor social indiscretion, best forgotten?

Slaves brought in silver platters laden with meats and vegetables. There was more meat than graced an Athenian dinner, and little seafood but for some trout and eels. Indeed, entire platters were carried in bearing nothing but boar, or deer, or other meats I couldn't identify.

As a slave put some sliced boar before her, Diotima leaned over to me and asked in a soft voice, "Was this meat properly dedicated?"

I whispered back, "I doubt it."

"I can't eat unsanctified meat," she said in horror.

"You'll have to," I told her, although I knew she was right. "Or else stick to the vegetables." An animal must be dedicated to the Gods before its life is taken for meat. Whether these Persians had done the right thing was doubtful.

Themistocles turned to a slave behind him and gave a low order. The slave produced a rhyton, a drinking horn, which he placed before me.

The horn was shaped like a boar's tusk, with a wounded boar at its base. I picked it up, bemused. It was made of some material I couldn't identify, heavy, cool to the touch, smooth. It was a solid object, but *I could see right through it*. I held it up close to my eye, unable to believe what I saw. Barzanes' face appeared through the solid material, distorted as if he had some terrible deformity. I lowered the rhyton, and he was back to normal.

Themistocles watched me do this and smiled. "Amazing, isn't it? It was a gift to me from the Great King, Artaxerxes, when I departed his court to take up my position here. You will drink from it tonight."

"What is this made of?"

Themistocles shrugged. "I didn't ask." Nicomache brought him a plate of meats and Themistocles turned his attention to it.

Cleophantus was seated next to me. He smiled and said, "Glad to meet you, Nicolaos. You brought Asia back to us when we thought we'd never see her again, and that makes you very welcome." No one would have missed the relationship with his elder brother and his father. The facial bones were the same, though Cleophantus was trim where Archeptolis was pudgy and Themistocles overweight. The hair of Cleophantus was darker and straighter and similar enough to Asia and Nicomache that I guessed it came from their mother. He wore a normal chiton and smelled of leather and horse.

I said, "It was no trouble."

"I'm sure Father will find a suitable reward. I hope the journey wasn't too arduous."

Cleophantus had given me the perfect opening. The Gods must have wanted me to follow my plan. I said, "Except for finding the dead body, everything went smoothly."

All conversation stopped. Even the Persians who spoke no Greek were staring at me. I felt a painful jab in my side from Diotima, which was her subtle way of saying I was the social equivalent of plague.

In the silence of the moment, Archeptolis said, "*What* dead body?"

"A man called Brion. He was executed not a thousand paces from here, on the road to Ephesus."

Every eye turned to Themistocles, who said, "If it had been an execution, every man in this room would know it." Themistocles raised his voice. "Does anyone here recall an execution?"

No one said a word.

Nicomache's hand went to her mouth and she gasped. Cleophantus looked left and right as if he were confused.

Mnesiptolema's hand, which was halfway to her mouth, stopped in midair. Blood from the lightly cooked pork dripped down her fingers. She said, "Brion the proxenos? He's dead?"

I said, "I'm sorry, I didn't realize he was a friend."

"An acquaintance," Mnesiptolema said. "Everyone knows the proxenos for Athens."

Archeptolis said, "He acted for Magnesia as well as Ephesus. Magnesia doesn't have a proxenos because"—he glanced at his father—"well, because. Brion fills the position for most of Ionia."

Nicomache said, "Any sudden death is a shock. Who would have done such a horrible thing?"

Themistocles grunted. "Common robbers is the likely answer."

"Cruel ones."

I said, "Had Brion been visiting Magnesia?"

"I wouldn't know," Themistocles said. "My officials have better things to do than keep track of everyone who enters the city. Especially since, without a wall, it would be an impossible task."

I doubted Barzanes took the same relaxed view, but he chose not to correct his satrap.

Themistocles waved a hand in dismissal. "We will leave it to Barzanes to look into and say no more."

I opened my mouth, on the verge of offering to help, then closed it. Themistocles had shut down the subject.

"I congratulate you on your position," Barzanes said to me, leaking deepest insincerity.

I said, "It's a pleasure to be here," returning the emotion.

He wore a simple, unadorned tunic and no jewelry or display of any kind, yet stood out at this table of well-dressed officers and overdressed civilians. The ringleted beard, the curled, black hair, the piercing dark eyes, and the hawklike nose gave him the air of a predator.

"I hope there are no hard feelings over our previous encounter. The Great King himself, may Ahura Mazda preserve and protect him, charged me with the safety of our empire. A man must perform his duty."

"I have no hard feelings," I lied. "I feel sure, were our positions reversed, I would have done the same, with much the same emotions as I'm sure you experienced."

Barzanes smiled. "We understand each other then."

Archeptolis ceased grabbing food while Barzanes and I spoke. I suppose he'd heard the underlying venom of our exchange. Their body language told a story. Archeptolis and Barzanes were sitting side by side, yet Archeptolis leaned away from his neighbor as if Barzanes had a disease. The lean took Archeptolis toward his father, as if he hoped for protection from Themistocles. Cleophantus, on the other hand, listened with an air of puzzlement. Themistocles watched with a slight smile beneath his bushy beard. He hadn't intervened.

Barzanes ignored me after that and turned all his attention to Nicomache, showing her little attentions, offering her choice morsels, pouring wine for her with his own hand. If Nicomache had a husband present, no one mentioned him. If he existed, he would certainly have objected to Barzanes' behavior. Her clothing, demeanor, and style were those of a modest maiden, which, considering she must have been almost twenty, was a considerable achievement. Themistocles must have noticed my raised eyebrows because he said, "Nicomache is betrothed to my future son-in-law, Barzanes."

Nicomache wasn't smiling, but Barzanes' eyes and his possessive manner spoke volumes. Barzanes was a man in love.

Before I had time to consider the implications, Archeptolis said, "This is not the normal dining arrangement." He speared some meat from a silver platter with a knife. "Normally the family dines alone or with any distinguished visitors, and of course Barzanes."

Archeptolis had made his statement in such a way as to be almost but not quite an insult. I let it pass, but Cleophantus did not. "Your meaning?" he asked.

Archeptolis shrugged. "Merely that our guest should not expect to see so many officers and officials at table, should he be invited again."

"That's terrible." Asia spoke up for the first time. "It was Nicolaos who saved me, brother. Father, you wouldn't let Nicolaos eat with the staff, would you?"

Themistocles smiled and reached over to pat her on the head with his beefy hand. "You are not old enough to dine with us in any case, little Asia, except during celebrations. You will return to eating in the women's quarters, as a child should."

Asia lifted her chin in a mannerism that struck me as similar to Themistocles himself. "He's an honored guest," she insisted.

Themistocles considered me. "I am inclined to agree with you. There, you have what want. Let the matter rest."

Asia smiled prettily and said, "Thank you, Father," in the nicest way. She glanced at me and immediately lowered her eyes, as if to say, *There, I have delivered you a present.*

Up and down the table, slaves were carrying full cups of wine to the guests. Themistocles and the family had their cups placed before them by Nicomache and Mnesiptolema, with Asia assisting.

"You drink with the meal?"

Cleophantus said, "The Persians begin the wine sooner than we do."

I nibbled at everything, intensely curious about the food. Something was odd about the ox meat, the lamb, the trout, the eel, the lentils, and the beans. They were all foods with which I was familiar, yet they tasted different, and I couldn't place why. Cleophantus leaned over and asked, "Anything wrong?"

"No. Well, everything tastes a little . . . not off, but strange."

"It's the oil. They don't cook with olive oil like we do. They use sesame oil instead. The taste is different."

"What in Hades is a sesame?"

"I have no idea. Oh, be careful of the wine."

"Don't tell me there's sesame oil in that too?"

"No, but there isn't any water either."

"They didn't cut the wine?" I said, aghast.

Barzanes had eaten sparingly of the meat. Now he scooped out ladles of the sauced vegetables while he listened to every word I said.

Diotima turned to Nicomache. "Your garden is very beautiful."

"It is, isn't it?" Nicomache replied. "They call it a *paradise*, which means 'surrounded-by-wall' in their language. I like to sit in the pavilions and watch the flowers. Do please use the paradise any time."

Slaves flowed into the room bearing food that looked unfamiliar.

"What's this?"

"This is dessert," Archeptolis said. "What we have here is"—he pointed at the bowl in front of him—"sweet grape jelly. Those are candied turnips, then next are capers and radishes with salt, candied fruits over here, and the last bowl is pistachio nuts."

I picked at the candied fruits. They were the sweetest, most delicious things I'd tasted in my whole life, like honey, but different. I scooped out more, as much as decency allowed, then scooped again.

"This is fantastic."

An officer beside Diotima said, "That's why you Hellenes are so skinny. Once you're done with the meat, there's nothing left to eat. If you had decent desserts like us, you wouldn't stop eating."

Diotima said, "Dessert is a luxury, and we Hellenes don't have enough food to go around as it is. I couldn't eat a dessert if I knew a child was hungry."

"Is food so scarce then where you live?"

"Yes, though it used to be much worse. I've heard it said that long ago, there was so little to eat that men when they reached their sixtieth birthday had to drink poison."

"I don't believe it," the Persian officer said.

"The story is true." We all looked to the head of the table, where Themistocles had been listening to us. He said, "I once spoke to the poet Simonides—a very great man—who told me such was the case on his own island in his father's day. The old were expected to remove themselves to make way for the young. Indeed Simonides told me he was present when his own father took the cup at a family dinner. The father bade his children farewell and then drank hemlock."

Slaves were constantly removing dishes and bringing more.

I wondered when it would stop, for surely everyone had eaten enough? Diners emptied their cups at a speed that would have done credit to any symposium and rushed to refill as fast as they could go.

Men stood and walked out of the room, only to return a while later, sit down, and continue eating without anyone taking the slightest notice. In Athens such behavior would have been considered rude. I asked Cleophantus, "Where are they going?"

"Outside, to piss."

"What's wrong with pissing in a bowl in the corner?"

"The Persians like to be alone for such things."

"Weird."

Themistocles made an effort to call out to each man present from time to time. It was clear he knew every man by name and something about each. One had recently lost a boy-child through illness, though as the father said, fortunately the child had been only four and so the father had never met him.

I leaned over to Cleophantus and whispered, "Is he serious? He'd never seen his own son?"

"It's the custom," Cleophantus whispered back. "The Persians leave their boy-children with the women until they're five, so if the boy dies the father won't grieve overmuch."

"Judging by his attitude, I'd say the system works," Diotima said coldly.

Mnesiptolema had been fidgeting throughout the banquet, and now she said, "Nicolaos, this murder, when did it happen?"

"A few days ago, as far as we could judge."

"Oh." She seemed to relax.

Themistocles said, "Nessie, that subject is closed."

"Yes Father." A moment later she leaned toward me and murmured so only she and I and Cleophantus and Diotima could hear. "Asia says you're an agent. Is it true?"

Diotima said quite loudly, "I can tell you a funny tale of

Nicolaos. When we were on the way here, he led the horse out the gates and then he . . ." She regaled everyone present with my failed attempt to ride Ajax, while I became redder, and redder. The whole table stopped to listen. Those who couldn't understand Greek listened to a translation from their neighbors.

Diotima came to my second attempt to ride Ajax when Asia interrupted, "You forgot the bit when he called to the horse like it was a dog!" More laughter all around. I had no choice but to join in, or be seen as someone who couldn't take a joke, but I was secretly furious.

When Diotima finished, the Persian officers laughed, Barzanes watched me as he always seemed to, and Cleophantus said, "You can't ride? Then I must show you. Let it be my gift to you for returning Asia."

"I'm not as bad as Diotima makes out." I knew I sounded harsher than was good.

"I'm sure you're not," he said hastily. "But riding is my best skill." He glanced at his father. "Some would say my only skill, and I'd love to have someone to ride with. I've picked up a few Persian techniques they don't teach in Athens. I'd be happy to pass them on to a fellow rider."

Themistocles thumped the table and everyone stopped to listen. "My friends, my children. I sit with you in this palace, enjoying your excellent company, eating the good food of the land, and drinking the best wine. Do I owe these fine things to the Athenians, whose gratitude I might have expected for saving their lives and their city? No! When the Athenians tried my judicial murder, I had no choice but to run to my enemy, who proved himself a better friend than my own neighbors. I owe everything you see here to the Great King Artaxerxes, a man higher in honor than any Athenian, in whose name I rule this land."

Asia beamed upon Themistocles in a clear case of father worship. The Persian officers cheered. Archeptolis and Mnesiptolema laughed loudly and artificially. Nicomache seemed sad.

Cleophantus whispered to me with a brittle smile, "He makes the same joke and the same toast at every dinner."

So much for a sign that Themistocles regretted his choice.

Themistocles raised his cup in the air. "Yes, my children, we would have none of this, had the Athenians not turned against me, and every day I thank the Gods that they did. We would have been undone, had we not been undone!"

12

*There is a fullness of all things,
even of sleep and love.*

"He doesn't regret it in the least," I said. "He's actually *pleased* to be a traitor."

"Because he's been rewarded," Diotima replied.

"I notice Themistocles profits from treason while I suffer for doing my duty."

"Life wasn't meant to be easy, Nico."

"Does it say that in Heraclitus?"

At the end of dinner, I'd grabbed Diotima by the hand and led her out into the paradise for some fresh air to clear my head and sort out my thoughts. I needed some clarity, but it was hard to come by while my stomach felt like a block of lead with all the food that had been stuffed into it, and my mind was in a weird state. It was the middle of the night, but the three-quarter full moon was bright enough to see by. We were the only ones still out. Every single Persian had had to be carried off to bed, except for Barzanes. He had thanked Themistocles, who was slumped comatose, and walked off.

"Thanks very much for telling everyone I fell off Ajax," I said to Diotima.

"My pleasure."

"It's not as if I *mind* having a roomful of men laughing at me."

"Barzanes had you in chains this afternoon because he suspected you. Tonight you were less than subtle during dinner when you talked about Brion, and then Mnesiptolema—Nessie, I think they called her—she asks you outright about being an agent. You need to look harmless, Nico. How many dangerous men do you know who can't ride a horse?"

"What's that smell?"

Our random wandering had brought us to a large hole in a distant corner of the gardens. Even as we watched a slave walked up bearing two buckets, one filled with scraps from the dinner, the other with slops and human waste. He emptied each bucket in turn and walked away. The hole was large. With that much fertilizer, no wonder the garden grew so well.

"I wouldn't mind having one of these back home," I said, as we walked on.

"A sullage pit?"

"A paradise. I can imagine walking around my own gardens after dinner, relaxing. Even a small one would be nice."

"You can't afford it."

"No. What did you think of the reactions to the death of Brion?" I asked.

"More complex than I expected. Any one of them could be hiding anything."

"Are we sure there's something to hide?"

"It's hard to see how your friend Thorion could have been traitorous without someone at this end to help him."

I nodded. "Maybe I should've mentioned Thorion's death as well."

"No, it would have given you away."

"All right then, who do you think killed Brion?"

"Your friend Araxes," she replied at once. "Because of that accursed secret letter."

"Probably, but who commissioned Araxes?"

Diotima thought about it for a moment. "Themistocles? Barzanes? Both of them?"

"They wouldn't need to hide a crime," I objected. "They could kill anyone they felt like at high noon in the middle of the agora, call it empire business, and who's going to complain?"

"What about motive then? The letter, I suppose. We won't know anything until we find out what was in the letter. Some threat? Some dire personal secret, maybe? Or blackmail? It could be anything or anyone."

"Anyone. Right. No doubt we'll discover Nicomache is behind the evil plot as part of her plans for world domination."

"Poor Nicomache," Diotima said. "She hates the man she's going to marry."

"Barzanes is probably nobility, and a marriage would cement Themistocles' position with the Persians. Anyone would call that a good match."

"Any *man* would. Didn't you see her shrinking from him?"

"It's irrelevant. When was the last time a woman got to choose whom she married?"

"The daughters of Callias."

"Yes, Callias," I conceded. He'd mentioned it himself in passing at his symposium. "Not every father is Callias."

We'd come to one of the pavilions Nicomache had spoken of. Someone had placed three dining couches in the middle. I could imagine in the heat of day it would be a fine place to relax. The pavilion sparkled because a pond next to it reflected bright moonlight. The reflections silhouetted Diotima in such a way that I could see the outline of her body beneath the fine linen of her chiton. The outline of the tops of her breasts was particularly clear.

"I feel as if my head were floating," I complained. This slow walk had done me little good.

"How many of those candied fruits did you eat?"

"Those very sweet things? Lots. Every time I took a bite, I felt like taking another. I couldn't stop myself."

She nodded. "The same thing happened to me, when Brion fed me some back in Ephesus. You get a feeling like you're full of energy, like you want to run?"

"That's it."

"It'll go away eventually."

"What should I do?"

"Do something energetic. Use up the energy."

I grabbed Diotima and kissed her.

I'd been wanting to do that for a long time.

Diotima was surprised, then she kissed back and I stroked her, and everything was progressing nicely until she pushed me away.

"No, Nicolaos."

"We're far from home. Who's going to know?"

"My future husband, I should think."

"I won't tell him if you don't."

"Would *you* marry a girl who wasn't a virgin?"

"No, of course not."

"Right."

"Unless, of course, it was you," I wheedled.

"I wasn't born yesterday. Believe me, if I had any choice I'd have you right now. I've avoided marriage longer than any girl could hope, but I can feel it catching up with me. I *need* a husband, and it's not you."

"Isn't that why you became a priestess?"

"Yes, and I suppose I could go somewhere where the priestesses don't have to be married, the Temple of Artemis at Brauron maybe. But Nico, I've discovered there's a problem with that."

"Oh?"

Even in the dim light I could see her blush. "I, umm, rather like the idea of men."

"Unfortunate." I couldn't help grinning.

"Don't laugh. You were talking about life being unfair. Well, try this: I was raised to be an Athenian lady, except my mother is anything but. How in Hades am I going to marry within my class? You said there are men who'd have me, and so there are, but I won't have them. I'm educated, I can read. I can think. I'm not going to be the wife of a poor farmer. Can you see me selling vegetables in the agora? I'd sooner slit my own throat." She shook her head. "I have to believe that somewhere in the world there's a man who suits me, but if there is, he isn't in Athens, and that, Nico, means we're not going to bed, at least not the same one."

Diotima walked back into the palace, alone, leaving me to watch her retreating back while I cursed my father and the rules of marriage, all thoughts of murder and treason evaporated. Geros had called me a slave to my lusts. Well, he was right.

I was summoned to the presence of the satrap late next morning, which I welcomed since it would give me a chance to fulfill Pericles' demand that I report on Themistocles. Philodios led me to an office high in the palace, a large room with many windows overlooking the gardens to the south. Themistocles reclined on a dining couch that had been set in the sunshine streaming through the window. He wore Persian dress. Two slaves sat before him taking notes. His dictation ceased the moment I was let in by the two soldiers at the door. Another two stood within the room. Themistocles was well guarded, even within his own palace.

He gestured at another couch. "Sit down. Relax."

I sat down and didn't relax.

"You are the first visitor I've had from Athens since I came here."

He paused for a response from me and didn't get one.

He continued, "Know much about politics? Follow it, do you?"

The sweat trickled in my armpits. I said, offhand, "I know as much as the next man, perhaps a little more."

"Tell me, what do they say of me in the agora?"

I was so relieved and surprised at the question, I told him the truth.

"They don't talk of you all, Themistocles."

He almost lifted off the couch. "They *what*!"

"Sorry."

"Doesn't anyone talk about what will happen when Themistocles returns?"

"No."

"Why not?" he demanded. "Many men have been ostracized, served their time, and returned to Athens to play as large a part in the city as they did before."

"Yes, everything you say is true, Themistocles," I said, attempting to be as tactful as I could manage. "Perhaps the difference in your case is . . . er . . . the difference is . . ." So much for not upsetting him.

"The difference is I am condemned for treason." He said it in a flat tone.

"No one expects you to return." I winced.

"We'll see about that."

I blinked.

"It is not all bad news," I hurried on. "The people of Piraeus remember you with love and respect." I repeated to Themistocles what the port captain had said to me.

"Do they now? Do they now?" He entered on a dissertation of the virtues of the men of Piraeus.

As Themistocles spoke my eyes began to wander, and I saw something astonishing. In each corner of the room was a krater, and all four were in the same shape, the same style, the same colors, and decorated with the same geometric patterns as the two amphorae I'd found in Thorion's office and the stash in the warehouse at Ephesus. It was the connection I needed.

"Themistocles," I broke in. "I can't stop admiring your kraters."

He stopped his monologue to say, "You have fine taste then. You are looking at the only remaining items from the lost treasure of Polycrates." He said it as if I should recognize the name.

"Who?"

Themistocles stared at me in shock. "If you've never heard of Polycrates, then you don't know one of the greatest men we Hellenes ever produced." He tried to heave himself up, failed, and waved at the two guards behind him. They helped him to stand. "Come with me."

Themistocles led me down the stairs and out to the paradise, to a corner where stood the statue of a man in his late middle years, balding but with a trim beard. Words engraved on the plinth proclaimed, "I am Polycrates, tyrant of Samos, first to rule the Aegean Sea."

Themistocles said, "Sometimes I walk out here at night. I've stood exactly where you're standing now and looked up at this statue, and wept."

"Oh. Was Polycrates a friend of yours?"

"Never met the man. He died when I was a small child, sixty years ago if I've reckoned it correctly, which I think I have. Never has a man risen so high, nor fallen so far," he said, oddly echoing what Callias had said of Themistocles himself.

"Polycrates ruled as tyrant on the island of Samos. He made the people of the island wealthy. Then he built the largest fleet in the world and used it to extend his power over the other islands in the Aegean. At his height, Polycrates ruled more Hellenes than any man before him. His empire bordered the empire of the Persians, much the same as the situation between Athens and Persia today."

Themistocles eased himself down onto a bench. "Polycrates was murdered. You're standing on the spot where he died."

He said it with such immediacy, as if the death were recent, that I looked about me for the body. Of course, only the statue marked the scene of the crime.

"Who killed him?"

"A man called Oroetes. In those days, Oroetes was the satrap of this region, the same position I hold today. Oroetes tricked Polycrates into coming to Magnesia. Oroetes said he was in fear of his life at the hands of the Great King and asked Polycrates for asylum, in return for which he would hand over his own large treasure.

"Polycrates was blinded by the thought of the wealth a man like Oroetes might bring, and would have left for Magnesia immediately, had not his friends and his daughter begged him to show more caution. So instead Polycrates sent an advance agent to Magnesia. Oroetes was ready for him. The agent was shown chest after chest of gold coins and silver. What he didn't know was each chest contained genuine coins only to a shallow depth, and thereafter nothing but stone or lead.

"The agent reported that the wealth of Oroetes was vast indeed. Polycrates hastened to Magnesia, bringing with him many expensive gifts for Oroetes. Oroetes captured Polycrates at once. Oroetes raised the pole and Polycrates was impaled. They say he spent many days dying in the greatest agony."

I blinked. "Polycrates and Brion died the same way?"

"If they meet in Hades they'll be able to compare assholes."

"They died within a short distance of each other too," I said.

"But sixty years apart. Some say Oroetes killed Polycrates for wealth and fame, but I think he murdered out of jealousy, because Polycrates was the better man."

I wondered if there was a connection.

Themistocles said, "I admire any man who can carry off such a devious plot. Oroetes did a good job of it, didn't he?"

"You admire an evil man because he does a good job of backstabbing a man you like?"

"Welcome to power politics. If a man could trick *me* like that, I'd have to admire his skills."

"Oroetes won his wealth and fame then."

"Not for long. He was assassinated a month later on the orders of the King, for the crime of being a little too powerful, a little too much of a threat." Themistocles laughed. "Oroetes should have begged for genuine asylum. Oh, the Gods do like to make fools of us men."

"The treasure of Polycrates, what happened to it?"

"It disappeared without a trace. Locals say it was hidden in a place only Oroetes knew. All that remains are a few pieces, like the ones you saw in my office."

Themistocles looked up to the stone Polycrates and said, "He was the most powerful man of his day, yet you've never heard of him. If a man like Polycrates can be forgotten in only sixty miserable years, what hope is there for any man?"

I'd agreed to ride with Cleophantus. I hoped it would be a chance to talk to one of the family alone and get a few leads on who killed Brion. I met him at the stables, where he had the horses ready and waiting. The horse he'd selected for me was like the animal I'd been taught on as an ephebe: older, smaller, and more docile than Ajax.

Cleophantus stood beside the tethered horses. He wore—I could barely believe it, but it was true—he wore . . . trousers.

"Here, put these on," he proffered me a copy of his bizarre garment.

I boggled. "You're not serious, are you?"

"Sure I am. Listen, Nico, I told you the other day the Persians are better on a horse than we Hellenes. One of the reasons is they wear these things. Your chiton just wraps around you; when you sit a horse there isn't much between you and the horse's back, so anything faster than a walk makes your balls bounce around a lot. You know how uncomfortable it is. Trousers fix all that by holding all the necessary bits in place, and there's all this tough material between you and the animal. You'll feel better for it. Trust me, I've been doing this for years."

I looked at the trousers dubiously. One of the worst insults you can throw at an Athenian is to accuse him of wearing trousers. It's a way of saying he's Medized, gone over to the enemy.

"I can't," I said. "You know the old saying."

Then I went bright red. For Cleophantus' father had Medized, and Cleophantus lived off his father's traitorous actions, and Cleophantus wore trousers.

The poor man stood there, silent. He knew how it looked.

"I'm sorry, Cleophantus. I didn't mean it like that. I just meant, well, you know . . . Oh Hades, just hand me the accursed things." I snatched the trousers from him.

I held them up and studied the holes for a moment. I knew what I had to do, in theory. I raised my left foot, balancing on the other. To get the foot in I had to lower the trousers, which made me overbalance. I tried again, using a hand to hold on to the stable gate for balance. That was when I discovered you need both hands to hold open the top hole. Both hands then, and do it quickly before there's time to fall.

My foot became stuck halfway down the leg. I fell flat on my bottom.

A squeal of laughter pealed from the hayloft. I looked up. Asia rolled back and forth, unable to contain her mirth.

"It's all very well for you to laugh, girl. You don't have to wear these things."

Asia jumped down from the loft. She wore trousers.

"Do you want me to show you how?"

"No," I said hurriedly. I stayed on my bottom, stuck my legs in the air, and laboriously threaded my feet through the tubes.

Undignified, but I had no farther to fall. I should have done it that way the first time.

"You're supposed to take your sandals off first," Asia said judiciously.

I ignored her, pulled myself up on the horse next to Cleophantus, and rode away as quickly as I could.

Cleophantus took my arm as we departed the palace gates and said quietly, "Nico? What you said about wearing trousers. It's true. I know it's true. But what do you do when it's your own father? And when everything's going so well?"

"When he's providing you with a life of luxury? I understand, Cleophantus. I don't know what I'd do if I were you."

He muttered, "Unfortunately, I do," more to himself than me.

By mutual consent we dropped the subject and rode on in the pleasant sunshine. It was a glorious day, a good day to be alive.

Cleophantus knew the countryside well. We rode along the main road heading east, until we came to a rough trail that went due south. Cleophantus urged his mount along it and I followed, more I suspect because my horse was used to following than for any command of mine. Rough shrub soon gave way to green and fertile pasture, disturbed only by low, rolling hills that presented no difficulty.

Cleophantus must have been mulling over the talk of Medizing, because as we rode side by side he said, "It's this land. It corrupts you."

"What do you mean?"

He shrugged and looked away, and I thought for a moment he wouldn't answer. Then he said, "Here we are at the eastern end of Ionia. We're not in Hellas, but we're not in Persia either. We're in the lands between, where the Hellene ways and the Persian are all mixed together. Persian habits, Hellene habits, people can pick and choose. They might have taken the best of both, but usually it's the worst."

"You really don't like the Persians?"

He shrugged. "There's a lot to admire about them; the way they sit their horses, for one. They have an obsession for telling the truth, which I like. You've seen some of their wealth; if you traveled on to Susa, it would astonish you. You've eaten their desserts."

"But?"

"But the casual brutality of their laws, the arrogance they display in their might without seeming even to realize; when you get down to it, they're just not us. I like you, Nicolaos. I like having a man here I can relate to, with the likes and habits of a decent Athenian."

"What about Archeptolis?"

"He's . . . well, he doesn't have the habits of an Athenian." Cleophantus couldn't bring himself to say "Medized." "I try hard, but I can't bring myself to like the Persians or their ways."

"Except for the trousers." I smiled.

"Except for the trousers." He laughed. "But that's practicality, not . . . not . . . how men are."

"I know what you mean," I assured him.

Cleophantus hesitated for a moment, then said, "I mean no offense, Nicolaos, you seem like a regular fellow, but a few times at dinner, you seemed to have a hint of the same air of secrecy and sudden death about you that surrounds Father all the time . . . and Barzanes." Cleophantus shivered.

"You don't like Barzanes?"

"Does anyone?"

"Nicomache perhaps?"

He laughed, but grimly. "She hates him more than anyone else. Barzanes is infatuated with her, has been since the day he arrived. He walked into the palace and he was supposed to be talking to Father, but he couldn't keep his eyes off my sister. I thought then the man must be human. Goes to show how wrong you can be."

"Then why the betrothal?"

"If you were an exiled Athenian, would you pass up the chance to become related to the royal house, no matter how distantly? It doesn't matter how unhappy Nicomache is, that wedding's going to happen." What he said closely matched what I'd said to Diotima.

He shifted in his seat, which for a horseman like Cleophantus was an admission of great inner turmoil. "Barzanes scares me, and I don't mind admitting it. Meanwhile my father's shut in his office working night and day. Why couldn't I have had a normal father?"

"My father's a sculptor. When he's in the middle of a piece he likes, he bars the door and won't allow anyone to disturb him. I've known him to work through the night by the light of a torch. I've known him polish and cut and polish for days like a man obsessed."

Cleophantus sighed. "I wish my father was a sculptor. You don't know how lucky you are. Being the son of the mighty Themistocles is a burden: the man who saved Hellas, the smartest man in the world, some call him. The Great King thinks so. Did you know, after the wars, the Great King set a bounty on Father's head of two hundred talents? Two hundred talents. Can you imagine any man worth that much? Father earned it merely by walking into the court of the man who most wanted him dead. When he walked into the Persian court of his own will, the Great King embraced Father and gave him the bounty he'd offered for his capture or death.

"How's a normal man like me supposed to live up to a hero like that? If I achieve anything, anything at all, perform any deed, I know I'll be compared to what Father did, and I'll be found wanting. I'm not stupid, but I know I'm no smarter than the next man. I'll always be the inferior son."

"It's a problem," I conceded. "So what are you going to do?"

Cleophantus shrugged. "If I'll never be good enough, why do anything at all?"

That explained why Cleophantus wasted his time here, living off the fat of his father's success. We'd rounded the top of a hill and spread out before us was—"What in Hades is that?" I asked.

Cleophantus looked at me as if I were mad. "It's a river, of course." Then, "Why, that's right, I should have realized. You're from Athens. You've never seen a large river before. The Illisos in Athens is a small stream compared to this."

I sat on my mare for some time, letting her crop the grass of the hilltop, while I watched the huge flowing mass of water pass by us below. So this was a river. I thought of the words of Heraclitus: "You can't step in the same river twice." I mentioned it to Cleophantus. He laughed. When he forgot to be depressed, Cleophantus had a happy, carefree laugh. He said, "If your philosopher meant this river then he was dead right. The damned thing changes direction every year. We haven't been here that long, less than ten years, and it's changed its banks more often than I can count."

"What do you mean, changes its banks?"

"See those great loops?"

I did indeed. The river swerved left and right in sweeping arcs, never going in a straight line. I said, "It flows like a drunken sailor."

"Right. Those loops change all the time. Usually they get bigger and bigger, pushing outward. Sometimes the loop becomes so large it collapses, and the water takes a shortcut across what used to be dry land, before the new path begins looping out again. It plays havoc with the farmers, I can tell you. That land you're looking at right below us is new. A whole loop collapsed here six months ago. The farmers love it when that happens because the new soil is always rich. See how green and strong the plants are? Of course, it was bad luck for the farmer who owned this land."

"Owned? Past tense?"

"He fell into the new waterway at night and drowned. It's easy to do in the dark when the riverbank isn't where it used to be."

"What's this river named?"

"They call it the Maeander."

We rode the trails for the rest of the day. It was a pleasant way to spend the time, and I found Cleophantus was good company. He was older, but compared to me he was an inexperienced child.

As we rode back toward the palace late that afternoon, side by side, Cleophantus said without any preamble, "I suppose you know a lot of ways to kill people."

"I do?"

"Well, it's only a guess." He sounded diffident. I would be too if I said crazy things like that.

He continued with, "I know why you came to Magnesia."

"To deliver your sister back to your father."

"You don't have to pretend with me, Nicolaos. I *know*."

"Know what?"

"So you're saying your presence here has nothing to do with a certain letter, which may have arrived in Athens?"

That stopped me dead. "What letter?"

This had to be a trap. Barzanes must have coerced Cleophantus into asking these questions, hoping I'd loosen up with a fellow Hellene. No real conspirator could be as clumsy as Cleophantus.

Our path had taken us into the foothills, close to the necropolis, the city of the dead.

I realized then we had taken a very indirect route home. I hadn't thought anything of it until that moment. After all, this was supposed to be a fun ride.

Cleophantus said, "This way," and turned his mount sharply, straight into the necropolis. It occurred to me a necropolis is the perfect place to hide a body. I followed after a moment's hesitation, but while his back was to me I used my right hand to check that my dagger was in place, as was the backup I kept hidden beneath my chiton.

We passed row after row of stele, memorial stones, all poking out of the ground and inscribed to speak to the passerby. Some were engraved with an image of the dead.

A woman standing with an arm raised in greeting: *Agesilla, wife of Timacrates, well deserving of him. She died bearing his son.*

Xaribolos lies here. I raised four sons and many daughters, and lived to seventy-five.

Some men, wealthier, had commissioned statues of the dead, or even monuments.

Two boys made of stone, standing side by side with an arm around each other: *Criton, son of Thrasybolous, erected this for his two sons, Dexiphanes, age five, and Criton, age four, who drowned in the river.*

Cleophantus wound past all of these graves, row upon row of the dead, and upward along the narrow path of trodden dirt, bordered by high, tough grass. The place was silent but for the whistle of the wind, the thud of hooves, and the occasional snort from our mounts. Well, in a necropolis, silence was preferable to the alternative.

Directly ahead, high above us, rock tombs were cut into the hills themselves. I'd heard of rock tombs, but never seen one; Athens doesn't have them. They are family graves that have been cut deep into the side of a solid hill by hand. The rock tombs of Magnesia stood in a ragged row, high and proud above the necropolis, with the outside faces chiseled, carved, and painted to resemble the façades of temples. All but one showed signs of wear: faded paint, or a certain loss of definition in the fine features where wind and rain had worn the carving. The exception was the last in the row, either new or freshly maintained. Its lines were sharp, complete; its paint bright; the effect astonishing. From a distance, I could have sworn it was the front of a real building.

I saw the path up the hill was a dead end, in more ways than one.

"Cleophantus, where are we going?"

He didn't answer, but dismounted at the first of the temple outlines. Now that we were closer I could inspect the work. As the son of a sculptor, I was fascinated. Someone had actually carved Ionic columns out of this solid rock, and temple roof outlines and metopes and friezes. This was quality artwork. I ran my fingers along the stone, feeling the erosion. They would have done better to have picked a hill made of marble, though I supposed valuable marble would have been mined. The paint-work up close was in poor condition, but that was to be expected, no paint could last on stone exposed as this rock face was. Even so, these tombs beat the burial urns we Athenians used any day. When I died, I wanted to be put in one of these.

There was a thick wooden door in the middle of the temple carving, hung on iron hinges. Cleophantus gripped the handle and pulled it back. It moved almost silently; someone had oiled the hinges.

Mnesiptolema sat inside, exposed to view as the door swung open. Her hard, angular face was sharpened by the contrast of light and dark.

I said, "I hope you're here to tell me who killed Brion."

"I rather thought you did." She pursed her lips. "I must say, you don't look like an assassin. But if Thorion sent you, I suppose you must be the best Athens has."

We sat on the stone benches carved into the walls, which should have held bodies but which had been long empty. It was cool and damp inside the tomb, and very private, which is what the children of Themistocles wanted. I sat opposite three of them: Mnesiptolema, Cleophantus, and Nicomache. Nicomache had been sitting unnoticed in the corner when the door opened. Invisibility seemed to be Nicomache's skill.

I said, for the third time, still not believing, "You want me to kill your *father*?"

"Surely Thorion explained this to you?" Mnesiptolema said, her impatience plain.

"So it was you three who sent the letter to Thorion?" I studiously avoided her question.

"Four. You forget my husband. Granted, that's easy to do."

"That's a good point. Why isn't Archeptolis here?" I asked.

"I speak for us both," Mnesiptolema said at once.

That was believable.

"Are you experienced at this sort of thing?" Mnesiptolema asked, as if I were an artisan interviewing for a commission.

"I haven't assassinated that many people."

"How many?"

"Well, none actually."

"None?" Cleophantus said. "We ask Athens for a killer, and they send *you*?"

"Athens didn't send me to kill anyone. I'm not an assassin; I'm an investigator, an agent."

"But we told Thorion—"

"Thorion's dead," I said.

Silence.

"How?" Mnesiptolema demanded.

"An assassin got him. A *real* one."

"I *told* Nessie this was a bad idea," Cleophantus said glumly.

I said, "The man who killed Thorion stole the letter before we could read it."

Nicomache gasped.

Cleophantus went pale. "Then whoever sent the assassin—"

"Has the letter. I don't know who he is."

"Barzanes, it has to be him," Nicomache said. "But if Barzanes knows, why hasn't he arrested us?"

We all turned to look at her. She went red when she realized the answer to her question. Even if Barzanes had perfect evidence, he would do nothing against his future wife.

"I suppose it could be someone else," she muttered.

Cleophantus sat down and held his head in his hands. "The one time in my life I try and do something positive, and this is what happens."

"If Thorion didn't send you, then why did you come?" Mnesiptolema said.

"To solve Thorion's murder. So you're telling me this letter said nothing of treason?"

"Certainly not treason against Athens. Treason against Persia, definitely."

"So Thorion *wasn't* a traitor."

Mnesiptolema shrugged. "If he was, it's nothing to do with us."

"And Brion?"

Nicomache muttered, "Poor Uncle Brion."

"*Uncle* Brion?"

"Well, not in fact, but that's what we called him when we were children."

"Oh, really? So much for him being a mere acquaintance like you said at dinner, Mnesiptolema."

Each looked at the others, waiting for someone to speak. Eventually Cleophantus said, "Nessie said that for our protection, Nicolaos. Please understand, we have a good reason to be nervous. But she didn't entirely lie. Brion was a friend on our mother's side of the family. There may have been a distant relationship; I'm not sure. He visited our home in Athens whenever he was in town on business, and Father received him. I couldn't say what the relationship was. You have to remember, we three were young children and Asia was a baby. Then when Father was condemned, it was a very scary time for all of us."

Nicomache nodded. "I don't think any of us ever got over it. I still have nightmares. The stigma . . ."

Mnesiptolema snorted.

Nicomache said, "It's true, Nessie. Just because *you* were happy to throw the stones back. . . ."

Cleophantus said, "The family became hated, you see. We were the children of a traitor. People spat on us. Other children threw stones. Father was already in exile. There was no protection."

His words reminded me of the persecution of Onteles, the son of Thorion, and the fate his family faced. I recalled the graffiti on their wall, which threatened to burn down their house with them in it. I nodded and said, "I know someone in a similar situation. I understand what you went through."

Cleophantus went on, "A man called Epicrates—a friend of Father's—smuggled us out in a cart. They killed him for it later, for helping us." Cleophantus paused and I could see, even in the dim light, the color in his face fade to an awful white. "It's awful knowing a man died for the *crime* of saving you when you were a child. Nicomache talked of nightmares; that's mine. Anyway, people think Epicrates took us all the way to Father, but he dropped us off at his farm estate. The man who took us the rest of the way was Brion."

"Themistocles must have been grateful to him for that."

"He never talked about it, but of course he must have been."

"I suppose he was a frequent visitor to you here then."

"Oddly, no. We never saw him again. Until recently, that is, when he began making trips to Magnesia."

"What for?"

"I don't know."

"What drove the three—four—of you to conspire to murder your own father? You do realize the Gods would curse you?"

Patricide is the worst possible crime for a Hellene, worse than any other form of murder. The only crime that comes close is bedding your own mother. Only one man ever committed both. That was Oedipus, and the Gods went out of their way to make him suffer.

Mnesiptolema smirked. "Our hands will be clean. We merely informed Athens of certain facts. The rest should have followed naturally."

I hoped for her sake the Gods saw it in the same cynical light she did.

"I gather this was your idea."

"You think these soppy fools could come up with a sensible scheme?"

"Nessie!" Nicomache objected.

I turned to Nicomache. "What could make a nice girl like you want to kill your own father?"

Nicomache clasped her hands together and rubbed them, as if she washed her hands in some invisible water. "I *don't*. I love Father. I don't wish him harm. But he's so determined to marry me to Barzanes. When I think of his hands on me I feel sick." She visibly shuddered.

I couldn't blame her. I wouldn't want that cold fish handling me either.

"I've pleaded with Father, and pleaded, and pleaded, but he says the marriage is a good one and I should be pleased. What he means is, the marriage is good for his ambitions. He doesn't care about my happiness at all."

"That's his right, you know, to make the judgment." As I knew all too well. Suddenly I felt a sympathy with Nicomache that I would never have expected.

"My brothers have promised me"—she looked to Cleophantus—"if Father dies, they'll annul the agreement with Barzanes and allow me to marry the man I love, my cousin Phrasicles of Athens."

"There's still the blood curse," I pointed out.

Nicomache said, "No, Nessie's explained it. If all we do is tell Athens of the threat to the city, then we aren't being bad at all. Quite the opposite: we're being good citizens."

Mnesiptolema said, "It's amazing how easy it is to persuade someone an action is moral when it's in their own best interests."

"Oh, be quiet, Nessie," Cleophantus said angrily. "Why must you always attack people? I don't want to be brother-by-marriage to Barzanes, any more than Nicomache wants to marry him."

"I see." I thought for a moment. "I think I've met this Phrasicles of yours, Nicomache."

Nicomache clasped her hands and said, "Oh, do please tell me, how is he? Is he well?" she asked with such a voice that I realized this was a lovelorn girl.

I shook my head. "It's only a passing acquaintance. What's your excuse, Mnesiptolema?"

"That's my business."

"Then explain to me why Athens should help you homicidal offspring commit murder."

They all three looked at each other in confusion, almost like comics playing in the agora.

Cleophantus said, "We explained it all in the letter."

"That would be the letter stolen from Thorion's dead body."

Cleophantus hung his head, shifted in his seat, and said, "Father's best days are behind him, his victory—despite everything, people still honor him for that—it would be terrible if he did something to destroy his greatest legacy. In a way, we'd be doing him a favor, because an honorable man in his situation would commit suic—"

"Oh, get on with it!" Mnesiptolema snarled at him. "Can't you do anything?" Mnesiptolema turned to me. "Our father is writing an invasion plan, and the Persians are going to use it. If someone doesn't do something, Athens will be conquered."

13

To spy upon the enemy,
alone in the dead of night,
it will be a deed of great daring.

I didn't hesitate. As soon as we returned the horses to the stable, I went straight to the agora in Magnesia and bought two wax tablets and leather cord, exactly as I had in Ephesus, and as before I took them back to my room, wound the cord about the pole, and began to write.

URGENT! THEMISTOCLES PREPARING INVASION PLAN OF HELLAS. PERSIAN ATTACK IMMINENT WHEN HE COMPLETES. PREPARE AT ONCE.

That ought to get Pericles' attention.

Twice before the Persians had tried to conquer Athens. The first time had been in the reign of King Darius, thirty years ago. Twenty-five thousand Persians had landed at Marathon. The Athenians, outnumbered three to one, had attacked, and the Persians were pushed back into the sea. It was a famous victory. Ten years later Xerxes, the son of Darius, launched his own massive invasion, and was defeated at the sea battle of Salamis, but not before taking Athens and razing it to the ground. No one doubted the Persians would try a third time if they could, and it seemed Artaxerxes, son of Xerxes, had decided that with Themistocles on their side the time was ripe.

I continued the coded message to Pericles, in smaller text, passing on all the details I'd learned from the homicidal siblings.

Back in the tomb I'd asked them, "How long has this been going on?"

Mnesiptolema said, "Months. Three months at least. Probably longer, but that's when we noticed."

Cleophantus added, "Usually he's open with us about whatever he's doing, I think because he wants us to take an interest—we've all disappointed him by not having any talent for statesmanship—the only one who pays attention is Asia. She dotes on Father."

Nicomache said, "Then one day as I cleaned the room—I'm the only one allowed, because I'm family—I chanced upon some notes. They talked about Persian forces in Hellas. I showed them to Cleophantus."

Cleophantus said, "I had a horrible feeling they were what they turned out to be. At which point we took Archeptolis and Nessie into our confidence."

"You came to this tomb to meet?"

"It's the only place we can be certain no one listens."

"But surely difficult to find a pretense to come here very often."

"It's no pretense," Nicomache said. "My mother—mine and Asia's—lies in the new crypt at the end of this row."

"Asia told me she was dead. I'm sorry."

"If she had lived, she would never have allowed Father to betroth me."

"How did you get the letter to Thorion?"

Mnesiptolema said, "Through Brion, of course. Brion handles so much correspondence to Athens, it was the simplest thing in the world to slip him the letter when he was in Magnesia. No one even blinked."

"Did Brion know what you'd written?"

"Not unless he's been reading our mail."

Which he may well have.

Mnesiptolema said, "When are you going to kill him?"

"Your father? I'm not."

"You must!"

"I'm not a murderer; I catch murderers."

"Well, *we* can't do it, we'd be cursed." She thought for a moment. "This man who killed Thorion, I wonder if he's for hire?"

"I'll tell you what I'll do. I'll write to Pericles telling him what's happening. He'll put Athens, maybe all of Hellas, onto a war footing and prepare for the coming invasion. The Athenians have beaten off the Persians twice before; they can do it a third time. He might do other things, who knows? He might even send a real assassin to solve your problem."

"It won't work. Barzanes will read your message for sure."

"He won't suspect a thing."

"Then don't mention us in your letter. We went to great trouble not to get caught last time. We have no wish to die with you."

I finished writing on the cord and put away the ink and thin brush. Now I placed the blank wax tablets before me and took up a bronze stylus to scratch words, beginning,

NICOLAOS GREETS HIS FATHER, SOPHRONISCUS, AND PRAYS TO ZEUS FOR HIS GOOD HEALTH. THE WEATHER HAS BEEN FINE. I HAVE SEEN MANY INTERESTING THINGS IN MAGNESIA . . .

I meandered—it seemed only fair given my location—around general topics for some time, enough to fill two tablets and justify the need for the cord. When I was done I sat back to gaze at my handiwork with pride. I confess I was pleased with what I'd achieved. I had discovered the contents of the missing scroll, precisely as Pericles had commissioned, and it had proven to be of paramount importance. How many other men had saved Athens, and probably all of Hellas, with a timely warning? Only one, and he had been a king of Sparta. If this didn't persuade Pericles to reinstate me, nothing would.

I wrapped the cord around the tablets and tied it tight. I would have to find a traveler to carry my message, one so inconspicuous no one would look at him twice. Fortunately I knew what to do, but before I did, I sent a slave to the women's quarters to find Diotima.

We met in the pavilion where I had tried to seduce her two nights before. The advantage was we could see if anyone approached. The disadvantage was I kept thinking of that night, when I should have been concentrating on the mission. Nevertheless I managed to give her a full account, speaking softly.

"You have to warn Athens at once," she said.

"I'm sending the message as soon as we part."

"Any chance we can carry it ourselves?"

"Themistocles made it very clear my life is forfeit if I step outside the city limits. I should think the same goes for you."

"I suppose the guards would spot us anyway."

"Yes, and if we sneak, they'll notice we're gone and ride us down long before we could make it to Ephesus."

"Not to mention Ephesus is technically part of the empire. We wouldn't be safe until we were on a boat out."

"The only way is to send an encoded message. I'm beginning to think Callias is some sort of prescient genius. How did he know the skytale would be so useful?"

"Because he's a diplomat. Nico, this could be a disaster. How many people were killed in the last war?"

"Tens of thousands of men in the fighting."

"And that's not counting the women and children lost in

the panic, and the elderly and sick who had to be left behind when Athens fell and the city was burned to the ground."

"There's nothing we can do except make sure the warning gets out. Then it's up to Pericles."

"You're right. What does this tell us about the murders? On the face of it, Araxes was sent to recover what amounted to a war warning from the children of Themistocles. You'd think then Araxes worked for Themistocles, wouldn't you? Yet Araxes carried Asia as a slave. As you said before, it doesn't make sense."

"Unless Barzanes sent Araxes? He couldn't send a Persian—the man would be spotted at once—and not many Hellenes would agree to such a mission. Araxes would have been the perfect choice."

"You need to explain why Barzanes thought it was a great idea to steal his boss's daughter."

"There is that."

Diotima chewed on her thumbnail, a sure sign she was thinking hard. "The children of Themistocles need to be looked into. Do you trust them?"

"I wouldn't trust Mnesiptolema as far as I could toss her."

"And I'm sure you'd enjoy handling her for the throw."

"Diotima!"

"I saw you ogling her at dinner. Nice body, I'll grant you, but that face. . . ."

"I guess I could close my eyes."

"All right, I'm teasing you. Go on."

I said, "Archeptolis is under his wife's thumb and it's an incestuous marriage."

"Yes, that disturbs me too."

"Nicomache is a nonentity. Cleophantus is either a simple, naïve young man, or else I look forward to seeing his performance on stage at the next Dionysia."

"I'm not so sure about Nicomache. Merely because she's quiet doesn't mean she's isn't dangerous."

"What are you thinking?"

"That someone knew the letter to Thorion needed to be retrieved. How?"

"I hate it when you ask good questions I can't answer."

"Leave it with me."

I wandered into the city, carrying the tablets. Magnesia was the sort of place people pass through; the city lay on the route connecting Ephesus with the center of the empire. Any man traveling from inland toward Ephesus would have to pass this way, and he would always stop in Magnesia, because the remaining distance to Ephesus was more than a man could make in a day unless he was on a fast horse.

The main route passed straight through the agora. Street kids spotted me in an instant as an out-of-towner. I felt little hands plucking about my chiton, which did them no good because, since I'm not stupid, I'd put my coins in my mouth before I left the palace. Nevertheless they were an irritant and I whacked a couple of them with my free hand and growled, "Go away."

It didn't deter them in the least. They dodged away like flies, and like flies returned the moment I stopped swinging my arm. At the same time they made offers such as:

"Hey, you not from here? Need an inn? I know a good one!"

"Come with me! Great food, good beds!"

"Hey mister, my sister's lonely! You wanna come with me?"

I replied to that one. "I don't need another woman, I have enough trouble with the one I've got."

"She's juicy!"

"How do you know?"

"That's easy, because—"

"Don't tell me! I don't want to know."

"What about your woman trouble then? If you need to get rid of her I can introduce you to a witch woman who can—"

"I have the opposite problem."

"I can get you a good deal on a love charm!"

Tempting, but, "No."

He was a street kid, filthy, wearing someone's torn, cast-off tunic, which he'd tucked up so it didn't trip him over. He either didn't have a mother, or more likely, his mother was the whore who'd sent him out to pimp for her.

"What's your name?"

"Macrobianos. Call me Mac, everyone does."

"All right, Mac, you want to earn some coins?"

His eyes lit up. "Does a cockroach want crumbs?"

"Er, right. I'm offering a drachma a day." That was about standard wages for a man. "You're my guide. Take me to the most expensive inn in town."

He looked me over dubiously and said, "You can't afford it. But I got a room we can rent you. It comes complete with—"

"Your sister. Yes, I know. Now take me to the expensive inn."

I left Mac standing outside Apollo's Retreat, which was by the main road, with orders to wait.

The inside of Apollo's was cool and dark. The entrance gave into a large public room with seats and couches. Immediately before me was a large courtyard with a pond. Beyond the courtyard I could see stables. It looked more like the home of a wealthy man than an inn.

A large party of Phoenicians kept to themselves and watched me from a distant corner. They were uncharacteristically far from the sea, all decked out in caps and beards, collars and armlets, and bracelets and torcs.

The innkeeper hurried up, looked behind me, failed to see any slaves, baggage, or signs of wealth, and wrinkled his nose in the way usually reserved for bits of lizard brought in by the cat. I hadn't stopped to wash or rest since the meeting with Mnesiptolema, Cleophantus, and Nicomache; I must have smelled of horse and sweat, and I hadn't completely shaken off the dust of the ride.

He said, "Do you want a room?" At the same time he motioned to a guard in preparation to throw me out.

"I don't need one. I'm staying at the palace."

"The palace?"

"Yes, I said to the Lord Satrap only yesterday I might look into town while I was here."

He stared at me and I could see him recalculate. His eyes widened and he said, "You're the guy who was dragged kicking and screaming from the agora."

I didn't quite remember it that way. Obviously the story had grown in the retelling.

"That little misunderstanding has been cleared up."

"Damn, this is awful."

"It is?"

"There'll be a lot of unhappy money change hands when they see *you* walking about."

"Someone is running a *book* on me?"

"Sure they are. This is Magnesia, people'll bet on anything. The way you came in with the Satrap's child—dear Gods, what a fuss when she went missing—and a Messenger's horse, and then Themistocles had you dragged off . . . all the smart money said we'd be looking up to you, but not in a good way. This is deeply disappointing. I've blown twenty drachmae."

"I'm sorry."

"I gotta say, wherever you get your luck, I wouldn't mind some of it."

"I'm asking after a friend of mine. A fellow called Brion. I believe he stayed here?"

"Well, he *was* here."

Of course he was. It had never occurred to me that Brion would stay anywhere other than the most expensive inn in town.

"But you can't see him; he's left."

"On a long journey. Yes, I know. Did he leave normally? Pay his bill? Didn't disappear without warning?"

"Sure." He looked at me strangely. Obviously word of Brion's demise had not reached the ears of the general populace.

"Did Brion come to Magnesia often?"

"Couple of times every month, I suppose."

"What did he do when he was here?"

"How should I know? We don't spy on our guests. He went out every day. He came back. Same as anyone, except for the mud."

"Mud?"

He shrugged. "I dunno. I just saw he came back a few times leaving muddy tracks for the slaves to clean up—you tend to notice on these pavers—and his hands were a bit grubby. Not the sort of thing we usually see in our clientele, not since Themistocles took over the city anyway."

Diotima had admired Brion because he always kept his fingernails clean.

"You like Themistocles?"

"You kidding? In the ten years he's been here he's done wonders. Magnesia used to be a dump. Themistocles cleaned up the streets—he hoisted crooks up on the poles until the rest realized he meant business—repaired the east bridge; restored the agora, which was run-down; lowered taxes to encourage trade, which worked, so now the city makes more money and people pay less tax. We get a better class of merchant stopping in. That man really knows how to run a city. Goes to show, don't it, how wise the Great King is. He knew a good man when he saw one and put him to work. The Athenians must have been mad to toss out Themistocles. Give me a wise king over a bunch of democratic idiots any day."

"Thanks for your help."

"When you get back to wherever you come from, recommend my place to anyone coming this way, will you?"

"I'll do that."

"Good. I figure you owe me for the twenty drachmae."

I emerged from Apollo's with my mind in a whirl, but I had to settle it down for the next job, the real reason I'd come to town. "All right, Mac, the next stop is a cheap inn.

"Plenty of those. And for an extra drachma I'll throw in my sister."

I paid him a half-drachma at once and promised another at the end of the day, as long as he didn't try to sell me his sister again.

As we passed though the agora I saw Barzanes. He stood before a troop of soldiers standing to attention. Barzanes harangued the troop, issuing orders in no uncertain terms, but my Persian wasn't good enough to understand. Barzanes saw me before I could move away and he gave me a stony look. I waved cheerily as I passed, like a tourist out to see the sights.

Mac took me to an inn on the main road going east, called the King's Rest, but if a king ever stopped here it was only because he couldn't wait to pee. It lay beside a bridge over the stream that flowed south into the Maeander. The King's Rest was the first place a man walking from inland toward the coast would see when he came to the city. A tired man who didn't know any better, or a poor one who did, would likely stop here. Mac had understood my wishes precisely.

It was a silent place, full of men sitting with their backs to the wall. Shifty eyes followed me from the moment I entered until I found the man I wanted in the far back corner, sitting on his own, the gray dust covering his sandals and feet and halfway up his legs, which told me he'd been walking hard all day. His nose and ears were sunburned, and he had the squint of a man who'd been looking into the sun too long, which meant he'd been walking west. He wore a heavy travelers' cape, and upon his head was a Phrygian cap, round, almost conical, made of soft leather, with the pointy top flopped over forward.

I bought two cups of wine and carried them across. A bowl of cheese and bread and beans lay mostly eaten before him. He was slumped over, massaging his calves and wincing.

"This might help." I put one of the cups in front of him. He glanced up at me, startled, but nodded and said, "That it might. What d'ye want?"

"I like a man who's direct. Which way are you headed?"

"No offense, stranger, but I can see right away you want something. I'm going to Ephesus. Got a load of cloth to sell in the agora. The donkey's got sorer feet than I."

"You sell cloth?"

"Make it. Quality stuff, mind."

"Is there money in that?"

"Not enough. But I got me five kids, and the wife says there's another on the way. I ain't got enough money to feed that many mouths. What's a man to do? Don't want to expose the kid, not if I can help it."

"Lots of men would." When a newborn is presented, the father accepts it by taking the child in his arms, or else he can order a slave to abandon the baby in the woods to die of exposure. No blood guilt attaches to the father because he didn't actually kill the child, all he did was fail to save it. Blood guilt requires a positive action.

The cloth seller grimaced. "I don't like the idea of leaving some child of mine outside for the wolves to eat. If I can get more for the rolls in Ephesus, maybe I won't have to."

"Good luck. Would this help?" I showed him a handful of coins, careful not to chink them since I had no wish to call attention. I didn't *know* there were thieves in the inn, in the same sense I didn't *know* there were fish in the nearby stream.

I said, "Could your donkey carry a little bit more? I have a package I want to send the direction you're going."

He looked down at the coins but said nothing.

I said, "The coins are Ephesian. Useful to a man going that way."

His squinty eyes looked into mine and he said, "How big is this package?"

I laid the tablets in front of him. "Nothing more than a letter home."

"Which is where?"

"Athens, but all you have to do is carry my letter to a man I know in Ephesus. Go to the commercial agora and ask for a merchant called Pollion. He will remember me. Give him two-thirds of the coins and ask him to put the letter on the next boat to Piraeus, to be taken to the man whose name is written on the outside here. That's my father." It was a convoluted arrangement, but messages were carried like this every day.

He shook his head. "A third for me ain't enough. I got a family to feed."

I'd offered him twice what I paid the sea captain on the docks at Ephesus, when I sent my first message. I sighed and put another handful in front of him. I shifted position so my back blocked the view for everyone in the room.

He nodded.

"I'll need you to swear."

"I ain't Hellene; I'm Phrygian."

"I guessed. Pick your deity."

He nodded. "I swear by Cybele to deliver your letter, an' if I don't, may she make my dyes run."

"It'll do." I pushed the coins across to him. "Thanks."

He scooped the coins into a bag and downed my wine in one swig, then stood, wincing as he did. He picked up the tablets. "No offense, stranger, but I gotta get me some sleep. Got an early start tomorrow."

"Have a safe trip."

"Hey, you didn't ask me my name."

"No, I didn't." He was safer that way. The cloth seller had

driven a hard bargain, but I didn't mind. I didn't want his child to die either.

Mission accomplished. Or this part, anyway. Now all I had to do was work out who killed Brion, uncover what part Thorion had played—I hoped a small one to save his family—and discover why Asia had been stolen.

The innkeeper offered me a meal—he said it was a local traditional dish—but I declined. As I walked out of the inn, the troop Barzanes had been addressing marched by in column. They took the bridge going east and kept on going.

I breathed a sigh of relief. It was all downhill from here.

14

To have a great man for an intimate friend
seems pleasant to those who have never tried it.
Those who have,
fear it.

The guard at the gate caught me the moment we returned and sent me straight to Barzanes. I was led to a room all too close to the prison.

Barzanes looked up from something he read and said, "You left the palace and walked about the city this morning. Why?"

"Merely looking around."

"Nothing else?"

"Would I lie to you?" I said, trying to look innocent.

"You Hellenes lie as easily as you breathe."

"And Persians are honest men?"

"We teach our children three things: to ride the horse, to shoot the bow, and always to speak the truth. Truth in our language is *arta*. The name of our Great King Artaxerxes, in our language, means, 'He whose reign is through truth.' Seek truth, Athenian, and your life will be judged well at its end."

"Speaking of truth, have you learned anything about the death of Brion?"

"I am dealing with it. The murder of the wretched merchant is a crime against the state."

"Then you agree it's murder."

"Of course I do." Barzanes scowled. "Disorder and crime is hateful to the Great King, and even more so to the Wise Lord, Ahura Mazda. This killer is beloved of the Daevas; his soul will writhe in a sea of molten iron for eternity."

"Daevas? Soul?" I asked. "What are they?"

Barzanes looked upon me in wonderment. "Ah, the Hellenes do not worship the Good Religion. It would do your soul good to learn the truth of Ahura Mazda."

"Sure," I said, disinterested, but there was no point in antagonizing him over some ritual.

"I notice in you, Athenian, an unfortunate tendency to meddle in affairs that don't concern you. In this place, it is I who delivers the King's justice. I advise you not to get in its way."

I returned to my room to find two things of great interest. The first was a command, couched in the form of an invitation, to have lunch with Themistocles. The invitation would normally have grabbed my full attention—and caused me to speculate about what he wanted—except the second thing I saw was two wax tablets, tied face-to-face, lying on my bed.

Had the cloth maker changed his mind and returned them? I picked up the package and saw my name, and the name of the inn I'd stayed at in Ephesus, written on the outside. The name of the inn had been crossed through and underneath it a different hand had written, Somewhere in Magnesia. Now I understood. I'd told the innkeeper at Ephesus where I would be and left payment for any messages to be forwarded. These tablets had arrived from Athens; the innkeeper had found someone traveling in this direction and they in turn had found me at the palace and left the tablets. It was exactly the sort of loose connection I relied on to get my warning to Pericles.

This was the reply to my first message, the one I had sent before leaving Ephesus, when all I knew was that Brion had disappeared. I wound the wrapping cord around the tube. It said:

PERICLES, SON OF XANTHIPPUS, HAS THIS TO SAY TO NICOLAOS, SON OF SOPHRONISCUS: WHAT IN HADES DO YOU THINK YOU'RE DOING? DEEPLY DISAPPOINTED TO LEARN NO PROGRESS TO DATE. ALL OF ATHENS NEEDS YOU TO DELIVER ON YOUR MISSION. SITUATION HERE EXTREMELY DIFFICULT. OUR ARMY IN EGYPT NOW FULLY COMMITTED. FLEET ENGAGED IN CYPRUS. RESERVES SO LOW WE'RE INDUCTING OLD MEN AND BOYS TO FIGHT. IF YOU DISCOVER THE THREAT, RETURN HOME WITH THE INFORMATION IMMEDIATELY, EVEN IF YOU HAVEN'T RECOVERED THE PROXENOS OR TRACKED DOWN ARAXES. *FIND THAT INFORMATION!* OR DON'T BOTHER COMING BACK. PERICLES.

Egypt? What in Hades was our army doing in *Egypt*? Pericles spoke as if it were common knowledge, which since Egypt was a satrapy of Persia it probably was. The Persians there had probably already noticed thousands of hoplites trying to kill them.

Pericles would get a shock when my letter arrived. If Athens was as overextended as Pericles described, then a squad of angry fishwives attacking from the east had a fair chance of taking the city, let alone tens of thousands of armed and dangerous Persians.

Most upsetting was Pericles' final order: "Or don't bother coming back." I dropped the tube in disgust. Of course, Pericles couldn't know how much I'd achieved since my first letter, but even Themistocles valued my abilities more than that.

I felt distinctly unloved.

"You told me long ago Brion owned an estate. Did it include a farm?" I asked Diotima.

"Several."

"In Magnesia?"

"No idea. I was his friend, not his estate manager. Why do you ask?"

"Because your clean friend had dirty nails." I told her what I'd learned at Apollo's Retreat.

"How odd," Diotima mused. "Brion with muddy feet. The mud doesn't have to come from an estate. Perhaps he went fishing in the stream?"

"Or the Maeander River. Maybe he fell in? Cleophantus tells me it's easy to—oh."

Diotima looked puzzled. "Oh?"

"There's a daimon whispering in my ear. He just gave me an idea."

"Are you going to tell me?"

"If you're nice to me."

Diotima poured cold water down my back until I told her the story I had from Cleophantus of the farmer drowning in the Maeander.

Diotima frowned. "It's an interesting thought. But if so, why?"

I shrugged. "We've plenty of facts, but few connections."

"Maybe we'll know more after we've searched Nessie's room."

"What?"

"I've been working. What would you say if I told you Mnesiptolema was seen leading Brion into the palace late at night?"

I sat up straighter. "This happened?"

"Yes."

"Then I'd say they were having an affair."

"So would I, but the slaves I had the story from—it was the two we saw dumping slops in the sullage pit the other night—say they saw her let a man in through a side gate and they only saw it only the once, though they empty garbage every night."

"Was it Brion they saw?"

"The description matches, but it's not certain."

"This incident wasn't just before Brion died, by any chance, was it?"

"You're right: it wasn't. It happened about three months ago."

"Oh." I thought for a moment. "Here's an idea: what if Archeptolis caught Brion with Mnesiptolema, and wreaked revenge?"

"If he did, there'd be no case to answer."

I nodded. Athenian law on this is simple. The male half of an adulterous couple may be killed on the spot as long as there are independent witnesses to back up the husband's claim. Of course the objection was, "But we aren't in Athens. What's the law here?"

"Whatever the Great King says it is, I should imagine. The important point is, at first Nessie denied a connection to Brion, then Nicomache revealed the family history, and Nessie admitted to it but no more. Now we find the connection between Nessie and Brion was stronger still. If there's any correspondence, it will be in her room."

"You're right, we have to search."

"When?"

"This afternoon, after I've had lunch with Themistocles."

"You're having lunch with Themistocles? Whatever for?"

"I have no idea."

"Aren't you worried?"

"He said I'm safe as long as I don't leave town."

"That was before you started sending out secret messages."

"If he suspected anything, lunch would be served in the dungeon. Anyway, I have other things to worry about. I have a message from Pericles." I told her what it said, unable to hold in the bitterness. "I've been thinking, Diotima. When this is over, I might freelance."

"A freelance agent?"

"Why not?"

"Because you'd starve to death waiting for work might be one reason."

"I don't see why. Araxes seems to be doing well enough for himself."

"You don't want to be like Araxes, do you?"

"No, but Pericles is cutting me off, that's my work gone. I'll be forced back to sculpting for my father, and he won't listen to me about anything important. So why go back?"

"Nico! You wouldn't leave Athens, would you?"

"Well, what's Athens done for me?"

Diotima said, "'Without a sign, his sword the brave man draws, and asks no omen, but his country's cause.'"

"What's that?"

"Homer, from the *Iliad*. Hector says it right before he goes out to face Achilles. I thought you might like a reminder."

Lunch with Themistocles was a mêlée of food and questions. The slaves brought one dish after another and removed the empties in a steady flow, while another slave filled my wine cup to the brim. Themistocles swirled his own wine and said, "Tell me, Nicolaos, what are your plans for the future?"

I said, "To be a leader in Athens, but my father doesn't have the money."

"You don't need money to get ahead in Athens. Look at me."

I did. The fleshy face, the overfed protruding stomach, the thick legs and arms. I suppose that's the risk you take when you're a satrap, governing a small province, living in a palace and eating sumptuous food brought to you by obsequious slaves. It was a risk I'd be willing to take if someone offered me the job.

"Let me tell you, young man, some advice my father, Neocles, gave me when I was the age you are now. We were walking along the beach at Phaleron, which in those days was the graveyard for ships too old or broken for service. Men had stripped them of everything useful and left the rest to decay. My father asked me as we walked what I intended for my future. I told him I wanted to be a leader of Athens.

"My father pointed to the abandoned hulks, bleached and rotting in the sun, and said, 'That, my boy, is how the Athenian people treat their leaders when they have no further use for them.'"

Themistocles sighed. "I didn't listen to him, of course. It's the way of things for young men to ignore their elders. In fact, if you paid any attention to the same warning I'm passing on to you, it would mean there was something wrong with you. The Gods give us young men to keep the world fresh and interesting." He held out his cup and a slave took it to refill.

"I don't understand, Themistocles. First you say I shouldn't let money stop me, then you warn me against my goal. Which would you have me do?"

"You must pursue power, of course. I merely warn you to be prepared for changing fortune. Any man's plan can fail, even mine: the Gods can turn against you; bad luck; poor judgment; important facts unknown; amazing coincidences; you never know what can go wrong. Always have an alternative plan."

"Such as escape to the Persians?"

"If necessary."

"But what of loyal—" I stopped, because I was about to say possibly the most stupid thing ever.

But Themistocles laughed and said, "What of loyalty to your city? This is the way your loyalties should run: first to yourself, second to your family."

"Then to your city," I finished for him with the standard Hellene triune.

"No, it finishes with family. Your city is an accident of birth, and why should something as important as loyalty be assigned by accident? What if Barzanes had been born in Athens and I in Susa. Would he then be loyal to Athens, and I to the Great King?"

"Yes, of course."

"Why?"

"Because . . ." I stopped. I had no idea.

"You see how arbitrary loyalty is? Every man should use his intelligence to decide his loyalty, rather than have it thrust upon him by wherever his mother happened to be lying when she spawned him. The only constant, lad, is family, the immutable, undeniable connection of blood."

He paused to drain his cup. At once a slave took it to refill. I noticed Themistocles' breathing was a trifle wheezy. Despite his bulk, Themistocles had drunk too much.

He said, "I'm sure someone has spilled the news to you I'm writing a plan for the next attack on Hellas. It's an open secret, impossible to hide."

"Yes, it's true."

"Everything I have, I owe to Artaxerxes. He welcomed me with open arms, even though defeating his father was my greatest achievement, the one thing for which I might be remembered. Now I'm helping Artaxerxes avenge his father against . . . me." He chuckled.

"I know I am safe telling you this, because you're ambitious, and you've seen enough of Athenian politics to know I gave good advice when I said the wise man keeps his options fluid. You might want to warn Athens, though you'd be a fool to try, Barzanes would catch you for sure—"

I smiled, knowing the message was already on its way.

"But you'll also help me, Nicolaos. Not because you love the Persians, but in case I become satrap of Athens. It's in the best interests of you and your family that I be in your debt."

I sat there stunned, then said, "Me? You want *me* to help *you*?"

"That's what I said."

"But that would be disloyal to—"

"I believe we've had that conversation. Use your head, Nicolaos. What's in your best interests?"

I had to think about it while he sat watching me.

Themistocles had given me a small lesson in how power politics really worked, and he was right, it made sense to leave myself a second way. If Athens survived the coming war I would be a hero for giving out the warning. If the Persians won, I would have Themistocles for a friend.

"What could I possibly do that would help the great Themistocles?" I asked, suspicious.

"In one way. I've been out of Athens for ten years, I don't know the administration of the city like I used to. You do, by association with Pericles if nothing else."

I felt relieved. There was very little I could tell him which he couldn't learn by asking any man in the agora, so what harm could I possibly do?

I nodded, and Themistocles smiled.

I would take the first step toward helping the Persians, but it was the first step only, and a small one. I could pull out at any time if he asked too much of me.

Themistocles signaled, and two slaves hurried to help him rise. "It is time for me to rest."

"Before you go, may I ask a final question, Themistocles?"

"Yes?"

"If you help the Great King you erase your own legacy, and sixty years from now you'll be as forgotten as Polycrates. So I don't understand. You're writing this plan because you want your power back, or because Artaxerxes demands it and you owe him?"

He looked at me for so long a time I thought he would not answer, until he said, "I am writing the invasion plan because I want to go home, and this is the only way I will ever get back to Athens."

15

There is nothing nobler or more admirable
than when two people who see eye to eye
keep house as man and wife,
confounding their enemies
and delighting their friends.

It wasn't until later that I realized what I'd done. I thought about it as I lay on my bed waiting for Diotima to tell me Archeptolis and Mnesiptolema had left their room.

The man who assists a traitor is himself a traitor. They'd executed Epicrates for less.

Back in Athens I'd said to Callias and Pericles that I couldn't understand the man who betrayed his city. Callias had alluded to intense pressures, but I had slipped into treachery as easily as a woman puts on her dress. Was this the way it had gone with Thorion?

Yet every word Themistocles said had made sense. It *was* in my interest to have a foot in both camps. Always leave a second way out, Themistocles had said.

My door opened. It was Diotima. "They're leaving their room."

I didn't tell Diotima about my deal with Themistocles. She wouldn't understand.

Archeptolis and Mnesiptolema had their rooms down the corridor from us. Diotima knocked. No one was home.

I knew what to do next; I'd spent an afternoon practicing on my own door. I pulled out a long, thin piece of metal with a hook at the end. This I put into the lock hole and felt about. Somewhere above was the latch. The hook scraped something. Ah yes, there it was.

"Hurry up," Diotima hissed. She stood with her back to me, watching for anyone coming.

"Don't tell me you're nervous?" I grinned. The latch gave, and the door opened a crack. The hinge squealed.

"Shh."

"I have to open the door, don't I?" I made a mental note to bring oil next time I committed burglary.

I pushed the door open enough to squeeze in, and Diotima pushed in behind me, shut the door, and replaced the latch.

There was a single, large room. A vast expanse of bed lay at the far end. A long divan ran the length of the inner wall. Divan and bed both were covered in overstuffed, embroidered cushions. Two windows overlooked the courtyard; diffuse light passed through curtains hung from the ceiling. Other thicker drapes decorated the walls.

My feet felt funny. I looked down. A thick rug of many colors, with intricate patterns, covered almost the entire floor. I'd never before seen a rug so deep my feet sank into it. It was as if a giant furry creature had died here. Everything stank of sweet scent.

Diotima stood in the middle with her hands on her hips. "I like it," she declared.

"You must be kidding."

"No, I mean it. I wouldn't mind having a room like this." She sat down on a couch and almost sank out of sight. "Of course, it's not very practical." She hauled herself out by holding on to a metal ring, set into the wall. "I wonder what these are for?" Other rings were dotted about the place.

"Probably what you used it for. Getting out of these effete, disgusting seats."

"Do I detect you don't approve of the décor?"

"I can understand a soft woman liking this—"

"Does Mnesiptolema strike you as being soft?"

"No, but I can't imagine any man suffering this abomination."

"Tsk-tsk. I suspect you have much to learn about married life."

I placed a chock of wood over the latch. If anyone tried to enter, it would feel like the latch was stuck.

Diotima opened an ornate chest of carved wood and buried her head inside. She rummaged about. "There's nothing in here except knives, and some stuff made of leather that looks like it's for fighting, and there's a sword at the bottom."

"That'll be Archeptolis' war chest," I grunted.

She closed the lid. "Do men really keep bridles in their chests?"

"I don't know. I never owned a horse until recently."

I'd checked the small chests to either side of the bed. And looked underneath. I opened two closely louvered doors. "I think this must be a cupboard. We might have better luck here."

It was indeed a cupboard, full of clothes and bags.

"What is this stuff?" Diotima ran her hands along one of the dresses, shiny like I'd never seen before. I put out a hand. The material was unbelievably smooth and cool to the touch.

Diotima continued, "Whatever it is, I want some. It's so light! Can you imagine wearing this?"

I could imagine Diotima wearing it. The idea was quite exciting.

The cupboard was quite spacious, deep and wide. Diotima and I worked our way through the contents without any luck.

The only thing left was an expensive-looking rack made of carved cedar. I opened the doors. "Here's a scroll rack. The cases are identical to the one stolen from Thorion. No surprise there, I suppose, but they were foolish to use their own when they wrote."

Voices were approaching from down the corridor. Mnesiptolema and Archeptolis. It was definitely them. We looked at each other in panic.

"They must have returned early," Diotima whispered. "Nicolaos, what will we do?"

There was no escape. We had no time to make it out the window, and even if we did, we'd be spotted immediately by the guards below. If we went out the door we'd run straight into Archeptolis and Mnesiptolema. There was no explaining our presence in their bedroom.

The footsteps stopped at the door.

"Just a moment . . ." I heard Archeptolis say. "Curse it, I dropped the key."

There was nothing for it. I pushed Diotima into the cupboard. I ran to the door, thanking the Gods for the quiet rug, snatched the block, and ran back to the cupboard, jumped inside, and pulled the doors shut behind me.

The door opened.

Diotima and I were wedged among the clothing. I could hear my own breathing, so loud despite my desperate attempts to silence it, I wondered they didn't open the cupboard to see what the noise was. But the surrounding cloth must have muffled the noise, because they didn't. I listened for Diotima. I couldn't hear her breathe, but I felt a rustle as she moved slightly. The louvers on the doors were canted downward. I didn't think they'd see us unless one of them crouched and peered upward or, please Gods no, opened a cupboard door. That thought made me ease back and place clothing between me and the light. It was small cover.

"I gave that slave something to remember, didn't I, Nessie?" Archeptolis boasted. "Striped his back for him."

"So you did, my dear." Mnesiptolema reassured Archeptolis. It was as if she were speaking to a child.

I heard the rustle of clothing. Were they undressing in the middle of the afternoon?

The lid of the war chest opened and shut. I longed to peek through the louvers, but didn't dare.

"Some of these cushions are stained," Archeptolis complained. "Oh, do look at this one. And it had my favorite scene too: slaves being tortured."

"You'll just have to embroider some more, dear." That was Mnesiptolema speaking.

Metal clinked, then snapped.

A whip cracked. "Please! No . . . no . . . aah!"

"Silence, slave. Did I give you permission to speak?"

"No mistress, but I—"

The whip cracked again. Archeptolis let out a yelp of pain, then groaned.

I could stand it no longer. I edged forward enough that I would see through a crack if I put my eye to it. Diotima was already forward. She had one eye screwed shut and the other glued to a gap between the louvers. She pulled back and looked at me, her eyes as wide as dinner plates and her mouth a giant O. She turned back to whatever it was she saw.

I found my own gap, and had to stifle a shout of surprise. Archeptolis was stark naked, facedown on the bed. His legs were spread, his ass pointed straight at us. The cheeks rose like twin mountains of quivering red flesh that reminded me of one of those Persian desserts. His wrists were shackled with slave bracelets, the chains were locked to a pair of the rings in the wall.

Mnesiptolema stood over him. She was dressed in the sort

of outfit worn by slave drivers—a leather belt from which to hang the whip and tools, and a leather jerkin—but hers were gleaming black with oil polish, and the silver studs gleamed. Her breasts pushed through holes in the leather. A variety of whips hung from her belt, like a slave overseer, and one she swung back and forth in her hand.

Mnesiptolema raised her arm and cracked the whip across the back of Archeptolis. I saw his back was already striped and realized the thin, white scars were the result of previous whippings.

"Do you still want a room like this?" I whispered to Diotima.

"I've changed my mind," she whispered back.

Mnesiptolema ceased her whipping when the blood began to drip from his back onto the bedcover. Archeptolis groaned constantly. Now Mnesiptolema began spanking Archeptolis on his behind. When the flesh became red she hit harder and harder. Every slap made a sharp cracking sound. Archeptolis moaned with obvious pleasure. Mnesiptolema grunted in rhythm with her strikes, her face a contortion of fury.

"Roll over, slave."

Archeptolis rolled over, his back raw and bloodied. No wonder the cushions were stained. It must have hurt, I wondered he didn't scream.

Mnesiptolema snapped silver bracelets round Archeptolis' ankles and chained his feet to the corners of the bed. She walked slowly along the side, bent over, and began to play with him.

Archeptolis moaned.

"Silence, slave." She cracked the whip across his thighs.

Archeptolis whimpered but shut up.

Watching Mnesiptolema play with Archeptolis caused a certain stirring in my own blood.

I glanced at Diotima to my side. Her eye was firm against

the gap in the door; she must be seeing everything. Her mouth was one large *O* of astonishment.

As I watched I could feel myself grow more and more excited. What they did on the bed was nothing like what I dreamed of doing, but it didn't matter. They were having sex, and that was the important thing.

Caught in the cupboard I noticed, as I had when we hid behind the tapestry at the warehouse in Ephesus, how very nice Diotima smelled. I put out my hand. She must have felt the movement because she took it in her own. I squeezed. She squeezed back, but she didn't taking her eye off the action. Did she hold my hand for comfort, or because she was excited too?

Mnesiptolema stepped up onto the bed and stood above Archeptolis.

It was all too much. I had to do something. Now or never. I let go of Diotima's hand and edged mine to Diotima's bottom. I waited for her reaction. She still peered through the crack, but I felt her press back the slightest amount. So I put my other hand on her breast.

She gasped, slapped my hand away, and turned to me. "No, Nicolaos. What are you doing?" She said it quietly but with force.

"I would have thought that was obvious," I whispered. "I want to have sex with you."

On the other side of the doors the bed creaked in rhythm. Mnesiptolema moaned loudly.

"In here?" Diotima fairly shrieked. Fortunately the groans on the other side drowned her out.

"Aren't you even a little bit excited, Diotima?"

"Oh! Oh! Oh!"

Diotima looked away. I saw her face was flushed, but whether the emotion was anger or something else I didn't know. She took a step toward me.

"Nicolaos, I—"

"Ooh!" That was Archeptolis.

"Aah!" That was Mnesiptolema.

At least *someone* got to have simultaneous orgasms, I thought sourly.

All was silence in the room. Diotima and I didn't dare continue our argument.

After a long pause Mnesiptolema said, "Time to dress for dinner, dear." She spoke in an entirely normal voice, as if the recent wild sex had never happened.

"Yes, dear," Archeptolis said. "I'm afraid your dress is stained."

"I'll get another."

Uh-oh. Diotima too realized the danger. I quickly pressed through the clothes until my back was to the wall. I edged along into the corner. Diotima squeezed into the other back corner. I took a deep breath and held it.

The cupboard door opened enough for an arm to reach in. A hand groped about, feeling the dresses.

"No, not that one," Mnesiptolema said to herself.

The door opened farther. Light spilled into the center. Only the large amount of cloth and the size of the cupboard prevented Diotima and me from being illuminated. Even so, I could see Diotima clearly, and she stared back at me in horror. If Mnesiptolema poked her head in . . .

The hand crept toward me, like a giant white tarantula. I shrank back as far as I could. She felt each dress as her hand moved along the line.

All our movement had stirred up dust. My nose began to tickle. I told myself firmly not to think about it. If I didn't think about sneezing, the feeling would go away. The hand crept closer. Thinking about not sneezing made me want to sneeze. My nose tickled more.

Her hand hesitated, and she stopped talking. Had she noticed something?

I was almost cross-eyed watching her fingers, but I didn't

dare move now. The fingers lifted, the tarantula was about to strike.

"Remind me to have the slave turn out this cupboard. I'm noticing dust in the air."

Don't sneeze . . . don't sneeze . . .

The fingers relaxed, felt along the top of the dress and caressed the material. If she went any farther I'd be—

"This is it."

She grabbed the dress off its hook, pulled it out, and shut the door.

The moment the light disappeared I put a hand to my nose and squeezed hard while I exhaled gently through my mouth. The tickle disappeared.

Mnesiptolema and Archeptolis dressed, and left the room. I could hear my heart pound in my ears.

We waited a few moments, to make sure they weren't coming back, then quickly exited the room ourselves. The corridor was empty. We stopped outside my door.

"What do we do now?" Diotima asked.

"You heard Mnesiptolema. It's time for dinner."

"The hard part will be to face them across a table without staring in horror or bursting out in laughter. Maybe both. Do you think Themistocles knows?"

"Who can say? Maybe it suits him to have a son and daughter behave like this."

"I can't imagine how."

"It gives him a certain hold over them. Mnesiptolema doesn't matter, but can you imagine the reaction if men knew about Archeptolis? He'd be mocked until he suicided."

"Are you sure? There are lots of Athenian men who get up to some pretty weird things with each other."

"But that's different, it's between men. To enjoy being beaten by a woman? No, it's either suicide or ridicule."

Diotima had an odd expression on her face. "But you think it would be all right, if it was between men?"

"Happens all the time. You know that," I said, as a matter of fact.

Diotima hesitated. "Nicolaos? You wouldn't . . . that is, with your men friends, do you . . . uh . . ."

Diotima blushed bright red. She couldn't even bring herself to ask the question. Diotima's morals were conservative enough to please the most prudish old woman. It comes of having a mother who's an erotic courtesan.

"Me? No. I like girls. I like you, Diotima."

Diotima's face was pure relief. "Keep it that way," she said firmly. "I'm going to my room to change. And you better wipe yourself down, and change your chiton."

I watched her swaying behind retreat into her room and the door shut behind her, and heard the bolt fall into place. Then I cursed myself for an opportunity lost. It had been the perfect moment to invite myself into her room. Or for her to invite me. What was wrong with the girl? Or was it me? Was I doing something wrong?

16

Whoever obeys the Gods,
to him they particularly listen.

I opened the window in my room next morning to see bright sunshine, and Barzanes in the garden, barefoot and wearing a pair of loose white trousers and a white vest of a material so thin and translucent it could not possibly have done him any good. As I watched, he bent to pick up sticks and twigs and place them in the stack in his arms, a task so menial no ranking Persian lord should have consented to it. I was intrigued, so I woke Diotima to go for a walk. By the time we arrived, we found him before a brazier, in which burned a fire.

The vest Barzanes wore was held by a girdle of fine white cloth wrapped about his waist three times and tied at the front and then the back. His chest was smooth and perfectly visible beneath the material. Knowing Diotima's penchant for male chests, I glanced at her to see what effect this one had, and I was relieved to see she wasn't staring overmuch.

As I watched, Barzanes untied his girdle. I thought he was about to take it off, but then he tied it again. He went to the brazier. A table stood beside, on which was a small pile of apples, a flask, a bowl, and two vases of flowers, one of hyacinths, the other of anemones, whose name means wind and whose petals are the color of fresh blood, and on the ground a pile of sticks and another of wood chips.

Barzanes added wood chips to the fire and poured in a thin stream of milk from the wooden flask into the brazier. The fire died with the milk and then flared up. Barzanes stared into the flames without blinking. The smoke from the fire was sweet and I realized the wood chips he'd thrown were cedar.

I didn't think he'd seen us approach from the side, but he said, "I will chant the prayer in Greek."

> *I curse the Daevas, the evil spirits.*
> *I declare myself a worshipper of Ahura Mazda,*
> *   a supporter of Zarathustra,*
> *Enemy of the Daevas, lover of Ahura Mazda and his*
> *   teaching,*
> *I praise the Amesha Spentas, the seven good angels,*
> *I worship the Amesha Spentas.*
> *All good comes from Ahura Mazda.*

He finished the prayer and threw the sticks he'd gathered onto the fire. No Hellene ritual is complete without the sacrifice of an animal; I looked around for Barzanes' sacrifice, but there was none, not so much as a rabbit or a pigeon. It seemed the wood was the sacrifice.

"It's a beautiful prayer, Barzanes," Diotima said.

"It is more than beautiful. It is truth, the prayer we call the Fravarane."

"You could not possibly have spoken so in our language unless the words were ready."

"I translated the Fravarane into Greek long ago, in the hope the Hellenes might hear the words of Zarathustra and believe. Despite my efforts, the Hellenes of Ionia do not comprehend."

"Ahura Mazda is your God?"

"Ahura Mazda means, in the ancient language, Wise Lord,

who created the world and all the good things in it, and all mankind, including you."

"Ahura Mazda must be Zeus then."

"Was it not Zeus who killed his own father?" Barzanes asked.

Diotima hesitated before saying, "Well, yes, but there was a good reason. You see—"

"He raped several women."

"Not all at once! But yes, there were one or two incidents—"

"Four or five, and your King of the Gods once arranged for a man to have his liver eaten out for all eternity."

"Prometheus had it coming to him."

"A man must choose between Ahura Mazda and the Lie," Barzanes carried on over her, seemingly unaware he had angered Diotima. "It is surely obvious your Zeus could never compare to Ahura Mazda who is above all earthly passions."

Diotima said, "Oh, come now. Can you really look around you, Barzanes, and tell me Love and War and Lust and Death don't rule our lives? Wisdom and chaos and motherhood and the madness of wine and the beauty of music, they and the seasons and the sun are what we Hellenes worship, and anyone with the wit to open his eyes can see they're as real as a smack in the face."

I grabbed Diotima's hand in case she decided to demonstrate the reality of a smack in the face.

"You fail to mention ethics," Barzanes said. "A typical Hellene omission."

"Ethics come of philosophy."

"Your philosophy is the imaginings of mortal men, and therefore incapable of perfection."

"I'll have you know, Barzanes, I am a philosopher." Diotima was openly angry now.

He said, "It is religion which defines right behavior. My vest contains a pocket. You see it here in the middle of my chest?"

"The empty one? Yes."

"It is not empty. Within this pocket are all the good deeds I have done, and all the evil I have committed. I hope, when I take them out and examine them, that the good will outnumber the bad."

His hand chopped through the air like an axe and his voice rose. "Your Gods are little better than bandits. They lie, and cheat, and fornicate with whomever they can catch."

"When you're a God, you can get away with these things," I said.

"Not even your Gods can escape judgment. It is sung in the Gâthâs, all who die are led by the angels to a narrow bridge across a vast chasm. The angel Mithra, who walks in shadow and dispenses justice, waits upon the bridge, and judges the hearts of those who cross. Friends of the Lie will be cast off the bridge into the chasm of molten iron to spend eternity in Worst Existence, but if you are a friend of the Truth, you will pass on to the House of Best Purpose."

"Mithra, who walks in shadow and dispenses justice" . . . it sounded like his own job. Did Barzanes think he was Mithra?

As we walked away Diotima whispered, "Is he sane? I've never seen anyone so convinced of his own righteousness."

"I'm thinking of that pocket he's wearing. I wish we could get a look inside to see what's there."

"It's a metaphor."

"We know that, but does he?"

"He believes every word he said. He really thinks his God will judge what he does."

"Yes," I said, glum. "Would a man do evil if he thought his God would punish him for it? If that sort of thing catches on, we investigators will be out of a job."

We retreated to a faraway corner of the paradise, well away from Barzanes.

"The dirty fingernails have to be significant," Diotima said. "We've been assuming Brion was killed because he was a link in the chain that sent the letter to Athens. Maybe there's another reason."

I said, "Why was Brion consulting the book in the temple?"

"We're not all ignorant like you. Even practical merchants can love philosophy, you know. Why else would anyone read Heraclitus?"

"Tell me about Heraclitus."

"Brilliant philosopher. Deeply obscure. His theory of the *logos*—"

"Yes, yes, I'm sure," I interrupted. "Now tell me about him as a man."

"A man?" Diotima repeated, as if this were a strange new thought. "Oh, he was quite mad."

"You don't say."

"He wandered about the hills outside Ephesus for years, ate nothing but grass and refused to come down. Got sick of it, of course, was forced to return to the city and dropped dead soon after. They buried him in the middle of the agora, as you know. Why do you ask?"

"I don't know. What I do know is, Brion spent days studying Heraclitus. Then he came to Magnesia and got his hands dirty."

"Mnesiptolema said he had business interests here."

"She did, but couldn't say what."

"Or wouldn't," Diotima added.

"Why did Araxes warn me against taking Asia back to Magnesia?"

"Probably for the same reason Araxes carried her off in the first place. Whatever that is."

"Something else: why did Brion react as he did when he saw her?"

"I wondered about that myself," Diotima said. "Brion seemed to point to Ephesus." She paused in thought. "Maybe he wanted us to take her there?"

"Why?"

"Beats me."

"If Araxes killed Brion, why would they agree about Asia?"

"That is a little weird, isn't it?" Diotima said. Neither of us had an idea.

"All right, what about the pots in Themistocles' office? They're the same style as the ones we found in the warehouse, and Themistocles says his amphorae are the only remains of the treasure Polycrates brought with him when he came here and was murdered."

"I still have those coins." She rummaged around in her priestess pouch and held them out on her palm. We both stared down at the electrum coins with the lion heads, willing them to tell us something.

Diotima said, "We're looking at the lost treasure of Polycrates."

"Obviously. Brion got it from somewhere around here." I had an idea where too, but I wasn't going to say until I'd proved it.

"It's why he suddenly began his visits to Magnesia. Then he sent it to his trusted contact Thorion—"

"Because if he tried to off-load it anywhere in Ionia, the coins would be spotted immediately for what they were. The treasure's probably supposed to belong to the Great King. We're getting close, Nico. We almost have it." Diotima liked nothing so much as eliminating a problem. She laughed and kissed me. The kiss developed and—

"No." She pushed me away. "I didn't mean to do that."

"I wondered when you'd remember."

Asia came skipping through the low bushes. She stopped dead at the sight of Diotima and me holding each other, burst into tears, and ran away.

Diotima and I looked at each other.

"What's her problem?" I asked.

"I can guess," Diotima said darkly.

"I think you should talk to her," I said to Diotima.

"Me? What have I got to do with it? *You* were her master. *You're* the one she's mooning over."

"All the more reason for *you* to do the talking," I said. "It's a woman thing."

"You're a coward."

"No, I'm a man."

"Same thing."

"You want to go down *there*?" Cleophantus asked. His hair whipped across his face in the strong breeze.

Our horses stood upon the hill where I'd seen the Maeander River for the first time. I'd found Cleophantus in the palace, and practically dragged him to the stables and onto a horse.

Now I stared at the meandering flow and said, "Remember the farmer you told me about, the one who drowned, whose farmland changed? I want to see his property."

"Why?"

"I'm looking for buried treasure."

"No, seriously, why?"

I insisted, so Cleophantus went first and our mounts picked their way downslope to the muddy bottom. Their hooves sank into the ground with every step and I was glad it was them walking through this muck and not me.

Cleophantus asked, "What are we looking for?"

"A big hole, maybe, or a storage pit, or even a low building. I'm not sure."

We picked our way over the surface, finding nothing.

"We could ask at the farmhouse," Cleophantus said.

"Is there one?"

"This way." He led me across the field until, around a cluster of tall bushes on firmer ground, I saw an old, small house in a sad state of disrepair.

"Wait, Nico, what's this?" Cleophantus slid off his horse

and bent to pick something out of the mud. He rubbed at it, then held it up to show me the dull yellow-white of an electrum stater. Cleophantus looked upon it in wonder. "How did you know to come here?" he asked.

"I knew your uncle Brion had found the lost treasure of Polycrates, and proceeded to smuggle it to Athens, where it would belong to him and not the Great King. My guess is sixty years ago, when Oroetes buried the treasure, this was dry land. The Maeander covered it after his death and didn't release its hold until now. The timing of Brion's discovery, and the Maeander revealing this patch of land, matched too closely to be coincidence."

"Brilliant, Nico."

"Also, the farmer shows the usual sign of someone who's met Araxes."

"What sign is that?"

"He's dead."

I looked him in the eye. "Cleophantus, you mustn't tell your father or Barzanes about this."

"I won't. Nico, there's nothing left but these few coins. Did Brion spirit the rest away before his death?"

"I doubt it, for two reasons. Firstly, the coin you found was on the surface of the mud. It would have sunk had it been there since Brion died, so it must have been dropped recently."

"Very good, and the second reason?"

"There are men standing behind you holding swords."

Cleophantus whirled to see what I'd just seen: men emerging from the dilapidated farmhouse. One of them had white hair.

"We're safe, Cleophantus. We have horses, they're on foot."

Two of the men raised bows.

"Run!"

The horses couldn't raise their hooves quickly enough in the mud. The best they could manage was a fast walk, and even that was only because we kicked and whacked their flanks without mercy.

Arrows fell around us. The distance and the strong breeze made it difficult for the archers, but it would only take one hit, and a horse is a big target.

Araxes and his men with swords began wading across the muddy field. The horses were faster, but not by much.

Cleophantus shouted, "Turn your back to them! It'll present the smallest profile!"

It seemed an insane thing to turn my back on an enemy, but Cleophantus was right.

"Lean forward!"

I leaned forward over the shoulders of my horse, barely in time because an arrow whistled over my shoulder. Sitting properly it would have taken me in the back.

"Nico!" Araxes shouted as he squelched after us.

"It's Nicolaos!" I shouted back.

"Nicolaos, you're starting to irritate me. It doesn't bode well for our relationship."

Araxes had stopped walking because our mounts had found firmer ground and were moving normally. We didn't stop, a lucky shot could still bring down one of our horses.

"I'll be back, Araxes."

"It won't do you the least good. We're finished here. Bring back soldiers if you like; we'll be gone."

Months passed. Two months, three, I'm not sure, because life in the palace was like living in a strange land where one day was much like another. None of my peers—the children of Themistocles—had a job that helped mark the passage of time. Mnesiptolema was a priestess of Cybele, apparently because the life of Themistocles had been saved by that goddess during his escape from Athens, and he had built a temple in the middle of Magnesia in gratitude. Archeptolis owned a small business to buy and export slaves, but it was a hobby more than a serious effort. Knowing what we did of their habits, Diotima and I were sure the enterprise was merely an excuse for Archeptolis and his dear Nessie to abuse the poor, unlucky slaves. Nicomache liked to clean up after the immediate family, and generally pretended that she lived a normal life in a household in Athens. Cleophantus pottered about with his horses and rarely ventured outside the stables.

During our ride home from the farm, after we had escaped Araxes and his bandits, Cleophantus and I had debated what to do, then had gone to see Barzanes to ask him for soldiers. We manufactured a story of stumbling across brigands while out for a ride. It was sufficient to bring out Barzanes and a squad of horsemen, without the need to tell him of the treasure, or that it was Araxes we chased.

But Araxes had told the truth. The farm was abandoned when we returned, and all we found to prove our story were discarded arrows. Barzanes put the incident down to highwaymen, and forgot about it.

There was little I could do to further the investigation. I'd never appreciated before how much my work depended on the authority to investigate. Likewise there was nothing I could do to help Athens. Even if there had been, it's not certain I would have, because as the time passed and I settled into life in the palace and the paradise, I became increasingly detached from my old life.

Cleophantus gave me riding lessons, which became increasingly more advanced until I was able to do tricks such as jump onto a moving horse and perform battlefield maneuvers. It was worth coming to Magnesia merely to learn these things.

Themistocles invited me for lunch on a regular basis. At these lunches he would quiz me about life in Athens since he had left, often asking after this man or that, frequently making acerbic remarks, or relating a scandalous story; or we would discuss the democracy, a subject on which I could hold forth with some expertise; or he would talk about politics and I would listen, learning from a master.

I always felt during these discussions that he was nostalgic for home. One day he said to me, "Truth to tell, Nicolaos, you are the first person to visit with even a slight knowledge of Athenian politics. I miss it." He sighed. "I don't suppose you could persuade Pericles to come here, could you? I'd love to talk with him now that he's a man."

"It doesn't seem likely, especially if he knows the story of Polycrates."

Themistocles laughed and said, "No, I suppose not."

I knew I passed over information at these talks—Themistocles took notes whenever I spoke of the democracy, or of people who had risen to power since his departure—but really, it was little more than gossip.

After many of these lunches had passed, I woke one morning to the realization I had learned more from Themistocles in a few weeks than ever I had from Pericles. At the start of our association, Pericles had promised to teach me his art of politics, and sometimes, grudgingly, he had talked to me, but never in the way Themistocles did, nor so willingly, nor with such familiarity. I was eventually emboldened to ask Themistocles a question that had been burning in my mind.

One day over wine after a fine meal I said, "Themistocles, there are those who say you were condemned out of jealousy, and those who say they feared you would make yourself tyrant, and those who say you helped the Persians. Tell me the truth; when the Athenians condemned you for treason, were you guilty?"

Themistocles picked up his wine cup and said, "You want to know *the truth*?"

"Yes."

"You sound like Barzanes, he's forever going on about truth. Personally I've always found that which men believe to be more important."

He paused. "The truth is, lad, I was innocent."

"Then how were you accused?"

"Because my friend Pausanias was guilty. The two best commanders in the war were myself from Athens and Pausanias of Sparta. Afterward Pausanias got himself into trouble with his fellow Spartans. They discovered he was in negotiations with the Great King."

"The charge was true?"

"Oh yes. Pausanias was ambitious and arrogant." Themistocles laughed. "Not like me at all. In any case, after he was found out, Pausanias took refuge in a temple where the Spartans couldn't touch him because of the sanctuary. They solved that problem by bricking up the entire building with Pausanias inside. He starved to death."

"Urrk."

"Indeed. After that unpleasant episode, all eyes turned to me, the reasoning being if one great general can betray Hellas, then so can two. The Spartans, who had always disliked me, provided incriminating letters—I swear they were forged—but with the example of the recently departed Pausanias to go by, I decided the bed of my oldest enemy was the safest place to sleep. So here I am, and all the better for it. I have wealth and comfort beyond anything I could have imagined had I remained in Hellas. I would have been undone, had I not been undone."

"You give that toast at every dinner."

"So I do." He drank off an entire cup of wine and laughed. "The irony is, Pausanias was rightly condemned for helping the Persians, while I was innocent. Yet here I am, the innocent man doing exactly what the guilty tried and failed."

———

I lay in bed one night thinking on this when the door opened. Mnesiptolema stood there, her figure silhouetted by the light streaming through the corridor windows.

"You've been a naughty boy, Nicolaos." She swayed into the room. She wore one of the shiny, smooth Persian dresses from her cupboard, and it actually clung to her skin. For all that the material covered her, she may as well have been naked.

I blinked. "I have?" I asked.

"Oh yes." She leaned forward and stroked me under the chin. "I like naughty boys, Nico."

I gulped.

"I know your secret, Nicolaos. You were in the cupboard, weren't you?"

"How do you kn—that is, what cupboard?"

She gave a throaty laugh and sat on the bed beside me, crossing her shapely legs.

I jumped up. "Have you noticed the room's a bit warm? I'll just open the shutters."

She pulled me back onto the bed beside her.

"Let's leave them shut," she said. "And I will answer your question. I could smell you, Nicolaos. I could smell your fear. I like the smell of fear. But you know that, don't you? You were watching."

Mnesiptolema laughed. "I enjoyed teasing you, edging my fingers closer and closer. Did you think I'd expose you?"

She reached up her hand and teased my hair, curling it around her fingers. She gave it a sharp tug.

"Do you want to know why I didn't? Archeptolis would have killed you, you know. He'd have had no choice."

"Wouldn't you have enjoyed doing it yourself?" I asked.

She gave the low, throaty laugh again. "I thought about it, as I stood there. But I have another plan for you, Nicolaos, one I've delayed for days while I fantasized. Desire withheld is all the more exciting, don't you think?"

"Not as such." A mental image of Diotima crowded my sight.

I didn't inquire about Mnesiptolema's plans. At least she hadn't mentioned Diotima. I had a feeling if Mnesiptolema had known Diotima was there too, her decision might have gone the other way.

"Since we're being personal, aren't you worried other men will find out what Archeptolis is really like?"

Mnesiptolema shrugged. "Slaves talk. No one listens. No man enters our room." She smirked. "And outside, Archeptolis is a bully."

"You like that, do you?"

Mnesiptolema put her hand on my thigh and leaned toward me. "What do you think?"

I could smell her breath. It was sweet. She must have been drinking rose water. Mnesiptolema rubbed her hand up and down my chest. I began to react.

"Aren't you worried about what Barzanes would say?"

"Barzanes? Yes, perceptive of you. But he lusts after weepy little Nicomache. Gods know why. I doubt Barzanes wants to upset the family while there's a chance Father will give Nicomache to him. But you, Nicolaos, you must fear Barzanes."

"Why?"

"Don't you know? He's the Eyes and Ears of the King."

"You mean he's a friend of Artaxerxes?" I had no idea what she meant.

Mnesiptolema stopped rubbing and looked at me in astonishment. "Didn't you learn *anything* about how the empire works before you came here?"

"The trip was on short notice."

"Artaxerxes has no friends. The Great King can't afford such luxuries. The Eyes and Ears report straight to the King. Even the satraps fear them. The King's Eyes and Ears are . . . auditors."

"That doesn't sound so bad."

"You think so? What they audit is the empire. The King can't be everywhere at once. He relies on the Eyes and Ears to tell him what his officers are doing, which satraps are more than usually corrupt, who's incompetent, who's abusing his position, who might be too ambitious. Barzanes watches everyone, including Father, *especially* Father."

"Informers," I said flatly.

"And hatchet men."

"Political agents?"

"That too. Spies. When the Great King has a sensitive problem that needs fixing, he calls for the Eyes and Ears. They're picked men, smart, trained, utterly trustworthy."

Barzanes was my opposite number, except he was a trained professional while I was an amateur feeling my way. Had Barzanes recognized me for what I was?

I said, "If I were a satrap I wouldn't want one of these men on my doorstep."

"They don't get a choice."

"So Themistocles doesn't want Barzanes here?"

"Who knows what my father thinks. Sometimes I think he even keeps secrets from himself."

"I wonder the satraps don't arrange accidents for them."

She laughed. "The Eyes and Ears of the King are the safest men in the Empire. If one of them dies on assignment, there's an army in that satrap's province before you can blink."

"So Themistocles has no choice but to be nice to Barzanes," I mused.

Mnesiptolema shrugged. "Father's not about to bite the hand that feeds him. Especially not a hand that could return him as satrap for Athens."

Mnesiptolema began to wind her fingers through my hair once more.

"I know why you were in that cupboard, Nicolaos."

I gulped. "You do?"

"You want me, don't you? No, don't pull away. There's no use denying it. Why else would you have been hiding, watching me whip that fat fool."

"Mnesiptolema—"

Mnesiptolema sneered. "He's fat and cries like a baby."

"Then why do you stay with him?"

"Divorce my own brother? What would Father say?"

"It is an unusual situation, isn't it?"

"Father insisted, you know, after I became pregnant by Archeptolis when I was twelve."

"Dear Gods, aren't you ashamed?"

"It's shocking, I know. My taste in men was abysmal." She laughed. "So, I fell pregnant and Father insisted we marry. I hated him for that."

"Archeptolis?"

"Father. He was the one who made me. I could have simply had the bloody child and then killed it. No one would have cared, people expose babies all the time. But Father gets weirdly sentimental about that sort of thing; can't stand to see a child hurt. That's why there are so many bloody girls in this family.

"Then I miscarried the baby, after all that fuss. It died in my womb and I had to push it out anyway. So there I was with a dead baby and a worthless husband."

"No other children?"

She shrugged. "Been pregnant a few times, but they always die."

"I'm sorry, Mnesiptolema."

"Probably because their father is such a weakling. But you, tough, strong, handsome Nicolaos, you wouldn't cry at the first hint of pain, would you? No, you'd endure, rise above it . . . yes, rise—"

Mnesiptolema pushed me back on the bed and jumped on

top. She kissed me deeply, then bit my lip hard. All the while her hands were fondling down below, which had exactly the effect she wanted.

She might have had a fine body, but the rest of Mnesiptolema didn't bear thinking about, particularly her mating habits. Thoughts of ice-cold water had no effect—her hands were too skilled—but the memory of what she'd done to Archeptolis—that she probably wanted to do to me—and the thought of a whip in her hand with me in my erect state had the desired effect.

I deflated.

I lay there and thought to myself, Diotima would be proud.

That was a mistake. The mental image of Diotima sent me back up, straight and hard.

"My Gods!" Mnesiptolema said in delight. "Thanks be to Aphrodite."

The door opened.

"What's going on here?"

Diotima stood in the doorway, hands on hips, where Mnesiptolema had stood not long before. She saw me lying flat on the bed, with the voluptuous and surprisingly strong Mnesiptolema straddled on top of me.

"Oh, hello Diotima," I said.

"This one's taken, dearie," Mnesiptolema said. "Try the next room."

"You haven't answered my question."

"You *are* innocent, aren't you, little girl? Nicolaos lusts after me."

"I don't believe you. Nicolaos would never cheat on me. Why don't you throw her out, Nico?"

"Are you going to let this woman tell you what to do?" Mnesiptolema demanded.

I pondered which answer would cause the least shouting.

When I said nothing (it seemed the safest choice), Mnesiptolema swung a calculating eye from me to Diotima and back again. "Well, you have reasonable taste, I'll say that for you, little girl."

"I'm not little, old woman," Diotima said.

Mnesiptolema sneered, "You're too young for some things, if the way Nicolaos responded to me is any sign."

"Oh, is that so?" Diotima glared at me.

Mnesiptolema said, "You need to service a man properly if you expect to keep him."

I watched Diotima's reaction to this with some interest. She went bright red.

Mnesiptolema climbed off—careful to knee me in the groin as she did—pointed and said, "Look at the poor man!"

Two female heads observed me as I lay on the bed in a rampant state. I stood, to regain what little dignity I could. Now I was both standing and . . . er . . . outstanding. I decided the only way to handle this was to throw out both women.

I said, "That's enough from both of you. Leave at—"

"You can give yourself all the airs of cleverness you like," Mnesiptolema spoke over me at Diotima. "But as a woman you're a total failure."

Diotima said, "Oh? Well I've seen what you do with that slab of rancid grease you call a husband. You want failure? Imagine the laughter when the whole world knows—"

Mnesiptolema slapped Diotima.

Diotima hit Mnesiptolema. She hit hard, but her aim was poor and the blow landed on Nessie's shoulder. It spun Nessie around but otherwise did no damage. Nessie staggered back a step, in surprise that Diotima had actually hit her, before she lurched forward to grab Diotima by the throat with both hands. Before I could intervene, Diotima went over backward and Mnesiptolema landed on top of her with an "Oomph."

I knew from experience how surprisingly heavy Mnesiptolema was. Diotima had been in fights before, but always at a distance with her bow, never hand-to-hand. She struggled under the weight. She turned her eyes to me and I could see the fear in my girl's eyes.

Mnesiptolema clawed her right hand in preparation to rake Diotima's face.

"No you don't!" I grabbed Mnesiptolema's raised arm from behind and yanked her off Diotima so hard, Mnesiptolema stumbled across the room and into the opposite wall.

I ordered, "Stop this, both of you."

Mnesiptolema pushed herself off the wall, and launched into a diving tackle, as if she were a boy in roughhouse play, except Nessie wasn't playing. She caught me around the midriff and it was my turn to go down. But unlike Diotima I knew what to do. I rolled back, letting her momentum drive me, so that I somersaulted backward and came up in one motion. Mnesiptolema had flown over my head. She came up as quickly and grabbed me from behind with an arm across my throat. She was tall enough that her face was at my neck and I wondered if she would bite me. I easily held back her arm from across my throat, but I was perplexed what to do next. It was obvious Nessie would keep coming at us. How was I to end this? I couldn't knock out the daughter of my host.

Diotima rose up from the floor, right before my eyes. She said, "Nico, duck."

I didn't. Instead I tilted my head to the side.

Diotima threw an almighty punch, exactly where my head had been.

She didn't miss this time. Diotima's fist whistled past my ear and struck Nessie square in the forehead. Mnesiptolema never saw it coming. She fell to the floor, unconscious.

Diotima shook her hand and said, "Ouch. That felt good."

"Are you all right?" I asked her.

Diotima looked down at the unmoving Mnesiptolema and asked, "Is she still alive?"

"You didn't hit her that hard."

"But I did hit her, Nico." Diotima sounded fearful, and with good reason, but there was no point worrying about it now.

"I'm glad you did," I reassured her. "She hurt you."

"If she tells Themistocles, I'll be in huge trouble."

"No, I will be, and I'll deal with it. It's my responsibility. You're my responsibility." I grabbed Diotima by both arms and looked into her eyes. "Diotima, I'll never let anyone hurt you. Never. You understand?"

"Yes, Nico."

I took her in my arms and hugged her tight.

While I held her I said, "I'm sorry about Mnesiptolema. You finding us like that. Believe me, nothing happened."

Diotima laughed. "I know that for sure, and I understand, Nico. Remember, days ago? It was *me* after all who said I knew you'd enjoy throwing her. For the record, punching had its moments too." She let go of me to look down at the body. "Er . . . what do we do with her now?"

"I don't know, but she won't be happy when she wakes up." I didn't mention that by tomorrow Nessie would have a lump on her forehead the size of an apple.

The door opened. "What's all the noise?"

Archeptolis stood there, fat and naked but for a loincloth. He looked down to see his wife, Nessie, out cold and naked at my feet, then looked back up at us. Diotima and I stared at him in horror. He smiled.

"Ooh, is it a party? Hit me too!" He tugged and dropped the loincloth, exposing himself, and licked his lips in Diotima's direction.

"Oh Gods!" Diotima swung her arm before I could stop her and punched out Archeptolis with a single blow to the jaw. He dropped to the ground beside his wife.

Diotima said, "I've had it with these perverts."

She stepped over his unconscious body and down the corridor.

I dragged the bodies of evidence back to their own room. It wasn't easy. Questions would be asked if I was spotted hauling the Satrap's unconscious children down the corridor by their feet. I had to pull the overweight Archeptolis by the ankles. I hefted Mnesiptolema in my arms with difficulty, a deadweight, and tried not to drop her, nor notice the breasts that pressed against my chest, and deposited her on their bed next to her husband.

I left a note beside them where they were sure to see it, pointing out that if the night's fun ever came to light then we would all be losers, and shut the door behind me.

I found Diotima in her room. She sat on her bed, with her head in her hands. Tears ran down her cheeks.

Diotima said sadly, "I shouldn't have done that, should I?"

"Do you mean when you threatened the daughter of our all-powerful host, when you brawled with her, or when you punched out his son? No, probably not."

"But the bitch was right, Nico. I'm a failure."

"You're the most competent woman I know. When you return to the Artemision—"

"I'm not going back to the Artemision. I failed there too."

"Oh. You mean the fight with the other priestesses?"

"Who told you?"

"Geros."

"There's something wrong with me, Nico. People just don't like me."

I reached out and held her hand. "I like you."

"Do you know how many other friends I have?"

I thought back over all the time we'd spent together. Who had she mentioned?

"Er . . ."

"That's right. Nobody. Never in my life have I had a girl-friend to talk to. No prospect of a decent husband—I had to flee my own city to even have a chance—no future in the temple because everyone hates me. I'm as doomed as any woman can be." She drew a deep breath. "You know where my life is going? I'll end up one of those withered old women who keep the temple clean and boss the slave girls, whom everyone pities because she never lived a proper life."

"I'm sure you won't."

"I'm sure I will." She stood and looked me in the eyes. "But I've decided something, Nico. If that's my fate, I'm going to please myself and have a life first."

"What's that mean?" I asked, worried. "Diotima, don't do anything rash."

"It means this."

Diotima reached up to the shoulder pins of her dress and pulled them out. She shrugged and her chiton fell to the floor. Diotima stood before me naked. My heart raced.

She said, "Get onto that bed."

I don't remember being tired in the days that followed, but I certainly should have been. Diotima and I spent our days in the pavilions of the paradise, and our nights in my room. I'm not sure how many, because I wasn't counting. The entire army of the Great King could have marched past, and as long as they didn't actually tread on us as we rolled in the grass I doubt I would have noticed. For all I knew, the Third Persian War had begun.

Whatever. I was sure Pericles could handle it. It was about time he did some useful work.

Our only concession to the real world was to avoid Archeptolis and Mnesiptolema as much as possible. Of course, we had to meet at dinner, where relations were formal but no worse. When we passed in the corridor, a frosty nod sufficed.

Diotima ceased chewing on her thumbnail. It looked almost normal. In between making love we reverted to habit: we talked about death. But neither of us could see how to make any headway. We were confident we knew the story of the pots and the treasure; it seemed reasonable to think Thorion was killed for the letter, but every other line had run cold. The letter and the smuggled pottery appeared to be unrelated, and above all, we still didn't know why Brion had to die.

"Hey, Nicolaos." A man approached: Philodios, the frustrated torturer. "Got a letter for you."

I sighed, let go of Diotima, and sat up, dragging my mind back to what passed for reality in Themistocles' palace, populated as it was by an incestuous couple, a brutal Persian spy who worried about ethics, and an overweight strategic genius suffering from relevance deprivation, not to mention Diotima and me totally in love. Roaming the streets outside the palace walls was the nicest assassin you could hope to meet. Somewhere among that bunch was the killer of Brion.

"A letter for me?" I opened the tablets at once and read the first line. "It's from my father."

SOPHRONISCUS SAYS THIS TO HIS SON NICOLAOS: GLAD TO HEAR YOU'VE COME TO YOUR SENSES. DELIGHTED WITH YOUR CHOICE OF GIRL.

"What does he say?" Diotima asked.

"He says he's delighted we're together. He must have changed his mind," I said, confused. "But, how did he know?"

"Got another message for you," said Philodios. "The Satrap wants to see you. At once."

Themistocles was in his office. He came to the point straight-away.

"I'm not a harsh man with my children, Nicolaos. You've probably noticed that. Some might say I've spoiled them, but I find it hard to say no."

"You're a father who loves his children, Themistocles. You give thought to their happiness, and that's a fine thing. More fathers should do it."

"I'm glad you see it that way, because Asia has asked me for you to be her husband. I take it you have no objections?"

"I . . . uh . . ." I choked. Everything went black. I can't have fainted, for Themistocles didn't notice, but when I came to my senses I heard, "You're young to be marrying, of course. Ideally you need another ten years, but you're a man of talent. When you arrived, Nicolaos, I confess I only spoke to you because I was homesick. Since then I've come to appreciate your quali-ties, particularly your ambition. In some ways, you remind me of me at the same age. You have promise, young man."

What would happen to me if I refused? Nothing good. This had to be done with tact.

"I'm deeply honored," I said. "Honored and surprised. But Themistocles, much as I admire Asia, I would have to ask my father for permission."

With any luck, my father would say no, and even if he didn't, the delay would buy me time to work out how to get out of this.

"I've already written to him," Themistocles said. "These things are for the elders to arrange, you know. Your father's reply arrived this moment. He said yes. I'm not surprised, the dowry I offered was generous, if I say so myself. Welcome to the family, son."

"I'll refuse."

As she wept Diotima said, "No, you have to marry Asia."

Diotima blew her nose and wiped her eyes. "She can give you position, status, wealth . . . everything I can't. Think about your future."

"What about yours?"

"I don't have one. I told you."

"We could run off together."

"And do what? I don't want you to live the life Araxes does. You were always ambitious, Nico. To rise high in Athens is what you've always wanted."

"Not if I marry Asia. It puts me in Themistocles' camp."

That stopped her. "Oh no, Nico, you can't! Thorion's family is waiting for you to clear his name."

"Do I have a choice? Asia's dowry includes a Persian alliance, obviously," I said. "It's not like Athens offers me much of a future, and Themistocles is very persuasive. There's only one problem. I don't want to marry Asia. I want you."

"Asia's the best offer you'll ever get," she said.

"I know."

"You should marry her and fight for Athens."

"I'd rather marry you and maybe fight for Persia."

"It's not an option, on both counts."

That night I was alone when I opened my bedroom door for the first time in many nights. I was so preoccupied I dropped my clothing on the floor and climbed onto the bed before I noticed a lump.

"Asia, what in Hades are you doing here?"

"Waiting for you, master."

"Oh." Of course. She was naked beneath the blanket. I could see the tops of her round and remarkably well-developed breasts and one nipple poking out.

"Well, you can't stay."

"But aren't we to be married, master?"

"We're not married yet, and please stop calling me master."

"I thought you liked it? You insisted after you bought me."

"Well, yes," I conceded. "But it's different now."

She nodded happily. "I'll be your wife."

"No, because you're the daughter of Themistocles. Call me Nicolaos. Or Nico."

"Yes, master." She grinned. "Nicolaos."

She'd folded her dress and left it lying on a couch. I picked it up and held it out to her. "Please put it on, Asia."

Asia jumped up stark naked and said. "Don't you want me, master? You think I'm ugly."

"I think you're remarkably pretty, and young, and available, and . . ." I looked her up and down and gulped and thought of cold water.

If Diotima was the embodiment of Artemis of the Hunt, then Asia was the tool of Eris, Goddess of Confusion. There was no fact so muddy, no situation so unclear, that Asia could not make it still worse by her mere presence.

"We're not going to be husband and wife until, well, we're husband and wife."

"That's not how Nessie behaved."

"So I gather. But you aren't Nessie, and I thank the Gods for that."

"I'm going to be the best wife I can be for you, Nicolaos. I'll help you with your investigations."

"I know you will."

"I wish Mother was still here so she'd know I got a good husband."

"You must be sad about her."

"Of course I was but"—she shrugged—"Mother had been ill for a very long time, and in pain, and she cried a lot because of it. She used to pray to the Gods to make it stop hurting, and eventually they did. Although if you ask me, they had help. I think that's why Nessie brought the man in the middle of the night. I think he was a doctor who helped her die. He visited, and two days later she was dead."

My hand proffering the clothing dropped. "Say that again?"

"Nessie brought a man into the women's quarters one night."

"Mnesiptolema didn't take the man to her own room?"

"No, to Mother's. I got up from bed and watched and they didn't see me. Nessie let him in but stood outside, and then some time later the door opened and he came out. I had to dive into bed because they came over to look at me and I pretended to be asleep. Then Nessie led him outside."

"Asia, is it possible the man you saw was the one we found on the pole?"

"I only saw him in the dark, and the man on the pole was . . . hard to recognize."

I knew she recalled the missing nose, it had turned his face into a horror mask.

She shivered.

Whatever my problems, they weren't this girl's fault. Callias himself had bought the husbands his daughters wanted. Themistocles had merely done the same, which made him a doting father. Asia knew how I felt about Diotima. No wonder she was anxious to please me.

I put the clothes around her and hugged her tight. "Asia, well done. If having a helpful partner means anything, then you're already being a good wife."

"I am?"

"You are. And tomorrow we're going investigating together."

Early next morning Asia and I walked out the palace gates and into the city, to investigate her own disappearance. The agora wasn't as crowded and chaotic as the one in Athens, but what it lost in color, atmosphere, and excitement it more than made up in dust and grime. I noticed Mac standing among a group of boys. He saw me too and approached, but I waved him away. He looked at me in surprise, probably because I'd decided to wear trousers. I might as well get used to them.

We found the lane Asia had described to me many days before on *Salaminia*, when she had recounted her kidnapping. It ran off a main road that adjoined the agora. The entrance was largely hidden by boxes and rubbish spewing out, and overlapping buildings to each side, so that from the street it looked more like the entrance to a building than the start of a passageway. Not even a man walking directly by on the main road could see inside. The lane was narrow, as she'd said, and there was plenty of litter lying in the dust. I could see a vertical crack of light in the distance, so at least it wasn't a dead end. "It was in here." Asia pointed. "I went down the lane, poked about among the stuff. "

"Stay here," I ordered. "I'll have a look."

"Didn't you say only an idiot would go down a dark alley on their own?"

"That doesn't apply to investigators. We do it all the time."

I squeezed past the rubbish and went in.

I kicked aside some of it in search of footprints that might tell me something, or perhaps something dropped during the struggle, but it had been too long ago, and there was no way to tell a clue from the rubbish. The lane ran between two walls that had once been whitewashed and now were filthy.

"Have you found anything?" Asia had disobeyed instructions and followed me.

"Only a girl who won't do as she's told. Go back."

She scoffed. "I'm more likely to be attacked in the main road than in here with you."

"Go back."

"Aarrgh. Yes, *master*." But she went.

I put my head down and continued the hunt for clues. What I found was a lot of rat droppings. Obviously this was a breeding ground for the local cuisine.

Behind me, in the lane, I heard a muffled scream, rapid movement. I jumped and turned. From somewhere an arm came down, something heavy hit me on the back of the head, and that's the last I remember.

When I came to, I was on the ground, my wrists bound behind my back, my ankles tied, and the sun shining on my face. My head was cradled in dirt. I tried not to move, to give myself time to think and see and find some way to escape.

I listened carefully. There were none of the noises of the city, no shouting, no traffic. Nor did I smell the ubiquitous city smells of garbage and donkey droppings. Somewhere birds were singing. I was in the country.

I heard the voices of two men. They were arguing, not about women or politics or any of the other things that men usually argue about. They were bickering over a pole.

"Hold it straight there!"

"It *is* straight, curse you."

"No t'ain't. It's leaning to the left, look I can see it."

"All right, how about that?"

"Now it's leaning to the right."

"If you can do better, why don't you?"

"Shut up, both of you," a third voice interjected, this one cultured, and the moment I heard it my blood froze. "The pole has to be perfectly vertical, or it won't take the weight. So look sharp about it and get it right. Have you set the bobs?"

"Aww . . ."

"Set them!"

I dared to open my eyelids, the merest slit. Two men knelt on the ground, dressed in rough leather jerkins and trousers made of some material that looked tough and was certainly filthy. One had a headband that was soaked with sweat, the other had rivulets running down his face and neck. Both had hands that were covered with grime.

A large wooden pole lay between them, to which they attached four pieces of twine, each with a pebble tied at the bottom. They nailed one on each side of the pole. This is a trick builders use to ensure an upright beam is truly vertical. When all four pieces of twine fall exactly down along the beam, the builder knows it's right.

"Make sure there are plenty of heavy rocks about the base, then pack the hole with gravel and dirt. Make sure of the rocks, I don't want any slippage." The third man walked into view. It was Araxes, as I feared.

"All right, that should do it. Cheiro, you raise the pole and Durgo, you sight it."

Cheiro and Durgo grumbled and pushed and swore and finally placed the pole. There was a rounded, smooth point at the top. That made me sit up.

"Ah, you're awake. Good." Araxes bent over me, his white hair shining with the sun behind it.

"What are you doing?" I demanded.

"I'm terribly sorry about this, but we're about to impale you."

My imagination ran away with me. Already I could feel the rough wood sliding up, my insides expanding as if there were a giant turd in me. My anus clenched shut. I trembled.

"I did warn you this was likely to happen, dear fellow. I have a client who, it grieves me to say, does not like you very much."

"Why? What did I do?"

"I am reliably informed by my client that you are a deadly assassin. You could have fooled me, but there you are. I confess I'm a trifle put out with you myself. You killed one of my men."

"I did? What man?"

"Oh come now. The guard at the warehouse."

"He was yours?"

"As if you didn't know. He was found with his throat slit and the goods looted. I knew you were on the way the moment I heard the news."

I blinked. So the one-armed beggar had got away with it.

Araxes said, "You're not going to deny it was you, are you?"

I shook my head. The beggar deserved his chance, and it wasn't as if I could do anything to make my predicament worse.

We watched in silence as the pole settled into place with a solid thunk. The narrowed end pointed straight up. Araxes chuckled. "Actually, I think the client's emotions may run to a stronger sentiment than dislike. He specifically demanded this end for you . . . *end!* Get the *point?* He ordered this *end.*" Araxes chuckled at his own demented joke.

"I normally find a quick sword thrust does the job with least fuss and pain. Most clients are satisfied by that arrangement. Either you have been particularly annoying, or else your enemy, my dear Nico—may I call you Nico? I feel we're forming a bond—your enemy, as I say, is a person of remarkable vindictiveness."

"I don't even know who he is."

"Client confidentiality is my watchword."

"It's Barzanes, isn't it? Barzanes set you on to me."

"I told you in Ephesus the wise hound creeps around the lion. Nor does he play with vipers."

"What of the girl?"

"The girl? Oh yes, the girl. Rather odd having her back, it's so rare that I get repeat business."

"You have her too?"

"You will be pleased to hear the girl ran away during the excitement of hauling you in. I considered you the greater threat. That may have been an error. She bit deep into the hand of one of my men and he foolishly released her long enough to make her escape."

Who had done this to me? Who hated me enough to want to kill me in this horrible manner? Perhaps Themistocles, if he had discovered my purpose; perhaps Barzanes, despite Araxes' denial; or maybe Archeptolis. He and Mnesiptolema had a good reason to hate both me and Diotima. Then a horrible thought hit me. What about Asia? Who else knew we were going to the alley? Was it reasonable that a girl could escape when I was captured?

Now that I sat upright I could see a group of men behind me—perhaps ten or twelve—dressed similarly to Cheiro and Durgo. Some of the men spoke Persian, some Greek. Two had the appearance of local peasants, some were light-skinned, some dusky. A typical pack of brigands. They lounged about watching the other two work. Their horses were tethered to sparse bushes in the minimal shade.

I searched about for something—anything—that might save me. Perhaps if I could see the road I might shout to a passerby. But no, the road was nowhere in sight. We were surrounded by low hills, covered in gravel and rocks and a few suffering bushes sufficient to block my view of beyond.

The main road could have been two hundred paces away and I wouldn't have known it. Even if I did attract the attention of a passerby, it would be a foolish man who came to investigate with a dozen cutthroats in plain view.

"Ready, Boss," Cheiro called.

"Put him on," Araxes said without emotion.

I screamed, hoping against hope that someone might hear. The only effect was for the dozen loungers to guffaw and make insulting comments. I kept screaming.

Araxes shook his head and said, "Come, come, Nico, this does you no credit at all. Would you die like a woman?"

"I wouldn't die at all."

"I'm afraid that option isn't available. You should follow the example of Thorion; he died cursing me. Carry on, men."

Cheiro and Durgo complained. "We're tired, Araxes. We dug the hole, someone else should do the rest."

Araxes nodded. "A fair comment. Take a break. You two." He pointed at the nearest two cutthroats. "Stick him on, but do it gently, I don't want him dying too fast."

Two ugly men grinned, stood, dusted themselves off, and approached me.

I yelled, "Wait! Only the Great King and his officers are allowed to execute like this. If they catch you, you'll be in big trouble."

Araxes said, "Oh goodness! I've never been in trouble with the law before." He waved an arm at his goons. "Drop him on."

They stood each side and pulled me up by the arms and thighs. My heart raced and I was dizzy, I felt like I was about to vomit.

I called out, "Araxes, if you have any decency you'll kill me before you put me on the pole. That sword thrust—"

"There is no degree of pleading that can weaken my resolve. I've heard it all before, Nico: the false bravado of the brave as they stare down fate, the whines of weak men, and the desperate entreaties of women clutching their children. I wish I hadn't heard those things, but life gives us few choices. If I could ignore them, I can certainly ignore you. The commission specifies impalement, so impalement it must be."

"He'll never know, whoever he is. Kill me first. Lie to him."

"What if he comes to inspect? He might, you know, before you're gone. It takes a few days to die."

I thought of the impaled man by the road, how I had watched him in his agony and, on the advice of Asia, been ready to walk away. I cursed myself.

"I'll kill myself quicker by pushing down."

"No, you won't. I've heard that one before, but once they're on the pole they always change their minds. They fight for every moment, every agonizing extra moment."

"I'll pay you. I'll pay you money if you make it quick."

Araxes stepped back as if I'd struck him. "What do you take me for? That would be unethical!"

Another man stepped up with a large jar. He put the jar on the ground, took off the lid, and reached in with both hands. The hands emerged with two enormous handfuls of dripping pig fat. He smeared this over the point of the pole and, when the top was smothered, reached into the jar again and smeared more greasy fat down the sides.

"This isn't the best of fits," Araxes explained. "The Gods did not create the human rectum to be able to take a large piece of wood a handsbreadth across, so we must have grease to ease it in. I'm afraid it will attract ants, which will add to your discomfort, but it can't be helped."

I began to struggle seriously now. There was no hope for me, but at least I could fight to the end.

They hoisted me higher as if I were an ungainly sack. Then, with a grunt, they pushed me up so that my bottom was higher than the point of the stake. Their grip was like fighting iron bonds. They walked me over. The stake came closer with every step, I couldn't take my eyes off it. I think I sobbed, but I don't remember. My mind insisted this wasn't real. My heart thudded so heavily it seemed to shake the ground.

Then I realized, it was no illusion. The ground really did shake. Cavalry appeared around the hill, a troop of Persians.

The cutthroats shouted in alarm and raced for their own horses. The two carrying me let go. I fell with a bone-jarring crack and my head hit a rock. I could feel it bleed but I didn't care. I rolled to get a view of the fight.

The two who'd held me turned to face the newcomers. A horseman saw them and broke from the pack. He leveled his spear and charged. The spear took the first man in the chest, but the second brigand swept his sword into the horse's neck. The wounded animal reared and threw his rider, who landed right beside me. The brigand killed the prone soldier with one quick thrust.

On the outside of the mêlée I could see Cleophantus sitting his horse as if he were on a parade ground. He thrust with his spear. I saw him kill one man and then prance his mount backward out of the chaos.

The black scowling face of Barzanes appeared in the center of things before he was obscured by the rising dust. I thought there must be twelve men among the attackers, plus Barzanes and Cleophantus, and that was more than enough to save me.

Cleophantus spotted Durgo, standing his ground with bloodied sword in hand. The son of Themistocles kicked his mount forward. He leaned in with his spear to catch Durgo on the right. But Durgo knew his business; at the last moment he jumped to the unprotected left of Cleophantus.

Cleophantus leaned far down the right of his mount, the opposite side to Durgo. Durgo's sword passed over the back of Cleophantus by a whisker.

Cleophantus wheeled on the spot, yelled a war cry, and thrust. The spear took Durgo in the throat. His eyes bulged and he vomited blood as he collapsed. I was impressed; the playboy knew what he was about when it came to riding in battle.

I lost sight of Araxes until I saw him run at Cleophantus from the rear. I screamed, "Cleophantus, behind you!" With my arms still bound I scrambled to my feet and ran at them.

The Gods were with Cleophantus. He had the sense to look behind him. He swung his spear in alarm so it connected with the blade of Araxes, which was within a moment of taking him in the back. This was enough time for me to reach them and I shoulder-charged Araxes. He dropped the sword, bounced off the hindquarters of Cleophantus' horse, and came back at me with a well-placed kick to my groin. I went down in agony.

Cleophantus tried a thrust with his spear, aiming at Araxes' shoulder, but Araxes—a true professional—stepped aside, grabbed the shaft, and pulled. Cleophantus toppled forward, right on top of me.

Araxes used the moment. He jumped onto Cleophantus' horse and kicked him into a gallop.

The dust in the air settled. Four Persian soldiers were down: one dead, two with injuries that were probably fatal, and one who would live.

"Thank the Gods you're here," I said to Cleophantus as he picked himself up. "How did you find me?"

"Asia ran back to the palace and broke in on a public audience. She announced what had happened in front of everyone and created quite a stir. Father ordered Barzanes to search. There are men all over the city looking for you, including that priestess. She started tearing the town apart."

"Diotima?" I said, alarmed. "Is she all right?"

"She's fine, but Father ordered her back to the palace. The guards who had to carry her—" He shook his head. "I suppose they'll heal.

"Then some pushy kid called Macrobianos turned up at the palace and reported seeing you." Cleophantus screwed up his face. "He demanded up-front payment. Father refused. You owe me a small fortune.

"The boy said a group of horsemen left the city, and we followed. Barzanes didn't want me with the soldiers, and Father tried to dissuade me, but I insisted. We rode with scouts to both sides of the road. One of the scouts heard your . . . ah . . . calls for attention." He looked over at the erect pole with its shiny, greased point waiting for a victim. Cleophantus shuddered. "I don't blame you. I would have screamed too."

"Ahura Mazda has been kind to you," Barzanes said, walking up to Cleophantus and myself. "As for these"—he spat upon the bloodied corpse of Durgo—"these are the spawn of the Daevas, and their souls will rot in Worst Existence."

"Thank you for rescuing me."

"Unlawful death is hateful to the Great King and must be punished. As the King commands, so I do."

"Lord Barzanes! This man lives."

One of the surviving Persians held up a defeated brigand. It was Cheiro, who had erected the pole but been too tired to impale me.

Barzanes studied Cheiro with his usual dispassion. After several heartbeats that seemed like a lifetime, Barzanes said, "Use the pole."

"Noooo!"

The Persians dragged Cheiro and ripped down his trousers. I said, "Barzanes, this is too cruel."

"It is the penalty for his crime. If I send him back to Magnesia, the Satrap must pronounce the same sentence, but in a day or two. That would be cruel indeed, to leave a man waiting when his fate is assured. I am the Eyes and Ears of the King. It is within my power to pronounce sentence at once."

I looked away as they put him on. To cover the noise of his screams I said, "The man who rode off, his name is Araxes. You want him. He's the man who took Asia."

Cleophantus took the mount of one of the men who'd fallen and pulled himself up. "That's it then, he dies."

Barzanes said, "Wait, Cleophantus. The Satrap gave no orders—"

"You think my father would hesitate if he knew? Come on if you like, or not, but I'm going after the man who stole my sister. I'll report back when I'm done."

Was this the effete playboy Callias had told me was a coward?

Barzanes swore, "Evil Daevas!" He had no choice, and indeed he shouldn't have needed one. He detailed four men to get the injured back to the city and ordered the remaining two to follow Cleophantus.

I was the last to leave. Before I did, I walked over to Cheiro. He stood with the stake deep inside him. Cheiro watched as I picked up a sword of the fallen brigands.

He said, "Thank you. In the heart, if you please."

"Can we catch him?" I asked after I caught up with the others.

Cleophantus said, "Not on the road. He's on the best horse in Magnesia. I should know, I bought and trained him myself."

"What if Araxes turns off the road?"

"He won't," Cleophantus said with authority. "Once he's in the rough, chance comes into play. Who knows when a galloping horse could put a hoof in a rabbit hole? No, he'll keep his comfortable lead until we get to Ephesus."

Barzanes nodded. "At Ephesus the criminal faces difficulty. It will take him time to pass through their gates, and the lords of Ephesus will give me what I demand. I do not think he can escape us."

Araxes was visible in the distance. Every now and then he turned to keep an eye on us. Once I believe he waved at me in mock salute.

It was a strange sort of chase. We all trotted rather than galloped, even Araxes. Hunter and prey both needed their mounts to make the same long distance.

Cleophantus said, "Did you see me in the fight, Nicolaos?"

"Yes."

"That's the first time I've killed a man." His eyes shone. "The first fight I've been in too, and I did well. Nico, I did well."

He glanced at Barzanes and the soldiers, who were a few

lengths ahead of us, and he said quietly, "What I said on our trail ride—it seems like ages ago now—about me and Father and Medizing. When we return to Magnesia, I'm telling Father I must return to fight for Athens."

"Good fortune to you then," was all I could say. I had no confidence his determination would stand up to the full glare of Themistocles' personality. Mine certainly hadn't.

"I'm sorry we involved you. I realize now a man has to solve his own problems, no matter what the consequences."

The ride became tedious. The sun rose to its full height and sweat ran down my back, arms, and legs.

"My bottom's sore," I moaned to Cleophantus.

"It's not as sore as it would be if we hadn't found you."

"Good point. Have I thanked you for saving me?"

"Several times, but feel free to say it again. If they'd got you on the pole, even for a moment, you would have died. No one ever survives once it's in them."

"I see Ephesus," Barzanes announced from the lead. "We have him now."

The horses breathed heavily and were in obvious distress, but the tough beasts had stayed the course.

Now I could see the city gates too. A knot of men and donkeys waited to pass. They would certainly hold up Araxes long enough for us to catch him.

Whether Araxes saw the problem too I don't know, but I think he already knew his plan, because he didn't pause.

"Why is he veering away?" Cleophantus asked, puzzled.

Araxes rode a path that cut a graceful arc to the right, away from the city gates toward the north. It was a path I'd seen before.

I shouted, "The bastard's not going for Ephesus, he's running for the sanctuary!"

"What?" Cleophantus said.

But Barzanes understood. "He runs for the Hellene temple called the Artemision. If he reaches it, they will not permit us to take him. We must catch the criminal before he arrives."

Barzanes kicked his mount and accelerated. He cut the corner into the rough.

"Yah!" Cleophantus effortlessly pushed his mount to a gallop.

The Persian soldiers followed.

I stayed with the soldiers, then got a little ahead. My body bounced hard. It was like being kicked in the groin over and over.

It was a thousand paces to the Artemision.

I saw the guards atop the gates of Ephesus point at us. They saw a man on horseback being chased by men on horseback. More figures appeared atop the wall as men climbed to watch the race.

We rode recklessly through the scrub.

A leg snapped. I thought it was my horse and flinched, but the Persian behind me went down.

Three of us emerged onto the temple road.

Araxes was twenty lengths ahead. He hammered his feet into the animal's sides and beat its hindquarters with a stick.

The temple was dead ahead.

The soldier bouncing beside me lost his seat. Gone like he'd fallen down a hole to Hades.

The horse ran on riderless.

"Let me through!" Cleophantus yelled.

His mount surged past Barzanes and made for Araxes as if he were fresh for an Olympic race.

Cleophantus rode low along the neck, reaching forward with his spear held at arm's length.

Araxes saw the threat. He stayed his course and didn't look behind him again.

The Artemision loomed close.

Cleophantus couldn't make it. He tossed his spear.

The spear caught between the legs of Araxes' mount.

The horse of Araxes went down headfirst. The animal bellowed a last dying cry of rage as its neck snapped.

Araxes flew through the air. He landed with a resounding thump. He lay there for a moment. Then he pushed himself to his feet and began to run.

Cleophantus raced by and kicked Araxes down.

Cleophantus wheeled and drew his sword.

Barzanes and I caught up.

We all dripped with sweat. I was so exhausted I shook. I wanted to get off my horse, but I didn't know if I had the strength.

Cleophantus raised the sword and said, "This is for Asia."

I shouted, "No, Cleophantus, we need him alive!"

Cleophantus began his swing.

"Halt!" a man's voice commanded. "This man is in sanctuary and may not be harmed. Nor may you take him."

It was one of the priests of the Artemision. Our violent approach had attracted interest from the people at the temple. Men, women, and eunuchs were lined up along the front steps watching. The priest pointed behind us. Sure enough, a stone painted white lay not more than a man's length from where Araxes was sprawled.

The horse in his moment of death had tossed Araxes far enough to live.

I could have cried.

Cleophantus burst out, "But he's a murderer!"

Time passed while Cleophantus and I both argued with the priest. Barzanes looked on and said nothing. Araxes sat on the ground while the men standing over him decided his fate.

The priest was obdurate.

"The sanctuary rule must be enforced no matter what the

man's crime. He is welcome to remain here for as long as he wishes." He looked to Barzanes, obviously recognizing that he was the senior man among us. "Even the Great King has decreed the sanctuary of Artemis is to be respected."

Barzanes nodded. "You speak truth. Then, Priest, we shall wait outside the bounds. I will have soldiers patrol the border. Unless the man wishes to spend the rest of his life here, we must surely have him."

"You have the power to order this?"

"I am the Eyes and Ears of the Great King."

The priest had the look of someone who finds he's swallowed a bug in his wine.

Barzanes asked, "You will feed this man?"

The priest, suddenly more helpful, said, "There is no requirement for the temple to feed the man, merely to protect him. His friends may bring him food, if he has any friends, that is."

"I will ring this temple with troops. He will emerge when he is hungry enough, and then he will pay the price for his crimes."

Araxes was bruised and bleeding, his clothing stained by sweat and horse, but he smiled and said in his pleasant voice, "May Artemis honor you, Priest. I'm willing to stay here as long as necessary for them to go away. Even if they camp outside forever, better a slow death within than what Barzanes would do to me without."

"No less than you were prepared to do to me," I growled.

"Practically the same," he agreed amiably. "Gentlemen, it is obvious whatever activities I may have engaged in are over forever. You want me for only two things: revenge and information. Let us make this easy for each other. If you put away your revenge, I will present you with the information you want, on the understanding I will be permitted to depart Ephesus on the first ship out."

"You're willing to sell out your employer?" I asked.

"I won't be hanging around for the retribution. I wonder

what the weather's like in Carthage?" he mused. "That should be far away enough . . . I hope."

Barzanes said, without consulting, "It is unacceptable. You killed the merchant on the lands of the Great King, you must be punished for it."

"I didn't kill Brion."

"You lie."

"Wait, Barzanes," I said. "I have more reason to hate him than most, but this might be our best chance to uncover the whole truth."

"No." Barzanes refused to make a deal.

I objected, "But he could identify the criminal."

"He *is* the criminal. That there may be another does not exonerate him. Do you Hellenes let half your criminals go free because they informed on the other half? No, of course not; no honorable man could agree to this. Any city which did such a thing would collapse in lawlessness."

"All right, what you say is true."

"I ride to the city for men to surround the sanctuary. Cleophantus, you and the Athenian keep watch." Barzanes rode off down the road.

Araxes said, "I'm thirsty, I haven't had a drink since the morning."

Cleophantus held up his water skin, beyond the white stone. "Come on over. I have plenty."

Araxes smiled but said nothing. He walked around the temple and I followed, wanting to keep him in sight. Cleophantus mounted his horse and watched us from the border.

A channel had been cut to divert water from the stream that split around the temple. It emptied through a fountain. Araxes used a ladle to drink his fill, then turned in to enter the temple.

He found a niche in a distant corner, which was hung about with tapestries that gave us some privacy.

"Listen, Nicolaos—"

"Call me Nico."

Araxes smiled. "Nico, I'm probably going to die soon. I've seen too many men die to want to go any way but fast. I'll fall on a knife before I let them put me on the pole."

I hesitated, then, "What if I can give you a way to not die?"

"I'd take it of course. What do I have to do?"

"Tell me the whole, complete truth, and if I believe you, I'll let you go. You'll still have Cleophantus to avoid, but that's your problem."

"What happened to men of honor not treating with thieves?"

"That's Barzanes. I'm much more interested in results. I admit I wanted you very badly at the start, but now I realize you're like me, Araxes, just some poor fool acting for someone else. The man I want is the one behind it all. But you'll have to be quick, because Barzanes will be back any moment."

"How will you explain my escape?"

"You surprised me, knocked me out, and tied me up."

"I accept."

"It started with the river, didn't it? The Maeander River, and the dead farmer."

Araxes nodded. "I must say you did well to work that out. The farmer found some coins and an old jar. He took it to Ephesus to sell. People do, around here, because they can get more than in Magnesia. Brion saw the amphora—he understood old pots and furniture—and recognized it as valuable. When he saw the picture on the coins he got excited.

"Brion quizzed the farmer closely. The man was guarded about where he'd found the stuff—it was obvious he planned to dig some more himself—but anyone could guess the man had found the stuff on his own land. Brion had to do some research to work out what he had, he found what he needed in the book they keep here in the temple."

"The part in the Book of Heraclitus about not being able to step into the same river twice, Brion used it to prove he'd found the lost treasure of Polycrates. What everyone takes to be profound philosophy is actually the raving of a madman who knew where the treasure lay buried."

"So Brion told me. I didn't pay any attention myself."

"The philosophers are going to be upset when I tell them," I said, looking forward to deflating Diotima and Anaxagoras.

He chuckled. "They won't believe you."

He was probably right.

Araxes continued, "Brion needed someone to deal with the messier aspects; fortunately he knew someone who introduced him to me."

"So you dealt with the farmer."

"It was a quick drowning, perfectly natural for the area. No one questioned it. Afterward, the widow was only too happy to be paid decent money for the property. We packed her off to her brother's house in Sardis."

"No unfortunate accident for her?"

"No need."

"Then you began digging up the stuff and exporting it to Athens. Brion's trade connections would have been perfect for that. It had to be sent away because any attempt to sell Polycrates' treasure locally would be spotted at once by people who knew the story."

"Brion handled that end of it. He hid the coins and gold and silver items in the old amphorae, which he plugged. We split the profits three ways."

"What went wrong?"

"I don't know. Brion did something to destroy the operation. The next thing I knew, I had Themistocles on my back. I told you even the toughest hound slinks around a lion, but when the lion has his paw on your neck, you obey. Themistocles ordered me to chase down the letter—well, you know that."

"You said Thorion died cursing you. You spoke to him?"

"Thorion laughed in my face, even as I had him in a death

grip. He said his death didn't matter, because he'd got word out of the coming invasion. It was news to me; Themistocles had told me nothing."

If Thorion thought the note he'd written to Pericles was sufficient then he had an odd idea of what constituted a warning. But then, the man was about to die, and if his admission of treason was enough to ease his passing then who was I to argue. I'd faced death myself that day and knew what it did to a man's mind. The knowledge that he'd confessed his crime might have been his only comfort.

I said, "Thorion spoke of being a traitor."

"Then it must have been his guilty conscience. I'm told some men have them. Thorion's only crime was common larceny on a grand scale, fencing stolen antiquities."

Araxes sat with his back against the wall of the Artemision, the sweat running off him, and caked in the grime of his flight on horseback. "You know, Nicolaos, if Thorion hadn't got that note off, you would have been none the wiser, you would never have come here, and I would not be sitting in this accursed temple awaiting my end."

Perhaps Thorion had done a better job for Athens than I gave him credit for. I said, "Thorion saved Athens."

"That remains to be seen. He certainly gave your people a chance." Araxes wiped the sweat off his brow. "Themistocles allowed me to finish clearing the site as a reward and to make sure I kept my mouth shut. I told the truth, by the way, when I said you won't find any more. We cleared it out with the last load."

"Why did you steal Asia?"

"I didn't. Themistocles gave her away."

"What?"

"I *told* you she was in the greatest danger if you returned her, didn't I? Themistocles told me to make it look like child theft, and his orders were to 'dispose' of her. I chose to interpret that loosely. When I saw her, I couldn't bring myself to harm the child." He laughed without humor. "The one time I try to do a good deed, and it destroys me. There's a moral to be had there. I can tell you, my client was not best pleased when the girl reappeared in your company."

"Why in Hades would Themistocles do such a thing to his own daughter?"

"Dear boy, the Satrap held my life in his hands. This was not the moment to be making personal inquiries."

"But why sell her in Athens?"

"I had a tight schedule to keep. Ephesus was impossible for obvious reasons. I had to track the courier, preferably before he had a chance to hand over the scroll, but regardless to eliminate anyone who saw it."

I said, "What I don't understand is, why Themistocles would want me dead. Why now? The man betroths me to his daughter, and *then* decides to kill me? It doesn't make sense."

"My dear boy, can't you guess? I'm a man of business. What businessman has only one client?"

"What?"

"Themistocles didn't hire me to kill you. It was—"

"Wait." I held up my hand. "Let me guess."

That made Araxes smile. "By all means let us have guessing games. It's not as if we have anything else to do."

I cursed myself for an idiot. Of course it wasn't Themistocles. Hadn't I myself named all those good objections? Now that I was rid of prejudice, only one person made sense.

I said a name.

Araxes nodded.

The tapestries moved. I thought it would be Barzanes returning, but it was Geros who slipped through, the eunuch who guarded the Book of Heraclitus.

Araxes said, "Well, you took your time getting here. I've been stalling for ages."

I looked from one to the other.

"I had to prepare the horses, brother," Geros replied.

Uh-oh. I said to Araxes, "The one who introduced you to Brion; it had to be someone who knew what Brion was up to, didn't it? Someone who was required to be in the room with him whenever he read the book."

Geros said, "We talked, and when I learned what he was about, and what he needed, I introduced him to my brother."

Araxes said, "I mentioned, didn't I, my brother was taken from me at an early age? He was taken for the temple." Araxes looked thoughtful. "Of course, this will make your story more credible."

I said to Geros, "The only good news out of this is I get to say, 'I Told You So' to Diotima."

"The priestess is in love with you."

"Yes, I know. There's no accounting for taste."

"It's why I did not hurt you before. You must marry the priestess and make her happy, or I will hurt you."

Araxes chuckled. "Haven't you heard, brother? Nico is betrothed to the girl Asia."

Geros hit me. Hard.

When I came to I was tied tight with a rag stuffed in my mouth, and that's how they found me some time later. To say I was not Barzanes' favorite person would be putting it mildly.

After he finished raving, Barzanes told me two men on horseback had burst from the stables when Cleophantus was on the other side of the temple. Cleophantus had given chase, but they swept around the city wall to the edge of the harbor, where they splashed along the edge of the sea, around the wall, to the docks, then boarded the first boat out.

Barzanes sent Cleophantus galloping ahead to Magnesia with

the news of what had happened, an assignment that horse-crazed Cleophantus was happy to accept. For the first time in his life, during the chase, his one skill had proven to be important.

This left me riding back to Magnesia with Barzanes beside me and a small troop of Persian soldiers at my back. Barzanes and I were the only ones of the party who spoke Greek. We were free to discuss whatever we wished.

I said, "Barzanes, the story Araxes told me. You knew, didn't you? Themistocles had murdered Brion, and you did nothing about it."

"The word of the criminal is meaningless. He told you this story to distract you, so his brother could walk up and strike you like a dumb ox."

"You know it's true, Barzanes. Everything fits."

Barzanes said nothing.

I said, "Do you realize, if I'm to marry Asia, then you and I will be brothers-in-law?"

"I am surprised you agreed to this. Do not think I failed to notice your, shall we say, attachment, to the priestess."

"The fathers have arranged it. This is the way it's going to be." I paused. "Asia's a good girl. So, *brother,* what is to be done with our father-in-law? You did know, didn't you? Admit it."

"It was obvious from the moment I saw the impaled body of the merchant. I needed only question the local guards until I found the ones who acted under Themistocles' orders. In fact, you saw me in the agora that day as I gave them new orders. I have transferred the squad that killed the merchant to a post on the other side of the empire. They will not talk."

"No molten iron for Themistocles, eh? What happened to crime and disorder being hateful to the Great King? What happened to cleaving to the Truth and abjuring the Lie? What would this Wise Lord of yours say, Barzanes, if he knew?"

"Ahura Mazda knows." Barzanes shifted in his seat. "Everything you say is true, Athenian. These same thoughts flay me every time I pray. As for Themistocles, I have no doubt Mithra will cast him off the bridge when his time comes, but for now I find myself with conflicting duties. I have the King's mission to ensure the plan of attack is completed. I know the Satrap has told you of this, and only he can do it. I have too the requirement to enforce the Great King's just rule by his satraps. In this case I cannot do both."

"So you abandoned justice."

"I delay it. The Great King will be informed of the Satrap's crime after the war has begun."

"Oh, right! And if the war succeeds and the Athenians are conquered, do you think he's going to be fussed about one little extra death?"

"I have considered the same thing, but it is for my King to decide, not me."

"And the angel Mithra, when you cross that bridge. Think you're going to make it to Best Purpose?"

"Believe me, Athenian, it is something about which I wonder, constantly. I have done things as an agent of the Great King that are hateful to Ahura Mazda." He shrugged. "I said to you and the priestess before the fire, when I inspect the contents of my prayer pocket, I must hope the good outnumbers the bad. What I did not say was that for me, my only chance is to do very great good before I die, in the hope it outweighs the evil I know is already within."

"I hope that pocket is a big one."

"Whatever the size, it will not prevent me from serving my King, nor from protecting the people from lawlessness and disorder. Remember it."

Diotima threw herself at me the moment we arrived. "Oh Nico, I was so worried! Are you hurt?"

"I'm fine."

"It's my fault. I should have gone with you even if that girl was there."

I soon found myself wearing Persian dress—trousers and tunic—because my Hellene clothing had been shredded and ruined. I felt much the same myself, but unfortunately nobody kept replacement bodies. I pulled on the trousers without hesitation or the slightest thought.

I took Diotima aside and told her all I'd learned, ending with the one thing neither of us had expected: that Themistocles had arranged the kidnapping of his own daughter.

Diotima's thumbnail received a mauling as I related all this. When I finished, she said, "No wonder we failed to solve that part. Who'd have thought it?" She pondered some more, before saying, "Nico, the late-night meeting when Mnesiptolema brought Brion into the palace."

I nodded. "Yes, and Brion helped the family escape Athens all those years ago."

She said, "There's only one possible conclusion."

"Yes, of course. This is the answer."

Diotima nodded.

"I'll have to confront him."

"Be careful, Nico."

I found Themistocles in the paradise, where he rested on a couch within a pavilion dictating in Persian to two slaves. Two soldiers, bodyguards, stood at his back.

I said, "Themistocles, we need to discuss my fiancée."

He stopped in midflow and said, "Yes?"

"Or rather, I want to discuss the father of my fiancée."

His eyebrows rose. It is perfectly normal to speak in front of slaves as if they were not there, but Themistocles paused, and for a moment I wondered if he'd refuse, Then he pushed down on the couch to rise. I stepped forward to help him, but a guard stepped before me, while the other pulled Themistocles up with one hand.

Themistocles led the way to the stables, where a handful of slaves were mucking out. Themistocles dismissed them with a word and they went running. He ordered the soldiers to stand sentry at the door.

"We're free to talk here, Barzanes has no spy holes in the stables."

I blinked at that one. "You mean he has in the palace?"

"Wouldn't you, if you were in his position? I don't know where they are, but I assume they're there."

We seemed to have a triangle of players, all hiding something from the others; perhaps a square, if you counted Mnesiptolema.

Themistocles said, "I take it you know Asia is not my daughter."

"She's the daughter of Brion, isn't she? That's what triggered the whole sequence."

"If that pest Barzanes hadn't arrived, I could have killed Brion in the open and there would have been none dare complain, but Barzanes is the Eyes and Ears of the King, with direct access to Artaxerxes, and I am a Hellene among Persians. If Barzanes reported I had abused my position it would have become difficult. Artaxerxes is like Barzanes; they're both irritatingly moral."

"You could have let Brion go on living."

"A man who not only cuckolded me, but sired a child for me to raise? Don't be ridiculous. You know as well as I do I'd have been well within my rights to kill them both if I'd caught them in the act, and expose the child."

"You were fourteen years too late."

"Better late than never."

"Not for Asia. She's not a baby you can expose with impunity anymore. None of this is her fault."

Themistocles sighed. "I told you before, sometimes even I make mistakes. I see now I was hotheaded when I sent the girl away, and she is the best of the brood. It was a mistake made in anger."

He hadn't "sent her away." Themistocles had ordered her disposed of. Now he rewrote history in his own favor.

"Sometimes at night you stand beside the statue of Polycrates. You told me so. My guess is you were standing there the night Mnesiptolema let Brion into the palace."

Themistocles nodded. "Yes. I thought they must be having an affair. When I checked discreetly next morning and discovered instead she'd taken Brion to meet my wife, I realized it was more complex. I confronted my wife, who on her deathbed admitted the truth."

I wondered if Themistocles had assisted his wife on her way after hearing her confession, but instead I said, "So you took a troop of soldiers with you, to put Brion on the pole. Is that when you learned of the letter?"

"He begged for his life. A man facing the pole will say or do anything to avoid it."

I remembered my own behavior and shuddered. "Yes, I know."

"He babbled something about a letter, offered to tell me of it in return for his life. This was the first I'd heard of the mess my idiot children had made."

"I see."

"It was a problem! The letter had to be retrieved, but I couldn't admit its existence to Barzanes. Nor could I use Persian resources, for the same reason. I stood there in the countryside, wondering what to do, while Brion knelt before me and babbled anything and everything he hoped might buy him life. Then he let slip about Araxes and his fascinating operation."

"Aha!"

"Yes, the solution suggested itself at once. My soldiers burst in on Araxes at that farmhouse he'd appropriated, and easily overpowered his gang. I offered the scoundrel a continued life of crime in return for recovering the letter."

"You seem to have a relaxed attitude to disloyal children."

Themistocles smiled. "Did I not once explain to you that blood comes first? Besides, all cause for conflict with my children will be over the moment the invasion begins, which I can tell you will be soon, because the plan is finished. I can easily keep myself alive until then. You know my children, Nico; I love them as a father should, but we both know that none of them have the slightest competence to carry off a decent plot."

I nodded glumly. "You've got that right."

Themistocles laughed. "You know, when you first turned up, I thought you must be the assassin they'd called for."

"I promise you I wasn't, but what changed your mind?"

"As I said at the time, what assassin in his right mind would call attention to himself as you did: approach his victim with a kidnapped child on a stolen horse? Besides, Araxes assured me the only man who'd read the letter was dead."

Clearly Araxes had neglected to mention the note Thorion had sent. Well, I wasn't about to enlighten Themistocles.

"Does this mean Barzanes still has no idea?"

"About the letter? As far as I know, he never found out. If he had, I'm sure I would have heard of it. He's a strange man, but a powerful one; I could barely believe my luck when he offered for Nicomache."

"Maybe he's in love."

"That cold fish?"

"I feel Barzanes is deeper than he seems."

Themistocles grunted.

"Themistocles, if Brion traded the information for his life, how come he's dead?"

"I lied. I kept Brion until Araxes reported back with the letter. When I was sure I no longer needed him, onto the pole Brion went."

His duplicity was staggering. Themistocles must have read the look on my face because he said, "I want you to know, Nicolaos, I wish you only well. It wasn't me who hired Araxes to kill you."

"I know who it was, Themistocles, and I think you do too."

"I suspect so."

"I don't suppose you have any advice?"

"Do I look like someone who can advise about woman trouble? But it's my order you'll do her no harm."

"We'll have a chat, that's all."

"And ensure this little problem doesn't happen again?"

"Yes."

"Fine, but if you hurt her, you'll answer to me."

"I understand." I paused. "Asia has no idea about her paternity. Will you tell her?"

"No. Amazing, isn't it? Of all my children, she's the one I could have sworn was most like me, and yet there isn't a drop of my blood in her veins. I do honestly regret ordering Araxes to take her. It was done in the heat of the moment. Of course, you're upset. I offered you a wife with a defect. Your father would be within his rights to refuse her if you told him. Let me sweeten the deal—"

"Father?"

Themistocles and I jumped as if we'd been hailed by the Gods. The voice had come from above, but it wasn't male. There in the hayloft, her head poking over the edge, was Asia.

She dropped down, landing in front of Themistocles with a light spring in her knees. She wore the trousers I'd seen before. "You don't mean that. You're only saying that to Nicolaos for some trick, aren't you?"

If Themistocles had been condemned to death, his expression could not have been more tortured. It was the first time I saw from him a reaction that I knew was not calculated.

He said, "I'm not your father."

Asia hid her face in her hands and rushed from the stable.

Themistocles and I looked at each other in horror. I said, "I'm sorry, I never thought . . . I was never going to tell her. I only needed to confirm for myself. I didn't think she'd be here."

"Nor I," Themistocles agreed. "Well, we cannot recall the river that flows. I doubt she wants to see me, perhaps she never will again. Go to her, Nicolaos. Tell her I would not have had this happen. But before you go to her . . . my children have been something of a disappointment to me."

Themistocles had a talent for understatement.

"My own sons, well, you've seen for yourself. I know what Archeptolis is. None of them show any interest in politics. When I become Satrap of Athens, I'll need good lieutenants, reliable magistrates. They must be people I can trust, and what you've achieved is impressive. I can use a man like you." Themistocles looked me in the eye. "There is something else I might mention. I shouldn't, because technically you are still the enemy, but this news might help you decide. I had word, days ago, that Athens has invaded Egypt. The news is fresh, it was delivered by the King's Messengers. Do you know what this means, Nicolaos?"

So the message from Pericles was true. I'd wondered why the Athenians would do such a thing, but now I saw the plan. I said, "Pericles draws a Persian army to defend Egypt; an army that otherwise might be invading Greece."

"I see you paid attention in our talks," said Themistocles.

"So the Persians will send an army south."

Themistocles snorted. "That's what Artaxerxes said in his message to me. But he's wrong. Even now I compose the reply that will persuade him to do otherwise. Tell me, Nicolaos, if many Athenian soldiers are in Egypt, then where are they *not*?"

"Dear Gods," I exclaimed. "Athens is exposed."

"Good lad. Pericles didn't see it, nor does Artaxerxes, but I do. Which means the time for the Persians to attack, and for me to become Satrap of Athens, is right now. I must have your answer at once."

Themistocles offered me not merely his daughter, but power within Athens for her dowry. What I'd always said I wanted. Themistocles would be Satrap of Athens when the Persians took the city. When he died or retired—it couldn't be too many years—then who knew what might happen? The cost was to support a war against Athens, and support a murderer who sold a child.

If I allied with Themistocles, I might very well end up the city's ruler.

"What can I say? I accept, of course."

I went to look for Asia, and to tell Diotima what had happened, but the soldiers found me first.

They presented themselves as I dried myself off and pulled on a fresh chitoniskos. A tall one with a bad eye, and a short one with a split nose. Neither looked the type of man you would wish to annoy. The shorter of the two said. "The Lord Barzanes commands you come."

"Tell the lord I'll come as soon as I've carried out a task for the Satrap."

"You're ordered to come at once."

"Didn't you hear me? I said the task for Themist—" They drew their swords.

"—ocles will just have to wait until I've spoken with your lord. All right, let's go."

The short one walked before me, the taller behind with his sword drawn. They led me through corridors I'd been dragged down once before. We were coming depressingly close to the dungeon. Luckily for my nerves, we turned off before we reached it. The guards showed me into a room and pulled the door shut behind me. I heard the clank from the corridor as they took post outside.

"Ah, Athenian. Come, look at this."

Barzanes stood behind a bench. Lying before him were the tablets I had given to the cloth seller to send to Pericles. They had been pulled to pieces. The wax from the tablets had somehow been cut from their frame still intact. The frames of the two tablets had been disassembled, and the strips of wood placed in their positions, as if ready to be put back together. In the middle of each disassembled frame was its backing board.

To the side lay the thong I'd used to tie the package together; the thong on which I'd written the true message. I told myself not to look at it, and to make sure I didn't, stared into the eyes of Barzanes, the Eyes and Ears of the King.

"Ahura Mazda, the Wise Lord, commands us to love the Truth and abjure the Lie. Do you love the Truth, Athenian?"

I tried to read his tone of voice, but I couldn't decide what he knew or didn't know. I swallowed, then licked my lips. "I don't follow your God, Barzanes. You said it yourself when you called me Athenian. I follow the Gods of my own people."

"I have spent my life dealing with the Hellenes. I know many of you would lie for your own advantage. So I do not think it too much to ask this simple question. Do you venerate the Lie, Athenian?"

"Life is never that simple, Barzanes. People are honest most of the time; sometimes they might tell a few lies. Even our Gods and Goddesses have been known to trick people, or each other . . ."

"Ah, trick. Yes. But you see, Athenian, the Wise Lord never lies, and through his prophet Zarathustra he commands us to follow this rule. Do you know, since becoming a man, I have never told a lie?" He shook his head. "There is a great deal of misunderstanding between our peoples, and it comes down to this: the Hellenes think it right to—what word do you use?—to *prevaricate* when you do not like the truth. For this we hate you. You lie to each other in your own courts, telling one falsehood after another to persuade a jury to vote your way. Your diplomats tell lies to each other. They tell lies to *us*."

"Athens has never broken an oath to Persia."

"You are wrong. In the days of our fathers the Spartans marched upon Athens, and the Athenians in their fear sent to the Satrap of Lydia to ask for his protection. The Satrap agreed, but only if the Athenians joined the empire by pledging *earth and water* to the Great King. The ambassadors accepted at once, every man of the court heard it. But then the Spartans returned home and the Athenians repudiated their promise. They *lied*, Athenian."

"I've never heard of this, Barzanes."

"I am not surprised. It is not something the Athenians would want their children to know, that their fathers break their oaths to kings. When the Athenians pledged earth and water, Athens became a part of the Persian Empire, legally and morally. All that followed has simply been the Great King claiming what is rightfully his." Barzanes glanced down at the pieces on the bench. "But, here we are talking of the acts of men now dead, when we have practical matters to deal with. You see here the package you sent to your father in Athens?"

"It did rather come to my attention. I suppose, since you never lie, the courier accidentally dropped it? I can't say I'm too impressed with the mail service."

"I intercepted your tablets. I have been working many days now to decide if you are a friend of the Truth, or of the Lie."

"My letter home is unlikely to tell you."

"At first I thought there must be some code in the words you used." He picked a sheet of parchment and stared at it. "I made copies to work upon. I tried every trick known to me, and that is many. I read off every second word, every third, every fourth, fifth, and sixth. Nothing worked. I looked for secret signs in the wax. I stared at it under strong light for something embedded in the wax. I found nothing.

"I was eventually forced to conclude that your message was no more than it seemed; the near-illiterate ramblings of a young man with nothing to say. But this did not satisfy me. Would you like to know why?"

"What would you do if I said no?"

"Because never, in the history of the world, has there been a young man who wrote to his father merely to send his greetings. Not even the most dutiful of sons does this. Sons write for many reasons; to ask for money; to explain an embarrassing incident before it reaches the ears of the sire from someone else; to announce to the sire he is about to become a grandfather, usually to his surprise since the son is not married. But no son, ever, has thought it important to write to say"— Barzanes picked up the parchment and read from it—"'The weather has been fine. I have seen many interesting things in Magnesia.'"

He put down the parchment.

"No, Athenian, if you want to cover a secret message, you will need to write something better than this offal."

I swore silently.

"I ask you again, to venerate the Truth and abjure the Lie. Tell me where is the message."

"I'm sorry you don't like my writing, Barzanes, but that doesn't mean there has to be anything more behind it."

"Ah, behind it. Yes." Barzanes picked up the backing boards. "In the time of the Great King Xerxes, before the wars between our people began, there resided in the court of the Great King a certain Demeratos of Sparta. This Demeratos had been king in his own land, but had been exiled by his people and accepted a guest's obligations at the court of the Persians. When

Demeratos learned of Xerxes' plan to invade Hellas, he decided to betray his host, a crime in any land, no?

"Knowing his perfidy dare not be caught, Demeratos took a writing tablet, scraped away the wax and scratched into the backing board his warning to the Spartans. Then he replaced the wax and sent the tablet with no message."

Barzanes paused. "Do you know how this story ends, Athenian?"

"Of course I do. Every boy in Hellas does. When the blank tablet arrived in Sparta, everyone was perplexed, except for Gorgo, the clever wife of King Leonidas. She realized since the wax surface was blank, there must be a message hidden beneath, and so the Hellenes had warning the Persians were on the way."

"Just so. Are you another Demeratos, Athenian?"

"You can look at the tablet and any part of it you like, for as long as you like, Barzanes. You will find no secret message." That, at least, I could say with confidence.

"I fear you are right." He dropped the backing boards. They hit the ground with a bang that startled me, though I saw it coming. "I have studied the boards, and there is nothing on them. I also looked at the wax itself, most closely. Perhaps there were pinpricks over certain letters, to spell out a message within a message."

If Barzanes wanted a reaction from me, he faced disappointment. This was obviously a test, mentioning one possibility after another to gauge my reaction. As long as I gave him nothing to work with, I was safe.

He continued, "But no, I found no pinpricks on the wax, nor any other intelligible sign. So I looked within the frame, to see if a slip of parchment was secreted there, or perhaps something scratched into the inside of the wood."

He picked up a piece of frame and peered at its inner side, then back to me. "Nothing."

I said, "Wasn't there a satrap who tattooed a message onto a trusted slave's scalp, and then waited for the hair to grow back?"

"There was, and his name was Histaeus of Miletus, yet another Hellene who betrayed the trust put in him by a Persian king. You see, Athenian, a certain pattern in the relationship between the Persians and the Hellenes? Like Demeratos, this Histaeus succeeded in his treachery, for a time at any rate. He was captured in the end and impaled upon the pole."

Perhaps I shouldn't have mentioned that example, but how was I to know the man had fooled some idiot king? There was no going back. "It's a wonder you didn't check the traveler I gave the tablets to for tattoos." I said, speaking in jest.

"I did."

Barzanes strode to the end of the room and pulled back the curtain that hung there. It revealed yet more room, and within was the cloth seller to whom I'd given the tablets. He was chained against the wall with his feet dangling, as I had been when Barzanes had me strung up. A rag was stuffed in the man's mouth and his eyes rolled in fear. His hair had been cut back to the scalp, and his skin had been shaved wherever hair hid it, including about the man's genitals.

"I looked most closely, but found nothing," Barzanes said, as calmly as if we discussed a dropped coin.

The poor cloth seller focused on me for the first time and he recognized me. In his eyes I saw accusation and raging hatred.

I mouthed at him, "I'm sorry."

I'd done it again. I'd made a terrible blunder, and now other people were to die for my mistake, just as the guards had back in Athens. Pericles was right to sack me; I wasn't fit for this.

Something was wrong with the way the cloth seller looked—not counting the fact that he was chained to a dungeon wall in fear of his life—and it took me a moment to realize what it was. At the ends of his feet were blank spaces where his toes should have been. Blood had pooled and dried on the stone floor directly below.

Barzanes must have seen the direction of my gaze, and the horror on my face, because he said, "It was necessary to discover if you had passed on any verbal message. He is not crippled; you see the large toes have been left and the middle ones, so he can still walk."

"Dear Gods, Barzanes, instead of torturing this innocent man, why didn't you simply ask me?"

"I have asked you, Athenian, in this room, many times, and every time you have proven friend to the Lie."

"Then think about this: by stopping that man and mutilating him, you've killed his unborn child. He was on his way to Ephesus to make money so he could afford their next child. Without the money they'll have to expose the baby."

"The cloth seller will be released with twice what he would have earned at market. I will pay this from my own wealth."

Barzanes walked back to the table. "After all this effort, I came to a surprising conclusion. Was it possible that this letter was what it seemed, entirely innocent? I was almost persuaded to release the cloth seller and drop the matter, but after our conversation on the ride back from Ephesus I thought it wise to make one last attempt."

Barzanes reached into a box beneath the bench with both hands, and pulled out two armfuls of wooden rods of different widths. He put them on the bench where they rolled about. He said, "I almost threw out the binding. In fact I made the mistake of cutting it instead of untying the knots. It was only when, having exhausted every other possibility, that I inspected the cord and noticed tiny scratches that might have been letters in your language. Then it was only a matter of finding how to reassemble the words." Barzanes searched through the rods, selected one, and began to wind.

I should have been terrified, but I was angry. "You deliberately put me through all this for your own pleasure!"

Barzanes had maintained his composure and kept a calm, neutral tone throughout the whole interview, but now his face contorted and he shouted, "No, Athenian, you have not listened to a word I said! I gave you every possible chance to repudiate the Lie. And did you? No! Instead you prove yourself its closest friend. You are Demeratos all over again, only this time, I thank Ahura Mazda for giving me the wisdom to prevent your crime. When the time comes for you to die, and you cross the narrow bridge to the House of Paradise, Mithra who judges the hearts of men will cast you into the chasm of flowing iron."

My heart almost stopped in fear, not because of this bizarre superstitious talk of angels and paradise and eternal punishment, but because it seemed to me at any moment Barzanes might call to the guards outside to take me away and kill me.

Barzanes strode across the room and flung open the door. He barked an order in Persian.

Diotima appeared from down the corridor, dragged between two Persian soldiers who held her arms in a lock. Her mouth had been stuffed with rag. She had a swelling black eye and a cut on her cheek. They hadn't taken her without a fight, but she was in pain; her head was bowed. She looked up and our eyes met, and the look in hers was anger, not fear. I know she saw fear in mine.

I'd promised I would never let anyone hurt her.

"The priestess is being held against your behavior."

I said, "You're holding the life of an innocent woman to protect a murderer, because you need the murderer to wage a war."

"Do not think I take pleasure in this, Athenian."

"You don't have to enjoy evil to do it, Barzanes, and I thought you were the ethical one. How's that pocket in your vest? Shall we take a look inside?"

"How I balance the good and evil I do is my problem." His voice was returned to neutral calm, but I heard the slightest tremor. "I have a duty to the Great King."

"Looks to me like I'll be seeing you in the boiling iron."

Barzanes winced as if I'd slapped him.

He gave me plenty of time to view the disaster, then said, "Marry the Satrap's daughter. Become his son, as shall I, and we will be brothers. Become his lieutenant when the Great King gives Athens to Themistocles. Rise high within the empire. All these things you can do. But if you make another attempt to save the Athenians, the priestess will die."

17

The difficulty is not so great to die for a friend,
as to find a friend worth dying for.

"Open up."

The two guards at the entrance to the cells looked at each other.

One began, "We must ask Lord Barzanes if—"

"You know who I am?" I interrupted.

They nodded. I was the Athenian traitor who spent so much time closeted with Themistocles, another Athenian traitor. Everyone knew I was to marry the Satrap's daughter.

The one I'd spoken over said, "What's in the basket?"

"Fruit, from the paradise."

He held out his hand. "Your dagger, and we must see the basket."

They were so interested in looking for hidden tools that they forgot to search me. Unfortunately I'd never counted on that. I'd brought nothing to help Diotima.

They opened a thick, wooden door that creaked into a narrow corridor with enough dust in the air to make me sneeze.

"Nico, what's happening?" A voice from a small cell on the left. The cell door was made of planks with gaps wide enough to pass a hand through and so allow air and a little light, which was necessary because there were neither windows nor ventilation within the cell itself. The corridor ended only a few paces along in a blank stone wall. I looked for any gap, anything that might give us a chance at a jailbreak. I saw nothing.

I said, "Pericles has no idea what's coming. Barzanes intercepted our invasion warning."

"Then our families are in the path, and a hundred thousand other Hellenes."

"Yes."

Diotima leaned close to the bars and whispered, "Nico, you must kill Themistocles."

"If I do, you'll die." I didn't bother to mention I was unlikely to escape either.

"So what? Can you save my life and let thousands and thousands die? And Athens conquered? And everyone we know a slave to the Persians? My family? Yours? Besides, he killed Brion and I want him to pay for that. You have to do it."

"You know what the local fashion is in executions, don't you? You want to spend days on a pole?"

"Give me your knife."

That shocked me. "I don't have it. The guards took it when I entered."

"Don't lie to me, Nicolaos. I know you better than that. Give me your backup, the one you have hidden beneath your tunic."

With the greatest reluctance, but unable to deny the logic of her demand, I reached behind and handed over the small, jagged knife. Diotima tested the edge with her finger before secreting it between her breasts underneath her clothing.

She whispered, quieter than ever, "If they come for me, I'll slit my throat. It'll be fast and painless."

"Diotima!"

"It's better than three days on the pole. You said so yourself."

I knew Diotima could give herself a quick death. As a priestess she had sacrificed many times, and once she had slit the throat of a human enemy.

I said, alarmed, "Do *not* do anything unless you are absolutely sure it's your last chance. Hear me, Diotima?"

"Yes, Nico."

On the spot, I came to a decision that amazed me. I didn't even know I would say the words until I heard them coming from my mouth, but my heart lifted as I said them.

"Diotima, I want you to take the knife, right now, and cut off some of your hair."

Diotima looked puzzled, uncomprehending. "But, I'm not in mourning. Not yet, anyway, and it's my death we're talking about. There's no need for me to do it."

"I want you to cut your hair, and then sacrifice it to Artemis."

There was no need to say more. Diotima knew the rituals far better than I. Her mouth and eyes became three large circles of astonishment. "Oh, Nico, do you mean this?"

"Yes, I do."

"But, we don't have everything we need according to the rites . . ."

"Just do it, Diotima. Please."

Diotima hesitated for a moment, then felt about her hair with her left hand. She decided on some locks at the back of her head, bent her neck, and sawed them off. They should have been burned, according to the ritual, but we had no fire. She kneeled on the floor and, intoning the prayers that she knew by heart, used the knife to slice her dark locks into tiny pieces. They became mixed with the dirt of the floor.

"Now hand me your girdle." All unmarried Athenian women

wear a girdle. The woman gives it up at the time of her marriage. Diotima stood and, without a word, removed the girdle and passed it through the bars to me. It should have been handed to her mother, but I was the only choice.

There was a bucket of water at the end of the corridor. We should both have bathed in the fountain of Kallirrhoe, but this would have to do. I took the scoop from the bucket and poured a trickle over my head. Diotima, more solemn than I had ever seen her, bent her head close to the view hole, and I reached through to pour a trickle on her too.

Diotima should have been carried in a chariot from her father's home to mine, dressed in fine robes for all the people to admire, and as she did she would eat an apple. We didn't have the chariot, nor her mother to walk behind holding torches, nor the fine robes, but I picked up one of the apples I had brought from the paradise and offered it to her.

There were tears in her eyes as she reached through the view hole and took it from my hands. She bit into it, and could barely chew or swallow, because now she was crying, but she finished it, all except for one bite that she left for me. That wasn't according to the ritual, but I liked it. I took the last bite and kept the core.

We reached up and held hands together.

"We can't do the most important bit," she said, and smiled through her tears.

"We already have."

We had performed as much of the marriage ceremony as a man and woman can when separated by a prison door and without their families or any of the trappings that go with a wedding.

"What will your father say when he finds out?"

"He'll get over it."

"He might not. He could repudiate this, you know."

"No, he won't, my wife. I promise you." He would never find out, because we were both going to die here.

The strength of her hold on me increased. "What will you do, Nicolaos, my husband?"

It felt like a hundred years since I'd attended the symposium of Callias. Back then, I'd wished for a Marathon of my own to fight. Now I faced something every bit as bad, and I cursed myself for a fool.

"I have no idea, my wife."

Diotima was the one for me. I'd known it since the day I met her. But in choosing Diotima over Asia I'd broken with Themistocles, and insulted him. He didn't know it yet, but he'd learn soon enough when I turned down the nuptials with Asia, and to make it worse, I knew too much about the coming attack on Athens. Themistocles would want me dead, and this was the man who was about to become Satrap of Athens.

But if I stopped Themistocles—and the only way to stop him now was to assassinate him—then Barzanes would execute Diotima. My two objectives were mutually exclusive, like that principle of logic Socrates had gone on about, back in our home at Athens.

To save Diotima, or to save Athens. What should I do?

Homer had described my problem, in the *Iliad*. The hero Hector, knowing he faced almost certain defeat, had parted from his wife and gone to face the enemy with the words, "One omen is best: to fight for your country."

I would follow Hector.

Of course, Hector had been slaughtered that same day. I would try not to follow him in all things.

I found Mac in the agora.

"Mac, I want to hire your services again."

He looked at me doubtfully. "I'm doubling the fee."

"Fine. Take me to that witch woman you mentioned."

He grinned. "Still got woman trouble?"

"I fixed that. Now it's man trouble."

"You get around!"

Mac led me to a dingy street on the outskirts of the northern part of the city, where the houses began to give way to farms. An old, shriveled woman sat in a hut that was little better than cast-off wooden pales, stuck together with daubs of mud. Something bubbled and boiled in a pot, over a small hearth she had lined with mud bricks. She peered at me closely—she was shortsighted—and grinned with near-toothless gums. Her skin was mottled and her hair was thin.

Mac said, "He's all right, Mina. He's a customer."

She cackled. (I'd always imagined ancient witches cackled, and now I knew it was true.) "And what does he want?"

"Poison," I said simply.

She didn't even blink. "Fast, or slow?"

"Fast."

"Painful death, or easy?"

I shrugged. "I'm not fussed. I want simple to deliver and no mistakes." With guards constantly hovering over Themistocles, there wasn't the slightest chance of stopping him with a dagger.

She nodded. "He should reach for Mina the box high atop yonder shelf."

I handed it to her and she undid the lid. I saw inside many small vials of different shapes and markings. She handed me one. "That he holds is the juice of many peach kernels. 'Tis stronger than the snakebite. No, he must not open the lid. Even the smell is strong and may make a grown man faint."

I quickly replaced the stopper. "Will it work on a dart?" I asked.

Mina shrugged. "Mina knows not. He can but try. But for

certain sure the concoction in a man's drink will carry him to Hades faster than a knife to the heart."

"There are bits of poison in *peaches*?" I asked, incredulous.

"He trusts Mina not," she said to Mac. "Aye, 'tis the peach, but the seed alone. Many in the greatest number, all together, and boiled to be the juice of the seed, and left to the air so that the Gods take the water and leave behind that which kills."

So Anaxagoras was right after all with his crazy talk of mixed-up particles. Who'd have thought it? I made a mental note never to eat a peach again.

"Thanks for trying to kill me."

"I'm amazed you survived," Mnesiptolema said, without the slightest trace of embarrassment. I'd tracked her down as soon as I returned to the palace and, to her surprise, dragged her into her own bedroom. It was the one place I could be sure there were no listeners.

I said, "It wasn't for lack of effort on Araxes' part."

"That bastard! I'll demand my money back. You just can't get decent help these days."

"I feel for you."

"I suppose it was Araxes who gave me away."

"No, I worked it out myself." It was a half truth, but Mnesiptolema needed more respect for my powers.

I said, "Araxes let slip that the person who wanted me dead had called me a highly trained assassin. You're the only person who ever used that phrase. Also, you once wondered whether Araxes might be for hire. You were thinking about your father then, but it wasn't much of a leap to transfer your attention to me, was it?"

"Do you know why?"

"Revenge for the scene in my bedroom. Why did you wait until now?"

"Father announced Asia's betrothal. I wanted my revenge before you became a brother. Besides, it means Father still favors that little bitch, despite everything."

"Listen, Mnesiptolema, I'd as soon kill you as look at you, but we need each other."

"For what?" she asked suspiciously.

"To kill your father. Tonight. That's why you sent the letter, isn't it? But we must be able to trust each other."

Mnesiptolema laughed, loud and cynical.

"Hear me out. I know enough to put you on the pole. Barzanes wouldn't hesitate, and Themistocles couldn't stop him. We can settle our differences later, but like it or not, right now we're stuck with each other."

Mnesiptolema thought about it. "I agree. We can kill each other after we both have what we need from Father's death."

Mnesiptolema called together the children of Themistocles. All except Asia. We crowded into the bedroom of Archeptolis and Mnesiptolema. I sat on the edge of the bed—I avoided the stains—and waited for the others to settle themselves on the abominably soft red cushions on the bench along the wall, except for Mnesiptolema, who chose to stand. Then I explained my plan to them, and ended with, "I need your help."

"No." Nicomache and Cleophantus together. Archeptolis coughed. Mnesiptolema narrowed her eyes.

"Listen to me," I said. "Nicomache, do you want to marry Barzanes?"

"No, of course not."

"Well you will. Unless you work with me. Cleophantus, I see you enjoy being a traitor to Athens."

"You know I loathe it," he said, angry. "Nico, what is this?"

"If Themistocles succeeds with his plan, that's what you'll be for the rest of your life. But you really want to be a respected gentleman of Athens, don't you?"

Cleophantus looked away.

Nicomache said, "The blood curse—"

"The blood curse is my problem," I interrupted. "You said it yourself, when we sat in the tomb. I've made the decision, I'm doing the deed. You don't need to do a thing. In fact, you have to *not* do something. You have to *not* take a cup. Before dinner tonight, you, Mnesiptolema, will take one of the wine cups from the kitchen, into which I will pour wine and add crystals of poison. I'll put a slight chip in the base so we all know which one it is. Mnesiptolema, make sure you are the one to carry the drinks tonight. Each of us will take a cup, leaving the chipped one for Themistocles. Let me emphasize, for this scheme to work, all that's required is for each of you to *not* do something. There is no blood guilt for you, only for me."

It was a thin line, but a familiar one to any Hellene, the same as the logic that allowed us to expose our unwanted babies.

Nicomache said, as angry as I'd ever heard her, "You refused to do this before. I was ready, I'd steeled myself up for it. Then you refused and I was able to relax. Why must you raise the whole awful thing again and upset me when I thought it was all over?"

I hesitated, but realized the truth couldn't hurt.

"Because I've married for love."

Mnesiptolema gagged.

I ignored her. I explained what had happened and finished, "If I can marry for love, so can you, Nicomache. Think of your lover Phrasicles. You still want him, don't you?"

Nicomache nodded, but she wasn't happy. Neither was I, but I'd made my choice, and now I had to force my choice on the children of Themistocles.

"The slaves and the guards who stand at his back will swear none of us touched his cup. Barzanes will investigate the kitchen and find no one there responsible. He will, however, find a suicide note in Themistocles' own hand."

"Impossible," Cleophantus said.

"I've already written it. I copied the writing on a note he sent me."

Mnesiptolema thought about it. "It might work," she said, and Archeptolis nodded in agreement. "We can do this."

"I still don't like it," Nicomache said.

Mnesiptolema snorted in disgust. "Too late to back out now."

Cleophantus said, "It's what we agreed, Nicomache. Think of what happened to us after Father was condemned. Do you want to go through it all over again? Imagine walking down the street if Father becomes Satrap of Athens. They won't dare spit on us with the Persians protecting us, but you know they'll want to."

They all of them nodded. But I couldn't stop for a moment.

There were still preparations to make, and very little time in which to make them.

18

Without a sign,
his sword the brave man draws,
and asks no omen,
but his country's cause.

Six of us sat down to dinner. Themistocles at the head of the table, Archeptolis to his right, then Mnesiptolema and Nicomache. Cleophantus to Themistocles' left, and then me.

The food was on the table, and although Themistocles ate heartily, his children seemed to have less appetite. Mnesiptolema entered bearing the tray of six cups of wine. She had pulled one of the cups from the kitchen shortly before, and I had returned it to her filled with wine and chipped. Now she offered me my choice of cups from the tray, and I took one nonchalantly, examined it closely to make absolutely sure there was no chip. Never before or since have I displayed such an interest in crockery.

Nicomache's turn was next. Her hand shook as she reached out, and I was sure Themistocles must see through the plot. I glanced at him but he seemed preoccupied. He frowned, his chin resting in his right hand and his eyes downcast.

Nicomache's hand shook so much she dropped hers. Wine the color of blood flowed across the table.

Mnesiptolema hissed, "Idiot!" She signaled to a slave to come sop up the mess while she moved on to Archeptolis. He took the nearest cup and sipped, without even a glance to ensure he was not taking poison. I realized he and Mnesiptolema had arranged she would present a safe cup nearest, but even so I marveled at his sangfroid. He and Mnesiptolema were fine conspirators; I felt honored to be plotting with them, and made a mental note never to trust either.

Cleophantus, looking like he was about to cry but resolute nevertheless, reached for his cup when, "I hope I'm not interrupting." Barzanes stood in the doorway.

Themistocles looked up. "Interrupting? Dinner is just starting. Do join us."

"With pleasure." Barzanes took the empty seat next to me and held out his hand for wine. "Oh, but I see there is only one cup for each, and I am one too many."

"No, no, take mine," said Themistocles. "I'll order another for myself."

Cleophantus and Mnesiptolema had been frozen. Now Cleophantus clutched a cup in a spasm and Mnesiptolema's face registered consternation and fear. She hesitated.

Themistocles said, "Mnesiptolema, what ails you, girl? Offer Barzanes a cup."

Mnesiptolema woodenly stepped forward and bent down to Barzanes with the two remaining cups. As she did she twisted the tray in her hands so that one particular cup was closest to him.

Good try, I thought to myself. That showed presence of mind. Barzanes' hand touched the first cup, and hesitated. "There is one here chipped," he said. "As the last present I shall take the least presentable." He reached forward and took the second cup.

Mnesiptolema opened her mouth, shut it again, placed the last cup before her own seat, and sat down. She looked over to me as if to ask, What do we do now? I think Barzanes caught the look. He held up his cup, inspecting the decoration. To the table at large he said, "Would you indulge a Persian at a table of Hellenes? You have a custom, I know, called the Loving Cup where the guests pass a cup of wine one to the next. In Persia we might offer our food to another. In this company though, I think the Hellene custom best, particularly since a Hellene is to be my wife." He smiled at Nicomache, the first I had seen him do so. Nicomache's answering smile was brittle. She said nothing.

Barzanes continued, "So in the spirit of the Loving Cup of the Hellenes, I begin by giving the first taste to my neighbor, my future brother-in-law."

Barzanes passed along the chipped cup. Now all eyes were upon me. Barzanes had arranged it so there was no possible way I could avoid drinking.

Nicomache whimpered.

There was nothing else I could do. I closed my eyes and drank.

Instantly I clutched my throat and choked and coughed for a moment, before I was able to say, "I'm sorry. It went down the wrong way." I passed the cup on to Cleophantus. "Your turn."

Cleophantus stared at me as if I were one of Barzanes' Daevas. "But . . . but . . ."

A slave carried in the transparent drinking horn from which I had drunk at the banquet, and set it before Themistocles. Themistocles raised it and offered his favorite toast. "We would have been undone, had we not been undone."

Themistocles downed the wine and set the cup upon the table. He began to speak, but instead clutched a hand over his heart and looked at us as if surprised.

He said, "I need to lie down."

He rose and swayed, visibly struggling to stay upright. Two slaves rushed to hold him.

Themistocles stared at each of us around the table. His eyes locked with mine for what seemed an age. He smiled and said, "Polycrates . . ." Then he choked.

I recalled his words of months before. Of the death of Polycrates he'd said, "I admire any man who can carry off such a devious plot. . . . If a man could trick *me* like that, I'd have to admire his skills."

The weight was too much for the slaves. Themistocles fell.

"Cursed Daevas!" Barzanes kneeled at Themistocles' side. The rest of us crowded around. Themistocles convulsed on the floor. There was nothing we could do except hold him down, but eventually the twitchings slowed to nothing, and as they did, his breathing became ragged and his face turned bright red. A moment later he lay still. The old witch had been right; it was like a knife to the heart.

Barzanes looked for any sign of breath. "He's dead."

Behind me, Nicomache wept.

Barzanes said, "How did this thing happen? A sudden illness? What is this?" He picked up a scroll case lying beside Themistocles. He turned it around in his hand, puzzled, before unfurling the contents.

The scroll case had come from the rack in Archeptolis and Mnesiptolema's room. This was the scroll on which I'd forged a suicide note. I'd dropped it and kicked it along the floor while everyone watched Themistocles die.

Barzanes read, "'My children, the war against the Persians was the greatest triumph of my life. I cannot bring myself to undo it, but nor can I refuse the orders of Artaxerxes. I therefore choose the only honorable path, in the hope he will understand and maintain you in your positions. Farewell.'

"An odd way to commit suicide," Barzanes said. "Before one's family, without warning, during a dinner."

"Not so odd, perhaps," I said. "Among some Hellenes it was

once the custom for a man to take hemlock when he reached sixty years. The family would stand by the man as he reached for the cup."

"But he offered no forewarning."

"Perhaps he felt, if you knew, you would have stopped him?"

"It would have been my duty, yes."

He looked me in the eye. I looked back, keeping tight rein on my thoughts. I knew what decision Barzanes had to make, and it was important I didn't appear to help him.

Barzanes said, his voice low, "You could not have known I would come here. You *could not.* I did not decide myself until the last moment. You could not have known Themistocles would call for another cup."

"No, of course not."

"You *could not* have known," he said as if to convince himself. "There will be an investigation, but first, the Great King must hear of this at once." Barzanes strode to the exit.

I almost shouted in the silence of the room, "Barzanes! Before you go."

He stopped and turned to me. "Yes?"

"You have a long ride ahead of you. Why not lighten your load in one pocket?"

He was puzzled for a moment before he took my meaning and said, "You speak truth." He turned to one of the guards at the door. "Release the priestess."

Barzanes turned back to me and said, "What's done is done. I thank you, Athenian. My pocket is indeed much lighter." Everyone in the room must have thought Barzanes meant my reminder to release Diotima, the need to hold her having passed, but I wondered if Barzanes had thanked me for something more sinister. If he could convince himself Themistocles had died by his own hand, but left behind a workable battle plan, then all his ethical problems were over.

Barzanes left the room at a run. I could hear him running up the steps of the palace two at a time in the direction of Themistocles' office.

The children of Themistocles were dazed.

"What happened?" Cleophantus asked, and "Who invited Barzanes?"

"I did," I said simply. "I sent him an anonymous note that a plot against the life of Themistocles would be carried out during dinner. I told the truth, after all, didn't I?"

All four of them stared at me in shock. "Traitor," Mnesiptolema hissed. Archeptolis' hand went to his side; I'm sure he would have drawn a weapon and slain me on the spot, had he one. Cleophantus was ashen and Nicomache shaking.

Cleophantus asked, "But why? Why make everything go wrong? Barzanes might have taken the poisoned cup. He did take the cup, curse it, and you drank it. Why aren't you dead?"

"None of the cups Mnesiptolema brought in were poisoned," I said. "I had to make it absolutely certain, in Barzanes' eyes, that I could not possibly have committed this crime. What's more, I couldn't trust you amateurs to get it right. I had to make sure the poison was in the one and only cup that would go straight to Themistocles. That would be the one he called for himself."

"But you were here at the table the whole time. You couldn't possibly have poisoned his wine. So if it wasn't you, then who?"

"The only person I could trust," I said.

"I did it." They all turned to see Asia standing in the doorway. She fainted.

19

A small rock holds back a great wave.

Araxes had been right, returning Asia to her home had turned her into a player in the game. Yet if she hadn't been there, my mission would have failed, Athens may have fallen, and a murder would have gone unavenged. Now she lay in a fever in the women's quarters. Diotima assured me she'd recover, given time.

Barzanes had grabbed the scroll box of Themistocles' master plan, had ordered up Ajax, the most powerful beast in the stables, and had ridden into the night with the precious box, and a squad of horse soldiers to protect it. He would not stop until he arrived at the Great King's palace in Susa. There he would be disappointed to discover that Nicomache, in the afternoon, on my instruction, had replaced her father's battle plan with Diotima's copy of the Book of Heraclitus. I hoped the Great King found it educational.

I'd held in my hands the most precious and sensitive document in the world: the master plan of how to conquer Hellas. I read it through once, exclaiming from time to time as I did, and memorized every word. Who knew, maybe one day I would need this plan myself. Themistocles had taught me an important lesson: always leave a second way.

When I finished, I handed it to Cleophantus, who carried the scroll to the burning brazier of Barzanes' God. Cleophantus tore off pieces of parchment and fed them to the fire until every scrap of it was ashes.

Barzanes was sure to be in a bad mood when he returned, and I didn't want to be here to suffer it, but Diotima insisted we stay a few days while she nursed Asia. The two of them spent every waking moment talking. They'd discovered they had a lot in common.

The Olympic Games were due to begin any day, with a general truce, declared by three runners who crisscross the Hellene lands. The runners didn't come as far as Magnesia, but we knew. Diotima and I planned to take ship and sail direct to Elis, and thence to Olympia, where Pericles was sure to be. This was a mission report I couldn't wait to deliver.

The family had begun the preparations to bury Themistocles the next morning, even as the populace of Magnesia gathered at the gates to wail and grieve for the man whose leadership had improved their lives. The people built a pyre in the middle of the agora, and the family gathered his ashes.

Cleophantus and I waited outside the palace, for Diotima to join us. He'd given us mounts for the journey to Ephesus. He said, "The people are already talking about erecting a statue to Father in the agora. I think it's a good idea. He did good work here, for all that he felt Magnesia was his low point. I don't know what we'll do with his ashes. He wanted to be taken back to Athens, but . . ." Cleophantus shrugged. "I don't know that the Athenians would have him back, even dead."

"Can I make a suggestion? Take him to Piraeus. Piraeus was his triumph. The people there will welcome him." I thought of the harbormaster who revered Themistocles. "Erect a monument to him on the headland. Then he can watch the most powerful fleet in the world come and go, the fleet he created, with which he defeated the Persians."

"That's a good idea. I'll talk to the others about it. Your plot was brilliant, Nico. Brilliant, and simple and devious and ruthless all at the same time; the sort of thing I'd have expected from Father. I can barely believe you fooled the Persian."

"I did what any Hellene would do. I lied to him."

"And you said you weren't an assassin!" Cleophantus laughed and clapped me on the back.

"I'll assume you mean that as a compliment."

"I do." Cleophantus paused, then said, "Nico, speaking of lying . . ."

"Yes?"

"I . . . all his children . . . would rather people remembered Father for the good he did. When you return to Athens, could you perhaps not mention that he plotted to invade Hellas?"

"Hide what happened here?"

"Yes. If people knew . . ." He flinched.

That was an easy decision. "I honor his memory too, Cleophantus. I must tell Pericles, but no one else will ever know."

"Thank you."

"Er . . . in return, it would be nice if you didn't mention to anyone that I killed him."

Cleophantus nodded. "That seems fair. As long as you don't reveal we children asked you to do it."

"Agreed. As long as you don't tell anyone I screamed when I was about to die on the pole."

"Consider it forgotten. And if you could forget about Asia's illegitimate parentage—"

"Done. If you don't tell anyone I almost went over to the Persians."

"Agreed. And if you could keep the secret of Mnesiptolema and Archeptolis and their . . . er . . . unusual habits—"

"Oh no!" I protested. "That one I'll be retelling at symposia for years to come."

Cleophantus laughed. "I don't like them either. All right Nico, it's a deal."

So many secrets to be kept, and one more. I would never reveal, not even to Diotima, that Asia had *insisted* she be the one to poison Themistocles. She had avenged her true father against the man who killed him. It would remain our secret, for the sake of her relationship with her brothers and sisters, and to enable her to find a husband in the future, and even for her own safety.

I said, "I'm sorry about Asia, but it was the only way. "

Cleophantus nodded. "We'll do our best to help her. I'm sorry too, Nico, about the letter. If we'd never sent it, you wouldn't have been drawn here and endangered, and Thorion would still be alive."

"And Hellas might have fallen to the Persians. Don't be sorry. Thorion died defending Athens as surely as any man in the front rank of the army. When I return I'll be sure to tell his son so." It would make all the difference for him and his family.

Cleophantus said, "May the Gods favor you." We hugged.

Diotima walked out of the front entrance of the palace. She smiled at me and said, "Are we ready to go, Nico?"

I took her hand. "We're ready, my wife."

AUTHOR'S NOTE

Warning! This author note
discusses the real history behind
the story. It's chockablock full of
spoilers. If you haven't read the
book yet, I suggest you turn to the
front. I hope you enjoy the book,
and I'll see you back here
in a while.

To the people who lived at the start of the Golden Age of Greece, Themistocles was the smartest guy in the room.

Themistocles was a man who showed an unmistakable natural genius; in this respect he was quite exceptional, and beyond all others deserves our admiration. . . . He was particularly remarkable at looking into the future and seeing there the hidden possibilities for good or evil. To sum him up in a few words, it may be said that through force of genius and by rapidity of action this man was supreme at doing precisely the right thing at precisely the right moment.

That quote was written by the great historian Thucydides. He personally knew both Pericles and Socrates, but he doesn't hesitate to rank Themistocles first for intelligence.

The only modern man to compare with Themistocles is Sir Winston Churchill. Indeed, Themistocles and Churchill had much in common. They were both renowned for their ready wit, they both had foresight beyond their fellow mortals, they both had the courage to act in the face of fierce opposition, and they both had egos the size of a mountain. I'm pretty sure if the two men had lived at the same time, the universe would have exploded.

Just as Churchill foresaw the coming of World War II, so Themistocles foresaw the Persian Wars. He persuaded the Athenians to build the most powerful fleet the world had yet seen—of two hundred triremes—which was ready in time when the Persians invaded. The Greek fleet destroyed the otherwise overwhelming Persian force, and changed the course of history. It was all the doing of Themistocles.

Themistocles made no secret that he considered himself a genius. The fact that he was correct did nothing to endear him to his fellow citizens. So when the Spartans, who feared and hated Themistocles, produced dodgy evidence that Themistocles had colluded with the enemy, the Athenians were only too ready to believe it.

Themistocles clearly was not someone you would wish to have plotting against you, but that is precisely the position the Athenians found themselves in after they ostracized the genius they feared was evil. To put a cherry on top, they condemned him to death for treason, based on the (probably faked) Spartan evidence. When he went over to the enemy, the Greeks, and the Athenians in particular, had everything to fear.

The Athenian fleet in 460 BC, when *The Ionia Sanction* takes place, was grossly overcommitted in Cyprus and Egypt. The

Athenian army was scattered to deal with multiple ongoing wars. When fighting suddenly flared up against Corinth in the west, Athens had nothing left to send but old men and boys. The old men and boys vanquished the army of Corinth(!), but it meant Athens was totally exposed to the east.

At that one delicate moment in history, if Themistocles had made his move, it seems certain Athens would have fallen, and with it, the future of Western civilization.

But Themistocles didn't make his move. Instead, he dropped dead.

His death came as a result of an illness; though there are some people who say that he committed suicide by taking poison, when he found that it was impossible to keep the promises that he had made to the King [to invade Greece]. In any case, there is a monument to him in the market-place of Magnesia in Asia. This was the district over which he ruled; for the King gave him Magnesia for his bread (and it brought in fifty talents a year), Lampsacus for his wine (which was considered at the time to be the best wine district of all), and Myos for his meat. It is said that his bones were, at his desire, brought home by his relations and buried secretly in Attica. The secrecy was necessary since it is against the law to bury in Attica the bones of one who has been exiled for treason.

This from Thucydides, book I, section 138, of the *Peloponnesian War* from the excellent Penguin edition. You can see in this one quote where much of my story comes from. An exile who wants his bones buried back in native soil is homesick. A strategic genius with an empire to back him, and a king demanding an attack plan, is in a position to get himself home. A man with three cities dedicated to feeding him probably has high cholesterol.

You see then that the death of Themistocles was unbelievable good luck for Athens. Either that, or, someone helped him along.

The blind poet, Homer, is the source of the quotes at the top of each chapter in *The Ionia Sanction*. Most major cultures in history have had their own great religious text: the Bible, the *Tao Te Ching, The Book of the Dead*. The Greeks had no book of religion at all. Instead they revered two great literary works: the *Iliad* and the *Odyssey.*

The city of Troy, of which Homer wrote, lay in the land named Ionia: the coastal region that is now western Turkey. The Greeks had colonized Ionia hundreds of years before; the colonies subsequently came under Persian rule. The Greeks, and the Athenians in particular, supported an Ionian uprising, which the Persians ruthlessly repressed. Athenian support for Ionian freedom was one of the reasons the Persians decided to deal with Athens, and which led to the Persian Wars.

Thorion the proxenos had one of the most interesting official jobs a man could have in Classical Greece. Thorion himself is my invention, but the job of proxenos was very real indeed.

The proxenoi acted rather like the modern system of consulates, but in reverse. Imagine if all foreign consulates were staffed and run not by citizens of the foreign nation, but by local citizens well disposed to the foreign nation for whom they acted. The *pro* means *for,* the *xenos* means *foreigner.* Hence *proxenos* means someone who acted on behalf of foreigners.

The proxenoi appear to have been at least as effective as the consulates of modern times. With the hundreds of Greek city-states, and their intricate political and trade alliances, the proxenoi must have formed a complex and fascinating network of men.

There is no record that the proxenoi ran an intercity mail service, but I think that they must have. With the amount of correspondence each proxenos sent to his client city, what more natural thing than to use a single courier to carry it all? And what more natural thing than for his fellow citizens to give the proxenos any letters they want sent in the same direction?

Today, Piraeus is the largest port in Greece, thanks to Themistocles, who in about 480 BC, twenty years before this story, decided that Piraeus was the perfect base for his shiny new fleet.

The Long Walls, down which Nico and Araxes fight atop a slippery cart, sound like something from an epic fantasy, but they were quite real. Athens was a walled city. Piraeus was an armed and fortified base for the fleet. It was Themistocles' idea to enclose the entire road from Athens to Piraeus within the Long Walls, so that Athens, Piraeus, and the road between became one vast fortification. It meant Athens could never be cut off from her fleet.

Nico's favorite food is eel in garos sauce. Eel was considered a delicacy and was expensive to buy in the agora. Garos sauce was the ketchup of the ancient world, hugely popular in both Greece and Rome (the Romans called it garum).

The original Greek version of garos was made from leftover fish entrails. When fishwives gutted the morning catch, they discarded the entrails into large vats where seawater was added, and the whole goopy mess allowed to ferment in the sun over weeks or months into yummy garos. The garos would have been transported up to Athens in amphorae loaded on to carts, exactly like the one Nico finds himself fighting upon.

It seems to be a common belief that British Worcestershire sauce is descended from garos or garum. It's not so. Worcestershire sauce is an accident derived from an Indian sauce. There is no chance that Worcestershire sauce tastes like garos, because the Greeks are known to have disliked anchovies. Also Worcestershire includes molasses, chilies, and sugar, none of which the Greeks had.

It's sometimes said that the closest modern equivalent to garos is an Asian fish sauce called *nuoc mam*. For all I know, it might even be true.

Modern readers expect to find fenugreek on their pizzas and in their curries. The Greeks put it in their wine. Fenugreek means, literally, "Greek hay." The Greeks put 1 percent to 2 percent seawater in their wine for a very practical reason: in a world without sulphur, salt makes the next best preservative.

Greeks *always* watered down their wine. To drink wine neat was the mark of the worst sort of barbarian. The ratios Nico gives during the symposium are correct; normal everyday drinking called for three parts water to one of wine.

Anaxagoras was the world's first professional philosopher, in the sense that Pericles paid for his upkeep in return for the wisdom of his thoughts. Historians of philosophy have long wondered whether Anaxagoras might have taught the young Socrates, but generally discount the idea because of the big difference in their ages. I'm glad that with this book we can finally reveal the truth of the matter.

Speaking of matter, the theory of matter that Anaxagoras espouses at the symposium is the beginning of atomic theory, and it happened in Athens, 2,500 years ago. The Greeks were much exercised by the question: if things were made of tiny particles, then what moved the particles? The answer of Anaxagoras was something he called Mind. The Greek word for mind is *nous,* which remains a word in English. The Mind proposed by Anaxagoras was a cosmic intelligence that decided what was to happen. In other words, a God. In these days when science and religion are so often at loggerheads, it's ironic that the world's first atomic theory was used to prove that a God existed.

The greatest philosopher of the age was Heraclitus of Ephesus. You might never have heard of him before, but you've certainly heard his most famous thought: "You cannot step twice into the same river." By which he meant that nothing ever stays the same; everything flows and changes.

Heraclitus was descended from the ancient kings of Ephesus, and himself was offered the crown. He turned it down, because to be a philosopher walking the hills of Ephesus stark naked and eating nothing but grass was so much more cool. Heraclitus caught dropsy, probably from eating the grass, which he then tried to cure by coating himself in cow poo and lying in the sun. You can guess how well this turned out. He was buried in the middle of the agora of Ephesus, where Nico trips over his funeral stone.

Heraclitus donated the one and only copy of the book he wrote to the Artemision, where people came from far and wide to read it and make copies. The small side temple that contains the Book of Heraclitus is my invention, but there must have been a keeper of the book.

Salaminia was the Air Force One of the ancient world. She really did exist, a special trireme fitted with only the best equipment, crewed only by citizens, and reserved for only the most delicate missions.

Most people these days know of Ephesus from the Bible. Think Paul's Epistles to the Ephesians. Those with a classical bent will know of Ephesus as home to one of the Seven Wonders of the Ancient World: the Temple of Artemis. The commercial agora at Ephesus, which Nico visits, is considered by some to be the world's first stock market.

Ephesus was abandoned in medieval times because silt built up in the harbor. Today, the ruins of Ephesus are many miles inland. The ruins are absolutely magnificent and a must-see if you're in the area. The city layout is precisely as Nico describes it. The brothel on Marble Road into which he blunders is real and can be walked through.

Artemis of Ephesus was a mother goddess, her cult statue covered in breasts, much to Nico's appreciation, whereas the Artemis of Athens was the Huntress.

Diotima has her facts right (as usual) when she describes the history of the Artemision, but for some slight errors caused by the Greeks not knowing their past as well as we know it today. There was a temple on the site of the Artemision dating back at least to the Bronze Age, no doubt rebuilt many times. The Amazons were indeed believed to have worshipped there before the fall of Troy.

All Greek temples had sanctuaries in much the same way as medieval cathedrals. The sanctuary of the Artemision of Ephesus was considered particularly strong, and so important that even the Great King of the Persians respected it. The belief in the sanctuary was such that at an earlier date during a siege, the Ephesians tried to save themselves by chaining the city to the temple.

The Artemision is one of the temples associated with sacred prostitution by both the ancient Greek travel writer Pausanias and by the Bible. The claim is contentious, and for my money, it's wrong. The evidence simply isn't there, and more to the point, how could the commercial brothel on Marble Road have done the thriving business it obviously did, if there was ecumenically approved nookie up at the temple?

A more probable claim is that the Artemision was served by eunuchs. The Greeks were about as uncomfortable with eunuchy as modern men, but Ephesus lies in Asia Minor where a large non-Hellene population had lived since prehistoric times, and the Asian peoples of the area were definitely pro-eunuch. The Persians regularly used eunuch slaves. Strabo says point-blank there were eunuchs at the Artemision and that they were called the Megabyzoi. I've accepted the Megabyzoi as true and the temple prostitutes as false. As with all historical interpretation, your mileage may vary.

Brion comes to a very sticky end, but one by no means unusual for the times. Impalement was a common method of state execution across the Middle East. The Hittites, Assyrians, Egyptians, and Persians all practiced it, although never the Greeks. There are even ancient "decorations" that show it done. The British Museum has a frieze that exhibits Assyrians impaling people.

Whiney, bleeding heart, soft-on-crime liberals eventually complained that anal impalement was too cruel. (I can't imagine why.) So they introduced the soft option of crucifixion. Crucifixion was an instant hit and replaced anal impalement altogether, until it was revived centuries later by that well-known traditionalist, Vlad the Impaler. Vlad is immortalized in popular culture as the inspiration for Count Dracula.

The King's Messengers, from whom Nico's horse, Ajax, was stolen, was a real organization. The King's Messengers are mentioned in Herodotus' *The Histories* (book VIII, section 98, if you're interested).

No mortal thing travels faster than these Persian couriers.
The whole idea is a Persian invention, and works like this: riders

*are stationed along the road, equal in number to the number
of days the journey takes—a man and a horse for each day.
Nothing stops these couriers from covering their allotted stage
in the quickest possible time—neither snow, rain, heat, nor
darkness. The first, at the end of his stage, passes his dispatch
to the second, the second to the third, and so on down the
line . . .*

U.S. readers might have noticed something familiar in the
quote from Herodotus. The unofficial creed of the U.S. Postal
Service is "Neither snow nor rain nor heat nor gloom of night
stays these couriers from the swift completion of their appointed
rounds." That's right. The U.S. Postal Service creed comes straight
from the King's Messengers of the Persian Empire.

Nico and Diotima see many strange things in Asia Minor,
but perhaps the strangest are glass and silk. A Persian drinking
horn fashioned out of glass has been found that dates to this
period. It is perfectly possible that Themistocles, as a favored
friend of the Great King, might have received one as a gift. The
idea of using glass to make windows lies far in the future, for
the present it's enough of a shock that there's a solid material
you can see through.

The Silk Road is open at this very early date. Silk has reached
the Persian lands, but probably no farther. The daughters of
Themistocles, a wealthy and powerful man who has recently
been at the Persian Court in Susa, were in a position to bring
bolts of silk with them when he moved to Magnesia. Diotima
acquires some silk dresses at the end of the book, her just reward for the perils she faced. When she returns to Athens she'll
be the envy of every woman. In the coming century a few Athenian women with wealthy husbands will be able to afford the
new wonder material.

In the unlikely event that this book is ever assigned as a school text, I'll save the poor student a lot of time by telling you now that the underlying theme is the nature of loyalty. When Nicolaos says that loyalty is first to oneself, then one's family, and lastly to one's city, he gives the standard Greek view.

The Greeks had no concept of national loyalty as we know it. None at all. Yet despite that the Greeks, and the Athenians in particular, are the people we have to thank for our underlying modern political philosophy. The Athenians believed, overwhelmingly, in the importance and priority of individual freedom. They took this view to its logical conclusion.

The Persians believed, overwhelmingly, in the importance and priority of the state and the need to maintain social order. In the Persian system the Great King ruled and every other man was his slave, his position defined in a strict hierarchy.

The Greek concept of moral responsibility was quite different to ours. When the children of Themistocles decide to arrange the death of their father, they tread a fine but not impossible moral line. The children make known to the Athenians certain facts about their father, they have not *actually* tried to kill him. If the Athenians send an assassin as a result of their letter, well, that was the decision of the Athenians, not the children.

Their logic is precisely the same doublethink as applied throughout Greece to the exposure of babies. The Greeks, with their terrible population pressure and scarce resources, exposed newborn babies if the family hadn't enough food to go around. Indeed, in the book, the cloth seller from Phrygia has precisely this problem.

To the Greek mind, abandoning a baby avoided blood guilt. But under no circumstances would the father of the house kill the baby himself. That would have been murder! To them the moral distinction was clear. The children of Themistocles make full use of it.

There is no historical record of the children of Themistocles attempting to harm him in any way. My story traduces a family that in all probability was happy and loving. The irregular paternity of Asia is also my own invention. If the living descendants could be identified—and there must surely be some considering how many children Themistocles had—then I suppose they could sue me for defamation.

The incestuous marriage of Mnesiptolema and Archeptolis, however, is real. The Greeks weren't too fussed about such things—unions between cousins and uncle-daughter marriages happened—but it seems odd that a man of Themistocles' position would have allowed a brother-sister marriage without an overriding reason. So I invented a reason.

The Greek libido was up for almost any combination of sexual athletics you care to think of—some of the pottery decoration of the time has to be seen to be believed—but I've never come across a single reference to Greeks practicing sexual bondage and discipline, I suppose because such a thing would have been considered demeaning to the man. It was therefore the *only* sexual activity I could think of which Mnesiptolema and Archeptolis might conceivably have cause to be ashamed (other than sneaking a donkey into the room, but there are practicalities to be considered).

Secret writing was very much a part of Greek political plots. The modern term for it—*steganography*—is precisely the ancient Greek word and means literally secret writing. The story of the slave with a message tattooed on his scalp, and the story of Demeratos sending a war warning scratched into the backing board of a wax tablet, both appear in Herodotus. The skytale that Nico uses, with a leather strip wrapped about a rod and written on lengthways, was a common Greek device.

The fact that the Greeks were so sophisticated in such things speaks volumes about their tendency to backstab, plot, and conspire. It's all good stuff if you happen to be a writer of Classical Greek mysteries.

Barzanes works for the Eyes and Ears of the King. It sounds like something from high fantasy, but I promise the Eyes and Ears of the King was a for-real organization, and not one you would want to mess with.

The Persian social structure was very hierarchical. At the top was the Great King. Directly below him were the satraps, chosen almost always from Persian nobility. Each satrap ruled a satrapy, being a province, of which there were many. Each satrap in turn had many officers in his province.

Everyone lived within the social hierarchy, obeying the next guy up the line, *except for* the Eyes and Ears. If you were a member of this elite organization, then your job was to keep an eye on how the empire was ticking over, and report directly to the Great King, bypassing the entire system. Most important of all, the local satrap had no power over you. This little detail is hugely important to the story: Themistocles had no power to control Barzanes, or what he might discover.

The Eyes and Ears of the King kept an eye on what the local satraps were up to, how they managed the army, and put down rebellions. They watched how tribute was collected from client states to make sure it all made its way to the king's coffers. (Satraps who enriched themselves were liable to rebel.) If the taxation didn't add up, the Eyes and Ears investigated to find out who was diddling the accounts. If a satrap broke the law, the Eyes and Ears reported the crime to the Great King.

The Eyes and Ears of the King was, in essence, the Persian FBI.

Greek and Old Persian was wildly different, and whenever the Greeks tried to say a Persian name they mangled it horribly. Because our histories were written by Greeks, we know all these great Persian men by their mangled but not their real names.

The Great King of the Persians at the time of this story was Artaxerxes (pronounced ART-A-ZERK-SEEZ), or at least that's what the Greeks called him. His real name was Artakhshaça. The father of Artaxerxes was Xerxes (ZERK-SEEZ). It was Xerxes who invaded Greece, so it's not surprising he gets really bad press from all ancient historians. His real name was Khshayarsha.

Many Greeks could speak Persian, especially those in Ionia, but the name mangling suggests most of them spoke it with an atrocious accent. So when Nico says the name of his adversary is Barzanes, that's him mangling a quite different name.

The story of the rich and powerful tyrant Polycrates, and his terrible death in Magnesia at the hands of Oroetes, is true and can be found in Herodotus. The lost treasure is my own addition.

The Maeander River, which plays such a central role in the mystery, is the selfsame river which gives us the English verb to meander. The Maeander River does indeed meander as Cleophantus describes to Nico.

The betrothal of the Greek Nicomache to the Persian Barzanes was by no means unusual. What might be slightly controversial is that Barzanes was a Zoroastrian. Modern Zoroastrians believe that at no time have their people married outside their faith.

Zoroastrianism was the state religion of the kings of Persia. It's a religion that has practicing members to this day. Zoroastrianism was the first dualistic religion in history, which is to say, there are good and evil spiritual forces that oppose each other in an eternal struggle. Men and women should support the good against the bad.

Ahura Mazda is the Good God of the Zoroastrians, and his name means Wise Lord. He is attended by many good spirits, or angels, the only one of which I mention is Mithra. Mithra went on to become the basis of his own religion, which at its height in Roman times was bigger than Christianity.

Ahriman opposes Ahura Mazda, with the help of evil spirits called the daevas. It is no coincidence that daeva sounds like the Hindu deva and the Christian devil. Nor is it likely to be a coincidence that in Zoroastrianism there is a judgment of the soul, which results in going to either a hellish sea of molten metal, or to a paradise.

The Zoroastrian prayers and practices were not written down until some time in the seventh century AD, more than a thousand years after this story. I am indebted to Tehmina Goskar, a medieval historian who also happens to be a member of the Zoroastrian faith, for her advice on early Zoroastrianism. Any errors in the text are certainly mine.

The idea of supporting a good god against an evil one seems very natural to the modern Christian mind-set, but it was 100 percent utterly foreign to the Greek worldview, for whom the gods were forces of nature to be placated. It's my personal belief that the wide gap between Persian and Greek morality, as expressed by their religions, was one of the reasons these two great peoples never managed to get along.

The last half of the book takes place in Magnesia-on-the-Maeander. Incredibly, there were *three* cities named Magnesia within walking distance of one another. Some genius thought this was a great idea.

The first was Magnesia-on-the-Sipylum, which has nothing to do with this story. The second was Magnesia-on-the-Maeander, where the story takes place.

Our Magnesia, the one on the Maeander, was moved wholesale by the citizens to somewhere up the road in about 399 BC, which was more than sixty years after Themistocles died. That's the third Magnesia.

Diodorus Siculus says, from the Loeb Library edition of his book:

"Thibron [a Spartan general with an army in 399 BC] . . . came to Magnesia. . . . And since the city was unwalled . . . he transferred it to a neighboring hill which men call Thorax."

The third Magnesia has known ruins. The Magnesia of this book is a genuine Lost City, though with all the available clues to its whereabouts I don't imagine it would stay lost for long if someone put their mind and money to finding it. The one point from Diodorus Siculus of importance to the book is the observation that our Magnesia didn't have a defensive wall, unlike virtually every other city of its time. This is why Araxes and his gang were able to come and go unhindered.

Witch women like Mina were alive and well in Classical Greece. A Greek witch was called a *pharmakis,* from which we have the modern pharmacist and pharmacology. The familiar name tells you what their basic job was. The Classical Greek witch dealt in herbs, medicines, and poison. The odds are very good that a sick person might go see the local witch woman rather than an expensive doctor.

The poison which Mina sells to Nico is hydrogen cyanide. The method she describes to extract cyanide from peach kernels actually works. Don't try this at home, kids, you're likely to poison yourselves. There's no record of the Greeks using cyanide, but the ancient Hittites used it as one of their many cruel methods of execution, and the Hittites once ruled the land of Ionia. It's reasonable for Mina to know how to make it. I wondered whether it was a good idea to give a working formula in the book, then realized anyone these days with the help of easily accessible advice on the Internet could make much worse, using only the bottles stored under the kitchen sink. If someone did use peach kernel cyanide these days then the peach DNA in the poison would be spotted at once and the police would have little trouble searching out the distilling equipment.

Not much is known about the children of Themistocles after his death, although we do know his descendants were honored in Magnesia for generations to come.

Cleophantus went on to become a well-known gentleman in Athens, although he was looked down on with contempt by the philosophers. About eighty years after the events of this story, Plato in his book *Meno* causes Socrates to say, "Cleophantus, the famous horseman . . . he could stand upright on horseback and shoot javelins from there and do many other remarkable things. . . . But have you ever heard anyone, young or old, say that Cleophantus, the son of Themistocles, was clever or wise?"

Romantics will be pleased to hear that Nicomache got her man. History records that one of the first acts of the sons of Themistocles after his death was to betroth her to Phrasicles of Athens. Phrasicles arrived promptly in Magnesia to claim his bride.

Asia, the little rock who held back a great wave, was taken to Athens to be raised by Nicomache and her new husband. From there Asia disappears into the mists of history, and is never heard from again.

A NOTE ON NAMES

The Greeks had only a single name each, which we would think of as a first name. Greek names were usually two everyday words stuck together to form a meaning. A lot of the trick to saying them is to spot the word boundary, then say and think of them as two words.

Let me use as an example someone you've heard of: Cleopatra.

Cleopatra may have been Queen of Egypt, but her name was very typically Greek. If you can cope with Cleopatra, you can cope with any Greek name. Cleopatra is CLEO + PATRA. Cleo means *glory*, and patra means *of the father*. Glory of the father. The ending in –a makes it a feminine name.

With that in mind, here are a few of the major characters with interesting names:

Nicolaos is NICO + LAOS. Nico is a variant of Nike, which means *victory*. Laos is *of the people*. Victory of the people. Nicolaos is a common name in Greece to this day, and is quite obviously the origin of the western Nicholas. There was a St. Nicolaos who is better known as Santa Claus. The Claus part comes from the –colaos of Nicolaos. Nico is our modern Nick.

Diotima is DIOS + TIMA. The Greek *Dios* is the Latin *Deus*, which if you've ever heard a Latin prayer in church you will know means God. *Tima* means honored. Diotima is *honored by God*. A suitable name for any priestess.

Boy names end in –os, –us, –es, –is, or –on. Girl names end in –a, –ia, or –ache. You can switch the sex of any name by switching the ending.

Archeptolis looks tough but is amazingly simple. Archeptolis is almost the same as *architect*, a very common English word. Say *architect*. Now take off the *tect* and add on a *tolis*. Done!

The *pt* in Greek always sounds like a plain old English *t*. Every modern child knows the flying reptile called a pterodactyl. It's the same thing.

The Greek *ch* can always be said like an English *k* (as in architect). But if you want to go for slightly more authenticity, try saying it like the *ch* in Scottish or German, which is to say like a *k* while choking on a fish bone.

Themistocles is THEMISTOS + CLEO. Themistos is *law*. The final *s* is removed to join the word to Cleo, which we already know means *glory*. The *o* of cleo is removed to make way for the male –*es* ending. Themistocles is *glory of the law*.

The –*cles* ending was very common, because glory was something every male aspired to. Parents naturally wanted their children to have positive, happy sounding names, and so frequently picked from the same small pool of image-reinforcing words. That's also why so many Greek names begin *Aristo*-. Aristos means *best*. Hence the English word *aristocrat*.

For the graduation exercise, let's look at **Mnesiptolema**. I confess I wouldn't have used this one except that Mnesiptolema was a real historical person, like about half of my characters. The word boundary is MNESI + PTOLEMA. *Mn* makes a plain old English *N* sound, like the English word mnemonic. Indeed Mnesi and Mnem both come from *memory*. Ptolemaios means *warlike* or *aggressive*. So Mnesiptolema is *memory of war*. Say her name as Nessie + Tolema. Her friends call her Nessie.